D. Ross Stewart

The Law of Horses

D. Ross Stewart

The Law of Horses

ISBN/EAN: 9783742809889

Manufactured in Europe, USA, Canada, Australia, Japa

Cover: Foto ©Andreas Hilbeck / pixelio.de

Manufactured and distributed by brebook publishing software
(www.brebook.com)

D. Ross Stewart

The Law of Horses

THE

LAW OF HORSES.

BY

D. ROSS STEWART, M.A., LL.B.,

ADVOCATE.

EDINBURGH:

WILLIAM GREEN & SONS,

Law Publishers.

1892.

PRINTED BY LORIMER AND GILLIES

FOR

WILLIAM GREEN AND SONS, EDINBURGH.

AGENTS IN LONDON—STEVENS AND HAYNES.
AGENTS IN GLASGOW—JOHN SMITH AND SON.

PREFACE.

—◆--

My object in undertaking the following work has been to bring within a volume of moderate size a view of the principles, enactments, and cases in Scots Law that relate to horses. In endeavouring to do this to the full, I have thought it right to go, when necessary, beyond the narrow limitation of the subject; to refer, for example, to English authorities in illustration of the law of Scotland; to point out differences between the legal systems of the two countries; and to cite cases relating to other subjects than horses as authority for the general principles of contract, fraud, and negligence which emerge in transactions about horses. The work thus aims, while dealing with a restricted subject, at treating it completely. I desire to acknowledge the obligations I am under to Mr. A. Orr Deas, advocate, who has kindly revised the proof sheets, and to him and other friends for many valuable and practical suggestions.

D. R. S.

21 NORTHUMBERLAND STREET,
EDINBURGH, *July*, 1892.

TABLE OF CONTENTS.

CHAPTER I.

SALE.

CHAPTER II.

WARRANTY AND SALE FOR SPECIFIC PURPOSE.

CHAPTER III.

HIRING AND LOAN.

CHAPTER IV.

CUSTODY—VETERINARY TREATMENT—HYPOTHEC AND DILIGENCE.

CHAPTER V.

CARRIAGE BY LAND AND WATER.

CHAPTER VI.

RESPONSIBILITY FOR THE NEGLIGENT USE OF HORSES.

CHAPTER VII.

DEFENCES TO ACTIONS OF DAMAGES FOR INJURY TO HORSES AND CAUSED BY THEM.

CHAPTER VIII.

DAMAGES.

CHAPTER IX.

INSURANCE.

APPENDIX.

INDEX OF CASES CITED.

THE LAW OF HORSES.

CHAPTER I.

SALE.

Nature of the Contract, 1. Horses as the subject of Sale, 2. Completion of the Contract, 3. Essential Error, 4. Proof of the Contract, 5. Offer and Acceptance, 6. Order, 7. Risk, 8. Implied Conditions as to Quality, 9. Price and Payment, 10-12. Delivery, 13-19. Respective Remedies on Breach of Sale, 20. Sale on Approbation, Sale and Return, and Hire and Sale, 21. Retention, 22. Stoppage *in Transitu*, 23-24. Sale by Auction, 25-28. Rejection on Insolvency, 29. Fraudulent Transactions, 30-35. Rescission, 36.

THE sale of horses differs little from the sale of other commodities ; and the general principles of the contract of sale, as far as they apply to the subject under consideration, will be treated very briefly. There are certain peculiarities in the sale of horses, however, of greater importance, such—*e.g.*, as warranties and sale for a specific purpose,(a) which will be treated hereafter at greater length.

1. The Contract.—Sale is a consensual contract, completed by consent alone. The consent must be given by one capable of consenting; it must be free, serious, and deliberate,(b) and where either of the parties is incapacitated by nonage,(c) insanity,(d) or intoxication,(e) or if there be

(a) See Chap. ii.
(b) B.C. i. 313, 458 ; Stair, i. 14, 1 ; Ersk. iii. 3, 2, see § 30, *et seq.*
(c) B.C. i. 128.   (d) B. Pr. 10.   (e) See § 34.

B

error,(a) constraint,(b) or fraud,(c) of such a degree as to show that the consent and engagement have not been the deliberate act of the parties, the sale is void,(d) and may be set aside.(e)

The seller binds himself, under the contract of sale, to deliver the animal purchased, and the buyer to pay the price; but the property does not pass till he has delivered the animal to the buyer, or to some one on his behalf.(f)

2. Horses as the subject of Sale.—It is necessary to the validity of the contract of sale that the horse or horses purchased be determinate, or capable of being determined; but it is not necessary to the contract that they be identified (g), —that is to say, the horse or horses may be specific animals, clearly distinguished, or set apart, out of a lot, for the buyer; or they may be a determinate number of animals, described generically, as occurs—e.g., in the case of a sale of so many out of a consignment of ponies. When a definite, or specific horse, capable of being identified, is sold, it lies at the buyer's risk; the property of it passes, according to English law; and the title to demand it, passes to the buyer, in Scotland, but not the property till it is delivered.(h) But where a certain number of ponies, say, is sold, neither the property in England, nor the right to them in Scotland, passes, nor does the risk of them fall on the buyer, until the stipulated number is measured off and separated from the bulk.(i) When a pair of animals is sold, or a greater num-

---

(a) B.C. i. 314, §§ 4, 30.

(b) B.C. i. 314.

(c) B.C. i. 316, §§ 30-35.

(d) As to when the contract is not void, but only voidable, see § 30.

(e) See § 36.

(f) Ersk. iii. 3, 2. In England, the property passes when the contract is complete, 2 Blackst. 398.

(g) B. Pr. 91 ; B.C. i. 461, note.

(h) §§ 13-18, provided that in sale in open market, in England, the conditions of sale have been adhered to.

(i) B. Pr. 91 ; Ersk. iii. 3, 7 ; Brown on Sale, 44, et seq.

ber at a slump sum the bargain is entire, there being no evidence as to the price of each,(a) and is not final, unless accepted as a whole ; and, consequently, the buyer cannot, at the same time, reject one and keep the rest, but must keep or reject all ;(b) but if the animals are purchased each at a fixed price, or there be anything to show that the sale of each is contemplated as a separate bargain, and the seller's title to any of them should fail, the buyer may keep the rest at the price fixed.(c)   The mere fact of the price a pair or two separate animals being proved to have been spoken of as at so much per head, is not conclusive evidence of a definite price for each, and yields to evidence of the intention of parties to buy or sell both or neither.(d)   An unborn foal may be the subject of sale ;(e) but in such a case the contract is an agreement to sell, not an actual sale, and the risk is with the seller.(f)

By the law of Scotland the *vitium reale* attaching to stolen horses is indelible till its return to the original owner. Consequently a horse stolen in Scotland is recoverable from a *bona fide* purchaser.   By the law of England and Ireland, however, it is removed by subsequent sale in market overt ; but it is not decided that the *vitium reale* attaches in Scotland when the theft has taken place in a foreign country. This question was raised, but not decided, in a recent case, where a farmer in Ireland raised an action against a farmer in Scotland for delivery of a horse in the possession of the defender, which the pursuer alleged had been stolen from him in Ireland.   The defender stated that the horse had been bought by him in Scotland from a man who had purchased it in open market in Ireland.   The pursuer

---

(a) *Dig. de lege Aquilia*, 9, 2, *Lex* 22, 1. See Lord Rutherfurd Clark in *Sinclair* v. *M'Ewan*, 1887, 25 S.L.R. 76 ; and Badgly (J.), in *M'Connel* v. *Murphy*, 1873, L.R. 5 P.C. 205, 209.

(b) *Cleghorn* v. *Taylor*, 1856, 18 D. 664.

(c) B. Pr. 91 ; B.C. i. 462. See also *Hamilton* v. *Hart*, 1830, 8 S. 596, as to rejection.

(d) *Stewart* v. *M'Nicoll*, 1814, Hume, 701.

(e) B. Pr. 91 (2) ; Ersk. iii. 3, 3.   (f) Benj. 82.

admitted, that according to the law of Ireland, a person from whom a horse had been stolen, which was afterwards sold with certain formalities in open market there, could not claim it from the purchaser unless he had within six months prosecuted the thief to conviction, and that no conviction had taken place in this case. On consideration of the evidence, it was held that the sale took place in open market in Ireland, and that as the pursuer had neither averred nor proved that the sale in open market was defective in any of the requisite formalities, the defender was entitled to absolvitor.(a)

3. Completion of the Contract.—The contract is complete when the parties have come to an agreement : the buyer to pay a definite price, the seller to deliver a certain horse; (b) and where there is a bargain to deliver before a certain time, and one party renounces and declares the bargain off, that is a breach of contract; and the other party may sue for specific implement or damages.(c) These two elements,— the certain article and the price,—are the essentials of all sales; and, therefore, if there be any essential error as to these, there is no contract.(d)

4. Essential Error.—If one buys too dear or sells too cheap, the law will give him no relief against his folly, provided there be no fraud on the part of the seller.(e) But when an error, either as to the horse or horses bought, or as to the price paid, or to be paid, for it or them, is of such a kind as to prevent a bargain being concluded according to the intention of the parties, it is essential error,(f) and is a ground for the contract being annulled, or for what has been

(a) *Todd* v. *Armour*, 1882, 9 R. 901.
(b) B. Pr. 89.
(c) *Danube* v. *Xenos*, 1862, 31 L.J., C.P. 284.
(d) Ersk. iii. 1, 16 ; Stair, i. 10, 14 ; B. Pr. 90.
(e) B. Pr. 11.
(f) Stair, i. 10, 13 ; Ersk. iii. 1, 16.

paid or delivered being recovered ;(*a*) and in pleading, it is necessary to specify precisely the nature of the error alleged, and if several errors are set forth, a separate issue must be taken for each.(*b*)

Thus, if one horse be mistaken for another;(*c*) or there be a mistake as to the number or quality of those sold ;(*d*) or if a man ignorantly purchase what is his own already;(*e*) or if there be an essential error about the price; either party may resile, or the contract may be reduced (*f*) at the instance of either party ; but to ground an action of reduction, the error must be either common to both parties, or have been induced by the conduct of him who seeks to maintain the contract.(*g*)

5. Proof of the Contract.—Writing is not necessary to the purchase of horses(*h*) in Scotland, but it is so in England, under the Statute of Frauds ;(*i*) and the bargain may be proved *prout de jure*—*i.e.*, by a general proof of facts and circumstances not limited to the writ or oath of the defender.(*j*) If the bargain be made verbally between the parties themselves, the evidence of two witnesses is usually required, but one is sufficient if there are circumstances corroborative of it ;(*k*) if by letter, the letters holograph, or signed by the parties, are sufficient evidence of the contract.(*l*)

If the sale be through a broker, his authority must be

(*a*) B. Pr. 11 ; Lord Justice-Clerk Hope in *Purdon v. Rowatt's Trustees*, 1856, 19 D. 206, p. 220. See also Lord Deas in *Rough v. Moir*, 1875, 2 R. 529, 535.

(*b*) *Ritchie v. Ritchie's Trustees*, 1866, 4 M. 292.

(*c*) *Hamilton v. Western Bank*, 1861, 23 D. 1033.

(*d*) Bank. Ersk. Pr. iii. 1, 6.

(*e*) *Bingham*, 1748, 1 Ves. 126.

(*f*) § 35.

(*g*) *Stewart v. Kennedy*, 1890, 15 App. Ca. 108 ; 17 R., H.L. 1.

(*h*) Ersk. iv. 2, 20.

(*i*) See § 13.

(*j*) *Pollock v. M'Andrew*, 1828, 7 S. 189 ; *Wilson v. Walker*, 1856, 18 D. 673 ; Dickson on Evidence, § 553.

(*k*) B. Pr. 89.

(*l*) B. Pr. 89 ; Dickson on Evidence, §§ 793-796.

proved.(a)   A bought and sold note (b) is evidence of the
bargain ; and it is not necessary in Scotland for a signed
note to be entered in the broker's books.(c)   Should the
broker not previously communicate the buyer's name, the
seller may, on its disclosure, reject the bargain within a
reasonable time, if he find the buyer's credit bad.(d)

6. Offer and Acceptance.—An offer is an obligation pro-
visional on acceptance.   It is presumed to continue till
acceptance, but may be recalled before acceptance.(e)
It may be made by parole, by letter, or tacitly, as when
horses are sent without or contrary to order, in which cases
acquiescence is acceptance.(f)

An absent offerer is understood to say : " If you receive
no notice to the contrary, you shall be entitled to hold
me as continuing my offer up to the time of posting or
despatching your acceptance ; which, if done *debito tempore*,
shall bind the contract."(g)

If, in construing an offer, it is found that it amounts to
a promise binding the offerer for a reasonable or specified
time, the offeree may claim specific performance of his
contract, or damages for its breach ; but, if not, there is
locus pœnitentiæ, and the offerer may resile ;(h) but the
recall of an offer has no effect unless communicated before
acceptance.(i)

Acceptance is either tacit or express.   It is tacit where
a horse is sent on approval and kept, if the proposal be
so made as to require rejection if the buyer do not mean

(a) Bell's Pr. 89 ; Benj. 249 *et seq.*

(b) These are not common in Scotland; for their form and effect, see Benj.
253 *et seq.*

(c) B. Pr. 89 ; but it is necessary in England, *Grant* v. *Fletcher*, 1826, 5 B.
and Cr. 436 ; *Thornton* v. *Charles*, 1842, 9 M. and W. 802.

(d) *Hodgson* v. *Davies*, 1810, 2 Camp. 530.

(e) B.C. i. 343 ; Stair, i. 3, 9 ; Ersk. iii. 3, 88.

(f) B. Pr. 74 ; see § 21, sale and return.

(g) Lord Deas in *Thomson* v. *James*, 1855, 18 D. 1, 25.

(h) *Walker* v. *Milne*, 1823, 2 S. 379 ; Lord Deas in *Allan* v. *Gilchrist*, 1875,
2 R. 587-590.

(i) *Thomson*, cit.

to keep it.(a) If there be express acceptance, it must precisely meet the offer.(b) If it contain any condition, the alteration is equivalent to a new offer requiring acceptance.(c)

The acceptance completes the contract if despatched before the receipt of a retractation of the offer(d) within the time limited by the offer, or within reasonable time if none be specified; provided no change of circumstances has taken place so as to make the offer "unsuitable and absurd."(e) The acceptance should be communicated in course of post, or according to the usage of trade. Once posted, the acceptance is complete, even though it should not reach the offerer;(f) but the acceptance may be recalled by telegram received before, or simultaneously with the acceptance.(g)

7. Order.(h)—Offer and acceptance thus differs from an "order in trade," which is part of the law of mandate.(i) An order in trade requires no acceptance; and must be immediately rejected, else it is binding on the person to whom it is addressed. It need not be in writing, and may be proved by parole evidence.(j) It must be executed in the terms of the order, otherwise it is not binding on the orderer; but if he acquiesce in the mode of execution, he is bound by it.(k) If an order be sent by telegram, the

(a) B. Pr. 76.
(b) Rank. Ersk. Pr. iii. 1, 6 ; B. Pr. 77.
(c) *Johnstone* v. *Clark*, 1855, 18 D. 70 ; *Wylie & Lochead* v. *M'Ilroy*, 1873, 1 R. 41.
(d) *Thomson* v. *James*, 1855, 18 D. 1 ; *Wylie*, cit. ; *Higgins & Son* v. *Dunlop*, 1847, 9 D. 1407 ; 6 B. App. 195.
(e) Lord President Inglis in *Macrae* v. *Edinburgh Tramway Company*, 1885, 13 R. 265, 269.
(f) *Higgins*, cit.
(g) *Thomson*, cit.
(h) Orders in trade are frequently given in the case of donkeys, ponies, &c.
(i) B. Pr. 80.
(j) B. Pr. 80-82 ; but it must be in writing in England.
(k) *Richardson* v. *Riscoe & Rigg*, 1837, 15 S. 952 ; *Van Oppen* v. *Arbuckle*, 1855, 18 D. 113.

sender is not liable for a mistake in transmission, and, unless the message be correct, there is no contract.(a)

If an order be given for a pair of horses or more, the buyer is entitled to consider it as one order, and decline to accept one unless the whole are delivered;(b) but not if the contract contemplates the possible delivery of a part only, or if the buyer acquiesce in partial delivery as fulfilment of the contract to that extent.(c)

8. The Risk.—The risk of the horse sold but not delivered is with the buyer.(d) The engagement of the seller being to deliver, and the buyer's right being to the specific animal purchased, the engagement is discharged, and the right extinguished if the animal perish through no fault of the seller ; and similarly it is no answer to a claim for the price that the horse has not been delivered, if it have perished without fault of the seller.(e)

The risk remains with the seller—1, If he specially undertake it, or where he undertakes it by implication, as to deliver it at a certain place ; (f) 2, if there is undue delay in delivery without fault on the buyer's part; (g) 3, where the seller neglects to give notice to the buyer to enable him to insure ; (h) or fails to put the animal in such a course of conveyance as to let the buyer obtain indemnity against loss in carriage ; (i) 4, or where anything remains to be done in identifying the animal or animals sold, as—e.g., where so many ponies out of a lot are sold.(j)

(a) *Verdin Brothers* v. *Robertson*, 1871, 10 M. 35.
(b) § 2 ; *Richardson*, cit. ; *Joffé* v. *Ritchie*, 1860, 23 D. 242, 249.
(c) *Smith* v. *Napier*, 1804 ; Hume, 338 ; B. 38 ; B. Pr. 91 (6).
(d) Stair, i. 14, 7 ; Ersk. iii. 3, 7 ; B.C. i. 461, n.
(e) B. Pr. 87.
(f) *Milne & Co.* v. *Miller*, 1809, 15 F.C. 127 ; *Henckell du Buisson & Co.* v. *Swan*, 1889, 17 R. 252.
(g) *Fleet* v. *Morrison*, 1854, 16 D. 1122.
(h) *Fleet* cit., see also *Hastie* v. *Campbell*, 1857, 19 D. 557 ; B.C. i. 475.
(i) B.C. i. 474-475 ; Benj. 703.
(j) *Hansen* v. *Craig*, 1859, 21 D. 432, see § 2 ; B. Pr. 88, note (f) ; *Anderson* v. *Walls*, 1870, 9 M. 122-125.

9. Implied Conditions as to Quality.—When a purchaser buys a horse without a warranty, there is a condition implied in the contract of sale that the animal is reasonably fit for the purpose for which it is sold ; that is to say, it must be a merchantable animal, and such as it is represented to be according to the fair intention and understanding of the parties.(*a*) If the buyer has seen and examined the horse, the rule *caveat emptor* applies, "his eye is his merchant," and he must take it with all its faults, unless there be fraud on the part of the seller, or the concealment (*b*) of any defect known to him material to the contract and not obvious on inspection.(*c*) A seller, however, is not bound to disclose any patent defects in a horse he is going to sell, unless this duty is imposed upon him by the buyer's asking about them : he may remain silent and allow the buyer to inspect the animal and judge for himself; mere silence does not *per se* amount either to implied warranty or concealment.(*d*) If the buyer, however, has not seen or had an opportunity of seeing the horse, the rule *caveat emptor* does not apply, and the buyer can reject it, and demand repayment of the price if it has been paid, in the event of its not being a merchantable animal.(*e*) If a defect be undiscoverable on inspection, the buyer is held both in England and Scotland to be aware of the possibility of its existence, and unless there be fraud on the part of the seller in concealing it, or the buyer get a warranty with his horse, he must take the risk.(*f*) " Where an article is sold with all its faults," said Lord Ellenborough, "I think it is quite immaterial how many belonged to it within the knowledge of the seller, unless he used some

(*a*) Ersk. iii. 3, 10 ; B.C. i. 463 ; *Ralston* v. *Robb*, 1808, M. *v.* Sale.

(*b*) See § 32.

(*c*) B. Pr. 96.

(*d*) Per Lord Jervis in *Keats* v. *Earl of Cadogan*, 1851, 10 C.B. 591 ; *Yeats v. Reid*, 1884, 21 S.L.R. 698, see this case also in § 28.

(*e*) B.C. i. 464 ; Ersk. iii. 3, 10.

(*f*) B. Pr. 97 ; Stair, i. 10, 15, citing *Brown* v. *Nicolson*, 1629, M. 8940. The former English rule that sound price implied sound quality, is overruled. *Jones* v. *Just*, 1868, L.R. 3 Q.B. 197.

artifice to disguise them, and to prevent their being discovered by the purchaser. The very object of such a stipulation is to put the purchaser on his guard, and to throw upon him the burden of examining all faults both secret and apparent. I may be possessed of a horse I know to have many faults, and I wish to get rid of him for whatever sum he will fetch. I desire my servant to dispose of him, and instead of giving a warranty of soundness, to sell him with all faults. Having thus laboriously freed myself from responsibility, am I to be liable if it be afterwards discovered that the horse was unsound?"(a)

It would also appear that specific animals sold by description may be rejected even when examined by the buyer, if of a different kind from those described, provided the difference was not apparent on inspection,(b) and if bought for a purpose known to the seller they must be reasonably fit for that purpose.(c)

By the Mercantile Law Amendment Act,(d) there is no longer an implied warranty against latent defects in the sale of horses, the actual condition of which may be ascertained by either party.(e)   Under § 5 of this statute, "where goods" (horses are held included under this term (f)) "shall, after the passing of this Act, be sold, the seller, if at the time of the sale he was without knowledge that the same were defective or of bad quality, shall not be held to have warranted their sufficiency; but the goods with all their faults shall be at the risk of the purchaser, unless the seller shall have given an express warranty (g) of the quality or sufficiency of such goods, or unless the goods have been

<hr/>

(a) Per Lord Ellenborough in *Baglehole* v. *Walters*, 1811, 3 Camp. 154, approved in *Ward* v. *Hobbs*, 1878, 4 App. Ca. 13, 27, 29.

(b) *Jaffé* v. *Ritchie*, 1860, 23 D. 242 ; *Carter* v. *Campbell*, 1885, 12 R. 1075.

(c) *Jones*, cit.   *Fleming* v. *Airdrie Iron Co.*, 1882, 9 R. 473 ; see § 58 where Mercantile Law Amendment Act applies.

(d) 19 & 20 Vict. c. 60.

(e) B. Pr. 97 A.

(f) *Young* v. *Giffen*, 1858, 21 D. 87.

(g) *Scott* v. *Steel*, 1857, 20 D. 253.

expressly sold for a specific and particular purpose, in which case the seller shall be considered without such warranty to warrant that the same are fit for such purpose.(*a*)

10. Price.—The rule is, No price, no sale.(*b*) If there be a material error as to price there is no sale ;(*c*) but if there be merely a misconception regarding the price, and delivery have taken place, the parties are held to have had in contemplation the market value of the animal sold.(*d*)

The price must also be certain in amount, or capable of being made certain by reference to some standard,(*e*) such as the award of a third party,(*f*) or the price to be fixed by the buyer,(*g*) or of one of the parties, subject to the control of equity (*h*) or the market value ; or again the price may, by the contract, be made to vary according to events. (*i*) It must not be illusory,(*j*) else the contract is one of barter, not sale, and it must be fixed in money payable in legal tender.(*k*)

A bargain, however, is frequently made where a horse and so much money is given for another horse. This is regarded as a sale ;(*l*) and where two horses were exchanged for one, delivery of one of the two does not preclude the owner's lien on the other till the delivery of the one horse for which the two were to be exchanged.(*m*)

11. Payment of Price.—When the bargain is simple and without special stipulation, the price must be paid immedi-

---

(*a*) See §§ 39, 58.
(*b*) Ersk. iii. 3, 4 ; Stair, i. 10, 13 ; 9, 14.
(*c*) *Sword* v. *Sinclairs*, 1771, M. 14,241.
(*d*) *Wilson* v. *Marquis of Breadalbane*, 1859, 21 D. 957 ; followed by *Stuart* v. *Kennedy*, 1885, 13 R. 221.
(*e*) Ersk. iii. 3, 4 ; *Hunter* v. *Duff*, 1831, 9 S. 703.
(*f*) Stair, i. 14, 1.
(*g*) *Lavaggi* v. *Pirie*, 1872, 10 M. 312.
(*h*) Ersk. iii. 3, 4.
(*i*) B. Pr. 92 (1).
(*j*) Ersk. cit. ; Stair, cit.　　　　　(*k*) 33 Vict. c. 10, § 6.
(*l*) *Brydon* v. *Macfarlane*, 1864, 3 M. 7.
(*m*) *Hanson* v. *Myer*, 1805, 6 East, 614.

ately,(*a*) and the seller is entitled to demand, and have an action for, payment on offering the horse, or on proof of delivery, or on showing that the thing has perished by accident.(*b*) If the sale be upon credit, and the buyer fail, or be *vergens ad inopiam*, the seller may resile,(*c*) or claim restitution of the horse, when delivery has been inadvertently made without payment, if not barred by delay or by giving credit.(*d*) The mere insolvency of the buyer does not rescind the contract ; (*e*) and his creditors (or trustee) may obtain delivery on payment ;(*f*) but the seller may retain (*g*) or stop *in transitu*,(*h*) if the buyer be declared insolvent. All mercantile contracts are construed according to the usage of trade ; and, accordingly, where there is a custom known to both parties of giving credit for a certain time, that will be held as part of the bargain; but if it is local and known to one of the parties only, it has no effect, nor is it admissible to prove a custom in contradiction of express contract.(*i*)

12. Express Conditions as to Payment.—If there be any express words or stipulations about payment, they will over-rule usage of trade.(*j*) If there be no time specified, payment is due on delivery, or when by usage of trade the price is due.(*k*) It must be in legal tender if insisted on,(*l*) or on such notes as may be received without objection, or which have been stipulated.(*m*)

When payment is made by note or cheque, the buyer is

(*a*) *Hall* v. *Scott*, 1860, 22 D. 413.
(*b*) Bell on Sale, 103, 78.
(*c*) B. Pr. 46, 71, 100.
(*d*) *Richmond* v. *Railton*, 1854, 16 D. 403.
(*e*) B. Pr. 100.
(*f*) B.C. i. 471.
(*g*) See § 22.
(*h*) See § 23.
(*i*) B. Pr. 83, 101 and cases there cited.
(*j*) B. Pr. 103.
(*k*) *Linn* v. *Shields*, 1863, 2 M. 88.
(*l*) 33 Vict. c. 10, § 6.
(*m*) *Caine* v. *Coulton*, 1863, 1 H. and C. 764 ; B. Pr. 127.

not free if the cheque be dishonoured ; (a) and if bank-notes, or the bill or note of a third party, are offered and taken as cash, without endorsation of, or recourse on the buyer, the seller has no remedy against the buyer unless he knew of the insolvency of the bank or third party, or unless he omitted something necessary for procuring payment.(b) Delivery may be refused till payment, in a ready-money transaction ; (c) but if a horse be delivered before payment, the buyer will be entitled to set off a sum due to him by the seller against the price demanded.(d)

If it be stipulated simply that a bill shall be given for the price, the bill must be sent within reasonable time ;(e) but such a condition as "to be sent in course" is absolute.(f) The stipulation that a bill shall be given for the price means the buyer's own bill.(g) But if the sale be made by a broker for the seller, the seller may object to the credit if he do so directly on ascertaining the buyer's credit,(h) or if there has been undue concealment, or a change in the condition of the buyer's credit between the time the bargain was made and the tendering of the bill.(i) A "discountable" bill means one that will fetch money at the banks, and an "approved bill" one which is unobjectionable.(j) A special condition of "ready money" suspends the passing of the property in a question with creditors.(k)

13. Delivery.—The primary obligation of the seller is to deliver the horse sold so as to complete the transfer ; and

(a) *Everet* v. *Collins*, 1810, 2 Camp. 515.
(b) *Camidge* v. *Allenby*, 1827, 1 Ross' L.C. 366 ; B. Pr. 127 ; *Fenn* v. *Harrison*, 1 Ross' L.C. 350.
(c) B. Pr. 127.
(d) Bell on Sale, 108.
(e) *Brodie* v. *Todd*, May, 1814, 17 F.C. 609.
(f) *Colvin* v. *Short*, 1857, 19 D. 890.
(g) B. Pr. 105.
(h) *Hodgson* v. *Davies*, 1810, 2 Camp. 530.
(i) *Brandt* v. *Dickson*, 1876, 3 R. 375.
(j) B. Pr. 106-107.
(k) B. Pr. 103.

there arises an implied warranty that the seller has a good title to sell,(a) and a claim for breach of warrandice arises on eviction.(b) Where a full price is paid, the warrandice is implied and is absolute.(c) Where the warrandice is express, it limits the implied warrandice; and the buyer is entitled to redress on eviction on giving notice of the challenge, and may claim under it such legal expenses as he may in good faith have been put to,(d) but he is not entitled to stop the bargain on pretence of want of title or on the mere possibility of a challenge.(e)

14. Time of Delivery.—The delivery must be made at the time, place, and in the manner specified in the contract, and, in the absence of stipulation, within reasonable time after payment.(f) Thus, where goods were to be delivered " forthwith, and to be paid for within fourteen days from the date of the contract," it was held that the parties intended that they should be delivered at some time within the fourteen days.(g) If there are no indications of a limit of time for delivery, " directly " means " speedily," or "as soon as practicable "—i.e., more expeditiously than within " reasonable time."(h) " As soon as possible " means without unreasonable delay, regard being had to the ability to deliver and the orders the seller has already in hand.(i) Again, where shipment of a cargo was to be made " during August next," Lord Shand was of opinion that, if a material part was not made during August, the purchaser was entitled to repudiate the contract.(j) If trouble and inconvenience be

---

(a) B. Pr. 114 ; Benj. 622 ; § 2 as to *vitium reale* attaching to stolen horse.
(b) Ersk. ii. 3, 25 ; B. Pr. 121.
(c) Ersk. ii. 3, 29.
(d) B. Pr. 126 ; Ersk. ii. 3, 20. (Stair and Bankton hold a different opinion, limiting the buyer's right to restitution simply.)
(e) B. Pr. 114.
(f) Benj. 686.
(g) *Staunton* v. *Wood*, 1851, 16 A. and E., Q.B. 486.
(h) *Duncan* v. *Topham*, 1849, M. G. and S. 8 C.B. 225.
(i) *Attwood* v. *Emery*, 1856, 26 L.J., C.P. 73.
(j) *Grieve & Co.* v. *König*, 1880, 7 R. 521.

sustained by the purchaser from delay on the seller's part to deliver, there arises a claim of damages on account of it ;(*a*) and if there be no stipulation as to time, a reasonable time is allowed for preparing to deliver when necessary.(*b*)

Where there is a stipulation that a horse is to remain with the seller till the buyer remove it, the seller is custodier for the buyer, and if the horse perish without his fault the loss is with the buyer ;(*c*) but if it is allowed to remain with the seller till after the term of payment has arrived, he may retain the horse,(*d*) unless he has given assent to a sub-sale by the buyer intimated to him(*e*).

15. Place of Delivery.—If no place be fixed where delivery is to be made, it is to be made where the horse is at the time of purchase ;(*f*) but if a certain place be stipulated, it must be made at that place ;(*g*) and the risk is with the seller till the horse is there, or is delivered to a proper carrier.(*h*) If, however, the buyer give directions as to the mode of transit, they must be fulfilled if possible,(*i*) and the buyer stands the loss.(*j*)

In any case, where a horse is given to a carrier for delivery, it must be despatched with due care to secure safe carriage,(*k*) and to give the buyer a claim upon a carrier,(*l*) and to enable him to insure it if he desire so to do.(*m*)

(*a*) Lord President Inglis in *Webster* v. *Cramond Iron Co.*, 1875, 2 R. 752.
(*b*) *Forbes* v. *Campbell*, 1885, 12 R. 1065.
(*c*) See § 8 ; B. Pr. 116.
(*d*) *Bloxam* v. *Sanders*, 2 Ross' L.C. 48.
(*e*) See under Retention, § 22 ; B.C. i. 243.
(*f*) Benj. 684.
(*g*) B. Pr. 117.
(*h*) *Dunlop & Co.* v. *Lambert*, 1839, 15 S. 884, 1232 ; rev. 1839, M'L. and R. 663.
(*i*) *Harle* v. *Ogilvie*, 1749, M. 10,095.
(*j*) *Vale* v. *Bayle*, 1775, Cowp. 294.
(*k*) *Sword* v. *Milloy*, Feb. 1813, 17 F.C. 209.
(*l*) *Hastie* v. *Campbell*, 1857, 19 D. 557.
(*m*) *Fleet* v. *Morrison*, 1854, 16 D. 1122 ; B.C. i. 474 ; B. Pr. 118.

16. Mode of Delivery.—If the horse be in the possession or custody of the seller, delivery takes place by handing over the animal to the purchaser or his servant ;(a) or by sending it to his stable ; or by sending it to any person authorised to receive it on his behalf ; or to any one whose stables are used by the buyer as his own ; or to a carrier by sea or land to be at the buyer's order ;(b) or by delivery to the buyer of the key of a stable where the horse is ;(c) or by delivery into the buyer's own ship, or one hired by time by the buyer, or entirely at his command.(d) In these cases the delivery is actual,(e) and the property is transferred beyond recall. The property, however, does not pass in a cash transaction by inadvertent transference of the horse into the possession of the buyer without payment being demanded, and the seller in such a case may demand restoration, but must do so immediately.(f)

17. Effect of Delivery.—In Scotland, the property being still untransferred till delivery, if the seller become bankrupt before delivery has taken place his creditors attach a horse sold, even after the price is paid.(g) The Mercantile Law Amendment Act(h) makes no change in this law, but it contains two enactments regarding it requiring observation. The first is, that " where goods sold but not delivered have been allowed to remain in the custody of" the seller, the diligence of his creditors is excluded in competition with the buyer enforcing his contract.(i) But, where not only the

(a) *Henry* v. *Dunlop*, 1842, 5 D. 3. Seller allowing cattle to be driven away by buyer's servant notwithstanding orders to his own servant not to let them be taken away.

(b) B. Pr. 1302. See § 23.

(c) Ersk. ii. 1, 19 ; *Maxwell & Co.* v. *Stevenson & Co.*, 1831, 5 W. and S. 269.

(d) Whether delivery to a common carrier is delivery to the consignee is a question of circumstances, a bill of lading not being conclusive upon this point. See B.C. i. 218.

(e) B. Pr., § 1302.   (f) B.C. i. 258.   (g) B. Pr. 1300.

(h) 19 & 20 Vict. c. 60, §§ 1, 4.

(i) *Wyper* v. *Harvey*, 1861, 23 D. 606 ; Lord President Inglis in *Black* v. *Incorporation of Bakers*, 1867, 6 M. 136.

custody but the beneficial use of a horse remains with the seller, so as to show that a true sale has not taken place, this section of the Act does not apply.(a)   The second is, that where a purchaser has not obtained delivery, a sub-purchaser from him is " entitled to demand that delivery . . . be made to him, and not to the original purchaser ; and the seller, on intimation being made to him of such subsequent sale, shall be bound to deliver on payment of the price, or performance of the obligations or conditions of the contract of sale.(b)

18. Constructive Delivery.(c)—Constructive delivery of a horse takes place where the actual or real possession cannot be, or is not, given to the buyer or his agent.   It is exemplified by such acts as setting a horse apart for the purchaser, or by the seller continuing to keep the horse subject to the buyer's right of property,(d) or by intimating a delivery order to the custodier.   Whether delivery has taken place or not is frequently to be judged according to whether or not the buyer has accepted it.

These following cases arose under the English Statute of Frauds,(e) which requires a purchaser to " accept " goods of the value of £10 and upwards if there be no signed written contract between the parties.   A seller, who was a livery stable-keeper and horse-dealer, sued the defendant for the price of horses purchased.   The defendant informed the seller that he bought the horses from him ; but having neither servant nor stable, he desired the seller to keep them for him, and he accordingly removed them from the sale-stable to another.   This was held to be a relinquish-

(a) *Sim* v. *Grant*, 1862, 24 D. 1033 ; *Edmond* v. *Mowat*, 1868, 7 M. 59 ; *Robertson* v. *Macintyre*, 1882, 9 R. 772.   This rule does not affect a landlord's hypothec, 19 & 20 Vict. c. 60, §§ 1, 4.
(b) 19 & 20 Vict. c. 60, § 2.   See also § 21.
(c) B. Pr. 1303.
(d) *Elmore* v. *Stone*, 1809, 1 Taunt. 458.
(e) 29 Car. II. c. 3.

C

ment of the seller's possession as owner, as the buyer had
thus ordered expense to be laid out upon them, and the
plaintiff had consented to keep them at livery. (a) Lord
Mansfield, C.J., said : " After the defendant had said that
the horses must stand at livery, and the plaintiff had that
order, it made no difference whether they stood at livery at
the vendor's stables, or whether they had been taken away
and put in some other stable. The plaintiff possessed
them from that time, not as owner of the horses, but
as any other livery-stable keeper might have them to
keep."

In another case of sale of a horse on credit, a seller agreed
to keep a horse for a buyer for thirty days for nothing, and
at the expiry of that time it was sent to grass at the defendant's request, " as the seller's horse," it was there held that
the acceptance had not taken place. (b)

Acts done for mere examination are not sufficient to effect
delivery ;(c) but an offer to re-sell a horse as his own is considered an act of appropriation by the buyer. (d)

Where a number of horses are sold on approbation and
return, (e) delivery of them to a carrier is not delivery to the
buyer, because there has been no opportunity for the exercise
of option. (f) Delivery is entirely independent of payment
or non-payment of price. (g)

If the horse be in the custody of a third party, delivery
takes place by giving notice that the third party shall hold
the horse for the buyer instead of the seller. Thus, a horse
in the hands of a carrier by land, or factor, is transferred by
his acceptance of the seller's notice to change the custody ;

(a) *Elmore*, cit.
(b) *Carter* v. *Touissant*, 1822, 1 D. and R. 515. See also *Tempest* v. *Fitzgerald*, 1820, 3 B. and Ald. 680.
(c) *Nicholson* v. *Bower*, 1857, 28 L.J., Q.B. 97.
(d) *Chaplin* v. *Rogers*, 1800, 1 East, 192 ; but see *Richard* v. *Moore*, 1878, 38 L.T., N.S. 841.
(e) § 21.
(f) *Coombs* v. *B. and E. Railway Company*, 1868, 27 L.J. Ex. 401.
(g) Per Lord President Blair in *Broughton* v. *Aitchison*, 1809, 15 F.C. 411. See also *Melrose* v. *Hastie*, 1851, 13 D. 880.

and when in the hands of a carrier by sea, by transfer of the bill of lading.(a)

The notice is given usually by a "delivery order," or by the indorsation of a warrant for delivery. The later decisions consider the delivery order as constructive delivery, giving a title to the property, and not merely an authority to change possession.(b) In England it would appear that the assents of seller, custodier, and buyer are all required to effect constructive delivery, the law regarding possession and delivery being different in England in this respect from what it is in Scotland.(c)

19. Express Conditions regarding Delivery.—When any express conditions are made regarding delivery they must be fulfilled.(d)

Thus, where horses are sold on "arrival of" or "by" a certain ship, the sale is suspended on the conditions of the arrival of the ship, and the horses being on board.(e) If the delivery is to be "on arrival not beyond" a certain day, it is essential that they arrive so as to be delivered by that day.(f) In the case of an entire contract for delivery of a number of horses within a certain time, and part is delivered, the buyer may return that part if the rest are not delivered, and the seller cannot demand payment until expiry of the fixed time, but if the term pass without return of the part delivered, the seller has a claim for what has been delivered.(g)

(a) B. Pr. 1305 ; 1 Smith's L.C. 502.

(b) *Anderson* v. *M'Call*, 1866, 4 M. 765 ; *Pochin* v. *Marjoribanks*, 1869, 7 M. 622 ; *Vickers* v. *Hertz*, 1871, 9 M., H.L. 65 ; *Distillers Company* v. *Russell's Trustee*, 1889, 16 R. 479. See also Factors Acts, 1823-1887 ; B. Pr. 1317 A.

(c) B.C. i. 194, *et seq* ; B. Pr. 1303, 1305 ; Benj. 786, 820.

(d) *Lang* v. *Bruce*, 1832, 10 S. 777. Condition as to cattle remaining so long with seller after sale by auction.

(e) *Johnson* v. *Macdonald*, 1842, 9 M. and W. 600 ; but if the contract note asserts that the horses are on board, then the only condition is the arrival of the ship, *Hale* v. *Rawson*, 1858, 4 C.B., N.S. 85.

(f) *Alwcyn* v. *Prior*, 1826, 1 Ry. and Moo. 406 (1 Ill. 107).

(g) *Turnbull* v. *M'Lean*, 1874, 1 R. 730 ; 2 Smith's L.C. 40, *et seq.* ; Benj. 545, *et seq.*

In all such cases the interpretation of the special conditions will depend upon the intention of the parties making them.(*a*)

20. Respective remedies on breach of Sale.—In Scotland the buyer's remedy on the seller's failure (in the absence of fraud or essential error) to deliver, is twofold—either to rescind the contract, withholding the price if unpaid, or claiming repetition of it if paid ; or to insist for performance with or without damages, as the case may be ; (*b*) but he cannot avail himself of both these remedies, (*c*)—that is to say, hold to the contract of sale, and claim damages for non-performance by the seller.   In England, however, the general rule that jurisdiction for specific performance is not entertained regarding personal property, is limited to cases "where a compensation in damages furnishes a complete and satisfactory remedy."(*d*)   In the majority of cases, therefore, in that country, a buyer must hold to his contract of sale, accepting damages for its breach ; but this rule is subject to many exceptions, and specific performance will be ordered by the Court wherever damages does not afford an adequate remedy.(*e*)

The seller's remedy is to retain the horse in security of the price.   Where the buyer refuses to take delivery, and the seller wishes to claim damages, he should in the general case apply to the Sheriff for a judicial warrant to sell (*f*), horses forming an exception to the general practice that no judicial warrant is necessary for reselling.(*g*)   If the seller do not wish to claim damages, he may sue for the price and

(*a*) See *Colvin* v. *Short*, 1857, 19 D. 890.
(*b*) B. Pr. 120, as to the effect of fraud, see § 36.
(*c*) *M'Cormick* v. *Rittmeyer*, 1869, 7 M. 854.
(*d*) Snell's Equity, 6, 35, *et seq.*
(*e*) White and Tudor's L.C. i. 912, *et seq.*, notes to *Cuddie* v. *Rutter.*
(*f*) Bell on Sale, 109. This, however, it is thought, is only an expedient to show that the sale is conducted *bona fide*, and does not appear absolutely necessary, B. Pr. 128. Lee's Sh. Ct. Styles, p. 375, note.
(*g*) B. Pr. 128.

its keep during the buyer's failure to take delivery, or put
the horse to livery at the buyer's order, the buyer in such a
case being liable in livery charges ;(a) but there is no
obligation to put a horse in neutral custody if the parties are
agreed that the horse is suitably cared for where it is.(b)

**21. Horses on approbation, on sale and return, and on
hire and sale.**—Frequently a number of horses or ponies are
sent on approbation to a dealer for him to elect to buy or
reject them, in which case, though the seller may be bound,
the sale is suspended, and the risk does not pass till the
buyer has declared his option of taking all or any of them.(c)
Or again, horses may be sent to a dealer on the understanding that only such as he can dispose of are to be sold to
him.(d)   In such a case the condition is suspensive,(e) and
horses on sale and return are not attachable by the consignee's creditors ; but any of them sold, are sold for the
benefit of the person having them on sale or return, and his
creditors will be entitled to the price, not the sender of the
animals.(f)   This contract is different from that in which
an animal is sold at a fixed price, and there is an agreement
to resell it to the seller at a subsequent period.(g)   It is still
an open question whether horses sent on sale and return are
subject to a landlord's hypothec.

When horses are on hire at a certain rate, with an option
of keeping them at a fixed price, they are at the risk of the
seller till purchased.(h)   Again, should a horse die or be
injured while in the hands of an intending purchaser, he has

(a) B. Pr. 128 ; B.C. i. 472.

(b) Per Lord Young in *Caledonian Railway Company* v. *Rankin*, 1882, 10 R.
63 ; *Hain* v. *Laing*. 1853, 15 D. 667.

(c) B. Pr. 109, 1315. See Lord Young in *Clarke & Company* v. *Miller's Trustees*,
1887, 12 R. 1035.

(d) More's Stair, lxxxviii. ; B.C. i. 288.

(e) *Macdonald* v. *Westren*, 1888, 15 R. 988, as distinguished from *Brown* v.
Marr, 1880, 7 R. 427.

(f) Bell on Sale, 111 ; *Macdonald*, cit. ; B. Pr. 1315, *note g.*

(g) *Graham* v. *Wilson*, 1836, 14 S. 866.

(h) *Marston* v. *Miller*, 1879, 6 R. 893.

the burden of proving that he was not to blame for the death
or injury, and is liable in the same degree of diligence as a
hirer of a horse. Thus, a horse was sent to an intending purchaser on trial, and it died. It had been overwrought a day or
two previous to being sent, but the overworking, although
proved to have a tendency to produce the disease of which
it died, was not proved to have been the cause of the death.
The owner failed to show that he was blameless, and it was
held that he must bear the loss, and it was observed that,
supposing there had been no proof of overworking or misuse,
the *onus* of proof still lay on the intending purchaser.(*a*)
Under the contract of hire and sale, if a horse be delivered
on terms that the customer shall pay so much on delivery and
a certain number of periodical instalments of price, and when
these conditions are fulfilled the horse shall belong to him,
the contract is one of sale with a suspensive condition, and
if the terms are not carried out, the seller is entitled to
recover it even from a *bona fide* purchaser of the customer.(*b*)

22. Retention in Sale.(*c*)—As long as a horse remains in
the seller's custody or possession, the seller's remedy is to
retain it in security of the price ; and until delivery, actual
or constructive, he is entitled to retain it against the buyer
and his assignees till every debt due to him by the buyer is
paid or satisfied.(*d*) This right depends entirely on possession ;(*e*) it ceases with the loss of it,(*f*) and does not revive
on recovery of possession, if it has once effectually ceased.(*g*)
As a general rule it is inseparable from the contract, out of
which it springs, and persons entitled to it cannot realise
the subject retained by sale or transference.(*h*) Thus, on a

(*a*) *Pullars* v. *Walker*, 1858, 20 D. 1238.

(*b*) *Murdoch* v. *Greig*, 1889, 16 R. 396.

(*c*) B.C. ii. 87-118.

(*d*) *Black* v. *Incorporation of Bakers*, 1867, 6 M. 136, where the distinction
between lien and retention is pointed out.

(*e*) *Meikle* v. *Pollard*, 1880, 8 R. 69.

(*f*) B. Pr. 1410 ; *Meikle* v. *Pollard*, cit.

(*g*) B. Pr. 116, 1410, 1416.   (*h*) B. Pr. 1417.

sale of horses detained by an inn-keeper for his bill, the lien ceased, and the true owner, not being the guest who incurred the bill, could have claimed the price from the buyer.(a) But a seller allowing a buyer to have a horse for a temporary ride, does not thereby lose his right of retention.(b) This right does not entitle the retainer to have the beneficial use of the horse any more than to sell or transfer it.(c) Should a seller desire to sell a retained horse, he must apply for a judicial warrant to enable him to do so.(d) A seller may also retain a horse when it is allowed to remain in his possession after the term of payment for it has arrived, if he is not barred by assenting to a sub-sale by the purchaser intimated to him.(e) Retention thus differs from the right of stoppage *in transitu*, which commences when possession has ceased, and continues till delivery takes place.(f) Under the Mercantile Law Amendment Act, where a sub-sale has been intimated by the purchaser to the seller, the seller is not entitled to retain a horse for any separate debt or obligation alleged to be due to the seller by the original purchaser; but the seller's right of retention for payment of the price, or for performance of the obligations or conditions of the contract of sale, or any right of retention competent to the seller, except as between him and the sub-purchaser, or as arising from express contract with the original purchaser, is not affected by the Act.(g)

23. Stoppage *in transitu.*—Stoppage *in transitu* is an equitable extension of the right to retain possession of goods sold till the price be paid.(h) It consists in the seller's recovering possession of the goods where the buyer has

(a) *Mulliner* v. *Florence*, 1878, 3 Q.B.D. 484.
(b) *Reeves* v. *Capper*, 1838, 5 Bing. N.C. 136.
(c) *Donald* v. *Suckling*, 1866, 35 L.J., Q.B. 232, per Lord Blackburn.
(d) § 20.
(e) B. Pr. 116 ; *Fleming* v. *Smith*, 1881, 8 R. 548.
(f) §§ 13-18.
(g) 19 & 20 Vict. c. 60, § 2 ; B. Pr. 1300 B.
(h) B.C. i. 223, *et seq.*

become bankrupt or insolvent, or is *vergens ad inopiam,*(*a*) after they are out of his possession, and before they come into the possession of the buyer,(*b*) and entitles him to retain them until payment or tender of the price.(*c*) Non-payment of the price is the basis of the right of stoppage; and it is competent only when the transit between the seller and the buyer is not at an end.(*d*) Transit begins by delivery to a carrier, or other depository for transmission, and ends where the buyer or his agent takes delivery from the middleman.(*e*) The rules as to the exercise of this right depend upon delivery. They are as follows :—1. Actual delivery(*f*) puts an end to the transit, and the right to stop. Except—(1) when the sale is for ready money, and delivery takes place before the price is paid ; or when the reciprocal obligations are contemporary, the delivery being then conditional ; (*g*) and (2) where the goods are taken into the buyer's custody for safety after insolvency.(*h*) 2. Constructive delivery to a third party for the buyer to abide his order puts an end to the right to stop,(*i*) but till an operation effecting appropriation or transference,(*j*) the seller may stop. Thus, a horse delivered into a purchaser's own ship, or a ship hired by him on a time bargain, cannot be stopped ; but if the ship be hired by the voyage it may, because the shipmaster in such a case is the ship-owner's servant, not the purchaser's.(*k*) 3. In all cases where delivery is made to a middleman, the right to stop is determined by the constructive possession of

(*a*) B. Pr. 1307.

(*b*) Ersk. iii. 3, 8, *n.*

(*c*) Rank. Ersk. iii. 3, 4, *a.*

(*d*) B. Pr. 1308 ; Benj. 843, 881, 904.

(*e*) Rank. Ersk. cit.

(*f*) § 16.

(*g*) B. Pr. 1308 ; *Watt* v. *Finlay,* 1846, 8 D. 529.

(*h*) *Steins* v. *Hutchison,* 1810, 16 F.C. 33 ; *Inglis* v. *Port Eglinton, &c., Company,* 1842, 4 D. 478.

(*i*) *Strachan* v. *Knox,* Jan. 1817, 19 F.C. 253 ; *Richardson* v. *Goss,* 1802, 3 B. and P. 119 ; *Black* v. *Cassells,* 1828, 6 S. 894.

(*j*) § 18.

(*k*) B. Pr. 1308, and cases there cited.

the consignee. (*a*)   4. It is barred by transfer of the
bills of lading, or other documents of title, by the buyer
to a third party, who is in good faith, and takes them
onerously ;(*b*) but the right is not defeated by part payment
of the price ;(*c*) nor by arrestment ;(*d*) nor by a claim by
a sub-vendee, unless under a *bona fide* indorsement of a bill
of lading, or a transference of document of title under the
Factors Act. (*e*)   5. It is only competent on the buyer's
declared insolvency or bankruptcy. (*f*)

The right to stop *in transitu* is competent only to seller
or consignor, or to the agent of a seller to whom a bill of
lading is transferred, (*g*) and it implies a countermand of the
order to deliver to the buyer, and a fresh order to deliver to
the seller which the carrier is bound to obey. (*h*)

24. Mode of Stopping.—The most effectual method of
stopping is by a warrant of a judge ordinary or a magistrate. It may be exercised by taking actual possession, (*i*)
or by written notice ; but verbal notice to the immediate
custodier of the horse is sufficient, (*j*) if given in such
a manner as he may with reasonable care direct his servants not to deliver the horse to the buyer ;(*k*) but a mere
notice to a creditor of the buyer is not sufficient. (*l*)   There
is no formality required, as any active steps for resuming

(*a*) The test is that the middleman must be independent of both seller and
buyer. Ersk. iii. 3, 8, *n.*

(*b*) *Lickbarrow* v. *Mason*, 2 Ross' L.C. 92 : 40 & 41 Vict. c. 39, § 5.

(*c*) *Hodgson* v. *Loy*, 1797, 7 T.R. 440 ; *Melrose* v. *Hastie*, 1851, 13 D. 880 ; 14
D. 268.

(*d*) *Louson* v. *Craik*, 1842, 4 D. 1452

(*e*) 40 & 41 Vict. c. 39, § 5.

(*f*) B.C. i. 242.

(*g*) *Morison* v. *Gray*, 1824, 2 Bing. 260.

(*h*) *Stoppel & Co.* v. *Stoddart*, 1850, 13 D. 61.   *Louson*, cit.

(*i*) *Morton* v. *Abercrombie*, 1858, 20 D. 362.

(*j*) *Robertsons* v. *Aitken*, 1801, Mor. v. Sale, Appx. No. 3.

(*k*) *Whitehead* v. *Anderson*, 1842, 9 M. and W. 518.

(*l*) *Robertsons*, cit.

possession seem sufficient. (*a*)   In Scotland stoppage *in transitu* does not rescind the contract so as to throw the risk back on the seller, and deprive him of the right to recover the price and charges, if these should exceed the market value of what is stopped.(*b*)

25. Sales of Horses by Auction.—(1.) *Nature of Contract.*—The contract in sale by auction is by offer and acceptance ; (*c*) the offer being by bidding, the acceptance by the fall of the hammer, or by close of the bidding by the auctioneer declaring the last offer to be accepted ; (*d*) but a bidder may retract his bid,(*e*) and the seller his authority,(*f*) before the hammer is down. The purchase of each lot is a separate contract ; (*g*) and a sale by auction is presumed to be for cash, unless it be otherwise stipulated ; and the auctioneer is not entitled to deliver a horse on credit.(*h*)

26. The Exposure.—An upset price may be fixed, below which a horse is not to be sold ; but if no price be fixed, the horse is to be sold at the pleasure of the bidders.(*i*) The owner himself should not bid, unless there be a power reserved to him for that purpose ; (*j*) but anyone else may bid who can purchase at a private sale.(*k*) All private interference by the exposer, such as by sending a third party to bid for him, and rushing up the price, has been condemned and regarded as fraudulent. (*l*) Where the sale is

(*a*) B.C. i. 248.

(*b*) *Stoppel & Co.*, cit. But see *contra*, B.C. i. 231.

(*c*) § 6.

(*d*) B. Pr. § 130. There is no implied contract by advertisement of sale by auction that all the goods advertised for sale will be exposed. *Harris v. Nickerson*, 1873, L.R. 8 Q.B. 286. See also *Spencer v. Harding*, 1870, L.R. 5 C.P. 561.

(*e*) *Payne v. Cave*, 1789, 3 T.R. 148.

(*f*) Per Martin, B., in *Warlow v. Harrison*, 1859, 29 L.J., Q.B. 14.

(*g*) *Chapman v. Couston*, 1871, 9 M. 675, affirmed 1872, 10 M. (H.L.) 74.

(*h*) Lord Justice-Clerk Moncreiff in *Macdonald v. Henderson*, 1882, 10 R. 95-100.

(*i*) B. Pr. 131.

(*j*) *Thom v. Macbeth*, 1875, 3 R. 161.

(*k*) *Shiell v. Guthrie's Trs.* 1874, 1 R. 1083.

(*l*) More's Notes to Stair, xci. ; Benj. 462.

" without reserve," or at the pleasure of the company, the plain meaning of this is that the seller shall not bid,(a) and the highest *bona fide* bidder is entitled to have the sale reduced against a fictitious bidder ; (b) or, if that is impossible, to have an action against the auctioneer.(c) Where a horse is bid up by a " white bonnet," and there is a condition that " the highest bidder is to be the buyer," the seller cannot recover the price.(d) In regard to this matter, Chief Justice Best said,(e) " A man goes to a sale, and is told that if he is the highest bidder he shall have the article. He bids a certain sum, and a person (employed by the seller), whom he does not know, attends the sale and puffs against him, and in consequence of that he is compelled to pay a much larger price than he would otherwise have paid. Is not this a gross fraud ? . . . I am of opinion that a person acts in opposition to the conditions of sale, where the highest bidder is to be the buyer, if he employs a person to bid for the purpose of enhancing the price."

In all cases the biddings must be fair and not collusive. Thus, where the offerers at a public sale had combined to smother competition, and thus enable one of their number to buy the subject at an under value, the proceeding was held fraudulent, and the sale was not only held void, but the guilty party was subjected in damages.(f) It is also unlawful to bribe another to refrain from bidding.(g)

An exposure by auction implies that the descriptions given shall not be deceitful.(h)

27. Duties of the Auctioneer.—The judge of the roup is

(a) *Faulds* v. *Corbet*, 1859, 21 D. 587.

(b) *Faulds*, cit.

(c) *Warlow* v. *Harrison*, 1859, 29 L.J., Q.B. 14.

(d) *Green* v. *Baverstock*, 1863, 32 L.J., C.P. 181.

(e) *Crowder* v. *Austin*, 1825, 2 C. and P. 208. See also *Wheeler* v. *Collier*, 1827, M. and M. 126 ; *Faulds*, cit. ; *Shiell*, cit.

(f) *Murray*, 1783, M. 9567.

(g) *Aitchison*, 1783, M. 9567.

(h) *Hill* v. *Gray*, 1816, 1 Starkie, 434 (1 Ill. 16).

not an arbiter to decide all questions arising out of the sale, but only to see fair play and decide matters arising while the sale is going on.(*a*) It is the implied duty of the auctioneer to give the buyers fair opportunity of bidding ; (*b*) but he is not responsible for any breach of the conditions of the sale, unless he has had knowledge of it.(*c*) He is personally liable for fulfilment of the contract if he does not disclose the exposer's name, (*d*) or if it appear that he is himself the seller.(*e*) The purchaser of a horse at an auction is not entitled to sue both the auctioneer and the principal, on an alleged breach of warranty. Such an action was dismissed against the auctioneer, in respect that the pursuer, having alleged that the principal had taken the horse back, must be held to have elected to sue the principal.(*f*) His position is that of factor for the seller till purchase, and then custodier for the buyer.(*g*) He has authority to receive payment, if there be nothing to the contrary in the conditions of sale ; but he has no implied authority to warrant a horse, and any warranty given by him without authority is given at his own risk entirely.(*h*) A statement that a horse is the property of the vendor made by himself or an agent is a sufficient warranty of the ownership, and an assertion by the auctioneer that all the horses in the sale are the *bona fide* property of the person whose stud he is selling vitiates a sale made on the faith of that representation, if such horse has been put into the sale without notice, because the purchaser would probably give a much higher price for a horse belonging to the stud in question than for one without a character.(*i*)

(*a*) *Strachan* v. *Auld*, 1884, 11 R. 756.

(*b*) *Burns* v. *Monypenny*, 1807, M. Appx. Sale 4 (1 Ill. 117).

(*c*) *Mainprice* v. *Westley*, 1865, 6 B. and S. 420 ; *Warlow* v. *Harrison*, 1859, 29 L.J., Q.B. 14.

(*d*) *Franklyn* v. *Lamond*, 1847, 4 C.B. 637 ; *Ferrier* v. *Dods*, 1865, 3 M. 561. For issues, see Appx. iii.

(*e*) *Wolfe* v. *Horne*, 1877, 2 Q.B.D. 355.

(*f*) *Ferrier*, cit.

(*g*) Benj. 247 ; *Warlow*, cit.

(*h*) *Payne* v. *Leconfield*, 1882, 51 L.J., Q.B. 642.

(*i*) *Bexwell* v. *Christie*, 1776, Cowp. 395.

Apart from exceptions in the conditions of sale, an auctioneer is responsible to the owner for the custody of a horse sent to him for sale till it is sold ; after sale he is custodier for the buyer ;(a) but if a horse is put up to auction and not sold, and the auctioneer request the owner to take it away, the custody of it reverts to the owner.(b) If there be an error in a catalogue, it may be corrected by the auctioneer ; and if the correction be heard by the purchaser, he cannot plead the error in defence to an action for the price.(c)

28. Conditions of Sale.(d)—Particular conditions are often introduced into sales of horses by auction. As, for example, that the exposer shall be allowed one or more biddings ; or that each bid shall exceed the previous one by a certain amount ; or that the bid of an offerer shall be binding on the failure of a higher offer; or that part payment must instantly be made ; or that horses returned as disconform to warranty must be accompanied by a V.S. certificate.(e) In nearly all auction sales of horses a time limit is fixed for rejection,(f) and almost invariably there is a condition to the effect that horses disconform to warranty shall be tried by the auctioneer, or some one appointed by him, whose decision shall be final.(g) All such conditions are to have their fair construction, and are not to be overruled by any verbal declaration of the auctioneer.(h) Thus, in a sale of cattle by auction, where an offer was made to prove that the auctioneer declared orally at the sale, that on the lots being knocked down they were to be held as delivered to the

(a) *Emmerson* v. *Heelis*, 1809, 2 Taunt. 38.
(b) *Renwick* v. *Von Rotberg*, 1875, 1 R. 855.
(c) *Eden* v. *Blake*, 1845, 13 M. and W. 614.
(d) See Appx. iv.
(e) *Bywater* v. *Richardson*, 1834, 1 A. and E. 508 ; *Mensard* v. *Aldridge*, 1801, 3 Esp. 271 ; *Hendrie* v. *Stewart*, 1842, 4 D. 1417.
(f) See § 43 ; also *Best* v. *Osborne*, 1824, 2 C. and P. 74 ; *Bywater*, cit.
(g) *Hinchcliffe* v. *Barwick*, 1880, L.R. 5 Ex. D. 177.
(h) *Horsfall* v. *Fauntleroy*, 1830, 10 B. and Cr. 755.

purchaser, it was held that such proof was incompetent, there being written articles of sale containing no such provision. (*a*)

In another case, a party made a purchase of horses at a sale by auction, one of the conditions of which was that, should the purchase money not be made good within twenty-four hours, the disposer was to be at liberty to resell the horses with or without notice to the purchaser, who should be debtor to the disposer for any loss arising out of the non-fulfilment of the bargain, including commission on the resale, keep, and all other charges. The purchaser failed to pay, and the horses were resold. It was held—1*st*, That the sale must be held to have taken place under the conditions of sale ; 2*nd*, that it was not necessary for the sellers to prove that these conditions had been read or publicly exhibited at the sale ; and 3*rd*, that the sellers were entitled to the difference of price, expense of keep, commission on resale, and other charges due to non-fulfilment. (*b*) Again, a condition of sale was in these terms, " Purchasers must satisfy themselves with the condition, quality, and description of the subjects previous to bidding, as no lot will be taken back or exchanged, or any other abatement made from the purchase price." A horse was sold without warranty or representation, but was known by the exposers to have certain defects which were not disclosed, and might have been discovered on examination. The purchaser refused to pay the price, but was held liable for it, there being no fraud by the exposers, inasmuch as the sale was with all faults. (*c*)

Sufficient notice of conditions of sale is given when they are printed along with the catalogue to be obtained in the sale-room ;(*d*) or if there are no printed conditions, when written conditions are pasted up on the auctioneer's box, or on the

(*a*) *Lang v. Bruce*, 1832, 10 S. 777.
(*b*) *Hain v. Laing*, 1853, 15 D. 667.
(*c*) *Yeats v. Reid*, 1884, 21 S.L.R. 698.
(*d*) *Hain*, cit. ; *Macdonald v. Henderson*, 1882, 10 R. 95.

walls or door of the market or place of auction.(*a*) Where there are no written or printed conditions, parole evidence is admissible to prove an additional condition alleged to have been made by the auctioneer.(*b*)

The remedy where there has been unfair bidding by or on behalf of the exposer is, if possible, to reduce all the offers after the last *bona fide* offer, and to hold the last *bona fide* purchaser to be the purchaser ;(*c*) but where that is impossible, the remedy is to reduce the sale *in toto*.(*d*) A sale by an auctioneer after the auction is over is an ordinary sale.(*e*)

An auctioneer has a lien over a horse for the price thereof,(*f*) and horses sent to an auctioneer are privileged from distress for rent.(*g*)

When property is sold in lots described particularly, a buyer is only affected with notice applicable to the lot he buys; and is not to be taken as having read all the particulars of all the lots.(*h*) In England, the price does not vest till expiry of the time of rejection on a warranty.(*i*) In Scotland, this is usually provided for in the conditions of sale.(*j*) When a sale by auction is advertised, and a purchaser is put to expense in coming to the sale he has no claim therefor if one or more of the horses advertised for sale be not put up to auction.(*k*)

29. Rejection on Insolvency.

—The buyer should reject a horse if he is insolvent or *vergens ad inopiam ;*(*l*) because if actual delivery of a horse is given, it cannot be rejected

(*a*) *Mensard*, cit., p. 29. See also *White & Co.* v. *Dougherty*, 1891, 18 R. 972.
(*b*) *Christie* v. *Hunter*, 1880, 7 R. 729.
(*c*) *Faulds* v. *Corbet*, 1859, 21 D. 587.
(*d*) *Shiell* v. *Guthrie's Trs.*, 1874, 1 R. 1083.
(*e*) *Mews* v. *Carr*, 1856, 26 L.J. Ex. 39.
(*f*) *Robinson* v. *Rutter*, 1855, 24 L.J., Q.B. 250 ; B. Pr. 1315.
(*g*) *Williams* v. *Holmes*, 1853, 22 L.J. Ex. 283. See § 89.
(*h*) *Curtis* v. *Thomas*, 1875, 33 L.T., N.S. 664.
(*i*) *Hardingham* v. *Allen*, 1848, C.B. 793.
(*j*) See Appx. iv.
(*k*) *Bexwell*, cit., 1776, Cowp. 397 ; *Harris* v. *Nickerson*, 1873, L.R. 8 Q.B. 286.
(*l*) *Watt* v. *Findlay*, 1846, 8 D. 529, 532 ; *Booker* v. *Milne*, 1870, 9 M. 314.

afterwards.(*a*) But if it be delivered to one not having
authority from the buyer to receive it,(*b*) it may still be
rejected ; and, similarly, if it be out of the seller's possession
and in the custody of a third party for his behalf, and no
constructive delivery have taken place, the seller's right is
preserved.(*c*) Intimation of rejection is necessary so as to
enable the seller by acceptance of it to rescind the contract,
and the test of the competency of rejection is whether or not
the buyer has taken possession or delivery of the horse.(*d*)

FRAUDULENT TRANSACTIONS.

30. Fraud.—Fraud, a term denoting moral turpitude,(*e*) is a
contrivance or machination to deceive,(*f*) and is a ground for
annulling obligations induced by it.(*g*) It manifests itself in
the sale of horses by false misrepresentation,(*h*) by active or
passive concealment,(*i*) by underhand dealing (*j*) or taking
advantage of persons intoxicated ; (*k*) or by circumvention or
undue influence upon a facile person.(*l*) When fraud enters
into any contract such as sale, it destroys the element of consent (*m*) necessary to the existence of a binding agreement.
It is not, however, for every kind of fraud that an injured
party will obtain redress by law. The fraud against which,
in mercantile dealings, no redress is given, is exemplified in
the concealment of such defect as the seller is not bound to
communicate unless he is asked about it, or in such petty

(*a*) *Mitchell* v. *Wright*, 1871, 9 M. 516.

(*b*) *Wallace* v. *Miller*, 1766, M. 8475 ; *Brandt* v. *Dickson*, 1876, 3 R. 375.

(*c*) B. Pr. 1310.

(*d*) *Drake* v. *M‘Millan*, 1807, Hume, 691 ; *Booker*, cit.

(*e*) Rank. Ersk. iii. 1, 6 A.

(*f*) D. Pr. 13, 13 A.

(*g*) Stair. i. 99 ; Ersk. iii. 1, 16 ; B.C. i. 263 ; *M‘Neill* v. *M‘Neill's Trustees*,
1824, 2 Sh. App. 206.

(*h*) § 31.

(*i*) § 32.

(*j*) § 33.

(*k*) § 34.

(*l*) § 35.

(*m*) Stair, i. 9, 9 ; Ersk. iii. 1, 16.

misrepresentations regarding the capabilities of his horses, and such praises as a seller is wont to bestow upon them so as to enhance their value. But once the buyer gives the seller to understand that he is relying on his statements, and that it is on the faith of them he is going to purchase, the law regards them as fraudulent, if false, and will give him remedies on such a contract.(a) The redress obtainable on the ground of fraud depends, in some cases, upon whether or not error has been combined with it regarding the horse purchased or the price.(b) When essential error is combined with fraud which gives rise to the contract, the contract is null *ab initio*,(c) but even where no material error co-exists, if it appears that a party would not have entered into a contract of sale had he not been fraudulently led into it, he is justly said to have been deceived ; and he may sue for a reduction of the contract on the ground of the fraud, or plead a personal exception when he is sued for the price, unless barred by delay ; though these pleas will have no effect in questions with *bona fide* assignees.(d) But a sale of a horse induced by fraud, where the fraud is such that it has given rise to it, is not void but voidable at the option of the injured party, provided there be no material error also.(e) The sale is consequently valid until rescinded, and the principle of rescission is *restitutio in integrum ;* to place both parties in the same position as they were before the sale took place.(f) This is accomplished by the return of horse and price, where it is still in the buyer's hands ; or, when that is impossible, as— *e.g.*, from death, or by his having sold it, by a claim of damages against the party committing the fraud.(g) When

(a) B. Pr. 111 ; B.C. i. 466, *n.*

(b) B. Pr. 13, 13 A, § 36.

(c) § 4. See Blackburn, J., in *Kennedy* v. *Panama, &c., Co.*, 1867, L.R. 2 Q.B. 580, 587.

(d) Ersk. iii. 1, 16.

(e) B.C. i. 262.

(f) *Western Bank* v. *Addie*, 1867, 5 M. (H.L.) 80 ; *Houldsworth* v. *City of Glasgow Bank*, 1880, 7 R.H.L. 53.

(g) Cases cit., *note f*, see B.C. i. 262 and *note ; Graham* v. *Western Bank*, 1865, 3 M. 617.

third parties have onerously acquired rights under a contract
induced by fraud, the remedy of the party defrauded is
limited to damages ; he cannot reduce the contract.(*a*)   And
where the fraud is merely incidental to the contract, and not
strictly speaking *dans causam contractui*, the injured party
cannot rescind the contract, but he has a claim of damages ;
and even in that case the fraud must be material.(*b*)

When, however, the fraud is that of a third party of which
the contracting party has no knowledge and derives no benefit, the remedy can only be obtained against such third
party.(*c*)   Thus a horse dealer who had entered into a plot
with others to sell an unsound horse as sound, was found liable
in relief to the purchaser, although the sale was not made by
him but by a coadjutor.(*d*)   But the fraud of an agent binds
his principal if the fraudulent act be within the scope of his
authority, or for his principal's benefit.(*e*)

31. Misrepresentation.—When misrepresentations of any
material facts are wilfully made, either to one who is to act
upon it, or to a third (*f*) party, with that end in view, with
the intent that they shall be acted on, either when known
by the party giving them to be untrue, or recklessly given
by him with an utter disregard as to their truth or falsity,
they are evidence from which fraud is to be inferred, and
are a good ground for annulling a bargain or claiming
damages.(*g*)   Thus, where a party advertised a horse for sale
by auction as " a remarkable good hack, and parted with for
no fault further than that the owner is going abroad and has
no further occasion for him," and a similar statement was

(*a*) B.C. i. 262 ; B. Pr. 13 A.
(*b*) B. Pr. 13 ; B.C. i. 262 ; *Attwood* v. *Small*, 1838, 6 Cl. and Fin. 232 ; *Ehrenbacher & Co.* v. *Kennedy*, 1874, 1 R. 1131, relevancy of averment of fraud.
(*c*) B. Pr. 13.
(*d*) *Hibbert* v. *Bruce*, 1822, 1 S. 422.
(*e*) B. Pr. 224 B., and authorities there cited, § 66.
(*f*) Bank. Ersk. Pr. iii. 1, 6 A ; *Attwood* v. *Small*, cit.
(*g*) Anson Contracts, 151 ; *Peck* v. *Gurney*, 1873, L.R. 6 H.L. 377 ; *Barry* v.
Croskey, 1861, 2 J. and H. 1 ; *Derry* v. *Peek*, 1889, 14 App. Ca. 337 ; *Wheelton* v.
Hardisty, 1858, 27 L.J., Q.B. 241. See pp. 51 and 52, *infra*.

made by the auctioneer when the horse was exposed and sold; it was held that, as the horse then was, and formerly had been lame in both shoulders, and had a sprained hind leg, which were old faults that were not visible at the sale by reason of the softness of the ground, and the seller declined to say who the gentleman to whom the horse belonged was, he was liable in repetition of the price.(a) Again, where the seller of a mare on being told by the buyer that he wanted "a quiet, useful and thankful animal," answered, "that the beast was canny and serviceable in every respect, and particularly in riding," whereupon she was bought at a fair price; it was held, although the evidence was contradictory, that as the seller was aware she had "tricks," he was bound to take her back and repay the price.(b) In these cases the facts misrepresented were held material; but in the following case, though there was misrepresentation, it was held not to be of a material fact. A party bought a horse under a written warranty, which described him as "my dark bay horse," and as "safe in harness;" and the seller had verbally represented that the horse had been sent to him for sale by a gentleman in England, whereas he had bought him from a gentleman in Leith, who parted with him because he had been on one occasion vicious in a gig, which the seller knew and did not disclose; and, after being kept for two months, the horse became restive in a gig, but this was attributable partly to the blame of the buyer. It was held on an action on the warranty, that the verbal misrepresentation as to the former owner of the horse was not sufficient to annul the sale (the written warranty being silent as to the former owner).(c) Lord Chancellor Eldon observed in that case :—"The object of the misrepresentation must have been to prevent inquiries which might lead to the rejection of the horse. But that mis-

(a) *Brown* v. *Gilbert*, 1791, Hume, 671.

(b) *Beddie* v. *Milroy*, 1812, Hume, 695.

(c) *Geddes* v. *Pennington*, 1814, 17 F.C. 606 ; aff. 1817, 6 Pat. App. 312.

representation will not invalidate the transaction if the horse was a fit horse for a gig at the time he was sold,"(a) and costs were consequently not allowed.

If, however, a misrepresentation be made which gives rise to a sale, and the seller believed the statements made to be true, he will not be liable,(b) nor if they are about matters connected with which the misled party exercised his own judgment ;(c) but this does not apply where there is essential error, or in the case of a warranty being given, because the warranty does not merely give rise to the sale, but is an absolute qualification of it ;(d) and where a misrepresentation is made which is capable of two interpretations, it lies on the party impugning it to show that he interpreted it in the sense in which it is false, and to show that he has been deceived by it. (e)

32. Concealment.—Provided there be a duty on a seller to reveal material facts or defects of which he is cognisant, concealment of them will amount to fraud.(f) This duty exists whenever a seller in the knowledge of a latent material defect, sells a horse for a full price without communicating the fact to the buyer.(g) In regard to what amounts to concealment Lord Currichill observes:—" Mere disingenuousness is not always of such a kind as is sufficient in law to annul the transaction in which it may have been practised.(h)

" In whatever manner a man may be deceived or misled, yet, if he was not deceived by relying upon the friendship and integrity of another, it is not a fraud. Fraud, therefore,

(a) *Geddes*, cit. p. 317.

(b) *Brownlie* v. *Miller*, 1878, 5 R. 1076, 1092 ; *Dunnet* v. *Mitchell*, 1887, 15 R. 131 ; Benj. 432, *et seq.*

(c) B. Pr. 14, and cases cited in *note (f)*.

(d) § 37.

(e) *Smith* v. *Chadwick*, 1884, L.R. 9 App. Ca. 187.

(f) B.C. i. 263.

(g) §§ 9, 39.

(h) *Gillespie* v. *Russell*, 1856, 18 D. 677, 686.

implies treachery, without which no artifice nor double-dealing can be termed fraud, in a proper sense."(*a*)

Except in circumstances in which one contracting party expressly, or by implication, pledges his veracity as to the truth of his representation to the other contracting party, the latter cannot complain of being defrauded by a failure in such veracity, however morally wrong it may be, and cannot insist on his contract being judicially rescinded on that ground.(*b*) An issue of concealment always imports a duty of communication. "There can be no relevant case of fraudulent concealment where there is no duty to disclose."(*c*) "Where there is a duty or an obligation to speak, and a man, in breach of that duty or obligation, holds his tongue, and does not speak and does not say the thing he was bound to say, and if that was done with the intention of inducing the other party to act upon the belief that the reason why he did not speak was because he had nothing to say, I should be inclined myself to hold that that was fraud also." "If, when a man thinks it is highly probable that a thing exists, he chooses to say he knows the thing exists, that is really asserting what is false—it is positive fraud. If you choose to say, and say without inquiry, 'I warrant,' that is a contract. If you say, 'I know it,' and if you say that in order to save yourself and the other party the trouble of inquiring, that is a false representation. You are saying what is false to induce him to act upon it."(*d*) " Active " concealment is virtually a misrepresentation,(*e*) as when one uses devices to conceal the defects of a horse sold, as by "gingering,"(*f*) " plugging," " pegging," " bishoping," or filling up a sandcrack or thrush ; or in failing, on discovery of

(*a*) Kames's Equity, i. 1, 4.

(*b*) *Broatch* v. *Jenkins*, 1866, 4 M. 1030.

(*c*) Per Lord Ardmillan in *Broatch* v. *Jenkins*, cit. p. 1032.

(*d*) Lord Blackburn in *Brownlie* v. *Miller*, 1880, 7 R. (H.L.) 66.

(*e*) *Schneider* v. *Heath*, 1813, 3 Camp. 506 ; *Hill* v. *Gray*, 1816, 1 Stark, 434 ; *Keates* v. *Earl of Cadogan*, 1851, 20 L.J., C.P. 76.

(*f*) *Cossar* v. *Marjoribanks*, 1826, 4 S. 685.

the error, to correct a misapprehension innocently caused ;(*a*) or by keeping silence as to facts which, if disclosed, would alter the whole effect of what has been stated.(*b*)   And even when a horse is sold, "with all faults," the seller is not protected against faults he has been at pains to disguise.(*c*)

33. Underhand Dealing.—Where there is such a course of underhand dealing, not precisely coming under misrepresentation or concealment, as above explained, it will depend very much on the facts of each particular case, on the relative situation of the parties, and on their means of information, whether it is, or is not, fraudulent.(*d*)

34. Intoxication.—Where a bargain has been entered into by a party in a state of intoxication, he may have redress ;(*e*) but the intoxication must amount to total incapacity of giving serious consent, and not mere facility from drink ;(*f*) and the issue generally framed leaves it to the jury to find whether the party pleading intoxication was so much intoxicated as to be "wholly incapable of understanding" what he was doing.(*g*)

Thus, in a case where a suspension of a charge upon a bill for the price of a horse, was brought on the ground that the suspender was intoxicated, it came out that, at the time of signing the bill, the purchaser not only was able to entertain his guests, but pressed them to take wine with him ; and, moreover, had recollections, the morning after, of having signed the bill, and it was held that he was not in such a

(*a*) *Reynell* v. *Sprye*, 1852, 1 De G. M. and G. 660.

(*b*) *Peek* v. *Gurney*, 1873, L.R. 6 H.L. 377.

(*c*) § 9.

(*d*) B. Pr. 14 ; Addison on Contracts, 116, see *Henry* v. *Wyper*, 1857, 20 D. 56. Circumstances in which a party, who alleged that he was merely a bystander, was held to be the principal in the sale of a horse, on a warranty, and liable on its proving unsound.

(*e*) Stair, i. 10, 13 ; Ersk. iii. 1, 16 ; *Duncan* v. *Martin*, 1839, M·F. 278 ; *Jardine* v. *Elliot*, 1803, Hume, 684 ; *Hunter* v. *Stevenson*, 1804, Hume, 686.

(*f*) *Taylor* v. *Provan*, 1864, 2 M. 1226.

(*g*) *Johnston* v. *Clark*, 1854, 17 D. 228.

state of intoxication as to entitle him to suspend the charge. (a)

If both parties be intoxicated, drunkenness may be proved to show that parties did not seriously consent. (b) It would appear, that a party seeking relief will be barred, unless he makes his challenge immediately after coming to his senses. (c).

35. Circumvention and Undue Influence.—When contracts have been obtained by artifice or fraud upon persons who are of a weak and facile disposition, by reason of age, disease, or other infirmity, or when force or fear is employed to obtain consent to them, such as will shake a mind of ordinary firmness, they are reducible. (d) Circumvention seems, in such cases, to have the same effect as fraud ; (e) but facility and lesion, without fraud or circumvention, are not of themselves grounds for setting aside obligations. (f) A grossly inadequate price, the buyer being in pecuniary difficulties, will not invalidate a sale, and will not, of itself, afford ground for annulling a sale, (g) although such circumstances are strong evidence in support of fraud or circumvention. Intimidation, however, combined with fraud and circumvention, in order to induce a person of facile disposition to enter into a contract, is a ground of reduction. (h)

36. Rescission of the Contract.—The nullity of a sale, on the grounds above referred to, must be judicially declared. The contract, ostensibly, is valid and regular, and it subsists till it is reduced. The Court, however, will not alter the

(a) *Pollok v. Burns*, 1875, 2 R. 497.
(b) *Jardine*, cit.
(c) *Pollok*, cit.
(d) B.C. i. 136 ; B. Pr. 14, and cases there cited.
(e) *Gray v. Binny*, 1879, 7 R. 332, 347 ; but see Lord Kinloch in *Love v. Marshall*, 1870, 9 M. 291, 297.
(f) *Scott v. Wilson*, 1825, 3 Mur. 518, 526.
(g) *M'Kirdy v. Anstruther*, 1839, 1 D. 855.
(h) *Cairns v. Marianski*, 1850, 12 D. 919, 1286 ; 1 M'Q. 212.

contract in accordance with the real intention of the parties, but will reduce it, subject, it may be, to conditions as to restitution and recompense. (a) In the absence of essential error, the defrauded party can only get the sale rescinded provided there be these three requisites(b) :—

(1.) That he can put the other party in the same position he was in before the transaction. Thus, if a horse have perished, the contract for its sale cannot be rescinded, but relief may be had in damages. (c)

(2.) That no third party has, in good faith, and for value, acquired rights under the contract.(c) But third parties having acquired rights gratuitously, or with notice of the fraud, cannot take benefit from a fraudulent transaction,(d) and under notice is included knowledge of all facts and circumstances as ought to have made them inquire into the author's title.(e)

(3.) That the wrong-doer's position is not materially altered by delay in challenging the contract. In the case of breach of the contract of sale, however, where there is fraud on the part of the seller, the purchaser is entitled, at his option, either to set aside the contract altogether, or demand such damages as he may have sustained through the fraudulent misrepresentation of the seller.(f) But, except there be fraud, he cannot both retain the horse and claim an abatement of the price; his remedy being to return it at once, and claim damages for breach of contract. (g)

(a) *Geddes* v. *Pennington*, 1814, 17 F.C. 606, aff. 1817, 5 Dow, 159.

(b) B. Pr. 13 A.

(c) § 20.

(d) *Wardlaw* v. *Mackenzie*, 1859, 21 D. 940.

(e) *Cook* v. *Eshelby*, 1887, 12 App. Ca. 271.

(f) *Amaan* v. *Handyside*, 1865, 3 M. 526 ; *Dobbie* v. *Duncanson*, 1872, 10 M. 810.

(g) *M'Cormick* v. *Rittmeyer*, 1869, 7 M. 854.

CHAPTER II.

37. Warranty Generally.(*a*)—In England a warranty in sale is a collateral undertaking, forming part of the contract by the agreement of parties, express or implied ; (*b*) in Scotland it is an essential condition forming part of the contract of sale ; consequently, if the warranty be broken, the sale is reducible ; (*c*) but in England it is a separate contract from the sale, and the sale stands though the warranty is broken, the buyer's remedy being damages for breach of it only, unless there be separate agreement that the horse is to be returned if not up to the warranty.(*d*)

As already indicated, the rule *caveat emptor* applies in the purchase of a horse,(*e*) and, unless a warranty be given, or there be fraud,(*f*) the buyer has no redress ; (*g*) and if a

(*a*) On this subject see Ersk. iii. 3, 10, *n* ; B.C. i. 466, *n* ; Smith's Mercantile Law, p. 649.
(*b*) Benj. 607.
(*c*) Rank. Ersk. Pr. iii. 3, 4. (*d*) See § 57. (*e*) See §§ 9, 7.
(*f*) §§ 30-35 ; *Rough* v. *Moir*, 1875, 2 R. 529.
(*g*) B. Pr. 97.

purchaser make no inquiries as to its soundness or qualities, and the horse turn out unfit for use, he cannot recover against the seller, as it must be assumed that he got it at a cheap rate.(*a*) But where a buyer has been so far warned by any disclosure which is incomplete, he must exercise his own judgment as to whether the horse is worth the price asked.(*b*)

Every affirmation previous to sale, provided it is so intended, is a warranty ; (*c*) but antecedent representations made as an inducement to buy are not warranties unless they form part of the contract when concluded.(*d*) When any statements are made previous to sale by private bargain, or are published in an auction catalogue, the question often arises whether what is said or written is a representation or a warranty,(*e*) for all affirmations made to a buyer as a ground of reliance are warranties, and are absolute qualifications of the sale.(*f*) It is not necessary that the statements be in writing. Words are sufficient ; and phrases such as " I warrant," or the like, are not required to constitute a warranty, for it is sufficient if the seller make representations which the purchaser has given him to understand are essential to his buying.(*g*) Further, the representations need not be made simultaneously with the bargain, provided they form part of it, they are warranties.(*h*) Thus, a plaintiff bought a horse without a warranty at auction. On the day previous to sale the following conversation took place, during the plaintiff's examination of the horse. The defendant said, " You have nothing to look for ; I assure you he is perfectly sound in every respect," to which the

(*a*) *Jones* v. *Bright*, 1829, 3 M. and P. 155, 175.
(*b*) *Brand* v. *Wight*, 1812, Hume, 697.
(*c*) Smith's L.C. i. 187, and cases there cited.
(*d*) Bell's Com. i. 466, *n.* 2.
(*e*) See § 40.
(*f*) B.C. 1, 466, *n.* 2 ; B. Pr. 111 ; *Pasley* v. *Freeman*, 1789, 3 T.R. 51, 59 ; *Stewart* v. *Jamieson*, 1863, 1 M. 525 ; *Shepherd* v. *Kain*, 1821, 5 B. and Ald. 240.
(*g*) *Scott* v. *Steel*, 1857, 20 D. 253 ; 2 Sm. L.C. 75, *et seq.*, as to agent's representations.
(*h*) *Stucley* v. *Bayley*, 1862, 1 H. and C. 405 ; B.C. 1, 466, *n.* 2.

plaintiff replied, "If you say so, I am satisfied." The horse turned out unsound, but the seller did not know it when he made the representation, so that there was no case of fraud. It was held that this was merely an expression of opinion.(a) It is no answer to a demand for the price of a horse rejected as disconform to warranty that the seller honestly believed the horse possessed of the qualities warranted, if it does not actually possess them.(b)

All warranties, whether express or implied, apply to the state of the horse at the time of sale; (c) except time warranties, such, for example, as "warranted sound for a month." Should a defect show itself soon after sale it is a question of evidence whether or not it amounts to a breach of warranty; and it lies on a purchaser to show positively that the horse truly had the disease on him prior to the sale; for if the horse become unsound after the date of the sale the purchaser has no ground of action against the seller.(d) Yet the warranty of a future event, if express, is valid whether given before or at the time of the sale.(e)

Thus, a seller after telling the buyer that one of two horses he was about to sell had a cold, agreed to deliver both at the end of a fortnight sound and free from blemish; at the end of the fortnight the horses were delivered, one with a cough, the other with a swelled leg, a fault that was also apparent at the time of the sale. The seller sued the buyer for the price and a verdict was given for the defendant and a new trial refused, on the ground that the warranty applied not to the time of sale but to a subsequent period.(f) In another case where a mare, warranted

(a) *Hopkins* v. *Tanqueray*, 1854, 15 C.B. 130.

(b) Per Lord Justice-Clerk Hope in *Scott*, cit. p. 256.

(c) *Ewart* v. *Hamilton*, 1791, Hume, 667; *Gilmer* v. *Galloway*, 1830, 8 S. 420; *M'Bey* v. *Reid*, 1842, 4 D. 349; *Hendrie* v. *Stewart*, 1842, 4 D. 1417; *Pollock* v. *Macadam*, 1840, 2 D. 1026. See also *Brown* v. *Boreland*, 1848, 10 D. 1460, where chronic disease became acute by the act of the purchaser.

(d) Lord Meadowbank in *Wright* v. *Blackwood*, 1833, 11 S. 722; Lord Benholme in *Dykes* v. *Hill*, 1860, 22 D. 1523.

(e) *Eden* v. *Parkinson*, 1781, 2 Doug. 732, a; *Pasley*, cit.

(f) *Liddard* v. *Kain*, 1824, 2 Bing. S.C. 183.

quiet, shied at meeting stage coaches, but was cured shortly after rejection, the purchaser was held entitled to reject and obtain repetition of the price.(a)

It is always a question for a jury, or a judge in his jury capacity, to determine whether a representation comes up to a warranty, and this is to be inferred from the nature of the sale, and the circumstances of each case.(b)

Warranties are of various kinds. According to their scope, they are "general" or "special."(c) A general warranty is such as is implied in the contract of sale, or it may be indicated by such a word as "warranted"; and it is an undertaking that a horse is what the party professes it to be; and, in such a sense, is distinguished from a special warranty which refers to a particular matter, such as age,(d) for example. According to their constitution, they are express or implied. An express warranty is a warranty strictly limited by its terms; whether these relate to soundness or freedom from vice, or anything else; while an implied warranty refers to the merchantable quality of fitness for work when a full price is given, or to fitness for a special purpose.(e)

38. Distinction between Representation and Warranty.(f)—The main distinction between a representation and a warranty is thus stated by Tindall, C.J. :—"In the case of a representation to render liable the party making it, the facts stated must be untrue to his knowledge; but in the case of a warranty he is liable whether they are in his knowledge or not."(g) A man may represent his horse as a

---

(a) *Begbie* v. *Robertson*, 1828, 6 S. 1014.

(b) B.C. i. 466.

(c) Oliphant, pp. 117, 118. See also B. Pr. 111.

(d) § 42. *Jones* v. *Cowley*, 1825, 4 B. and C. 445 ("Except a kick on the leg"); *Henning* v. *Parry*, 1834, 6 C. and P. 580 (Warranty "except one foot").

(e) As to the meaning of an express warranty in the Mercantile Law Amendment Act, see § 39, p. 50.

(f) On this subject generally see B.C. i. 466, n, and the judgment of Williams, J., in *Behn* v. *Burness*, 1863, 32 L.J., Q.B. 204.

(g) *Budd* v. *Fairmaner*, 1831, 5 C. and P. 78.

good goer, and praise it to any extent with a view of getting it sold, but vague statements of this kind do not of themselves constitute a warranty, and a buyer may take or reject these boastful recommendations according to his prudence.(a) But when a statement is made, and on the faith of it a sale is effected, which would not but for the faith in the statement have been effected, it amounts to a warranty.(b) The test in all cases where such words as "I warrant," or the like, are not used, is whether the person who entered into the bargain did so on the faith of the statements made, and that this was known, or must have been known, to the party making the representations. Thus A sold a horse to B. He tried it, and thereafter asked A whether the horse was steady and quiet to ride, and A said he was. The horse turned out unsteady and B offered to return it, but A declined and it was sold by judicial warrant. B raised an action against A for repetition of the price. Lord Wood in his judgment observed :—" On the evidence I think it clear that a representation was made on which the purchaser was entitled to rely and did rely—the representation so made, according to the law of Scotland, amounting to a warranty. Then I do not think that the trial at the time of sale took off the effect of it, and threw it on the purchaser to satisfy himself as to the qualities of the horse. For after the trial, and while writing out the cheque he said, ' Are you sure the horse is steady in harness, and quiet to ride ?' and thus the sale did not come to depend on the trial, but rested on the representation."   Lord Cowan also said :—" It is quite enough that the purchaser says he wishes a horse for a particular purpose, and that the seller says that the horse will suit for that purpose. That is quite as good as the use of express words of warrandice."(c) Thus, such words as " You may depend on it the horse is perfectly quiet and free

(a) B. Pr. 111.
(b) Chandelor v. Lopus, cited in Smith's L.C. i. 186, see § 30.
(c) Scott v. Steel, 1857, 20 D. 253, 257.

from vice" is a warranty, the element of reliance being present.(a) Again, a bare affirmation that a horse is sound is not *per se* a warranty. The parties must be shown to the satisfaction of a jury or a judge to have given and received the statements as a warranty, and not merely as a representation.(b)

Where the language used by a seller is mere expression of opinion, belief, or inference, there is no warranty ; (c) but if it amounts to the statement of a material fact and be relied on by the buyer, it is construed as a warranty. Thus, in *Wood* v. *Smith*,(d) a buyer said to the seller, "She is sound, of course?" "Yes," said the seller, "to the best of my knowledge." On being asked to warrant, he said further, "I never warrant. I would not even warrant myself." It was held that there was a qualified warranty given. In another case a buyer said he wanted a "quiet, useful and thankful animal," and the seller answered "that the beast was canny and serviceable in every respect and particularly in riding," and the mare was bought at a fair price. It was held, although the evidence was contradictory, that the seller was bound to take her back and repay the price on proof that he knew she had "tricks," and that she reared and plunged when ridden by strangers.(e) And where a seller did not know the age of a horse, the age marks being undiscoverable at the time of purchase, but had a written pedigree with him, and sold him according to that pedigree knowing nothing further about it than what was in the pedigree, it was held to be no warranty, and that he was not liable to an action on the pedigree turning out false.(f)

It would appear, however, that to found a plea upon a breach of warranty, the deviation from the warranty must be

(a) *Cave* v. *Coleman*, 1828, 3 M. and R. 2 ; in *Salmon* v. *Ward*, 1825, 2 C. and P. 211.

(b) Parsons on Contracts, i. 581, n, and cases there cited.

(c) *Hopkins* v. *Tanquery*, cit., p. 43 ; *M'Connel* v. *Murphy*, 1873, L.R. 5 P.C. 203.

(d) *Wood* v. *Smith*, 1829, 4 C. and P. 45.

(e) *Beddie* v. *Milroy*, 1812 ; Hume, 695.

(f) *Dunlop* v. *Waugh*, 1792, 1 Peake, 123.

material.(a)   Nowhere is this doctrine better illustrated than in the case of *Geddes* v. *Penington*.(b)   There, a party bought a horse under a written warranty, as " my dark bay horse, . . . safe in harness."   The seller represented that the horse had been sent to him for sale by a gentleman in England, whereas he had bought him from a gentleman in Leith, who parted with him because he had once proved vicious in a gig, and this fact was known to the seller.   After being kept two months, the horse became restive in a gig, partly because of the buyer's blame.   It was held that the misrepresentation as to the former owner of the horse was not sufficient to annul the sale, as the warranty was silent as to the former owner.(c)   In *Hardie* v. *Austin*,(d) a seedsman purchased one of two lots of turnip seed, represented by the seller as " East Lothian Swede. . . . Both lots were grown in East Lothian, and are first-class stock."   Delivery was given on 1st June.   On 13th August he wrote that he found the yield insufficient, and requested the seller to take it back, which he declined to do.   In an action for the price, it was observed that no express warranty was given by the above words ; but the representation being true, the seller was held not liable for the deficiency in germinating power.

As illustrating how narrow the distinction between a representation and a warranty may be, the case of *Rough* v. *Moir*(e) may be cited.   In that case (which was decided on the implied warranty of fitness for a special purpose) there was a representation in an auctioneer's catalogue of a horse as having been " driven regularly in double and single harness." Lords Deas and Mure held that this did not amount to

(a) 1 Smith's L.C. 190.

(b) *Geddes* v. *Penington*, 1814, 17 F.C. 606 ; aff. 1817, 5 Dow, 159 ; 6 Pat. App. 312 ; see also *Hardie, infra, note (d)*.

(c) There is a very instructive Sheriff-Court case, of an assurance against crib-biting and wind-sucking being construed as warranty, where no express warranty was given, *Vaucamps* v. *Campbell's Trustees*, 1889, 5 S.L. Rev. 353.

(d) *Hardie* v. *Austin & M'Aslan*, 1870, 8 M. 798.

(e) *Rough* v. *Moir*, 1875, 2 R. 529, see § 58.

a warranty, but Lord Ardmillan was of the contrary opinion.(a)

One who sends animals to a public market for sale does not impliedly represent that they are free from contagious disease dangerous to animal life; and will not, when they are sold "with all faults," be liable in an action either for breach of warranty or for false representation. The mere act of sending infected animals to market, although an offence against the Contagious Diseases Animals Act, does not amount to a representation by conduct on the vendor's part, that the animals are in fact free from disease.(b)

39. General, express, and implied Warranties.—A general warranty, as a rule, applies to a horse being sound, in the sense of its being fit for immediate work.(c)   A general warranty of soundness, however, does not cover patent defects — *i.e.*, defects which are so obvious that the buyer cannot help observing them; but a buyer who knows of the defect cannot sue the seller on the warranty.(d)   On the other hand, a buyer who relies on the warranty, and omits to make a minute examination, is protected against defects which, though not apparent, might have been detected.(e)   In other words : "The patent defects which the warranty does not cover, and to which the doctrine of *caveat emptor* applies, must be so manifest and palpable as to be necessarily within the knowledge of the purchaser, and also such defects as at the time of sale either are or will inevitably produce an unsoundness.(f) Whether a defect is patent or not is purely a jury question."

(a) See a case where a conversation prior to sale was construed as not amounting to a warranty, *Robeson* v. *Waugh*, 1874, 2 R. 63.

(b) *Ward* v. *Hobbs*, 1878, L.R. 4 App. Ca. 13.

(c) *Ralston* v. *Robb*, 1808 ; M. v. Sale, App. 6.

(d) § 46.

(e) *Maryetson* v. *Wright*, 1831, 5 M. and P. 606 (Crib-biting and Splint) ; *Holyday* v. *Morgan*, 1858, 28 L.J., Q.B. 9 (Shortsight) ; *Smith* v. *O'Bryan*, 1864, 11 L.T., N.S. 346 (Splint).

(f) Oliphant, 136.

Thus, in the case of a horse which was warranted sound, and was shortsighted from a peculiarity of the cornea that induced the habit of shying, Lord Campbell observed that this was not a defect which the purchaser was bound to have observed.(a) Again, where an action was brought on the purchase of a racehorse warranted "sound in wind and limb at this time," two defects—viz., crib-biting and a splint, were both discussed before purchase. The horse broke down, and on the case being tried, the buyer obtained a verdict. Tindal, C.J., in making a rule for a new trial absolute, said :—" In this case no fraud or deceit can be attributed to the defendant, as the horse's defect was manifest, the splint not only being apparent but made the subject of discussion before the bargain was made, . . . and the learned judge left it to the jury to say whether the horse was fit for ordinary purposes. His direction would have been less subject to misapprehension if he had left it to them in the terms of the warranty to say whether the horse was at the time of the bargain sound in wind and limb, saving those manifest and visible defects which were known to the parties."(b)   "A person buying a horse is often no judge of horses, and may say, ' I don't want to see the defects or blemishes of the horse, as I really know nothing about them ; I want and must have a written warranty.' . . . Some splints cause lameness, and others do not.   A splint, therefore, is not one of those patent defects against which a warranty is inoperative."(c)

An express warranty,(d) on the other hand, is strictly confined to what is expressed in it, and it must be made good to the letter, whether it refer to warranty of quality or fitness for a specified purpose.(e) So rigorous is this rule, that when one or more qualities are included in a warranty, there is an

---

(a) *Holyday*, cit.
(b) *Margetson*, cit., verdict on new trial for plaintiff.
(c) Per Pollock, C.B. in *Smith*, cit.
(d) Form of issue whether horse sold with express warranty, *Croall* v. *Hunter*, 1855, 17 D. 652, Appx. iii.
(e) B. Pr. 111.

implied exclusion of others not alluded to in the warranty.(a)   Thus—e.g., a horse is sold as "for life," or "alive" (a frequent term at auctions); this expression means that no warranty of any kind is given, and the buyer takes the horse with all its faults, visible and invisible, and the rule *caveat emptor* applies.   Again, if a horse is sold with a general warranty of "believed sound," such a warranty is limited to what the seller believed,(b) but will not exempt him from defects which he knew of, or must have known.   Again, an action was raised under the following warranty :—"To be sold, a black gelding, five years old; has been constantly driven in the plough; warranted."   It was held that the warranty applied only to soundness, and it was not necessary to prove the fact of its being constantly driven in the plough.(c)   Any warranty higher than this, such as "warranted sound," or "this horse is sound,"(d) is express, and will render the seller liable for any unsoundness except a patent defect.   This distinction is more sharply drawn in English than in Scotch law, where the term "express warranty" is more frequently used in contradistinction to the implied warranty of quality for a full price of the law previous to the Mercantile Amendment Act, 1856 ;(e) and, in reading English cases, it must always be kept in view that in English law it is competent, when there is stipulation to that effect, to hold to the sale, and also bring an action of damages on breach of warranty,(f) a remedy not available in Scotch law.(g)   Lord Justice-Clerk Moncreiff, referring to the Mercantile Law Amendment Act, said:—"The words 'express warranty' are used in the statute to exclude and alter the former law, which implied a war-

---

(a) § 40.
(b) *Wood* v. *Smith*, 1829, 4 C. and P. 45.
(c) *Richardson* v. *Brown*, 1823, 1 Bing. 344.
(d) Best, C.J., in *Salmon* v. *Ward*, 1825, 2 C. and P. 212.
(e) 19 & 20 Vict. c. 60.
(f) § 37.
(g) *M'Cormick* v. *Rittmeyer*, 1869, 7 M. 854 ; see as to fraud, § 36.

ranty of quality from a full price.   But in dealing with the
evidence of a warranty, it must be kept in view, first, that
the words must amount to an express warranty as contrasted
with representation, or assurance, or statements of belief of
quality; and secondly, it must be proved to what specific
element of quality the warranty was intended to apply."(a)
The 5th section of the statute in which these words occur
contains a proviso excluding implied warranties "where the
seller was without knowledge that the goods were defective
or of bad quality, . . . unless he has given an express warranty or sold them for a specific purpose," and it applies to
the sale of horses. (b)   Previous to this the Scotch was similar
to the English law, by which, when a warranty of soundness
is given generally, the seller is not liable for defects distinctly
obvious to the purchaser ; and, on the other hand, a buyer
who purchases on the faith of a warranty, and neglects to
make a minute examination, is protected against defects
which, though not apparent, might have been readily
detected by such an inspection. (c)   But what if a seller,
charging a full price with knowledge of defect, sell a horse
without an express warranty and not for a specific purpose ?
Does the implied warranty of the old law still apply ?   This
question was touched in a recent case, (d) which was decided
upon the ground of false representation, where a mare was
sold by auction with a description in the catalogue by the
seller's instructions as "having been driven regularly in
double and single harness."   In an action for the price it
was held, after a proof that the mare was not fit to be so
driven, and that the seller was aware of this, that he was not
entitled to recover—(1) in respect of the implied warrandice
at common law (the first branch of § 5 of the Mercantile
Law Amendment Act not being applicable, as the seller was
not without knowledge of the defect) ; and (2) of the implied

---

(a) *Rose* v. *Johnston*, 1878, 5 R. 600, 603.
(b) *Young* v. *Giffen*, 1858, 21 D. 87 ; for issues, see Appx. iii.
(c) § 9.
(d) *Rough* v. *Moir*, 1875, 2 R. 529 ; see § 58.

warrandice under the second branch of the same section, the mare having been sold as fit for a specific purpose. Lord Deas, holding that the pursuer had knowledge, said:—"The case comes within the class of cases in which the Act does not require an express warranty," and the common law of Scotland holds a seller not entitled to enforcement of the price. . . . He knew that she had not been driven regularly in double and single harness after having been properly broken, which was obviously the meaning in which the representation was calculated and intended to be understood. That I take to be a sale which the law holds to have been made on a false representation, known to be false, in a matter *in essentialibus* of the contract." It is thought that the implied warranty of quality would still subsist regarding patent defects(a) if the buyer had no opportunity of examination ; but, if he had, *caveat emptor* would apply.(b) If, however, the defect was latent and material, and undiscoverable till some time after trial, the buyer would be entitled to reject, or have the sale reduced.(c) Where there are any express conditions in warranties either regarding soundness, vices, or capabilities of a horse, they rule the question ; but vague assurances are not to be held as express agreements altering the implied engagements.(d) Express warranties usually refer to such matters as age, height, temper, time for rejection, &c. ; and where any peculiarity is to be guarded against, or included, it must be inserted specially in the warranty, and it is a question of evidence how far the condition has been fulfilled.(e)

40. The Construction of Warranties.—When a warranty is given with a horse, it may be given in writing or verbally ; and where there is writing, parole evidence is inadmissible to

(a) *Ralston* v. *Robb*, 1808, M. v. Sale, Appx. 6 ; *Hardie* v. *Austin*, 1870, 8 M. 798.
(b) *Scott* v. *Hannah*, 1815, Hume, 702.
(c) *Cooper & Aves* v. *Clydesdale Shipping Co.*, 1863, 1 M. 677. As to concealment, § 32.
(d) B. Pr. 129.
(e) *Scott* v. *Steel*, 1857, 20 D. 253 ; *Thomson* v. *Miller*, 1859, 21 D. 726.

limit or extend it.(a) Thus, where a horse was sold with a written warranty ("warranted sound, free from vice, steady in single and double harness") had a cough which was known to both buyer and seller, which developed into pleurisy, congestion of the lungs and bronchitis, and after protracted medical treatment it ultimately recovered, it was held to be unsound; and that the buyer having rejected it, the seller was held bound to receive it back and to pay the price with expenses of treatment.(b) It was argued that as the buyer knew of the cold at the time of purchase he must take the risk of the animal getting better; but Lord Gifford observed: "I cannot so read in law the written warranty; it is absolute and contains no exception, and it would be contrary to every principle to read the warrandice as if it had contained the words ' excepting always the cold under which the mare is labouring.' That would be to make a totally new bargain for the parties entirely different from that which they have made for themselves. If the defender had meant to except anything from his warranty he should have said so."

The following cases illustrate the strictness of the construction of warranties (c) :—A warranty, " Received £100 for a bay gelding got by ' Cheshire Cheese ' warranted sound," was held to cover soundness only, and not to apply to the pedigree.(d) A warranty that a horse is " a good drawer and pulls quietly in harness," will not be satisfied on proof that he is a good drawer.(e) Again, a horse warranted " sound and quiet in all respects," must be quiet in harness ;(f) but a warranty in these terms, " Received from A £60 for a black horse rising five years, quiet to ride and drive, and warranted

(a) *Pickering* v. *Dowson*, 1813, 4 Taunt. 785, Benj. 617 ; *Dickson* v. *Zizinia*, 1851, 20 L.J., C.P. 72.

(b) *Gardiner* v. *M'Leavy*, 1880, 7 R. 612.

(c) See *Richardson* v. *Brown*, cit., § 39, p. 50.

(d) *Dickinson* v. *Gapp*, 1821, cit. in *Budd*, 8 Bing. 50.

(e) *Coltherd* v. *Puncheon*, 1822, 2 D. and R. 10. The Court held these convertible terms.

(f) *Smith* v. *Parsons*, 1837, 8 C. and P. 199.

sound up to this date, or subject to the examination of a veterinary surgeon," was not held a warranty as to its being quiet to ride and drive, on the ground that what the warranty covered was soundness to the date or the opinion of the veterinary surgeon after examination, and that the age and quietness to ride and drive were descriptions and not warranties.(a)

"Sound to the best of my knowledge," or "sound as far as I know, but I never warrant," is not a warranty of absolute soundness, but is limited to the granter's knowledge.(b) To come up to a warranty of freedom from fault, a horse must obviously be sound, and also free from both vice and blemish.(c) In a recent case, horses were bought with a written warranty that they were "quiet in harness and saddle, and sound to the best of my knowledge." The purchaser claimed to return them as disconform to warranty, and alleged that there was an oral warranty given in addition to the written one. It was held on the evidence that the alleged oral warranty was nothing more than a representation of belief, not intended as a warranty; and that the words "to the best of my knowledge" qualified the whole of the written warranty, and not only the warranty of soundness.(d)

In a Sheriff Court case there was an advertisement and also an alleged statement by the auctioneer, that a mare was "in foal to a certain horse," and she was purchased accordingly; and the question turned upon whether the representation amounted to a warranty. Usage of trade being proved to the effect that in such cases the risk is with the buyer, the above words were held not to amount to an express warranty.(e) In another case also in the Sheriff Court, it was held that where a mare was advertised and sold by auction as "in foal to a certain horse," and it subse-

(a) *Anthony* v. *Halstead*, 1877, 37 L.T., N.S. 433.
(b) *Wood* v. *Smith*, 1829, 4 C. and P. 45.
(c) *Deuchars* v. *Shaw*, 1833, 11 S. 612.
(d) *Campbell* v. *Henderson*, 1886, 23 S.L.R. 712.
(e) *Routledge* v. *M'Clew's Trustees*, 1880, 5 S.L. Rev. 212.

quently turned out that she was in foal to a different
horse, such an error in its description did not nullify the
contract.(a)

41. Verbal Warranties.—In regard to verbal warranties
it is necessary not only to prove the express terms of the
warranty, but also the very words used. Thus, where a two-
year old filly was sold, and the only evidence of the verbal
warranty was that of the buyer and seller who were at vari-
ance on the facts, Lord President Inglis observed :—" A purchaser intending to rely on an express warranty must either
have it in writing or take care to have evidence sufficient to
prove the terms of the warranty, . . . and to prove an express
warranty it is not sufficient for witnesses to say that the
goods were warranted."(b) Again in another case,(c) the
same judge observed :—" If an express warranty is not reduced
to writing, there must at least be satisfactory evidence of
the words spoken—the very words spoken—which are
alleged to constitute such express warranty." In a case
where a verbal warranty was given, and after sale of the
horse was embodied in different terms in the receipt, Lord
Justice-Clerk Moncreiff observed :—" An express verbal
warranty may be proved as any other express verbal contract may be proved. It is a jury question and any
evidence which leads to that result is sufficient."(d)

42. Age Warranties.—A horse was sold at auction, " warranted six years old, and sound." It was rejected beyond
the specified limit of time in the conditions of sale, as disconform to age, and the Court held that the age was included in
the warranty, and observed, in reference to the time limit :—
" There is good sense in such a condition at public sales,
since, with all the care possible, many accidents happen to

(a) *Craig* v. *Brown*, 1889. 6 S.L. Rev. 49.
(b) *Mackie* v. *Riddell*, 1874, 2 R. 115.
(c) *Robeson* v. *Waugh*, 1874, 2 R. 63.
(d) *Rose* v. *Johnston*, 1878. 5 R. 600.

the horse between the time of sale and the time of return, if not limited ; but the age of a horse is not open to the same difficulty."(a)   But where the warranty was in the following terms :—" Receipt.   Received £10 for a grey four-year-old colt, warranted sound in every respect ;" it was held not to cover age,(b) on the ground that the first part of the receipt is a representation only, and not a warranty.   Again, an advertisement, " a horse, five years old, has been constantly driven in the plough, warranted," was construed as referring to soundness only ; and it was not found necessary to prove that it had been driven in the plough.(c)   A frequent term used by veterinary surgeons and horse-dealers is that a horse is "aged."   There is no precise definition of this term. After a horse reaches the age of eight years the teeth marks suffer very little alteration in the next few years.   Accordingly, where a horse is sold, warranted as eight years old, it is necessary to have skilled evidence regarding its age about that period, in order to prove it precisely ; and even the best evidence on this point may not be reliable.(d)

43. Time Warranties.—Strictly speaking, time warranties apply rather to the time within which a horse may be rejected as disconform to warranty, than to the warranty itself. Where a time warranty is given, it is construed strictly according to its limit.   Thus, a warranty given with a horse sold in these terms, "warranted sound for one month," was construed as a limitation of the seller's responsibility for such faults as were pointed out within the month, and he was not held liable for a defect which existed at the time of sale, but was not discovered till more than a month elapsed.(e)

44. Height Warranties.—Warranty of height is usually

(a) *Buchanan* v. *Pranshaw*, 1788, 2 T.R. 745.
(b) *Budd* v. *Fairmanner*, 1831, 8 Bing. 48, see also §§ 38-51.
(c) *Richardson* v. *Brown*, 1823, 1 Bing. 344.
(d) But see Galvayne on Horse Dentition.
(e) *Chapman* v. *Gwyther*, 1866, L.R. 1 Q.B. 463.   See as to rejection, §§ 60-63.

guarded in auctions, by a condition(*a*) that the buyer shall be the judge of it himself. The reason is obvious; the height of a horse may vary with the position in which it stands; and there are many purposes, such as racing, polo, &c., for which ponies are required, where they must not be above a certain limited height, else they will be debarred from competition. But where such a warranty is given, and a horse is rejected on disconformity to the warranty, skilled evidence would be required to prove the height precisely.(*b*)

45. Proof of Warranties.—Warranties are proved in the same manner as any other conditions of contracts.(*c*) When the warranty is in writing,(*d*) parole evidence is inadmissible to limit or extend its terms, and nothing which is not found in the writing can be considered as part of the contract.(*e*) It is also incompetent to modify a complete written contract by proof of previous written communings of the parties. (*f*) But where there is any ambiguity, parole evidence is competent to explain it.(*g*) Where technical terms are used, they will receive their technical signification, according to the usage of trade. In all cases of unfitness, whether under warranty, express, implied, or for a special purpose,(*h*) the alleged unfitness must be clearly proved.(*i*) Thus, where a horse died a few days after sale, and after dissection the lungs were found greatly inflamed, and the skilled veterinary evidence was conflicting as to the duration of the disease, it was held that the evidence must be such as posi-

---

(*a*) See Appx. iv.

(*b*) *Cossar* v. *Marjoribanks*, 1826, 4 S. 685, a case in which disconformity to height was raised, but without a warranty being given.

(*c*) § 5.

(*d*) *Rose* v. *Johnston*, 1878, 5 R. 600, where the question was raised as to how far, and in what circumstances, a written warranty, to which a seller, who cannot write, has adhibited his mark, is binding upon him.

(*e*) Abbot, C.J., in *Kain* v. *Old*, 1824, 2 B. and C. 627.

(*f*) *Inglis* v. *Buttery*, 1878, 5 R., H.L. 87.

(*g*) Dickson on Evidence, 1077, 1082-3.

(*h*) § 58.

(*i*) *Pickering* v. *Dowson*, 1813, 4 Taunt. 785.

tively to prove that the horse was unsound at the time of
the sale, not merely to raise a suspicion of unsoundness.(a)

Thus, it is advisable always to obtain a written warranty
of a horse, because the parties are bound by it alone,(b) and
it cannot be extended by implication.(c)

46. The Nature of Unsoundness. — In the case of
Gardiner,(d) it was urged that "unsoundness" has a wider
meaning in England than in Scotland, because the buyer can,
in certain cases, retain his horse and claim damages for disconformity to warranty, a remedy incompetent in Scotland.
On this point Lord Gifford observed :—"There may be room
for the distinction, although I am not aware of any case in
which it has been recognised." Accordingly, the construction of the word "unsoundness" accepted in England is
valuable, and is practically the same as that of the Scotch
law. A very distinct proposition was laid down in the case of
Dundas v. *Fairbairn*; "it is obvious that one who buys a
pair of horses for his carriage, covenants for animals which
are to be depended on for immediate service, and not for
such as may become serviceable with the help of time and
training. When he furnishes a pair of horses for such a
purpose, duly spoken out, the seller truly undertakes a warrandice of them in that respect."(e) This was followed by
the case of *Ralston* v. *Robb*,(f) in which it was held that,
"under a warrandice of the sale, whether derived from the
payment of the market price of a sound and unblemished
horse, or from the express stipulation of the parties, the purchaser is entitled to have a horse immediately fit for its
purpose. He is not understood, in law, to go to market with
the view of purchasing a commodity of which he cannot have

(a) *Eaves* v. *Dixon*, 1810, 2 Taunt. 343 ; *Wright* v. *Blackwood*, 1833, 11 S. 722.
(b) *Pickering* v. *Dowson*, 1813, 4 Taunt. 785.
(c) *Dickson* v. *Zizinia*, 1851, 20 L.J., C.P. 72.
(d) *Gardiner* v. *M'Leary*, 1880, 7 R. 612.
(e) *Dundas* v. *Fairbairn*, 1797 ; Hume, 677.
(f) *Ralston* v. *Robb*, 1808, M. v. Sale, Appx. 6.

the immediate use, which may require a course of medicine
and cure to render it fit for its purpose, and which demands
the exhibition of more than ordinary skill and expense to
preserve it in a state of usefulness or, perhaps, from utterly
perishing :" and many cases in Scotland have followed this
principle.

In England the leading case upon this point is *Kiddel*
v. *Burnard*,(*a*) in which the rules in prior cases were
reviewed. There Baron Parke observed :—"The rule I laid
down in *Coates* v. *Stevens* (*b*) is correctly reported, and I am
there stated to have said: 'I have always considered that
a man who buys a horse, "warranted sound," must be taken
as buying him for immediate use, and has a right to expect
one capable of that use, and of being immediately put to
any fair work the owner chooses. The rule as to soundness
is, that if at the time of sale the horse has any disease,
which either actually does diminish the natural usefulness of
the animal, so as to make him less capable of work of any
description, or which in its ordinary progress will diminish
the natural usefulness of the animal, or if the horse has
either from disease or accident undergone any alteration of
structure, that either actually does at the time, or in its
ordinary effects will diminish the natural usefulness of the
horse, such horse is unsound." It is to be observed that the
words "any disease" are used ; and, of course, under them
are comprehended constitutional and hereditary diseases,(*c*)
and to this definition was added, that the disqualification for
work may arise either from disease or accident.(*d*)

The application of that rule was further illustrated in the
same case, thus :—"For instance, if a horse had a slight
pimple on the skin it would not amount to an unsoundness,
but even if such a thing as a pimple were on some part of

(*a*) *Kiddel* v. *Burnard*, 1842, 9 M. and W. 668.
(*b*) *Coates* v. *Stephens*, 1838, 2 M. and Rob. 157.
(*c*) *Holyday* v. *Morgan*, 1858, 28 L.J., Q.B. 9.
(*d*) Baron Anderson in *Kiddel*, cit. p. 671.

the body where it might have the effect of impairing its natural usefulness, as, for instance, on the part which would prevent the putting a saddle or bridle on the animal, it would be different." Moreover, it is not necessary that a disorder be permanent or incurable, provided the animal be unfit for present service. This was laid down in a case of temporary lameness,(*a*) and also of cough ;(*b*) and Baron Parke, in *Kiddel* v. *Burnard*,(*c*) said : " A horse may have a cold which may be cured in a day, or a fever which may be cured in a month, and it would be difficult to say where to stop." All acute diseases, therefore, constitute unsoundness as long as they last, and also some vices, provided they are such as to impair a horse's usefulness. The question whether a horse is sound or not is often one of circumstances merely, and it is frequently very difficult to draw the line where unsoundness begins.

As a result of these and other cases,(*d*) it may be taken that a horse is sound when he is free from any disqualification for immediate or future use. This definition excludes diseases of all kinds, hereditary, constitutional, permanent, or temporary. When the latter character is such as to impair its usefulness, it would also cover disease which either does, or in its ordinary progress will, impair its future usefulness; and it also excludes any imperfection arising from the result of accident, and such vices as would in law amount to unsoundness. The question of soundness or vice is purely a jury question, and in judging of it the jury must consider whether a horse warranted sound was at the time of delivery unfit for immediate use to an ordinary person ; and the Court will not set aside a verdict merely on the ground of a slight preponderance of evidence.(*e*)

(*a*) *Elton* v. *Brogden*, 1815, 4 Camp. 281.
(*b*) *Elton* v. *Jordan*, 1815, 1 Starkie, N.P.C. 127.
(*c*) *Kiddel*, cit.
(*d*) Cited in §§ 49-53.
(*e*) *Lewis* v. *Peake*, 1816, 7 Taunt. 153 ; Justice Patteson in *Baylis* v. *Lawrence*, 1840, 11 Ad. and E. 920.

47. The causes of Unsoundness.—The diseases usually causing unsoundness in horses may be thus classified: —(1) Those affecting the soundness of wind; (2) those affecting soundness of limb; and (3) those affecting eyesight, skin, digestion, the brain and nervous system, or the glandular system ; including internal tumours and the like.

48. Diseases affecting the Wind. — All diseases which are permanently incurable constitute unsoundness, and where a horse is affected with a curable disease, it is a question of degree whether it be sound or not. While it lasts, almost every disease of wind is unsoundness sufficient to entitle rejection.

A horse suffering from broken wind is manifestly unsound,(a) as it is an incurable ailment; or from thick wind, for the like reason, if it be the result of chronic inflammation,(b) but not so if it be proved to be the result of a temporary cause.(c)

Bronchitis also, and inflammation of the lungs, amount to unsoundness.(d) Thus, where a horse sold died the day after sale of inflammation of lungs, and it was proved that it had a cold and coughed on the morning of sale, and was kept for some time in a warm stable, and there was no maltreatment by defender, unsoundness was upheld in defence to an action for the price.(e)

49. Cough and Sore Throat.—A cough at the time of sale is a good ground for immediate rejection, if permanent. But what if it be temporary ? (f) In England, the subsequent recovery is no defence to the action,(g) but it may be

---

(a) *Willan* v. *Carter Lancaster Spr. Ass.* 1853, cit., Oliphant, 79.
(b) *Atkinson* v. *Horridge Chester Spr. Ass.* 1847, cit., Oliphant, 472.
(c) Oliphant. p. 107, such as exercising it on a full stomach.
(d) Oliphant, p. 79, as to cold developing into these serious disorders, see § 49.
(e) *Fulton* v. *Watt*, 1850, 22 S. Jurist, 648.
(f) See § 46, p. 60.
(g) *Coates* v. *Stephens*, 1838, 2 M. and R. 157.

proved in mitigation of damages.(a) There are three import-
ant Scotch cases upon this matter. In *Dykes* v. *Hill*,(b)
a horse was sold under a warranty of soundness. Though
suffering from a cold, it was held sound at the date of sale,
notwithstanding that two days afterwards the symptoms
were much aggravated, and the cold passed into strangles,
extensive internal abscesses were formed, and the animal
died in twenty-one days. Lord Benholme observed :—"The
question is, at what period of time did the cold pass into
the other disease ? For a cold and sore throat do not constitute unsoundness, although under peculiar circumstances
and treatment the one may rapidly pass into the other."

In *Newlands* v. *Leggat* (c) a question arose regarding
unsoundness of a mare arising from cold, which the pursuer
was barred from pleading owing to his own treatment of her.
Lord Mure observed:—"It may be that a cough will entitle a
purchaser to return a horse if it is unfit for the work for
which it has been bought. If a horse has a cold with a
consequent loss of appetite, and is feverish and requires to be
blistered, he is for the time unfit for work, and a buyer
might be entitled to return him."

These cases may be contrasted with *Gardiner* v. *M'Leavy*,(d)
in which it was held that a mare affected with a severe cold
at time of sale, which developed in a few days into pleurisy,
congestion of the lungs, and bronchitis, amounted to
unsoundness, though the mare was ultimately cured. The
terms of the warranty were, "sound, free from vice, steady
in single and double harness." When the cold was discovered
to be serious, the mare was treated for three or four weeks
by a veterinary surgeon. Repeated notice was given to the
seller, but he never went to see the mare. She was sold
after recovery. It was held on the evidence that she was

(a) *Kiddel* v. *Burnard*, 1842, 9 M. and W. 668, overruling in one point *Bolden*
v. *Brogden*, 1838, 2 M. and Rob. 113.

(b) *Dykes* v. *Hill*, 1860, 22 D. 1523.

(c) *Newlands* v. *Leggat*, 1885, 12 R. 820.

(d) *Gardiner* v. *M'Leavy*, 1880, 7 R. 612.

unsound at the date of sale. Lord Gifford said:—" The existence of a mortal disease, that is, of a disease which ultimately
proved mortal, is certainly covered by the defender's warranty. It makes no difference whatever that in the present
case, the mare, instead of dying of the disease, ultimately
recovered, though with great risk and by means of skilful
and expensive treatment. . . . Where a warranty of soundness is given, and where there exists at the date of the
warranty a disease which renders the horse unfit for work for
weeks or months, which exposes its life to imminent danger,
and which is only cured by skilful, protracted, and expensive
medical treatment, that disease amounts to unsoundness."(a)
Lord Justice-Clerk Moncreiff also confirms the dictum of
Lord Benholme in *Dykes* v. *Hill*, that a cold and sore throat
do not constitute unsoundness in the ordinary case. " Where
a horse has a cold at the time it is purchased, if it is cured
in two or three days there is nothing in our law to justify
the contention that the cold amounts to breach of warranty ;
but where the animal's constitution is unable to bear the
effect of the malady without danger to its life it will be held
unsound even though it recover."

50. Roaring.—There can be little doubt that every roarer is
inconvenienced when in rapid action, and it would be difficult
to say in any case that it is merely a bad habit acquired
without some previous inflammation or alteration of structure.
In practice roaring is always very properly considered an
unsoundness.(b) Thus, in regard to roaring it was observed :
" If a horse be affected by any malady which renders him
less serviceable for a permanency, I have no doubt that it is
an unsoundness. I do not go by the noise but by the disorder ;"(c) and Lord Ellenborough said : "It has been held by

(a) *Gardiner*, cit. p. 617.
(b) Oliphant, p. 99. See a case of roaring held within the knowledge of a seller
of a horse warranted "sound as far as he knew," *M'Michael* v. *M'George*,
1886, 2 S.L. Rev. 446.
(c) *Onslow* v. *Eames*, 1817, 2 Starkie, 81.

very high authority (Sir J. Mansfield, C.J.) that roaring is not necessarily unsoundness, and I entirely concur in that opinion. If a horse emits a loud noise which is offensive to the ear, merely from a bad habit which he has contracted, or from any cause which does not interfere with his general health or muscular powers, he is still to be considered a sound horse." On the other hand, if roaring proceeds from any disease or organic infirmity which renders him incapable of performing the usual functions of a horse, then it does constitute unsoundness. To prove a breach of the warranty the plaintiff must go on to show that the roaring is symptomatic of disease.(a) The same reasoning will apply to such ailments as strangles, sore throat, wheezing, whistling, grunting, and the like. It has not been decided whether nasal gleet constitutes unsoundness.(b).

51. Diseases arising from Lameness.—Lameness, temporary or permanent, constitutes unsoundness. Thus, canker,(c) bone spavin, and blood spavin,(d) pumice feet,(e) ossification of the lateral cartilages, or side-bone,(f) laminitis,(g) navicular joint disease,(h) quittor,(i) true ring bone,(j) sand-crack,(k) are almost invariably indications of unsoundness, as they are not only very difficult of cure, but nearly all of

(a) *Basset* v. *Collis*, 1810, 2 Camp. 522.

(b) Oliphant is of opinion it would, p. 95, but it is very much a matter of degree.

(c) See Williams, Prin. Vet. Surgery, 384, *et seq*.

(d) *Pollock* v. *Macadam*, 1840, 2 D. 1026 ; *Hendrie* v. *Stewart*, 1842, 4 D. 1417 ; *Gardiner* v. *M'Leavy*, 1880, 7 R. 612 ; *Watson* v. *Denton*, 1835, 7 C. and P. 86 (bone spavin). Williams, 301, *et seq*.

(e) Oliphant, p. 97.

(f) But not in cart horses, Williams, 332.

(g) *Hall* v. *Rogerson*, Newcastle Spring Assizes, 1847, Oliphant, Appx. 468 ; *Smart* v. *Alison*, before Chief-Justice Wilde, Guildhall, 1847, Oliphant, Appx. 474.

(h) See *Robeson* v. *Waugh*, 1874, 2 R. 63 ; *Matthews* v. *Parker*, Gloucester Spring Assizes, 1847, Oliphant, Appx. 471. A nerved horse is always unsound, because, having no sensation in the foot, he may come down at any time. *Best* v. *Osborne*, 1825, R. and M. 290.

(i) Oliphant, 97 ; Williams, 389, *et seq*.; and *Bywater* v. *Richardson*, 1834, 1 A. and E. 508.

(j) On the same principle as bone spavin, but not always false ring bone, Williams, 285.

(k) Williams, 374.

them proceed from, or give rise to, such alteration of structure as will undoubtedly impair the animal's future usefulness. If a horse is warranted sound, and after sale throw out a curb, that does not constitute a breach of warranty; but if it be proved to have existed at the time of sale, a horse could be rejected on a general warranty of soundness.(*a*) Contracted hoof, too, has been held an unsoundness, when accompanied by a manifest alteration of structure, or inflammation of the foot.(*b*) Again, mere thinness of sole does not constitute unsoundness if it does not produce lameness.(*c*) There are, however, a large number of minor ailments which a horse may suffer from at the time of sale, and yet be perfectly sound in a few days after. These disorders, which in their aggravated forms culminate in lameness, such as wind-galls, thorough-pins, contracted feet, mallenders and sallenders, bog spavin, broken-knees after the wounds are completely healed so as to leave no after effects,(*d*) and the like, may, or may not, constitute unsoundness, according to the degree of virulence of the complaint. Thus, a party bought a horse, at a price implying soundness, and sold him a month afterwards to another, who returned him as lame, and it was proved he had been "hoof-bound" for, at least, a year; he was found liable in repetition of the price, and entitled to repetition from the original seller.(*e*) Thrush has been held an unsoundness.(*f*) Corns, when gravelled and suppurating, amount to unsoundness.(*g*) Crib-biting and wind sucking, when so inveterate as to cause injury to the digestive system, would appear to indicate unsoundness ; (*h*)

(*a*) *Brown* v. *Elkington*, 1841, 8 M. and W. 132.

(*b*) *Greenway* v. *Marshall*, Ex. Sitt., 9th Dec., 1845, cit. Oliphant, 81.

(*c*) *Bailey* v. *Forrest*, 1845, 2 C. and K. 131.

(*d*) Broken-knees before the wounds are healed usually constitute unsoundness ; and even afterwards, if the utility of the horse be impaired.

(*e*) *Ewart* v. *Hamilton*, 1791, Hume, 667.

(*f*) *Ralston* v. *Robb*, 1808, 14 F.C. 251 ; M. Sale, Appx. 6 ; see also *Fisher* v. *Ure*, 1846, 9 D. 17 ; *Jardine* v. *Campbell*, 1806, 14 F.C. 253, M. Sale, Appx. 6.

(*g*) *Hamilton* v. *Hart*, 1830, 8 S. 596.

(*h*) *Basset* v. *Collis*, 1810, 2 Camp. 522 ; *Broenenburgh* v. *Haycock*, 1817, 1 Ill. 116 ; Holt, N.P. 630.

but *Deuchars* v. *Shaw*,(a) an authority usually cited in support of the view that these vices constitute unsoundness, only goes the length of deciding that they are sufficient to warrant rejection under a warranty of "freedom from fault."

Again, splint may, or may not, be unsoundness, according to situation or amount of tenderness. Thus, Lord Chief-Justice Tindal said :—"It now appears that some splints cause lameness, and others not, and that the consequences of a splint cannot be apparent at the time. . . . We, therefore, think that, by the terms of this written warranty, the parties meant that this was not, at that time, a splint which would be the cause of future lameness, and that the jury have found it was. We, therefore, think the warranty was broken."(b)

String halt was, in one case, found by a jury to be unsoundness, on the direction of Mr. Justice Cresswell that, "if you are satisfied that it is a disease calculated to impair the natural usefulness of the horse, you must find for the plaintiff."(c) In another case it was proved that, on the buyer observing after the sale that a mare went lame, the seller said she had picked up a nail at the farrier's ; it was held that a temporary injury or hurt, capable of speedy cure, is not necessarily an unsoundness.(d)

52. Blindness and other Diseases.—When a warranty is given of "sound in eyesight," or "free from blindness," that, of course, must be complied with to the letter ; and blindness, if complete, is a ground for rejection on a warranty of soundness, provided it be undiscoverable by a purchaser who has examined the horse, whether it arise from cataract,(e)

(a) *Deuchars* v. *Shaw*, 1833, 11 S. 612.

(b) *Margetson* v. *Wright*, 1831, 7 Bing. 603 ; *Smith* v. *O'Bryan*, 1864, 11 L.T., N.S. 346 ; see § 39, p. 49.

(c) *Thompson* v. *Patteson Liverpool Sum. Ass.*, 1846, reported at length in Oliphant, p. 105 ; *Brand* v. *Wight*, 1813, Hume, 697, case of string halt.

(d) *Garment* v. *Barrs*, 1793, 2 Esp. 673.

(e) *Martin* v. *Ewart*, 1791, Hume, 703.

or opacity of the lens.(*a*) Glaucoma, also, is an unsoundness,(*b*) and also glass eye or gutta serena.(*c*) But where a horse, warranted sound, was sold by auction, having a blemish in one eye, open to the buyer's observation, notwithstanding the warranty, he was found liable for the price.(*d*) But where a buyer unskilfully doctored a horse for blindness, without notification to the seller, the seller was found not liable, under a warranty of "free from blindness."(*e*) If a horse takes megrims, mad or sleepy staggers,(*f*) it is manifestly unsound; and if it be a "shiverer,"(*g*) it is thought that, being unable to "back," it is unsound also. When a horse suffers from dropsy of the skin or heart,(*h*) glanders or farcy,(*i*) poll-evil,(*j*) enlargement of the parotid gland,(*k*) ringworm, mange, or scab,(*l*) it is without doubt unsound; and in regard to slight derangements of the liver,(*m*) or slight enlargement of the hock,(*n*) lampas,(*o*) pimples on the skin,(*p*) a ragged frog, or saddle galls,(*q*), it is a question as to how far its utility is, or is likely to be, impaired, whether it is unsound or not. Further, any vicious habit may amount to unsoundness, provided it impair the natural usefulness of the horse. Thus, backing and jibing, kicking, rearing, shying, crib-biting, roaring, if of

(*a*) *Higgs* v. *Thrale*, before Chief Baron Pollock, Guildhall, 18th Feb., 1850; *Briggs* v. *Baker*, before Chief-Justice Tindal, 1845; cit. Oliphant, 76.

(*b*) *Settle* v. *Garner*, before Martin, B., Westminster, 1857; Oliphant, 90.

(*c*) Oliphant, 91.

(*d*) *Scott* v. *Hannah*, 1815, Hume, 702.

(*e*) *Russell* v. *Ferrier*, 1792, Hume, 675.

(*f*) *Sheriff* v. *Marshall*, 1812, Hume, 697.

(*g*) *Pollock* v. *Macadam*, 1840, 2 D. 1026.

(*h*) *Eaves* v. *Dixon*, 1810, 2 Taunt. 343.

(*i*) See cases of glanders, *Baird* v. *Graham*, 1852, 14 D. 615; *Robertson* v. *Connolly*, 1851, 13 D. 779, 14 D. 315; see also §§ 66, 169.

(*j*) Oliphant, 97.

(*k*) Oliphant, 97.

(*l*) Oliphant, 94.

(*m*) If severe, it is unsoundness, *Hyde* v. *Davis*, Liv. Sp. Ass., 1849; *Buckingham* v. *Rogers*, 1864, Guildhall, Oliphant, Appx. 477, 479.

(*n*) Oliphant, 88.

(*o*) Oliphant, 94.

(*p*) See § 46.

(*q*) Oliphant, 100.

a sufficient degree of persistence, constitute unsoundness, if they diminish, as they usually do, a horse's natural useful-ness; and would, it is thought, entitle a buyer to reject a horse on a warranty of soundness, even although a special warranty of freedom from vice was not given.

53. Vice.—Under the heading of unsoundness, several vices have been treated, but there are still other vices which would entitle a buyer of a horse to reject it on the warranty of "freedom from vice," which he could not do under a warranty of soundness. A horse may be sound in wind and limb and a vicious biter when being groomed; he might have a habit of rearing, and yet be perfectly free from all disease ; he may be a steady worker alone, and restive in the presence of mares; he "may go steadily under the hands of persons of extraordinary skill, like hostlers, but the question is as to the horse's behaviour in ordinary circum-stances."(a) The distinction between vice and unsoundness must therefore be pointed out. The legal meaning of vice in a horse is a bad habit, either manifested in temper so as to render him dangerous, or diminish his usefulness, or a habit injurious to health.(b) As in unsoundness, so in vice ; it is frequently a difficult matter to fix the point at which a horse may be considered vicious ; and it is impossible to draw a hard and fast line, for each case must depend upon its own circumstances. Still, when a horse, otherwise perfectly sound, manifests any bad habit of the character indicated, there is such vice as will satisfy the law and entitle the buyer to reject it.(c)

Friskiness, or "riggishness" from imperfect gelding is evidence of vice in a horse, and in certain circumstances will entitle a buyer to reject it under a warranty of free from vice. On this point Lord Cuninghame observes in charging

---

(a) Per Lord Wood in *Scott* v. *Steel*, 1857, 20 D. 253, 257.
(b) *Scholefield* v. *Robb*, 1839, 2 M. and Rob. 210.
(c) See *Geddes* v. *Pennington*, 1817, 5 Dow, 159 ; 6 Pat. App. 312.

a jury, where an action was raised on a breach of warranty of a horse sold as "hale and sound and free from vice" :—
"Any imperfection in cutting the stones of the animal is not a breach of warranty, if in point of fact it does not affect the steadiness of the horse ; at the same time I can conceive many situations in which a horse may be bought, and in reference to which this might be a good objection under the warranty, as for example in the case of a horse bought for a lady or for other riding purposes.(a)

54. Dangerous Habits.—Under this category come habits of backing and jibbing, which, if persistent, undoubtedly amount to vice, and if permanently incurable, may even constitute unsoundness. Biting, kicking, rearing when incurable, and bolting without cause, if of sufficient persistence to amount to a habit, are vices,(b) but isolated instances of any such behaviour would not suffice to prove a horse vicious. Thus Pollock, C.B., observed(c) :—"A horse put into a new harness and an unaccustomed carriage once or twice may kick and yet be deserving of a warranty of being quiet in harness." Shying has been held a vice. Thus, where a mare was sold warranted quiet in harness but proving liable to shy greatly at stage coaches, it was held, though she was completely cured shortly after being returned, that the purchaser was entitled to reject her, and was not bound to break her in for the use for which she was warranted as fit at the time.(d)

Any other evil habit a horse may exhibit under the necessary operations of grooming, harnessing, or shoeing, if inveterate and dangerous to its attendant, is a breach of warranty of freedom from vice. Thus, Lord Justice-Clerk Hope observed (e) :—"Now, if any peculiar mode of attach-

(a) *Fisher* v. *Ure*, 1846, 9 D. 17.

(b) Oliphant, p. 75.

(c) *Buckingham* v. *Reeve*, N.P. Ex. 1857, cit. Oliphant, 122.

(d) *Begbie* v. *Robertson*, 1828, 6 S. 1014 ; see also *Rose* v. *Johnston*, 1878, 5 R. 600.

(e) *Scott* v. *Steel*, cit. 257.

ing the bridle was essential, a purchaser was entitled to notice. . . . It is a question of temper." When a mare "goes amiss" and the difficulty of mounting and dismounting is attended with danger, it would amount to a vice. (*a*)

55. Habits Injurious to Health.—Under this category fall habits of crib-biting and wind sucking, particularly when digestion is thereby impaired. (*b*) Capped hocks are evidence of vice if produced from kicking in stable, which is also a vice if detrimental to health. (*c*) "Weaving" also, as evincing an ill-will to confinement or control, and incessant fretfulness, would be evidence of vice. Rolling, also, harmless enough on grass, would, it is thought, be a vice if a confirmed habit in the stable, to the detriment of the animal itself, or to the disturbance of other horses. (*d*) And it is thought that when a horse so persistently refuses to lie down in stable, that its legs thereby become swelled, there would be sufficient evidence of vice. (As regards grunting, roaring and whistling, see § 50.) Cutting and speedy cut are not vices, nor do they constitute unsoundness. A horse could not be considered unsound in law merely from badness of shape. As long as he is uninjured he must be considered sound. When the injury is produced by the badness of his action, that injury constitutes the unsoundness. (*e*)

56. Blemishes.—When a horse is warranted "free from blemish" it can be rejected for a blemish, provided it be not manifest to the buyer at the time of sale, and even though discoverable if concealed. (*f*) Thus, although there was a visible blemish on the leg of a horse, yet as the seller did not explicitly state to the buyer that the horse was

(*a*) *Fraser* v. *Jones*, 1886, 2 S.L. Rev. 292.
(*b*) *Deuchars* v. *Shaw*, 1833, 11 S. 612; *Basset* v. *Collis*, 1810, 2 Camp. 532; *Scholefield*, cit. p. 68; *Vaucamps* v. *Campbell's Trustees*, 1889, 5 S.L. Rev. 353.
(*c*) Oliphant, p. 79.
(*d*) Oliphant, 100.
(*e*) Alderson, J., in *Dickinson* v. *Follet*, 1833, 1 M. and Rob. 299.
(*f*) § 36.

then lame by means of it, but rather led him to understand that he had formerly been so, and a full price was paid, it was held, on the horse proving lame, that the seller was bound to repeat the price. (a) This warranty is commonly combined with some other quality; and no case has turned upon the question of blemish alone. (b) If, however, a horse "warranted sound" have a blemish of such a character as to impair its usefulness, such blemish amounts to an unsoundness; (c) but if it merely amount to a lack of elegance or of beauty, or of graceful action, it could not be rejected on a warranty of unsoundness. Thus, chipped knees, capped hocks, angleberries, warts, &c., are all blemishes; but it is a question of degree whether they amount to unsoundness. When any special idiosyncrasy, vice, or blemish is desired to be guarded against, which does not come under those already mentioned, such—e.g., as clicking, or over-reach, or the like, it is well to have a special written warranty of freedom from it.

57. Effect of Breach of Warranty.—By the law of England, the buyer, when there is a breach of warranty, has a twofold remedy; he can either reject the horse, if there be a stipulation to that effect, and rescind the contract, or retain the horse and raise an action for the loss he has sustained by the breach of the warranty. (d) In Scotland, however, the buyer's only remedy is to return the horse to the seller, or to place it in neutral custody, at the seller's risk and disposal, (e) if the seller will not receive it, and then bring an action of reduction or of damages for breach of contract, according to circumstances. (f) A buyer cannot both retain

(a) *Durie* v. *Oswald*, 1791, Hume, 669; see also *Scott* v. *Hannah*, 1815; Hume, 702, see § 33.
(b) See cases where it is combined with other warranties. Lameness, *Durie*, cit.; blindness, *Russel* v. *Ferrier*, 1792, Hume, 675, see p. 67, *Scott*, cit.
(c) § 46.
(d) Benj. 647, *et seq.*
(e) *Gardiner* v. *M'Leavy*, 1880, 7 R. 612.
(f) B.C. i. 471, see §§ 36, 169.

the horse and claim an abatement on the price except there be an express agreement to that effect between him and the seller.(a) The principle in both countries is the same— viz., *restitutio in integrum*, the means adopted to secure the end alone are different. Lord Chelmsford said upon this matter :—" If a horse is sold with a warranty of soundness, and it turns out to be unsound, in England the purchaser cannot return the horse unless there is a stipulation in the agreement that if the horse does not answer to the warranty he shall be at liberty to return it, but all he can do is to offer to return the horse to the seller, and if the seller refuses to take it back, then he may sell the horse, and recover from the seller the difference in price between a sound and an unsound horse—that is to say, the difference between the price which the horse realised upon the sale, and the price which he had paid. In Scotland, as I understand, there is an absolute right to return the horse upon the discovery of its unsoundness without there being any stipulation to that effect in the agreement between the parties."(b) And when the seller of a horse improperly refused to take it back, when tendered, in terms of the bargain of sale, it was held that the purchaser did not incur liability for its subsequent deterioration whilst in his custody, unless imputable to his own act or gross negligence.(c)

58. Sale for a Specified Purpose.—Under the common law, previous to 1856, there was an implied warranty when a horse was sold for a particular purpose, that it must be reasonably fit for that purpose, whether the seller knew of the defect or not. Thus, a horse specially bought and sold as a quiet, well-tempered horse," fit to be ridden by a gentleman advanced in life," was found vicious and sulky, and apt to shy at vehicles, &c., and to rear and plunge ; it was found

---

(a) See §§ 20, 36, 39.

(b) *Couston & Co.* v. *Chapman*, 1872, 10 M., H.L. 74, 81.

(c) *Graham* v. *Wilson*, 1839, 1 D. 407.

unfit for the purpose, and the price was ordered to be repeated.(a) This case may be contrasted with another, where a young lady purchased a pair of young carriage horses, which she was apprised were "at grass, and of course not in good order;" she sent them to be broken, and rejected one as restive and refractory. It was sold judicially, and afterwards turned out an excellent carriage horse; the lady was found liable for the price.(b)

Again, a gentleman bought a pair of horses to work together in the same carriage, and was informed by the seller that, although he knew the one well, and would be answerable for it, he was not sure as to the other, as he had lately got it. On trial they would not work together; and it was held that, having been bought as a pair, and for immediate use, the above notice, and an allegation that on further training they worked well together, were irrelevant to relieve the seller of liability to repay the price.(c) And in an English case, a pole for a carriage was bought and supplied; it broke, and damaged the horses. It was held that the plaintiff was entitled to recover the price of the pole, and also a sum in name of damage to the horses, should a jury to whom the case was remitted find the damage to be the natural result of the breaking of the pole.(d)

By the Mercantile Law Amendment Act,(e) however, if a seller does not know of any defect in a horse he is not held to have warranted it; but if he sell it expressly for a specified and particular purpose, then he is held to have warranted it, and on disconformity to the warranty of fitness for that purpose the buyer can reject it. But to bring a case within this implied warranty, the specified and particular purpose for which a horse is sold must be something different from the ordinary purpose for which horses of the kind purchased

(a) *Campbell* v. *Mason*, 1801, Hume, 678.
(b) *Earl of Wemyss* v. *Seton*, 1802, Hume, 682.
(c) *Dundas* v. *Fairbairn*, 1797, Hume, 677.
(d) *Randall* v. *Newson*, 1877, L.R. 2 Q.B.D. 102.
(e) 19 & 20 Vict. c. 60, § 5.

are sold. Under the first head—viz., the knowledge of the defect by the seller, the case of *Rough* v. *Moir* (*a*) is instructive as showing in what circumstances knowledge of defects on the part of the seller is held proved. It was held that a horse represented in an auctioneer's catalogue as having "been driven regularly in double and single harness, and sold upon that representation, is expressly sold for a specified and particular purpose;" and if bought for that purpose, and found on trial to be unfit therefor, that the seller cannot recover the price or must refund it if paid.(*b*) Under the second head—viz., that the "specified and particular" purpose must be different from the ordinary purpose for which a horse is sold, the case of *Hamilton* v. *Robertson* is a leading one.(*c*) There, a party who advertised for "a good Clydesdale entire horse not over three years old for the Australian Colonies," agreed to purchase a horse which was stated by the seller to answer that description. He afterwards refused to take delivery on the ground that only one of the horse's testicles had descended from the abdomen into the scrotum. On proof it appeared that the pursuer was not aware of this peculiarity at the time of the sale. The buyer pleaded that the horse was not entire, and that having been sold for the specified and particular purpose of breeding, the sale was void as falling under the exception of the Mercantile Law Amendment Act. There was skilled veterinary evidence to show that a stallion was an entire horse when its generative organs had the defect in question, and was capable of getting foals. Lord Shand said:—" It is suggested that the horse was sold for the particular purpose of procreation. But every entire horse in this country is used for that purpose. The provision of the Act does not create or provide a warranty by the seller that the goods shall be suitable for the general purpose for which such goods are used, but for a specified and par-

---

(*a*) *Rough* v. *Moir*, 1875, 2 R. 529.

(*b*) Per Lord Mure in *Rough*, cit. p. 537.

(*c*) *Hamilton* v. *Robertson*, 1878, 5 R. 839.

ticular purpose when that purpose is expressly stated. If it had been represented that the horse, being entire, would run well in single harness, and the defender had bought him for that purpose, a question might have arisen in which the statutory provision would have applied. The contract as it stands does not fall under that branch of the clause at all, but simply under the first branch, which places the goods with all their faults, at the risk of the purchaser."(a) Lord President Inglis thus further elucidates this matter:—"The meaning of the clause is that there is to be an exception when the subject of sale is sold, not for the ordinary purpose, or for one of several ordinary purposes, but for a specified and particular purpose which is expressly mentioned in the contract. Thus, if you sell oats,(b) it may be to feed horses, or for oatmeal,(c) or for seed, and if you sell oats for seed,(d) and the contract bears that, and the seed will not germinate, no doubt the statute will hold you have warranted it. But you can never say that goods have been sold for a 'specified and particular purpose,' if they have been sold for the ordinary purpose for which all such goods are sold. Therefore, in my view of the clause, it does not apply to the present case. If the defender could have shown that this was not in any sense an entire horse, that might have raised a different question, though it would be difficult even then to get over the words of the statute, that the goods with all their faults shall be at the risk of the purchaser."(e) It was held accordingly that the defender was not entitled to reject the horse as having been sold for a particular and specified purpose for which he was unfit.

In another case a farmer bought from a cattle dealer a number of milch cows for dairy purposes. Two proved unfit for use, and the buyer refused to pay for them. In an action

---

(a) *Hamilton*, cit. p. 841.
(b) See *Hutchison* v. *Henry*, 1867, 6 M. 57.
(c) *Smart* v. *Reg*, 1852, 14 D. 912.
(d) See *Hardie* v. *Austin & M'Aslan*, 1870, 8 M. 798.
(e) *Hamilton*, cit. p. 842.

for the price, it was held that dairy purposes being the usual use to which milch cows were put, the cows had not been " expressly sold for a particular and specified purpose," within the meaning of the Act, and that therefore the buyer was liable for the price.(a)

59. Trial before Rejection.—When a horse is purchased either with or without a warranty, the trial by the purchaser must on the one hand be of such a character as fairly to test its capacity,(b) and on the other hand must not be such as to overstep this limit, or lead to the conclusion that the buyer means to keep it.

When there is no time limited by express condition or stipulation within which a horse is warranted, or within which it must be returned, the general rule is that it must be rejected immediately,(c) but a reasonable time is allowed in certain cases for trial.

Thus, in an action for breach of warranty of "quiet in saddle and harness," the buyer mounted a mare and rode her along the road and was satisfied with her in saddle. The bargain was then completed. After its completion the mare was brought to the buyer's stable. It was a Saturday, and the buyer's son tried the mare a short ride that night. Neither of those trials were alleged to have been unsatisfactory. On the Monday, however, and also on the Tuesday, the son rode the mare, and it plunged and reared and would not go ; and on the two following days the mare showed the same restiveness and plunging in harness. Here the trial

(a) *Dunlop* v. *Crawford*, 1886, 13 R. 973. The following cases may be referred to upon this matter—(i.) cases under the common law *Jaffé* v. *Ritchie*, 1860, 23 D. 242 ; *Hutchison*, cit., gives form of issue ; *Stewart* v. *Jamieson*, 1863, 1 M. 525 ; *Edinburgh & Leith Brewing Co.*, 1861, 24 D. 26 ; (ii.) under the statute *Hardie* v. *Austin & M'Aslan*, cit. ; *Macfarlane* v. *Taylor*, 1868, 6 M., H.L. 1 ; *Rough* v. *Moir*, cit. p. 74 ; *Rowan* v. *Coates Iron Co.*, 1885, 12 R. 395.

(b) Circumstances in which it was found not to have been proved after sufficient trial that a horse was not "a good worker" when sold, *M'Bey* v. *Reid*, 1842, 4 D. 349.

(c) See §§ 60, 62.

of the animal stopped, and Lord Cowan observed:—"No impartial trial of her, whether in saddle or harness, or by any other person, was made. . . . The two occasions when the pursuer took the animal out to ride, and the other two occasions when he drove her in a dogcart are held to be a sufficient test of the animal's unfitness, whether for saddle or harness. . . . It seems to me impossible to ascribe the animal's alleged misconduct in saddle and harness during these four days to unfitness for purposes for which she showed herself perfectly fit when in the possession of every-one but the pursuer."(a) The buyer, however, must examine his horse and make up his mind without delay, for if it suffer from a defect which is easily discoverable, he will lose his right of rejection if he delay unreasonably to exercise it.(b).

A horse sent on trial must not be subjected to further work than is sufficient for testing its capacity; and the buyer on trial must take as good care of it as if he had it on hire. Thus a horse died in the hands of an intending purchaser on trial; it had been overwrought a day or two previous to its death, and although it was not proved that the over-exertion was the cause of death, it was held that the purchaser was bound to show that the death was not due to his blame.(c) The overworking in this case amounted to a trial of how much the horse could do, and was proved to have been hazardous to the health of the horse, which was a young one; inasmuch as it induced incipient inflam-mation of the intestines, and while suffering from this the horse was further worked the day before its death. Lord Cowan observed:—"The true view, in my opinion, is that the horse was to get a fair trial, was to be used as the pursuer's other horses were, and with that degree of care and caution which a prudent man would exercise in the use of his own

(a) *Thomson* v. *Miller*, 1859, 21 D. 726.
(b) *Scott* v. *Steel*, 1857, 20 D. 253; *Smart* v. *Begg*, 1852, 14 D. 912; *Smith Bros.* v. *Scott*, 1875, 2 R. 601, effect of agreement as to rejection.
(c) *Pullars* v. *Walker*, 1858, 20 D. 1238.

horses." Lord Wood also said :—" I by no means think that the pursuers were tied down to exact nothing from the horse beyond some moderate work. But there is a great difference betwixt that and extra work of a severe kind, which, although it might not be more severe than other horses are occasionally put to and could do, it may be, with reasonable safety, must always be attended with some risk, more or less, even to a well-trained and completely seasoned horse." But if the seller request the buyer to keep the horse and give it further trial, and the buyer keeps it for a time and returns it as unfit for the purpose for which it is sold, then the *onus* of proving that the unfitness was caused by something occurring subsequent to the sale is thrown on the seller if he raise an action for the price.(*a*)

The trial of a horse sent with a view to purchase is not limited to the intending purchaser himself; he is at liberty to employ a competent person to ride it.(*b*)

60. Rejection.—"The time within which a horse ought to be returned depends very much upon the period when the defect is discovered."(*c*)   If it is manifest, the challenge must be made instantly, and when a fault is easily discoverable, by such examination as one skilled in horses usually makes, a buyer must try the horse and determine whether to keep or reject it without undue delay, the legal inference, if the challenge is not made immediately, being that the buyer is satisfied.(*d*)

If a buyer has had no opportunity of examining a horse, or if it suffers from a defect which is not apparent at first sight, the buyer does not lose his remedy by failure to reject

(a) See § 61, and *Crawford* v. *Hay*, 1888, 4 S.L. Rev. 270.

(b) *Camoys Ld.* v. *Scurr*, 1840, 9 C. and P. 383.

(c) Lord Eldon in *Geddes* v. *Pennington*, 1817, 5 Dow, 159, horse kept two months ; *Cossar* v. *Marjoribanks*, 1826, 4 S. 685.

(d) Ersk. iii. 3, 10 ; *Yates* v. *Pym*, 1816, 6 Taunt. 446 ; *Smart* v. *Reg*, 1852, 14 D. 912 ; B. Pr. 99.   See also *Clerk* v. *Eliot*, 1836, 15 S. 253, where the rule was applied that a party who takes back his carriage from the yard where it has been repaired, and uses it for a considerable time, is barred from refusing to pay the coachbuilder's account on alleged insufficiency of the repairs.

immediately; (a) nor, where horses have been ordered and are disconform to order, does the mere fact that the buyer has sold part of them before discovery of the defect bar his right of rejection; but he must restore the value and not the contract price of those returned.(b)

In one case, an action was raised for the price of a mare warranted "sound, quiet, and free from vice and blemish," which was bought for thirty guineas, and soon afterwards was discovered unsound and vicious. The buyer kept her three months and gave her medical treatment. He resold her, and after some time she was returned unsound by the sub-purchaser. On being returned she was refused, and died on the way back to the seller's stable, and on dissection was found to have been unsound twelve months before her death. No notice of unsoundness was given till rejection. A verdict was given for the plaintiff, and on a motion for a new trial the Court held the mare to have been unsound at the time of the sale, that the lapse of time before she was returned did not alter the nature of the contract, originally false, that the failure to give notice may be a strong presumption against the buyer, and will make his proof more difficult, and that here the evidence was with the jury.(c) Again an action was laid on a breach of a warranty of a pair of coach horses, warranted "perfectly sound and free from blemish and in no manner vicious, and if on trial they should have any of these faults, I agree to take them back again and repay the purchase money." One turned out vicious and the buyer informed the seller of the fact, but kept it for several months, partly on the seller's persuasion, then sent it to grass, and after having had it again in harness for a few days returned the pair, and demanded the price, it was there held that it was incumbent on the buyer to return the horse as soon as the fault was discovered, unless the seller

(a) B. Pr. 99 ; *Street* v. *Blay*, 1831, 2 B. and Ad. 456.

(b) *M'Cormick* v. *Rittmeyer*, 1869, 7 M. 854.

(c) *Fidder* v. *Starkin* (C.P.), 1788, 1 Hy. Blackst. 17 ; 1 Ill. 115.

by subsequent misrepresentation induced the buyer to prolong the trial; and that the length of a trial must be reasonable, and that six months was too long.(a)   In a recent case a party bought a horse on the 15th of January and took delivery on the 28th.   On 19th March he wrote the seller saying he did not know what to do about the horse as it was very vicious in saddle, that he had not made up his mind to part with him yet, and he desired to know if the seller would change him if he decided to do so.   On 24th March he wrote again, saying that the horse was vicious, and he must be quit of him at once.   On 1st April he wrote, threatening legal proceedings if the horse was not taken back and the price returned.   Thereafter he returned the horse, and brought an action for repetition of the price. The Court assoilzied the defender on the ground that the rejection was not timeous.(b)

But if a buyer use a horse as his own, he is barred from rejecting it;(c) and, in the case of a number of horses being sold, if he appropriate any of them he thereby bars his right to reject the rest,(d) unless there be an understanding or stipulation to the contrary, or unless the horses are sent on approbation or sale and return.(e)

In the absence of express stipulations as to a time limit to the right of rejection, a buyer, on being dissatisfied with a horse purchased either with or without a warranty, or for a special purpose, should instantly give notice to the seller, and as soon as possible return it to him.(f)

61. Acts barring Rejection.—A buyer loses his right of rejection,(g) and a seller his right of suing for the value of a returned horse, by using it as his own.   Thus, a cabowner

---

(a) *Adams* v. *Richards*, 1795, 1 Ill. 116.

(b) *Chaplin* v. *Jardine*, 1886, 23 S.L.R. 487.

(c) § 61.

(d) *Ransan* v. *Mitchell*, 1845, 7 D. 813.   (e) § 21.   See also § 2.

(f) *Caledonian Railway Company* v. *Rankin*, 1882, 10 R. 63, as to when to put a horse in neutral custody.

(g) Ersk. iii. 10.

bought a mare from a horse-dealer, which he returned next day as disconform to warranty. The seller wrote demanding implement, but worked the mare in his business. It was held that by so using it, he was barred from suing for the price.(a) Thus, also, where A sold a horse to B, who kept it ten days and resold it to C, who kept it twenty-seven days and returned it as unsound, B proposed to reject it, but was held barred by delay.(b) Again, a buyer of a horse having sold and repurchased it, cannot, on discovering that it was unsound when first sold, require the original purchaser to take it back.(c) Also, a buyer who rode a horse from Edinburgh to Suffolk and back, was held barred from rejecting it.(d) In another case a time limit of two days for trial was given in a sale by auction with a warranty " six years old and sound." The buyer kept the horse for ten days when it was discovered to be twelve years old. A jury found for the defender on the rejection being not timeous, but the Court granted a new trial on the question of non-conformity to the age warranty.(e)

A purchaser may, however, return a horse at any time within the time limited, even though it has by an accident become depreciated in value.(f)

Further, any act of appropriation, such as treating a horse medically, may bar rejection. Thus, where a buyer treated a horse for some months for blindness, the seller was relieved on the ground of the buyer's treatment.(g) Even neglecting

---

(a) *Croan* v. *Vallance*, 1881, 8 R. 700.

(b) *Bennoch* v. *M'Kail*, 1820, 20 F.C. 80.

(c) *Street* v. *Blay*, 1831, 2 B. and Ad. 456. As to effect of sale of goods when disconform to order, see § 60, p. 79.

(d) *Sheriff* v. *Marshall*, 1812, Hume, 697.

(e) *Buchanan* v. *Parnshaw*, 1788, 2 T.R. 745. See also *Budd* v. *Fairmaner*, 1831, 8 Bing. 48. As to age warranties, see § 42.

(f) *Head* v. *Tattersall*, 1871, L.R. 7 Ex. 7; *Hinchcliffe* v. *Barwick*, L.R. 5 Ex. D. 1880, 177; *Elphick* v. *Barnes*, 1880, L.R. 5 C.P.D. 321.

(g) *Russell* v. *Ferrier*, 1792, Hume, 675. Lord Eskgrove, in holding the warranty imprudent, both parties being aware of the defect, said, " I would lay hold of a small matter to release him from it."

G

to do so when that should be done has been considered an
act barring rejection. Thus, where a horse warranted sound
soon after sale showed symptoms of staggers, the buyer
would not physic him but bled him, and twenty-eight days
after, on the seller's refusal of him, put him to a livery stable
and he died, the seller was held not bound to repay.(a) Again,
a buyer of a mare warranted "sound in every way" blistered
her throat for cough and docked her tail while the cold was
still upon her. He did not call in a veterinary surgeon for
ten days, and the mare died twelve days after the sale ; the
buyer was held barred by his treatment of the mare from
suing for recovery of the price.(b) Again, where a purchaser
worked a horse without objection for six weeks, it having
meanwhile been in the hands of a third party, the seller was
held not bound to take it back.(c) And Lord Chief-Justice
Tenterden, while commenting on Lord Eldon's *dictum* that
where a horse is returned upon a seller, it must be in the same
state as when sold and not diminished in value,(d) observed
that a purchaser may return a warranted horse in the
ordinary case, and further said, "There is no authority to show
that the purchaser may return it where he has done more
than was consistent with the purpose of trial, where he has
exercised the dominion of an owner over it by selling and
parting with the property to another, and where he has
derived a pecuniary benefit from it ; . . . he cannot do so
after resale at a profit."(e)

If, however, it would injure the horse to send it back,
notice should immediately be given that it is to be kept at
the seller's risk ; and it would be better in such a case to
remove it into neutral custody, to lie at the seller's order ;
but a buyer acting as custodier for the seller must keep

(a) *Wilson* v. *Marshall*, 1812, Hume, 697.

(b) *Newlands* v. *Leggat*, 1885, 12 R. 820 ; but see *Pateshall* v. *Tranter*, 1835,
3 A. and E. 103.

(c) *Pollock* v. *Macadam*, 1840, 2 D. 1026.

(d) *Curtis* v. *Hannay*, 1800, 3 Esp. 83.

(e) *Street* v. *Blay*, 1831, 2 B. and Ad. 456, 463.

the horse intact till removal.(a) When the horse is received back, or the seller acquiesce in accepting the notice as a rejection, there is a mutual rescission of the contract.(b) But where the seller refuses to take back the horse, the buyer to preserve his remedy, is bound immediately to take steps to enforce the warrandice and to obtain a judicial warrant for sale of the animal from the Sheriff, meanwhile placing it in neutral custody.(c) Thus in *M'Bey* v. *Gardiner*,(d) where the purchaser merely intimated his rejection, and kept the horse for fifty-seven days without taking any proceedings on the notice, he was held barred from insisting on repetition of the price. But in the case of *The Caledonian Railway Company* v. *Rankin*,(e) the seller requested the buyer to keep the horse and to wait a little to see whether or not it would recover, and there was evidence that he was willing to take it back, and in these circumstances it was held that the buyer was not barred from recovering the price, even although he retained the horse six weeks after intimation of rejection.

62. Rejection where no time fixed for Trial.—If no time for trial be specified in the warranty, the rejection must be made immediately on the discovery of the defect, or at least as soon as is reasonable, for if a time elapse during which by ordinary diligence the defect could be discovered, the right to reject ceases.(f). Thus, where an action was laid on the warranty of a horse sold at £20, the warranty and unsoundness were proved, but there was no tender of return. The animal was placed at a livery stable, the keeper of which would not give it up without the price of its keep. It was held that all the plaintiff could recover was the price

---

(a) *Chapman* v. *Couston*, 1871, 9 M. 675.

(b) *Weston* v. *Downes*, 1778, Dougl. 24.

(c) B. Pr. 128, see Appendix ii.

(d) *M'Bey* v. *Gardiner*, 1858, 20 D. 1151.

(e) *Caledonian Railway Co.* v. *Rankin*, 1882, 10 R. 63.

(f) *Smith Bros.* v. *Scott*, 1875, 2 R. 601, effect of agreement on rejection.

of the horse and not its keep, because it was his own fault in not returning it.(a)

63. Rejection where a time is fixed for Trial.—If a time be fixed for trial and rejection, as is most usually done in auction sales, the time fixed between the parties must be adhered to.(b) Thus, in a repository, there was a notice in a conspicuous place that warranties were to continue in force till twelve o'clock next day, and a horse warranted sound was bought there by private bargain. The horse proved unsound, but no complaint was made till after twelve o'clock next day. It was held that the seller was free, although the fault was one which was undiscoverable till after that period.(c)

Under a time warranty, if a horse become disabled from any cause not connected with the warranty, the buyer can reject it.(d)

64. Requisites of Rejection.—In order to effectual rejection it is not necessary to go through any particular form. It is enough for the purpose of rejection that it shall be clearly indicated, and in some way notified to the seller.(e) But the rejection must be unequivocal and absolute ;(f) and if a horse be not timeously rejected, the buyer will not after an interval be heard on the plea that it was purchased for a specified purpose.(g)

65. Effect and Competency of Rejection.— Rejection is a privilege to be exercised at a buyer's pleasure, but there is no absolute duty on him to reject if not inclined to preserve

---

(a) *Caswell* v. *Coare*, 1809, 1 Taunt. 566, see § 65.

(b) *Mensard* v. *Aldridge*, 1801, 3 Esp. 271 ; *Buchanan* v. *Parnshaw*, 1788, 2 T.R. 745.

(c) *Bywater* v. *Richardson*, 1834, 1 A. and E. 508.

(d) *Head* v. *Tattersall*, 1871, L.R. 7 Ex. 7.

(e) Lord President Inglis in *Booker* v. *Milne*, 1870, 9 M. 314, 318.

(f) B. Pr. 99.

(g) *Edinburgh & Leith Brewing Co.*, 1861, 24 D. 26.

his right to rescind the contract,(a) even in contemplation of bankruptcy.(b)   The effect of rejection of a horse as disconform to warranty is, when accepted, to rescind the contract; it bars a buyer's retention for a claim of damages,(c) and even when refused, for the expenses of its keep.(d)   In England, if the seller refuse to take back the horse, the buyer should sell him for the best price that can be secured, and the seller is liable for his keep meanwhile for a reasonable length of time, the amount of which is a jury question.(e)   In Scotland, as already indicated, a judicial warrant is necessary.

Where more horses than one are bought at a slump sum, even though a separate warranty be given with each, and one or more prove disconform to warranty, the whole must be rejected ; but the rule is different where the parties intended the contract to be servcable.(f)   And where a pair of carriage horses(g) is sold, or two together, each at a lower price than would have been paid if they had been sold separately ; both may be rejected though bought at fixed prices, the bargain being considered an entire one in such cases.(h) Rejection is also competent where a buyer has not seen the horse, if no warranty be given ; but only on the ground of its not being a merchantable animal, or in those cases of sale for a specified purpose not falling under § 5 of the Mercantile Law Amendment Act.

66. Sale and Warranty by an Agent or Servant.(i)—

Where authority is given to an agent or servant by his principal or master to buy, sell, or warrant a horse, he cannot

(a) *Booker*, cit. p. 319.

(b) *Ehrenbacher* v. *Kennedy*, 1 R. 1135, see Lord President Inglis' observations upon this matter.

(c) *Padgett* v. *M'Nair*, 1852, 15 D. 76 ; *Melville* v. *Critchley*, 1856, 18 D. 643.

(d) *Barclay* v. *Guthrie*, 1886, 3 S.L. Rev. 103.

(e) *Chestermann* v. *Lamb*, 1834, 2 A. and E. 129 ; see also *Caswell* v. *Coare*, cit. § 62, p. 84.

(f) Sec. 2, *Stewart* v. *M'Nicol*, 1814, Hume, 701 ; Lord M'Laren in *Campbell* v. *Henderson*, 1886, 23 S.L.R. 712 ; see also § 2.

(g) *Dundas* v. *Fairbairn*, 1797, Hume, 677.

(h) *Hamilton* v. *Hart*, 1830, 5 S. 896.

(i) See further upon a servant's authority, §§ 150-155.

delegate this power to anyone else ; (a) and whether it is special or general the mandate given is held to include all the necessary and usual means of executing it with effect.(b)   The authority may be either general or special according to its extent ; and it is either express or implied, according as the agent has a definite duty to do, or acts in pursuance of his ordinary employment.   There is this distinction between the general mandate of an agent such as a horse dealer and the special mandate of a servant, that in the former case third parties dealing with him are not affected by any private instructions given him by the master, but in the latter case they must inquire as to the extent of his authority, or take the consequences if they do not.(c)

The agent cannot exceed his authority express or implied. Thus, he is not allowed to exchange one horse for another if his authority be limited to selling,(d) and if he is limited to selling he must receive the payment in money, and *primâ facie* has no authority to receive it otherwise,(e) but such authority may be inferred from usage (f) or special circumstances.(g)   Thus, when an agent was told to secure a pair of horses of a certain height and failed to do so, it was indicated that the principal against whom judgment was given, might have repudiated the bargain when the horses were not conform to height.(h)   Where the act is within his authority, the principal is bound by the act of his agent, even though it be fraudulent,(i) and is liable for damages for

---

(a) Ersk. iii. 3, 34.

(b) B.C. i. 516, also 511, n.

(c) Chitty on Contracts, 301, 302, see *infra*, p. 87 ; *Alexander* v. *Gibson*, 1811, 2 Camp. 555 ; *Brady* v. *Tod*, 1861, 9 C.B., N.S. 592, 605.

(d) *Guerreiro* v. *Peile*, 1820, 3 B. and Ald. 616.

(e) *Catterall* v. *Hindle*, 1867, L.R. 2 C.P. 368.

(f) Bailey, J., in *Pickering* v. *Busk*, 1812, 15 East. 38, 45.

(g) *Miller* v. *Lawton*, 1864, 15 C.B., N.S. 834.

(h) *Cossar* v. *Marjoribanks*, 1826, 4 S. 685.

(i) § 30.   *Cornfoot* v. *Fowke*, 1840, 9 M. and W. 358 ; Willes, J., in *Barwick* v. *Eng. J.-S. Bank*, 1867, L.R. 2 Ex. 259 ; but an agent is not liable for a misrepresentation innocently made, *Eaglesfield* v. *M. Londonderry*, 1875, L.R. 4 Ch. D. 693.   See § 31.

his negligence,(a) especially if he have benefited by it; (b) but unless the fraud or negligence falls within the actual or implied authority, it is not necessarily the fraud of the principal.(c)

When an agent selling a horse does not disclose his principal, he is personally bound to deliver it.(d) If a person sells goods under the belief at the time of contract that he is dealing with a principal, but afterwards discovers that the person with whom he is dealing is not the principal in the transaction, but agent for a third party, though he may in the meantime have debited the agent with it, he may afterwards recover the amount from the real principal.(e) When a servant is a *special* agent he is invested only with powers limited to the duty he has to perform, and it is the duty of parties contracting with him to ascertain the scope of his authority; for the principal will not be bound if the agent act beyond the powers expressed in or necessarily implied from the terms of his authority. The rules regarding this are(f) :—(1.) If the terms of the agency are express the limits are absolute. (2.) The agent's powers and duties are to be regulated by ordinary acts and skill and knowledge of the person in the particular line of business. (3.) Where any power is necessary or reasonable in order to the accomplishment of the purpose it is to be implied.(g)   But an auctioneer has no power to warrant a horse sent him for sale.(h) (4.) If agent be at a distance and in difficult circumstances he is not liable if he act with sound discretion. (5.) An agent has power to pledge or sell a horse of his principal for advances ; but not to borrow on his credit or bind him as a cautioner.   (6.) All mercantile mandates

(a) See §§ 150-156.
(b) Lord President Inglis in *Clydesdale Bank* v. *Paul*, 1887, 4 R. 626.
(c) *Coleman* v. *Rickes*, 1855, 16 C.B. 104.
(d) B.C. i. 536; Smith's Mercantile Law, i. 173.
(e) Per Lord Tenterden in *Thomson* v. *Davenport*, 1829, 9 B. and C. 78, 86.
(f) B. Pr. 225.
(g) *Brady*, cit. p. 86.
(h) § 27.

are extended or restricted by usage of trade.(a)   The following cases show pretty clearly what is within the implied
authority of servants in horse cases :—A servant employed
to buy a pair of carriage horses did so, and at the time his
attention was drawn to an obvious cause of lameness, and it
was held that the buyer having been put on his guard, was
bound to have thoroughly inspected and tested the animal,
and not having done so was not entitled to repetition of the
price.(b)   Again, a coachman went in his master's livery
and hired horses which his master afterwards used ; the
master was held liable for the hire of the horses (although
he had previously agreed to pay the coachman a large salary
to provide horses), unless it could be shown that the person
from whom the horses were hired had notice that the coachman hired them on his own account, and not for his master.(c)
Thus, also, a master, by agreement with his groom, allowed him
£5, 5s. a-year for shoeing and medicine.   A farrier employed
by the groom sued the master for medicines ; and was held
entitled to recover.   Lord Kenyon observed :—"That it was
no defence to the action unless the plaintiff knew of this agreement, and expressly trusted the groom. . . . A tradesman
has nothing to do with any private agreement between the
master and servant."(d)   Also, a master having sent his servant with a horse, to be sold at a fair, and the servant having,
on the journey, placed the horse in a stable, knowing that it
was diseased with glanders, and the horses in the stable
became infected and died ; it was held that a claim of
damages was relevant against the master, although his personal knowledge of the horse being diseased was not
averred.(e)   Again, the servant of a manufacturing chemist
purchased a horse, in the ordinary course of business, for its

---

(a) §§ 11, 40, p. 54.

(b) *Brand* v. *Wight*, 1813, Hume, 697.

(c) *Rimmel* v. *Sampayo*, 1824, 1 C. and P. 254.

(d) *Precious* v. *Abel*, 1795, 1 Esp. 350 ; contrast with *Hiscox* v. *Greenwood*, 1802, 4 Esp. 174.

(e) *Baird* v. *Graham*, 1852, 14 D. 615.

carcase, at midnight, and it was boiled down for manure before morning. It turned out that the horse had been stolen, and was worth £10 ; and it was held that the chemist was liable for the negligent buying on the part of his servant.(a)   A servant is not entitled to buy on his master's credit.   Thus, where a servant injured his master's carriage, and sent it for repairs to a coachmaker not usually employed by him, Lord Ellenborough held that, on the master's refusal to pay the account, the coachbuilder was not entitled to retain the carriage in security, on the ground that unless the master had been in the habit of employing the tradesman, the servant had no authority to bind his master to contracts he had no knowledge of.(b)

The question, how far a servant has power to sell,(c) or warrant his master's horse, has been the subject of several decisions in England. It depends what kind of service the servant is engaged in. Thus, " if a horse-dealer, or person keeping livery stables, expressly direct his servant not to warrant him, and he does so, the master is, nevertheless, bound by the warranty ; as it is within the general scope of his employment. But if the owner were to send a stranger to a fair, with express instructions not to warrant, and he did so, the master is not bound."(d)   This case was followed by another on the first point—viz., that a horse-dealer's servant has an implied power to warrant his master's horse in the face of express orders to the contrary, and bind him accordingly,(e) and Willes, J., says of the authority to warrant :—" It arose out of the general character of the transaction, and any person dealing with the agent of a horse-dealer has a right to assume it," and in a similar case the reason given was because . . . the master has not noti-

---

(a) *Faulds* v. *Townsend*, 1861, 23 D. 437.

(b) *Hiscox*, cit.

(c) *Morrison* v. *Statter*, 1885, 12 R. 1152, of the authority of a head shepherd to buy sheep.

(d) *Fenn* v. *Harrison*, 1790, 3 T.R. 757, per Athurst, J., 757, 760.

(e) *Howard* v. *Sheward*, 1866, L.R., 2 C.P. 148.

fied to the world that the general authority is circum-
scribed.(a)   But the servant of a private owner, not a
horse-dealer, entrusted to sell a horse on one occasion to a
private buyer, has not this authority, and the buyer takes the
risk of being able to prove that the servant had authority.(b)
Yet, if the servant of a private individual is to sell the horse
at a fair, the authority to warrant it is presumed ;(c) and the
same rule is applicable if the master is necessarily buying
and selling horses at the time ;(d) but where a master is un-
willing to adopt a warranty given by his servant, he is bound
to take back the horse and return the price.(e)

(a) Bayley, Justice, in *Pickering* v. *Busk*, 1812, 15 East, 37, 45.
(b) *Brady* v. *Todd*, 1861, 9 C.B., N.S. 592, 605.
(c) *Alexander* v. *Gibson*, 1811, 2 Camp. 555 ; *Brooks* v. *Hassal*, 1883, 49 L.T. 569.
(d) *Baldry* v. *Bates*, 1885, 52 L.T. 620.
(e) *Fenn*, cit. p. 89.

CHAPTER III.

HIRING AND LOAN.

67. Nature of the Contract.—The contract of hiring so closely resembles that of sale that it may be said to be "the sale of the use and benefit of the thing" hired. It is completed by consent alone, and when the parties have agreed regarding the horse, the sum to be paid, the use, and the time or particular journey, the contract is perfect ; and, to entitle either lessor or lessee to enforce his rights, neither delivery nor payment is necessary.(*a*) The distinction between this contract and sale is, that in hiring the risk and the property of the horse do not pass, whereas they do in sale ; and the loss falls on the owner of the horse, unless when caused by fault or negligence on the part of the lessee.(*b*) Under a contract of horse-hiring, reciprocal obligations arise between the lessor and the lessee.(*c*) These are—to deliver the horse, to pay the hire, and to return the horse when the period for which it is hired has expired, or when the occasion is past.(*d*) The contract may be proved by writing or parole ; but if writing exists the terms of it are not alterable by parole evidence.(*e*)

(*a*) Ersk. iii. 3, 14 ; Stair, i. 15 ; B.C. i. 481.
(*b*) See § 74.
(*c*) As to two parties hiring jointly ; and hiring of horse, and driver to drive owner's carriage, see § 155.
(*d*) B. Pr. § 135.
(*e*) Dickson on Evidence, 1015 *et seq.* ; *Pollock* v. *M'Andrew*, 1828, 7 S. 189.

The horse hired may be a particular animal, in which case the subject is certain, or an indeterminate and uncertain one, as in the case of a jobmaster furnishing horses for a carriage, where neither party has fixed upon the particular animals which are to be the subject of the contract.(a)

The hire must be certain, or ascertainable by reference to some standard ; for if there be no consideration, the contract is one of commodate.(b) The use may be either according to what is implied in the bargain,(c) or according to stipulation, as where one hires a horse for a particular purpose ; such as a horse for riding a definite distance or for a definite time.

68. The Lessor must supply a fit Horse.—The lessor is bound to supply a horse(d) or carriage(e) fit for immediate use, and if he omits to tell the lessee of any defect in the horse, which he knows or ought to know of, which renders it unfit for the purpose, he will be liable in damages.(f) Where a warranty is given along with a hired horse, it must be up to the terms of the warranty, as in the case of sale ;(g) but in general there is no implied warranty against latent defects.(h) So, when a horse(i) or carriage is hired for a particular journey, it is implied in the contract that the lessor warrants it fit for such journey. Lindley, J., observes : " A person who lets out carriages is not, in my opinion, responsible for all defects discoverable or not ; he is not an insurer against all defects ; nor is he bound to take more care than coach proprietors or railway companies who

---

(a) B.C. i. p. 482.

(b) Ersk. iii. 1, 18 ; see § 76.

(c) See §§ 71, 72.

(d) *Fowler* v. *Locke*, 1872, L.R. 7 C.P. 272 ; 10 *ib*. 90. See also *Johnstone* v. *Rankine*, 1687, M. 10,080.

(e) *Sutton* v. *Temple*, 1843, 12 M. and W. 52, 60.

(f) 1 Smith's L.C. 266 ; B. Pr. 141.

(g) §§ 37, 38, 39.

(h) B. Pr. 141 ; *Fowler* v. *Locke*, cit. ; *Hyman* v. *Nye*, cit. *infra*, p. 93.

(i) *Chew* v. *Jones*, 1847, 10 L.T. 231.

provide carriages for the public to travel in; but, in my opinion, he is bound to take as much care as they, and although not an insurer against all defects, he is an insurer against all defects which care and skill can guard against. His duty appears to me to be to supply a carriage as fit for the purpose for which it is hired as care and skill can render it; and if, whilst the carriage is being properly used for such a purpose, it breaks down, it becomes incumbent on the person who has let it out to show that the break down was in the proper sense of the word an accident, and not preventible by any care and skill."(a)

If the horse hired be a particular one and it accidentally die, the lessor is thereby discharged; and if it become temporarily useless by no fault of his own, the lessee can either abandon the contract or claim an abatement of the hire. But when the horse hired is an indefinite animal, as in jobbing out horses, the accidental death of the horse does not free the lessor; nor, when so many horses are hired out, does the accidental death of one discharge his obligation.(b)

69. The Lessor must Warrant the Use of the Horse Hired.

—Under a contract of hiring the lessor is bound to warrant the use of the horse hired. Therefore, a lessee has a claim of damages for eviction if he is deprived of the use of it.(c) A lessor is also bound to maintain the subject hired free from faults and defects, and fit for the purpose for which it is hired. Thus, where a vehicle is hired, the lessor is bound to pay for all repairs except ordinary tear and wear, or such damage as is the result of the lessee's fault,(d) and the lessee has the burden of showing that damage

---

(a) *Hyman* v. *Nye*, 1881, L.R. 6 Q.B.D. 685. See also *Christie* v. *Griggs*, 1809, 2 Coup. 79.

(b) B. Pr. § 141.

(c) The same principles regulate damages for eviction in hiring as in sale, see § 13.

(d) *Sutton* v. *Temple*, 1843, 12 M. and W. 52, 60.

occurring during the time of hire was not due to his fault.(a) In another case, the landlord of a country residence having, against the remonstrances of the tenant, made repairs upon the stable and coach-house, and left these premises in such a state of disrepair that the rain got in, was held liable for the expenses of keeping the tenant's horse at livery in the town to which he had meanwhile sent it, for the value of some hay and straw destroyed by rain, and for the expenses of a conveyance hired daily by the tenant to take him to town.(b)   How far apart from express contract the lessor is liable to maintain a horse in a fit condition when its unfitness is due to no fault of the lessee is not decided. Certainly he would be liable for veterinary attendance if the animal took ill, and for medical treatment during its illness, if the disease were of a severe character; but it is thought that if the ailment be merely temporary, the lessee must take the risk of it, and be satisfied with claiming abatement of the hire. In all cases where a lessee of a horse or carriage suffers loss occasioned by the want of it, or by supervening incapacity not due to inevitable accident, the lessor is bound to indemnify him, and to suffer an abatement of the hire if it accidentally become wholly or partially useless, without blame on the part of the lessee.(c)

Insolvency is no defence to an action for implement of a contract of hiring, but it will expose the lessor to an action of damages ; but impossibility of performing the contract is a good defence, as—e.g., by the death of a particular animal.(d) The risk remains with the owner ; and, if a horse perish, it perishes to the owner, unless the injury is traceable to the misconduct of the lessee. (e)

(a) See *Sutton*, cit. ; and see § 74.

(b) *Robertson v. Menzies*, 1828, 6 S. 452 ; but see §§ 170, 171.

(c) Ersk. iii. 3, 15 ; B.C. i. 482-483 ; *Fowler v. Locke*, 1872, L.R. 7 C.P. 272, 10 *ib.* 90.

(d) B.C. i. p. 482.

(e) Ersk. iii. 3, 15.

70. Obligations of the Lessee.—The lessee is bound to pay the stipulated hire, with deduction, if any, for temporary or partial deprivation of the use due to defect of the animal or vehicle, or to the fault of the lessor ;(a) to take only the stipulated or implied use of it according to the contract ; to indemnify the lessor for excessive use ; to take good care of it, and to return it when the occasion or period is over.(b)

The same rules which are applicable to payment in sale,(c) apply in the case of hiring, the general rule being that payment is due on returning the horse in the absence of express stipulation to the contrary.

71. Use of Horse on Hire by Agreement.—When the use is the subject of express agreement it is limited thereby. Thus, a merchant was held liable for the price of a horse killed by overburden, it being admitted that the "packs" were to be sixteen stones, whereas the animal was loaded with twenty-one stones.(d) Again, it was found relevant to infer responsibility that a horse was over-ridden by galloping, and that having been hired to go to Stirling it was further ridden to Dunblane.(e) In another case, a horse was hired at Edinburgh to go to Whitburn, and the hirer started riding it, but got into a stage-coach, and the horse was ridden alongside of it for several miles. He then got out and rode the horse on to Glasgow. Next morning he rode it back to Edinburgh, and within three miles thereof the horse was seized with flux, and was unable to travel farther. The lessee was found liable for the value of the horse.(f) Again, a party who hired a pair of horses and a coach to take recruits from Glasgow to Whitburn, but no further, and proceeded to Edinburgh, was found liable for the value of the horses, which died from over-fatigue.(g)

(a) Ersk. iii. 3, 16. (b) § 74. (c) §§ 10-11.
(d) Straiton, 1610, M. 3148.
(e) Moffat, 1624, M. 10,073 (Over-riding).
(f) Shaw v. Donaldson, 1792, Hume, 297.
(g) Gardeners v. M'Donald, 1792, Hume, 299.

Further, a party hiring a horse for a ride along the road is not allowed to take it for a gallop in a grass field ;(a) nor one who hires a horse for a lady to ride, to put it in harness.(b) And when a horse is hired to go from one place to another, no material deviation from the direct road is allowed, for if any damage ensues during such a deviation the lessee would seem to be liable therefor.(c)

72. Use implied in the Contract.—When a horse is hired for a special purpose, whether it be for a particular journey or on a time bargain, the lessor, in the absence of express stipulation, is bound to put it only to such use as will be presumed to be the intention of the parties to the contract. Thus, one who hired a horse and lent it to a friend, who rode it sixteen miles in an hour and a-half, left it in the open air for a quarter of an hour, and then gave it cold water, and four days afterwards the horse died, was held liable for the value of the horse and the expenses of medical attendance.(d) Again, a youth who hired a horse, and while intoxicated recklessly rode a race with it along a road with some companions, with the result that the horse fell and suffered severe injury, was found liable in damages.(e) The case, however, which has gone beyond all others in fixing liability for injuries to a hired horse, is that of *Seton* v. *Paterson*,(f) where it was held by the Second Division (Lord Gifford dissenting) that one who hired a horse for a ride on the road, and who took him into a grass field for a gallop, was liable for the value of the horse, which had its pastern bone broken in the field, and died six weeks afterwards from a twist of the colon and resulting inflammation, alleged to be

(a) *Seton* v. *Paterson*, 1880, 8 R. 236 ; see also § 107.

(b) *Gapp* v. *Gaudonati*, C.P. 1857, before Creswell, J., cit. Oliphant, 247.

(c) *Davis* v. *Garret*, 1830, 6 Bing. 716, case of lime damaged on a ship which deviated unnecessarily ; *Seton*, cit.

(d) *Campbell* v. *Kennedy*, 1828, 6 S. 806.

(e) *Macpherson* v. *Sutherland*, 1791, Hume, 296.

(f) *Seton* v. *Paterson*, 1880, 8 R. 236.

due to want of proper exercise. The case was laid on violent
and reckless riding, as well as deviation from stipulated use.
There was evidence that a higher charge would have been
made if the horse were to be galloped upon grass ; but there
was also skilled evidence that the twist in the colon was in
no way connected with the split pastern bone. This decision
seems very difficult to reconcile with a great number of other
cases decided on the maxim, *causa proxima non remota
spectatur*.

73. Reasonable Care of Horse Hired.—The lessee is bound
also to bestow due care upon the horse of which he has the
use, to provide it with food and shelter, and restore it to the
owner when the time has expired or the occasion is over.(*a*)
The care necessary is such as every prudent man should take
of his own animals,—the care of a *bonus paterfamilias*.(*b*)
Thus, a lessee is bound to pay for the keep of a hired
horse,(*c*) and for the shoeing of the horse when it is hired
on a time bargain, but not if for a journey to be driven by
the lessor's servants.(*d*)   Should a horse fall lame on a
journey, the lessee's duty is to put him up at the place
nearest to where he becomes unfit for use, and give notice
to the lessor, whose duty it is to send for him,(*e*) and the
expenses of its cure fall upon the lessor.(*f*)   Thus, a horse
was hired for £10, with an option of purchase at £50.   It had
a slight cold, and, on the last day of trial, after it had been
driven twenty miles, it was discovered that there was a
swelling under its throat, and it refused its feed.   The lessee
drove it other twelve miles whilst so suffering, and it was
returned in a much worse condition than when delivered for
hire.   There was veterinary evidence that to compel a horse

(*a*) B. Pr. 145.
(*b*) B.C. i. 483.   See also *Cooper* v. *Barton*, 1810, 3 Camp. 5, *n*.
(*c*) *Handford* v. *Palmer*, 1820, 2 Brod. and Bing. 359.
(*d*) Such is the opinion of Pothier. Louage, § 107, but there has been no case
decided on this point.
(*e*) *Chew* v. *Jones*, 1847, 10 L.T. 231 ; *Johnston* v. *Rankin*, 1687, M. 10,080.
(*f*) Story on Bailments, § 389.

to pursue its journey under such conditions for twelve miles, constituted a want of proper care and attention, and it was held that the lessee was not entitled to return it on payment of only £10, and a verdict was given for the full price. (a)

Again, a lessee must provide veterinary treatment for a horse if it fall ill, and, if he do so, that is sufficient; but if, instead of doing so, he prescribes medicines for it himself, he will be answerable if the treatment prove improper. Thus, the hirer of a horse, on its taking ill, prescribed improper medicines for it, and the horse died. Lord Ellenborough said :—" Had the defendant called in a farrier he would not have been answerable for the medicines the latter administered; but when he prescribes himself, he assumes a new degree of responsibility, and prescribing so improperly, I think he did not exercise that degree of care which might be expected from a prudent man towards his own horse, and was, in consequence, guilty of a breach of the implied undertaking he entered into when he hired the horse from the plaintiff."(b) In cases where there has been such necessary expenditure by the lessee, on behalf of a hired horse, as a prudent man would have made had the animal been his own, he will have recourse for it against the lessor, provided he can show that the expenditure was indispensably necessary, that notice was given to the lessor, and the occasion of the expenditure was not due to the lessee's fault.(c)

74. Restoration to the Lessor, and *onus* of Proof of Injury.—When the period for which a horse or carriage has been hired has expired, or the journey for which it was hired has been accomplished, the lessee is bound to return the horse or carriage to the lessor in as good condition as he got

(a) *Bray* v. *Mayne,* 1818, 1 Gow, 1.

(b) *Dean* v. *Keate,* 1811, 3 Camp. 4 ; see also *Campbell* v. *Lord Kennedy,* 1828, 6 S. 806 ; see *infra* as to custody of horses at grass, or for training, and at innkeepers, §§ 80-87.

(c) B.C. i. 482.

it.(a)   In Scotland, the lessee is responsible for his own negligence, for that of his family, and also for that of his servants,
whether it occurs in the ordinary course of their employment
or not, and the law throws upon him the burden of proving
that damage to the horse, while he has the use of it, is accidental and not negligent ; (b) in England, however, the
burden is on the lessor to prove negligence.(c)   Thus, a
defendant hired a carriage and horse from the plaintiffs, the
defendant's coachman, in place of taking them, as was his
duty, to the stable, drove, for his own purposes, in another
direction.   While he was thus engaged the carriage and
horse were injured, owing to his negligent driving.   It was
held that there had been a breach of contract, for which the
defendant was liable.(d)   Should a horse be returned in a
damaged condition, the lessee is bound to indemnify the
lessor for the damage, unless he can show that the injury
has been due to inevitable accident, and the later decisions
have increased this burden of proof so far as to make it compulsory upon the lessee to prove the cause of the accident or
injury, and also that he was not to blame for it.   Thus, one
who hires a horse, if it die or fall sick, must prove not merely
that he rode *modo debito*, and no farther than agreed upon,
but also by what accident, defect, or latent disease it failed,
otherwise he must pay the price.(e)   This case was followed
by *Robertson* v. *Ogle*,(f) where an action was raised on a
serviceable hired horse being returned unfit for service.
There was a report by two carriers and a veterinary surgeon, that over-riding and bad usage, while in the defender's
possession, was the cause of the damage.   The defence was
that it was unfit for the journey when lent on hire, and that

(a) B. Pr. 145.

(b) §§ 150-152, and cases there cited.

(c) *Cooper* v. *Barton*, 1810, 3 Camp. 5, n.

(d) *The Coupé Company* v. *Maddick*, L.R. [1891], 2 Q.B. 413, where the
difference between a lessee's liability to a wayfarer and to the lessor is explained.
See a criticism on this case by Beven Law Mag. and Rev., 4th Ser., 283, 1.
See also § 155.   (e) *Binny* v. *Veaux*, 1679, M. 10,079.

(f) *Robertson* v. *Ogle*, 1809, 15 F.C. 348.

it had been gently ridden and well used. The Court held that, if the horse's malady arose from any cause for which the defender was not blameable, the *onus probandi* lay upon him, and that the pursuer could not be expected to prove the treatment the horse had received while in the custody of the defender. This case, when contrasted with *Cooper* v. *Barton*,(a) exhibits very clearly the distinction, already indicated, between the English and Scotch law—viz., that in England the *onus* of proving that the lessee has been negligent lies upon the lessor, whereas, in Scotland, the *onus* is upon the lessee to disprove negligence.

In the case of *Marquis* v. *Ritchie*,(b) the strictness of the law laid down in *Binny* v. *Veaux* (c) was somewhat relaxed. The lessee, on returning a horse with its leg broken above the knee, failed to bring his proof up to the standard required, and the rule in *Robertson* v. *Ogle*(d) was thus construed :—" It is incumbent on the person by whom the horse has been hired, to establish that the injury sustained could not be prevented by due care and attention on his part, and was occasioned by that for which he was in no respect to blame." These two cases show that it would have been sufficient if the lessor could establish that he was not to blame, whether he could show the cause of injury or not. But in *Pyper* v. *Thomson*,(e) a case in which the lessee of a horse and gig established his freedom from blame, for the injury it received while under his care, it was observed, " that the lessee must be able to discharge himself of the care he was bound to bestow on the property of the other, by showing that he was not to blame in regard to the cause of the injury, and must, in the general case, be able to show how the injury occurred." The same doctrine was applied in

(a) *Cooper* v. *Barton*, 1810, 3 Camp. 5, *n*. In this case the plaintiff proved the hiring of the horse, and that it had often been out before and had never fallen, but gave no evidence of negligence, and was, accordingly, non-suited.

(b) *Marquis* v. *Ritchie*, 1823, 2 S. 386.

(c) Cit. *supra*.

(d) Cit. *supra*.

(e) *Pyper* v. *Thomson*, 1843, 5 D. 498.

Pullars v. *Walker*,(a) where a horse died in the hands of an intending purchaser. On trial, Lord Cowan observed:—"Fortunately the parties here are at one as regards the degree of diligence which applies to the case. It is that degree of diligence which applies to the hirer in a contract of location. . . . In this case, therefore, as in all such cases, the hirer must show the cause of death and that he was blameless."(b) This *dictum*, which thus extended the burden of proof, was approved of in *Wilson* v. *Orr*,(c) and the judgment in that case turned upon the very point of the defender's inability to show the cause of the accident. A farmer hired a horse for its keep, and it was proved, by *post-mortem* examination, that it died from the effects of a blow on the shoulder, received while in the lessee's custody. There was no evidence as to how it happened. The horse was delivered, to all appearance sound, upon the 20th of April, and he was kept without work from the 20th to the 26th. He was worked on the 27th and 28th on the defender's farm, and indicated on both days, especially on the second, a certain slowness and unsteadiness in his work. At four o'clock on the morning of the 29th, the defender found the horse's shoulder festered, and led it up and down the court. A veterinary surgeon saw it on 1st May, lanced the swelling on the 5th, and the horse died on the 7th. Lord Justice-Clerk Moncreiff observed:—"If the subject of the contract be not restored in the like good condition as that in which it was received, there is a certain burden of proof laid on the hirer. He must show the cause of injury or death; and, at least, produce *prima facie* proof that the cause was one for which he was not responsible,"(d) and Lord Gifford to the same effect said:—"I think it lay upon the defender to do a great deal more than merely to say, 'I cannot tell how the injury was received, but it was not owing to any fault in me or my servants. The animal may have injured itself in its stable—I cannot tell how—but here are my servants, every one of whom exoners himself of blame.' He has not sufficiently discharged himself of the duty and *onus* which lay upon him, and which lies upon all parties who, under a contract of hiring, or of any other contract, get the entire use, custody, and control of another person's property. If the property is found broken or destroyed, the custodier cannot content himself, without explanation, by a mere plea that he was not to blame."(*a*)

75. Defences available to Lessee.—If the lessee can establish that the injury or damage was the result of inevitable accident he will be free. Thus, whilst a horse hired for theatrical purposes was being ridden on to the stage, which was to all appearances safe, it fell through the flooring, and was injured. In an action brought by the lessor, it was held that there was no duty on the lessee to examine the premises, and there being no proof of negligence, the lessee was not held liable for the loss.(*b*) In another case, where a party hired a horse, and it was stolen from a livery stable, he was found not liable for the price of it, the breaking into the stable being considered an inevitable accident, which the lessee could by no means have averted;(*c*) but if the lessee negligently leave the door of his own stable open at night, and the horse be stolen, then he must answer for it.(*d*) Or, if the lessee can establish that the damage was entirely due to the fault of the horse itself, as—*e.g.*, by backing a gig into a river, he will be free.(*e*) Similarly, where a party hired a horse for a

(*a*) *Wilson*, cit. p. 269.

(*b*) *Tilling* v. *Balmain*, 1892, 8 *The Times'* L.R. 517.

(*c*) *Trotter* v. *Buchanan*, 1688, M. 10,080. This would not free an innkeeper or carrier, see §§ 87, 93, 116.

(*d*) Jones on Bailments, 88.

(*e*) *Pyper* v. *Thomson*, 1843, 5 D. 498.

journey, and put it into a stable, and it was taken ill and died, in consequence of want of proper treatment by the hostler, it was held that a person who hires a horse is not responsible for the *culpa* of those (hostlers of inns and others) to whom in the course of a journey he properly entrusts it.(*a*)

Where one gets possession of a horse, on the pretence of hiring it, and then offers it for sale, it is relevant to infer a charge of obtaining goods on false pretences, if not of theft ;(*b*) but in England if the sale is not effected the actual conversion of property has not taken place, and there is no felony.(*c*)

76. Loan.—When the use of a horse is given without hire, either on time or for a special occasion, the contract is one of commodate or loan.(*d*)   The loan is not complete till delivery, and when a horse is lent, the property remains with the lender, and so does the risk, unless the borrower be in fault.(*e*) The loan being gratuitous, and the beneficial use being for the borrower's benefit, he is bound to take reasonable care ;(*f*) but he is not liable for inevitable accident occurring in the use of the horse under the terms of the contract, or in ordinary use ; (*g*) but he is liable for negligence, his own, or that of one using the horse with his authority; (*h*) for misuse, for gross want of skill in use, and, above all, for anything that may be qualified as legal fraud.(*i*)   The lender, however, must communicate to the borrower any peculiarity which renders a horse perilous to use,(*j*) else he will be

(*a*) *Smith* v. *Melvin*, 1845, 8 D. 264.

(*b*) *Menzies*, 1842, 1 Broun, 419 ; *Hardinge*, 1863, 4 Irv. 347 ; Macdonald, Crim. Law, p. 22, *et seq*.

(*c*) *Reg* v. *Brooks*, 1838, 8 C. and P. 295.

(*d*) Ersk. iii. 1, 20. If it be lent at will the contract is called *Precarium*.

(*e*) B. Pr. 196.

(*f*) *Bain* v. *Strang*, 1888, 16 R. 186.

(*g*) As to what is ordinary use, see §§ 71, 72.

(*h*) *Wheatley* v. *Patrick*, 1837, 2 M. and W. 650.

(*i*) *Blakemore* v. *B. & E. Ry. Co.*, 1858, 8 E. and B. 1035, 1050.

(*j*) *Coggs* v. *Bernard*, 1 Smith's L.C. 201, 266 ; Story on Bailments, § 391 (*a*).

liable in damages. "Would it not be monstrous to hold that if the owner of a horse, knowing it to be vicious and unmanageable, should lend it to one ignorant of its bad qualities, and conceal them from him, and the rider, using ordinary care and skill, is thrown from it and injured, he should not be responsible? . . . By the necessarily implied purpose of a loan a duty is contracted towards the borrower not to conceal from him those defects, known to the lender, which may make the loan perilous or unprofitable to him."(a)   The terms on which the delivery of a horse lent has been or is to be made may be proved by parole.(b)

77. Use of Horse by the Borrower.

77. Use of Horse by the Borrower.—The borrower must limit his use to the express terms of the contract, or to what is implied in loan of the horse, else he will be liable to the owner in damages.(c) He must not lend the horse to another,(d) and he is also bound to restore it in the same condition as he got it at the expiry of the term of the contract, or, if no time be specified, when restoration is demanded; and, if he fail to do so, the owner has a claim for damages, or may, in certain circumstances, reject the horse and claim its value.(e) The borrower may, in Scotland, retain a horse lent to him in security for reimbursement of extraordinary expense laid out for its medical treatment, or other necessary outlay on its behalf, but not for anything extraneously caused; (f) but this does not seem to hold in England.(g)

78. Reasonable Care of Horse Lent.—The leading case in Scotland of reasonable care required of a borrower

(a) Per Justice Coleridge in *Blackmore* v. *B. & E. Railway Company*, 1858, 27 L.J., Q.B. 167.

(b) B. Pr. 196.

(c) *Coggs*, cit. ; 1 Smith, L.C. 201, 266, where the distinction between loan and hiring for a specified time and for a particular journey is pointed out ; see also *Camoys* v. *Scur*, cit. 7, § 59, p. 78.

(d) Even his servant, *Bringloe* v. *Morrice*, 1675, 1 Mod. Rep. 210.

(e) B. Pr. 197.   (f) B. Pr. 198.

(g) Shirley's L.C., C.M. 202.

of a horse is *Bain* v. *Strang.*(a) In that case, a party borrowed a horse, and while being driven along a road it stumbled and fell, and damages were claimed on its being returned with broken knees, it was held that there was an *onus* on the borrower to show that he had used reasonable care. There was uncontradicted evidence that the horse was driven discreetly. Lord President Inglis in that case observed :—" Now, one of the conditions undoubtedly is that the thing lent is not to be used except for the express purpose for which it is lent ; and, secondly, that in using the article for which it was lent, the borrower shall use reasonable care. There is what may be called an incidental condition of the contract also, which is rather to be gathered from decisions of the Court than from anything in the essence of the contract—viz., that if the article is returned in a damaged condition, there is an *onus* on the borrower to show that the damage did not arise through his fault. It is argued that the *onus* is heavier than that, and that he is bound to show what was the specific cause from which the injury arose. I am not disposed to decide that question, because I do not think there is any necessity to do so. We have, I think, sufficient evidence to show that reasonable care was used by the defender in dealing with the horse."(b) Lord Adam, however, indicated an opinion that even though the borrower cannot prove the specific cause of the accident, he should be absolved if he satisfy the Court that he took all reasonable care.(c) Professor Bell, however, holds that a borrower is bound by the very slightest fault, and must take the most vigilant care.(d) In England, when a gratuitous bailer of a horse acquires the sole benefit, he must exercise the most vigilant care, and is liable for slight negligence ; but the diligence required is not so exact if the lender is also

---

(a) *Bain* v. *Strang*, 1888, 16 R. 186.
(b) *Bain*, cit., p. 189.
(c) *Bain*, cit., p. 192.
(d) B. Pr. 199.

benefited by the loan.(*a*)   Where a party rode a horse gratuitously at the owner's request, for the purpose of showing
him for sale, it was held that he was bound in so doing to
use such skill as he actually possessed.   "The defendant,"
Parke, B., observed, " was shown to be a person conversant
with horses, and was therefore bound to use such skill as a
person conversant with horses might reasonably be expected
to use ; if he did not, he is guilty of negligence." (*b*)

(*a*) Shirley's L.C., C.M. 200-205.
(*b*) *Wilson* v. *Brett*, 1843, 11 M. and W. 113.

CHAPTER IV.

CUSTODY—VETERINARY TREATMENT—HYPOTHEC AND DILIGENCE.

79. Custody of Horses.—The degree of care required on the part of a lessee and borrower of a horse having been explained,(a) there now falls to be considered the custody of horses when the use of them is not given. This occurs when horses are put out at livery or to grass, or for training or medical treatment, or to an innkeeper, or to a carrier for carriage.(b)

80. Of the Safe Custody of Horses at Livery and at Grass.—As a general rule, the giving of horses into custody for safe keeping does not give the custodier the use of them for his own purposes, apart from stipulation to that effect. When horses are deposited for safe keeping for remuneration, a secure stable or other secure place of custody, is implied in the contract,(c) as is also proper labour in dressing and feeding. The livery stable must be wind and water tight, so as not to expose the horse to cold or wet, and the food supplied must be wholesome and

(a) See §§ 73, 78.
(b) The care required of carriers is treated in Chapter V.
(c) *Scarle* v. *Laverick*, 1874, 43 L.J., Q.B. 43.

107

sufficient, and the hostler fit for his undertaking.(a)   The conditions of custody, of course, may vary by express contract, or by acquiescence in any known peculiarity of conditions ; but, in the absence of agreement, where a horse is put to grass, the grazing field must be fenced against the escape of the horse, and against savage, dangerous, or infected animals, and must be free from pitfalls and dangers which may lame or injure it.   There is also implied the personal care of the custodier to prevent injury to the horse under his care ; and, if injury happen to it, there is laid upon him the burden of proving that it did not occur through his fault.(b)

The care required by livery stable keepers and those who graze horses for hire, is such as a diligent and prudent man will take of his own beasts.(c)   Thus, a horse which had been sent to be grazed for hire upon a farm, was killed by falling into a hole in a field in which it had been placed, which was situated over old mineral workings.   The hole was proved to have been noticed for some time before the accident by several persons in the neighbourhood.   The farmer was held liable for the value of the horse.(d)   Lord Shand said :—" The *onus* is in the first place upon the defender to account for the death of the horse, and I do not think he has satisfactorily discharged that *onus* by proving that the horse was killed by a cause for which he is not responsible.   It may no doubt be said that the defender treated his own horses in a similar manner, but in so doing he was clearly incurring a great risk, and one to which he was not entitled to expose his neighbour's horses when he was to receive hire for grazing them."(e)   Again, an action

---

(a) B.C. i. 488.

(b) B.C. cit., *Coggs* v. *Bernard*, and cases in Smith's L.C. 226.

(c) *Rooth* v. *Wilson*, 1817, 1 B. and Ald. 59 (case of gratuitous grazing); *Broadwater* v. *Blot*, 1817, Holt's Rep. 547 (leaving a gate open) ; *Smith* v. *Cook*, 1875, L.R. 1 Q.B.D. 79 (injury by bull goring a horse).

(d) *M'Lean* v. *Warlock*, 1883, 10 R. 1052 ; *Mack* v. *Allan & Simpson*, 1832, 10 S. 349 ; *Groucott* v. *Williams*, 1863, 32 L.J., Q.B. 237.

(e) *M'Lean*, cit. p. 1055.

of damages was raised for the loss of a chestnut gelding which had, while grazing in a grass park belonging to the defender, became infected with glanders or farcy, or both, from a pony, which the defender had, knowing it to be so infected, put into the same field with it. The pursuer, on finding his horse not looking well, took it home, and two other horses in his stable became infected from it, and grew so ill that they had to be destroyed. It was held, that if these facts were proved, the hirer of the parks would be liable, not only for the chestnut gelding, but also for the other horses which became infected and died. The case was afterwards tried, and there being no dispute about the facts, the jury were charged that it was not necessary to bring direct evidence of the knowledge of the disease on the part of the defender, but that presumptive evidence of it was sufficient to found liability.(a) In one case a defence was set up that the fact of the grazing park being bounded by a river which was fordable was not communicated to the owner of the horse. The Court remitted to the Lord Ordinary to inquire as to the usual care of cattle in the wood, and what care was taken of the horse in question, an opinion being indicated that if the defender showed no undue negligence in looking after the horse in so ill enclosed a field, or in giving immediate notice or in making due search on the loss, the action should be dismissed.(b) In another case, the keeper of a livery and sale stable retained a horse bought from him on the suggestion of the buyer with a view to resale, and one of the stable servants over-rode the horse and it died. The stable keeper pleaded ignorance of the horse's condition, and that he rode it at the owner's request ; but he was found liable for the value of the horse, Lord Justice-Clerk Boyle observing:—" I am clear that the keeper of a livery and sale stable has a duty and responsibility in reference to the horses committed to his

(a) *Robertson* v. *Connolly*, 1851, 13 D. 779, 14 D. 315.
(b) *Davidson*, 1749, M. 10,081.

charge, from which he cannot shake himself free by transferring it to his groom. He is answerable for the conduct of every person about his stables. The defender has no right to plead ignorance of the condition of the horse, he was bound to know it."(a)

81. Modification of Responsibility by Notice.—These conditions may be varied to any extent by express stipulation or even by notice. Thus, a gentleman sent his horse to a park for pasture and it strayed. He brought an action against the tenant of the park, who pleaded in defence that he had put up a placard intimating that he would not be liable for any horses put into the park "although they should be stolen or break their neck." No other condition was expressed in the contract and the defence was held relevant.(b) In two other cases relative to the same placard the same defence was sustained in the absence of proof that the tenant was accessory to the loss by fraud or negligence.(c)

82. Of the Responsibility of Breakers and Trainers of Horses.—The liability of a trainer or horse-breaker as far as custody is concerned, is the same as that of a stable keeper,(d) and he is liable for damage done to a horse through his negligence in breaking.(e) The owner of a mare sent her to a stable-keeper and horse-breaker to be broken. Whilst a servant of the stabler was riding the mare, it took fright and leaped among some benches which had been placed in the area of the stable, and it was so severely injured that it died, notwithstanding good treatment. It was held that the stabler ought to have taken better care that his stable should not be exposed to such accidents.(f)

(a) *Hagart* v. *Inglis*, 1832, 10 S. 506.
(b) *Whitehead* v. *Straiton*, 1667, M. 10,074.
(c) *Birnie*, 1680, M. 10,079 ; *Maxwell* v. *Todridge*, 1684, M. 10,079.
(d) § 80.   (e) Oliphant, 233.
(f) *Hay* v. *Wordsworth*, 1801, M. App., *Nauta*, &c.

A horse sent to be broken must be preserved from all accidents and not exposed to danger. Thus, where a stabler, who received a young mare to train into his stable, under which, he was aware, that a railway company were forming a tunnel by blasting rock, and who did not communicate that fact to the owner, was found liable for injury done to the mare in consequence of a fright occasioned by an explosion in the tunnel.(a)   Lord President Boyle observed :— " He is bound not only to train it, but to preserve it from all accidents, and the owner of the horse is entitled to rely on this being done. . . . By receiving the horse into his stable he took the risk of its safety on himself; " (b) and it was further observed that the stable keeper should have arranged with the railway company to get notice of the time of the explosions, and that, not having done so, he was liable because that was a measure of precaution that should not have been neglected, and also that the fact of the blasting explosions going on should have been communicated to the owner.

83. Responsibility of Veterinary Surgeons.—Where a horse is sent to a veterinary surgeon's, the sender is entitled to presume that he has the ordinary skill of a man who makes this business his profession, and his obligation is for a due application of the necessary attention, art and skill.   The rule is that if an apprentice only be employed, instead of a master, he is responsible for a fair exertion of his capacity, but that where a professional man is employed to perform any specific act, it must be done according to rule,—neither negligently nor unskilfully,—and if there be no settled rule but a known method of performing it, it must be followed.   Further, if an operation be intricate and difficult, a professional man, though he err, is not liable if he fairly exert the best of his skill and judgment ; but he

(a) *Laing* v. *Darling*, 1850, 12 D. 1279.
(b) *Laing*, cit. p. 1284.

has the *onus* of proving that injury received while in his
hands was not due to his fault. (*a*)   In regard to veterinary
treatment for disease, the same rules apply which govern
the treatment of persons by a medical man.   A veterinary
surgeon is bound to bring reasonable skill and fitness to the
subject under treatment, and he must exercise it with due
and proper care.   If he be deficient in fitness, or having the
requisite skill fail to exercise it properly and carefully, he is
liable for any damage which may ensue. (*b*)   And if he is
employed professionally and undertakes a case, that is
sufficient to render him liable for negligent treatment; (*c*)
accordingly, in a case of negligent treatment, it was not found
necessary to aver by whom the medical man was employed,
nor by whom he was to be paid. (*d*)   A surgeon, moreover,
is bound to exercise the same degree of care and skill by
whomsoever he may be called in. (*e*)

In regard to the granting of veterinary certificates of soundness, the rule appears to be that if a veterinary surgeon give
a warranty wrongfully, to render him liable, the case against
him must come up to this, that he acted as no intelligent
and properly educated veterinary surgeon would have done
when he examined the horse; in fact, that he did not
exercise a reasonable amount of skill and intelligence. (*f*)
His liability appears to be limited to the party by whom he
is employed.   Thus, if a buyer stipulates that a veterinary
surgeon's certificate of soundness is to be given with a horse
he is to purchase, and the seller provides one, which the
buyer can show was negligently given, he has no remedy
against the veterinary surgeon (*g*) unless he can prove that

---

(*a*) Bell's Pr. 154 ; Beven on Negligence, 820, *et seq.*

(*b*) *Collins* v. *Rodway*, 1845 ; Oliphant, 229.

(*c*) *Gladwell* v. *Steggall*, 1839, 8 Scott's C.P. 60.

(*d*) *Pippin* v. *Sheppard*, 1822, 11 Price, 400.

(*e*) Tindal, C.J., in *Gladwell*, cit.

(*f*) *Mann* v. *Stephens*, 1881, before Montague, Q.C., Penzance, 54 Veterinarian, 655.

(*g*) *Walker* v. *Barling*, 1884, N.P.C. Derby before Justice Denman, 57
Veterinarian, 202 ; *Robertson* v. *Fleming*, 1861, 4 Macq. 167.

between the veterinary surgeon and the seller there was a conspiracy to defraud. If, however, the veterinary surgeon is employed by the buyer, or jointly employed by the buyer and seller, he is liable to either party for gross negligence in granting a certificate.

84. Responsibility of a Smith and Farrier.—A smith or farrier is liable if he damage a horse in shoeing. In England a farrier cannot refuse to shoe a horse if brought at a reasonable time.(a) But in Scotland this is not compulsory, and a smith is at liberty to decline to shoe a horse brought to be shod. If, however, he undertakes to shoe it, he incurs responsibility if it is done negligently.(b) If a servant of a farrier shoe negligently, the master is liable,(c) but not if the injury be wilful, as by the servant's wilfully driving a nail into the hoof for the purpose of laming the horse. (d) If there be peculiar difficulties in shoeing they must be mentioned to the farrier.(e) Again, a farrier was found liable for the value of a colt killed by negligence in castration.(f)

The owner of a stallion, it is thought, must take the same care of a mare sent for cover as a livery stable keeper or farmer when grazing it ; (g) the custody being incidental to the special contract for service ; but this responsibility will be lessened where the owner of the mare sends his own groom with it.

85. Lien of Custodiers other than Innkeepers.—The owner of a stallion has a lien over the mare sent for

---

(a) See the various English statutes regarding farriery cited in Oliphant, p. 229.

(b) Coke, C.J., in *Everard* v. *Hopkins*, 2 Bulst, 332.

(c) § 150-1.

(d) § 150-1.

(e) See Pollock, C.B., in *Collins* v. *Rodway*, 1845, reported in Oliphant, 229, and in 14 Veterinarian, 102.

(f) *Peddie* v. *Rodger*, 1798, Hume, 304.

(g) § 80.

I

cover for the charges for service.(a) So have veterinary
surgeons for medical treatment ; and horsebreakers and
trainers by whose skill horses are rendered manageable
have also a lien for training and breaking.(b)   In England
a livery stable keeper or a grazier, if he is not also an
innkeeper, has no lien for the keep and expenses of veterinary treatment(c) of horses at livery(d) or at grass,(e) except
by special agreement.(f)   This point has not been decided
in Scotland ; (g) and it is thought that a livery stable keeper
or grazier has a right of lien for the keep of or attention
to the horse ; but not a general retention which would
entitle him to retain a horse for an account due for other
matters ; nor can he retain one horse for the keep and
attention bestowed on other horses.

86. Proof of the Contract of Custody.—The contract of
hiring of custody may be proved by parole or writing.(h)
In the case of innominate contracts, unless the contract is of
an anomalous character, proof may be *prout de jure*, and is
not limited to the writ or oath of the defender.   Thus, in an
action for payment of an account for stabling omnibus horses
for several years, the defence was that the pursuer had agreed
to stable the horses free of charge, in consideration of the
omnibus departing from and arriving at the stabler's inn on
its way to and from the railway station.   It was held that
the alleged contract might be proved *prout de jure*.(i)

(a) *Scarfe* v. *Morgan*, 1838, 4 M. and W. 270.

(b) *Bevan* v. *Waters*, 1828, 3 C. and P. 520 ; *Scarfe*, cit. ; *Forth* v. *Simpson*,
1 49, 13 Q.B. 680.

(c) *Orchard* v. *Rackstraw*, 1850, 9 C.B. 698.

(d) See *Parsons* v. *Gingell*, 1847, 4 C.B. 545 ; *Yorke* v. *Greenhaugh*, 2 Lord
Raym. 866, where it was also held that a livery stable keeper was answerable for
a horse stolen from his stables. *Smith* v. *Dearlove*, 1848, 6 C.B. 132.

(e) *Jackson* v. *Cummins*, 1839, 5 M. and W. 342, where the authorities are
collected.

(f) *Donatty* v. *Crowther*, 1826, 11 Moore's Rep., 479, and if it is defeated by
fraud of the owner he may regain possession of it, *Wallace* v. *Woodgate*, 1824
1 C. and P. 575.

(g) § 88.

(h) P. Pr. 136.

(i) *Forbes* v. *Caird*, 1877, 4 R. 1141.

A farmer, sued by an innkeeper for delivery of a horse wintered with him, alleged an express contract that it was lent for the whole winter, and was not to be redemanded till spring, and also founded on a local custom of horses being kept and used for farm purposes by farmers during winter and spring in exchange for their keep. It was held, on his failure to prove either the agreement or the alleged custom, that the contract was terminable at the will of either party.(a)

87. Of an Innkeeper's Custody.—The edict, *nautæ, cau·pones, stabularii,*(b) has so far been adopted in the law of Scotland as to render public carriers,(c) innkeepers, and stablers answerable for restitution of a horse in the same condition as they receive it ; unless it has perished, or has suffered injury by inevitable accident,(d) or by the negligence of the guest himself.(e) But it would appear from the edict itself(f) that stable-keepers are not within the clause unless they are also innkeepers who receive guests ; and therefore the edict applies only to innkeepers proper, and the responsibility of livery-stable keepers and graziers is limited to that of a *bonus paterfamilias,* as already explained,(g) while the responsibility of an innkeeper is very much higher than that of a stabler or grazier ; and furthermore, in regard to a horse or carriage, an innkeeper cannot obtain any benefit from the Innkeepers Act, which permits him on certain conditions to limit his responsibility, inasmuch as horses and carriages, and any gear appertaining to them, are expressly excluded from its operation.(h)   "The

---

(a) *Brown* v. *M'Connell*, 1876, 3 R. 788. Proof of what usually occurs is not proof of custom, per Lord Gifford.

(b) The meaning of this word is not a livery-stable keeper pure and simple, but an innkeeper who has stables, or an hostler. See Denman, J., in *Nugent* v. *Smith*, 1875, L.R. 1 C.P.D. 19, p. 29, n, and Blackburn, J., in *Searle*, cit., § 80.

(c) § 93.

(d) § 93, 108.

(e) *Armistead* v. *White*, 1851, 20 L.J., Q.B. 524 ; per Erle, C.J., Ex. Ch., *Cashill* v. *Wright*, 1856, 2 Jur., N.S., 1072.

(f) Dig. iv. 9, 5. See *Juridical Review,* vol. iii., 1891, p. 396.

(g) § 80.   (h) 26 & 27 Vict. c. 41.

law is express that if the goods" (and horses and carriages must be included under goods) " perish even without his fault, he is liable, unless the loss has happened *damno fatali ;* —*i.e.*, by an accident which could be neither foreseen nor withstood."(a) Where a guest leaves his horse at an innkeeper's and goes away himself, the innkeeper is still liable for any injury to the horse occurring in the absence of the owner, as he is a gainer by the transaction.(b)

By both Scotch and English law an act of God or the King's enemies is sufficient to relieve the innkeeper of his responsibility.(c) Lightning, storm, and tempest are *damna fatalia.*

Loss by robbery, it is thought, is an accident for which the innkeeper would be responsible ;(d) but the responsibility undoubtedly extends to theft.(e) Accidental fire, however, is regarded as a *damnum fatale,* and an innkeeper, if a fire break out in his stables, is not liable for the loss of his guests' horses, unless, of course, the fire was caused by his own or his servants' negligence. Thus, an innkeeper was held not liable for the value of three horses belonging to a guest, destroyed through the stable (which was lighted by a lantern of the ordinary construction) taking fire, although the last person in the stable was the guests' groom, who was intoxicated and smoked a pipe.(f) The Mercantile Law Amendment Act, which expressly made carriers liable for loss by fire of goods under their care,(g) makes no mention of innkeepers' liability, which affords additional weight to the decision referred to.

Though an innkeeper has the custody of a horse, he is not

(a) Ersk. iii. 1, 28. [Erskine there says, " If, *e.g.*, they have been lost by storm or carried off forcibly by pirates or *housebreakers,*" but he gives no case in support of this statement.]

(b) *York* v. *Grindstone,* 1 Salk. 388.

(c) As to what constitutes a *damnum fatale,* see Smith's L.C. i. 241. See also §§ 68, 74, 75, 93, 108, 116.

(d) Ersk. iii. 1, 28. But see B.C. i. 499, where this is doubted.

(e) *Williamson* v. *White,* 1810, 15 F.C. 712 ; *M'Pherson* v. *Christie,* 1841, 3 D. 930 ; *Yorke* v. *Greenhaugh,* 2 Lord Raymond, 866.

(f) *M'Donnell* v. *Ettles,* 1809, 15 F.C. 460.

(g) 19 & 20 Vict. c. 60, § 17.

allowed the use of it, except upon express agreement. In England, it has been held that an innkeeper is not liable for the loss of a guest's horse, put to grass at the owner's request, unless he is a party to the negligence causing the loss, but it would appear that he is answerable if he have put the horse out to grass without the owner's knowledge.(a) The presumption in the case of injury or loss is always against the innkeeper, and in England it is doubtful if anything short of actual negligence on the part of the guest can free the innkeeper.(b)

88. Of an Innkeeper's Lien.—An innkeeper has a lien over horses for their keep,(c) and for his bill for a guest's lodging,(d) and also over a vehicle, for standing room and labour bestowed on it, whether it be the property of the guest, or hired by him from a third party.(e) This lien operates even against the true owner of the horse, though it had been stolen by the person who brought it to the inn, the lien being strictly confined to the keep of the horse itself. (f) The lien is lost, and does not revive if the horse have once been allowed to go away,(g) but the mere fact of horses having been temporarily taken away to run races, even for days at a time, does not deprive the innkeeper of his lien.(h) Thus, a carrier who had been in the use to put up his horses at an inn owed £36 for their keep, and the innkeeper seized three of the horses and sold them. Judgment was given for the owner of the horses on two grounds : —first, because there was no power to sell, but only to detain ; and, second, because there was no lien after the

<hr>

(a) *Saunders* v. *Plummer*, 1662, Ord. Bridge, 227 ; Tenterden, C.J., in *Richmond* v. *Smith*, 1828, 8 B. and C. 9.

(b) Pollock, Chief Baron, in *Morgan* v. *Ravey*, 1861, 6 H. and N. 265, overruling *Dawson* v. *Chamney*, 1843, 5 Q.B. 164 ; *Bather* v. *Day*, 1863, 32 L.J., Ex. 171.

(c) B.C. ii. p. 99 ; *Smith* v. *Dearlove*, 1848, 6 C.B. 132.

(d) *Mulliner* v. *Florence*, 1878, L.R. 3 Q.B.D. 484.

(e) *Turrell* v. *Crawley*, 1849, 18 L.J., Q.B. 155.

(f) Platt, B., in *Broadwood* v. *Granara*, 1854, 10 Ex. 417 ; *Snead* v. *Watkins*, 1856, 26 L.J., C.P. 57.   (g) B. Pr. 1410.

(h) *Allen* v. *Smith*, 1863, 9 Jur. N.S. 230, 1284 ; Wilde, J., in *Parsons* v. *Gingell*, 1847, 4 C.B. 545.

horse was once allowed out.(a) The first ground—viz.,
power to sell, has been the subject of a legislative enactment
whereby, after six weeks, an innkeeper is empowered to sell
a horse or carriage of a guest in satisfaction of his bill.(b)
The second ground of the decision is based upon the doctrine
that the right of lien exists only as long as the subject is
retained; and that a cessation of possession is equivalent to
an abandonment of the claim.

Both in England and Scotland an innkeeper is bound to
take in a guest, and also his horse if he has accommodation.(c)
In England, however, a livery-stable keeper, not an innkeeper, is not bound to take in a horse, consequently, he is
denied a lien for its keep and attention, and a horse under
his charge is liable to distress for rent;(d) In Scotland the
question of lien has not been raised, but it is certainly the
practice to exercise it; and it is thought that horses sent to
livery are exempt from the landlord's hypothec.(e) In both
countries a guest's horse is exempt from distress for an innkeeper's rent, (f) and this holds where an innkeeper uses
premises belonging to a third party, for a particular
occasion.(g) The lien of an innkeeper also is, like all
rights of retention (except the general retention of a factor),
a personal right inseparable from the contract out of which
it arises; (h) and, accordingly, it has been held that, on a
sale of horses, detained by an innkeeper for his bill, the
lien ceased, and the true owner, not being the guest who incurred the bill, could have claimed the price from the buyer.(i)
It extends to a horse not the property of the guest.(j)

(a) *Jones* v. *Pearle*, 1 Strangr. 556.

(b) 41 & 42 Vict. c. 38, 1.

(c) B.C. ii. 99; Smith's L.C. i. 142, and cases there cited.

(d) *Parsons* v. *Gingell*, 1847, 4 C.B. 545; *Smith* v. *Dearlove*, cit., p. 117;
Yorke v. *Greenhaugh*, 2 Lord Raymond, 866.

(e) See § 89.

(f) § 89, English law, Co. Litt. 47; 34 & 35 Vict. c. 79.

(g) See Pollock, C.B., in *Williams* v. *Holmes*, 1852, 22 L.J., Ex. 283.

(h) B. Pr. 1417.

(i) *Mulliner* v. *Florence*, 1878, L.R. 3 Q.B.D. 484.

(j) *Threfall* v. *Borwick*, 1875, L.R. 10 Q.B. 210.

89. Hypothec.—In arable farms a landlord's hypothec is now of very little importance, on account of recent legislation; the Acts of 1867 and 1880, which do not affect urban leases, having practically abolished it. The right extends over horses upon the farm, and at common law could not be made effectual after the expiry of three months after the last conventional term of payment.(a) The Act of 1867(b) confirmed this, and further provided that the stock of a third party, taken to graze for a *bona fide* payment, should be liable up to the amount of the rent to the landlord's hypothec.(c) The Act of 1880(d) provides that, from and after 11th November, 1881, "the landlord's right of hypothec for the rent of any land, including the rent of any buildings thereon, exceeding two acres in extent, let for agriculture or pasture, shall cease and determine." Thus, in all leases of urban tenements, all agricultural leases entered into prior to 11th November, 1881, and all leases of lands, under two acres in extent, the law of hypothec is still in force. Where a landlord has not authorised or assented to a sub-lease, the sub-tenant's horses are liable for the principal tenant's rent; but if he has, the hypothec only extends to the amount of the sub-tenant's rent, and not even to that extent, if there is nothing in arrear.(e) Where horses and corn have been sequestrated, it is lawful to consume the corn thrashed, or part of it, in feeding the horses.(f)

In urban leases—*i.e.*, leases of buildings, whether in town or country, if not accessory to a farm, the landlord's hypothec extends over *invecta et illata*. It has not been decided whether horses fall within this category or not; but if they

---

(a) Ersk. ii. 6, 56 ; B.C. ii. 27 ; Rankine on Leases, 322, *et seq.* ; *Hepburn* v. *Richardson*, 1726, M. 6205 ; *Napier* v. *Kissock*, 1825, 4 S. 304 ; *Henderson* v. *Warden*, 1845, 17 Sc. Jur. 271.

(b) 30 & 31 Vict. c. 42, § 4.

(c) *Ibid.*, § 5 ; *Stewart* v. *Stables*, 1878, 5 R. 1024.

(d) 43 Vict. c. 12, § 1.

(e) Ersk. ii. 6, 63.

(f) *Gordon* v. *Suttie*, 1836, 14 S. 954 ; *Miller* v. *Paterson*, 1831, 9 S. 792.

should be so held, it is thought that the distinctions taken in the case of furniture(a) would be applicable, where horses are not the property of the tenant, but are only on hire or loan.

90. Horses the subject of Diligence.—Horses, being moveable property, are subject to the ordinary rules of diligence applicable to that class of property. Thus, they are arrestable; and may also be poinded, but plough horses cannot be poinded in the labouring season, when no search has been made for other goods.(b)   The provisions of the Mercantile Law Amendment Act regarding diligence(c) are applicable to horses.(d)   It has also been held that the first section of the Mercantile Law Amendment Act did not apply to a transaction or sale under which, as part of the agreement, a horse remained undelivered, and the seller had not only the custody, but continued in the use and possession of it, with a power to sell; and, therefore, that a poinding at the instance of a creditor of the seller was valid.(e)

(a) B. Pr. 1276; *Bell* v. *Andrews*, 1885, 12 R. 961.
(b) *Lord Advocate* v. *Forgan*, 1811, 16 F.C., Appx. No. 1; Ersk. iii. 6, 22.
(c) 19 & 20 Vict. c. 60, §§ 1, 3.
(d) *Young* v. *Giffen*, 1858, 21 D. 87.
(e) *Sim* v. *Grant*, 1862, 24 D. 1033.

CHAPTER V.

CARRIAGE BY LAND AND WATER.

91. Nature of the Contract.—The carriage of horses is either by land or water, and the contract for their conveyance may be either express, in which case it depends on the terms of the agreement verbal or written, or implied, as in the case of a common carrier.

92. Carriage by a Common Carrier.—A common carrier is one who for hire undertakes the carriage of goods for the public indiscriminately from a certain place within the realm to another either in or beyond the realm.(a)   He is bound

(a) *Macnamara*, Art. 19 ; B.C. i. 496 ; *Crouch* v. *L. & N.-W. Ry. Co.*, 1854, 14 C.B. 255 ; *Harrison* v. *L. & B. Ry. Co.*, 1860, 2 B. and S. 122 ; *Coggs* v. *Bernard*, 1 Smith's L.C. 201, and cases there cited. One terminus may be beyond the sea, *Nugent* v. *Smith*, 1875, 1 C.P.D, 243.

121

to carry horses for hire,(*a*) when offered at a reasonable time,(*b*) unless he does not profess to carry them, or has no convenient means of doing so ;(*c*) and, by holding himself out in a public character, he is under certain fixed responsibilities and obligations concerning what is entrusted to his care.(*d*) Thus railway, canal, and shipping companies are common carriers of live stock, apart from any limitation statutory(*e*) or stipulated. So are lightermen, wharfingers (*f*) and ferrymen. Thus, the lessees of a ferry were found liable for injury sustained by a horse in consequence of a side-rail of the landing slip giving way, although the horse was at the time under the control of its owner.(*g*)

93. The Liability of Common Carriers.(*h*)—A common carrier has, by the common law of both Scotland and England, a more enlarged responsibility than exists in the case of carrier by contract, being bound to make good all loss or damage to what is entrusted to him for carriage, although no fault or neglect can be proved against him, unless it is due to inevitable accident,(*i*) the act of God or the Queen's enemies, or inherent vice of the animal carried,(*j*) or the fault of the consignor or consignee, and the loss is *primâ facie* presumed to be due to a cause for which the carrier is responsible, the *onus probandi* being upon him to exempt himself from blame.(*k*) If, however, the owner assumes the care and custody of it himself, instead of

(*a*) Best, J., in *Riley* v. *Horne*, 1828, 5 Bing. 217.

(*b*) § 95.

(*c*) *Johnson* v. *Mid. Ry. Co.*, 1849, 4 Ex. 367 ; *Howey* v. *Lovel*, 1826, 4 S. 752.

(*d*) B. Pr. 160, § 93.

(*e*) 11 Geo. IV. and 1 Will. IV. c. 68 ; 28 & 29 Vict. c. 94 ; 17 & 18 Vict. c. 104, § 503 ; 17 & 18 Vict. c. 31.

(*f*) When they combine the trade of lightermen, but not unless ; B. Pr. 236.

(*g*) *Willoughby* v. *Horridge*, 1852, 12 C.B. 742.

(*h*) B.C. i. 496, *et seq.* ; 1 Smith's L.C. 236, *et seq.*

(*i*) § 108.

(*j*) § 109.

(*k*) *Macnamara*, Art. 54. See *Smith* v. *M. Ry. Co.*, 1887, 57 L.T. 813, where evidence was equally consistent with negligence and inherent vice of animals carried. Verdict for railway company.

entrusting it to the carrier, the carrier is not liable for the loss. This liability attaches as soon as the horse is delivered to and received by the carrier,(a) and it continues till the consignee had, or might have had, an opportunity of removing it.(b) The general rules applicable in the case of a common carrier by sea (c) are these :—" Where a shipowner receives goods to be carried for reward, whether in a general ship with goods of other shippers, or in a chartered ship whose services are entirely at the disposal of the one freighter, it is, apart from express contract, implied at common law, that he is to carry and deliver the goods in safety, answering for all loss or damage which may happen to them while they are in his hands as carrier, unless that has been caused by some act of God, or of the Queen's enemies, or of some defect or infirmity of the goods themselves,(d) or through a voluntary sacrifice for the general safety. And those exceptions are not to excuse him if he has not been reasonably careful to avoid or guard against the cause of loss or damage, or has met with it after a departure from his proper course, or if the loss or damage has been due to some unfitness of the ship to receive the cargo, or to unseaworthiness which existed when she commenced her voyage."(e)

94. Railway Companies as Carriers of Horses.—Railway companies may or may not be common carriers of live animals. If they hold themselves out to be so they are, and they may assume the responsibilities of a common carrier if they choose to do so. Under the Railway and Canal Traffic Act, 1854, while they are not common carriers of goods which they do not profess to carry,(f) railway and canal companies

(a) §§ 96, 97.

(b) § 100, and cases there cited.

(c) See also § 116.

(d) This applies to carriers by water within the kingdom such as hoymen, and carriers by canal. Also to ships carrying for the public generally, whether on coasting voyages or not, Carver, § 3.

(e) Carver, § 22.

(f) *Oxlade* v. *N.-E. Ry. Co.*, 1857, 1 C.B., N.S. 454, 498 ; *Richardson* v. *N.-E. Ry. Co.*, 1872, L.R. 7 C.P. 75.

must make proper arrangements and afford all reasonable facilities for the receiving, forwarding, and delivering of traffic (including animals) without unreasonable delay, and without prejudice or favour to any particular person or commodity; (a) and under their jurisdiction the commissioners, by these Acts, have power to award damages in cases of loss.(b)   A railway company is not bound to be a common carrier of animals, yet being bound by § 1 of the Act to afford facilities for their carriage, they can only limit their liability in respect thereof by reasonable conditions under § 7 of the Act.(c)

The liability of a railway company under this Act attaches whenever the horse is delivered.   Thus, a horse being led to a part of a railway company's yard by a groom, under the direction of a railway porter, was startled by another horse, and backed into some iron girders, and was so seriously injured that it had to be killed.   The jury found the company liable for negligently leaving the girders where they were.(d)

95. Railway Companies must receive Horses for carriage.

—Railway companies professing to carry live stock must receive a horse for carriage in the same manner as any other common carrier,(e) if it is offered to them at a reasonable time; (f) but their duty in this respect is limited to the convenience at their disposal.(g)   The company is entitled to be prepaid a reasonable hire for carriage in the absence of stipu-

(a) 17 & 18 Vict. c. 31, § 2 ; Dickson v. G. N. Ry. Co., 1886, 18 Q.B.D. 176.

(b) 36 & 37 Vict. c. 48, § 12 ; 51 & 52 Vict. c. 25, § 8, et seq.

(c) Dickson, cit., p. 123 ; see § 111.

(d) Hodgman v. W. Mid. Ry. Co., 1865, 6 B. and S. 560.   See this case further noticed, § 110.

(e) Lane v. Cotton, 1 Lord Raymond, 646, 652 ; M'Manus v. L. & Y. Ry. Co., 1859, 4 H. and N. 327 ; Johnson v. M. Ry. Co., 1849, 4 Ex. 367 ; Dickson, cit.

(f) Garton v. B. & E. Ry. Co., 1861, 30 L.J., Q.B. 273 ; Pickford v. G. J. Ry. Co., 1844, 12 M. and W., 766.

(g) Erle, J., in M'Manus, cit.

lation to the contrary ; (*a*) and delivery of the horse to the company or their authorised agent (*b*) at their usual place for receiving it (*c*) is sufficient, when accepted by the company, to fix them with responsibility for its safe carriage (*d*) till the destination is reached.(*e*)

96. Of Delivery to the Railway Company.—To render the company liable they must be charged with the horse by delivery of it to them,(*f*) or to some one empowered to act for them, either as agent or servant.(*g*) Such delivery must be in conformity with the known course of the company's business or it will not bind them.(*h*) The horse must be delivered in a state fit for carriage ; (*i*) yet if a defect in this respect be manifest and the company undertake the carriage notwithstanding, they are responsible.(*j*)

97. Obligations of a Railway Company.(*k*)—Railway companies as common carriers are bound not only to receive a horse for carriage,(*l*) but must provide a sufficient vehicle for its conveyance, tie it up properly, observe due care and exercise reasonable despatch in transit, and deliver it to the consignee.(*m*) They are bound also to follow out instructions given by the owner or his agent, when reasonably practicable.(*n*)

(*a*) *Batson* v. *Donovan*, 1820, 4 B. and Ald. 21, 28 ; Parke, B., in *Carr* v. *L. & Y. Ry. Co.*, 1852, 21 L.J. Ex. 261.

(*b*) *Macnamara*, Art. 35.

(*c*) *Macnamara*, Art. 31, as to usage.

(*d*) *Randleson* v. *Murray*, 1838, 8 A. and E. 109. *Macnamara*, Art. 96.

(*e*) *Muschamp* v. *L. & P. Ry. Co.*, 1841, 8 M. and W. 421.

(*f*) § 16.

(*g*) *Bain* v. *Sinclair*, 1825, 3 S. 533 ; *Bain* v. *Blackburn*, 1824, 3 S. 362 ; *Reid* v. *Mackie*, 1830, 8 S. 948. As to liability of forwarding agents and carriers' agents, see *Wight* v. *Inglis*, 1828, 6 S. 572 ; *Bates* v. *Cameron*, 1855, 18 D. 186 ; *Stewart* v. *Gordon*, 1852, 14 D. 434 ; *Macnamara*, Art. 43.

(*h*) *Slim* v. *G. N. Ry. Co.*, 1854, 14 C.B. 647.

(*i*) B. Pr. 162.

(*j*) *Stuart* v. *Crawley*, 1818, 2 Stark, 323.

(*k*) B. Pr. 164, 165.

(*l*) § 95.

(*m*) §§ 98, 116.

(*n*) *Streeter* v. *Horlock*, 1822, 1 Bing. 34, as to countermand of order to deliver during transit. See *Scotthorn* v. *S. S. Ry. Co.*, 1853, 22 L.J. Ex. 121.

98. A safe Vehicle for Transit.—A railway company is bound to supply a proper carriage or van, fitted with all reasonable equipments and fastenings for the conveyance of live stock, and they are responsible if loss ensue from the vehicle supplied not being reasonably fit for the purpose to which it is put, or from the incompetency of their servants.(*a*) Thus, where a horse was placed by a railway company in a truck which was insufficient, and the horse put its foot through a hole in the floor and was injured, the railway company were found liable in damages.(*b*) But it is sufficient if they provide a truck or van which without any extraordinary accident will probably perform the journey ; (*c*) and which is reasonably sufficient for the conveyance under the ordinary incidents of a railway journey.(*d*)

99. Statutory Provisions regarding Vehicles for the Carriage of Horses.—In the exercise of the powers vested in them under the Contagious Diseases (Animals) Act, 1878,(*e*) the Privy Council have made numerous regulations as to the construction of trucks, horse boxes, and other vehicles, and their appurtenances for railway transit, and as to the cleansing and disinfecting thereof. The powers which were formerly vested in the Privy Council are now transferred to the Board of Agriculture,(*f*) and the local authority for enforcing the order is the County Council.(*g*) The provisions of the Animals Order, 1886, will be found in the Appendix (*h*) along with those of the Contagious Diseases (Animals) Act regarding the provision of an adequate supply of food and water to

---

(*a*) B. Pr. 165 ; *Combe* v. *L. & S. W. Ry. Co.*, 1874, 31 L.T., N.S. 613 ; *Blower* v. *G. W. Ry. Co.*, 1872, L.R. 7 C.P. 655 ; *Chippendale* v. *L. & Y. Ry. Co.*, 1851, 21 L.J., Q.B. 22 ; *Redhead* v. *M. Ry. Co.*, 1867, L.R. 2 Q.B. 412.

(*b*) *M'Manus* v. *L. & Y. Ry.*, 1859, 4 H. and N. 327.

(*c*) *Amies* v. *Stevens*, 1 Str. 127.

(*d*) Willes, J., in *Blower*, cit.

(*e*) 41 & 42 Vict. c. 74.

(*f*) 52 & 53 Vict. c. 30, § 2 (*a*), Sch. 1, part 1.

(*g*) 52 & 53 Vict. c. 50, § 11, sub.-sec. 3.

(*h*) Appx. v., which contains the provisions of the Passenger Steamer Amendment Act regarding conveyance of horses.

horses during railway transit. A railway company having an Act of their own empowering them to charge a maximum rate for the conveyance of animals inclusive of every expense incidental to such conveyance, "except for any extraordinary services performed by the company, in respect of which they might make a reasonable extra charge," were not entitled to charge the owner of the animal with the cost of cleaning the truck, there being " a cattle plague order," to the effect that trucks should be cleaned once every twenty-four hours when being used for animal transit.(a)

100. Of Tying up the Horse in the Van.—It is the duty of the carrier or his servants properly to tie up the horse in the van, unless the consigner has undertaken that duty himself; (b) and even then, if the carrier could with ordinary diligence notice and remedy the faulty tying up by the consigner, he will not be discharged. Thus, a horse in good health was trucked at Drem for Tillicoultry, but was found dead at Edinburgh. It was tied up by one of the Company's servants in presence of the owner, and before the journey was ended the horse was found dead. It was proved that the cause of death was strangulation through the horse tugging at the rope by which it was fastened : and that the rope was too long, being between four and five feet, instead of only two. The Company pleaded they were not responsible for the method of tying up the horse, but this plea was repelled on the ground that they have the responsibility and the power of taking the necessary means for safe transit. Lord Justice-Clerk Moncreiff observed :—" I do not think that in the carriage of live animals a railway company are insurers to the extent that if the animal die in the course of transit, the value or loss must fall upon them. There may

---

(a) *Cox* v. *G. E. Ry. Co.*, 1869, 38 L.J., C.P. 151.
(b) B. Pr. 164, *Stuart* v. *Crawley*, 1818, Stark, ii. 323 ; *Richardson* v. *N.-E. Ry. Co.* 1872, L.R. 7 C.P. 75.

be presumptions, throwing the *onus* of proof of the cause of death on one side or the other."(*a*)   And where an owner of cattle bespoke a waggon of certain dimensions, took possession of it, overloaded it to save his own pocket, having signed conditions whereby he undertook all risk of loss in loading, unloading, conveyance, or otherwise, except such as shall arise from the gross negligence or default of the railway company or its servants, the company were found not liable in damages for injuries received by the cattle in transit.(*b*)

But railway companies are not responsible for accidents happening in the transit which are not of a kind that they were bound to have foreseen, if they take all reasonable precautions.   Thus, where a three-year-old horse which was fastened in the usual way in a railway horse-box, struggled through the feeding window into an adjoining compartment and was thereby injured, it was held that the accident was not of a kind the railway company were bound to have foreseen and to have provided against, and that they were not liable in damages.   It was argued that the aperture being twenty-five inches square was too large and the halter being three feet was too long ; but on the evidence given the aperture was found to be of the usual size, and that a horse getting through it was a most improbable and unprecedented occurrence.(*c*)

101. Of Reasonable Care in Transit.—A railway company is bound to carry with reasonable care.(*d*)   The standard of care is that which a prudent man would adopt if he were in the carrier's place, and had to deal with the animals under the circumstances and subject to the conditions in which the carrier is placed and under which he is called on to act. The precise degree of care varies with the circumstances of

(*a*) *Paxton* v. *N. B. Ry. Co.*, 1870, 9 M. 50.

(*b*) *Rain* v. *G. S.-W. Ry. Co.*, 1869, 7 M. 439.

(*c*) *Ralston* v. *Cal. Ry. Co.*, 1878, 5 R. 671, see observations of Lord President Inglis and Lord Deas upon tying up horses for railway transit.

(*d*) B. Pr. 167, and cases there cited.

every case, some animals requiring more care and management than others, according to their nature, habits, and conditions. A condition that a railway company will not be responsible "for loss . . . occasioned by kicking, plunging, or restiveness of the animal," does not relieve them of the duty of using reasonable care, and "the exception goes to limit the liability, not the duty." It is the duty of the carrier to do what he can to avoid all perils, including the excepted perils.(a)

Railway companies in the habit of carrying live animals are under a certain responsibility, not only toward the owner of the animals but also towards the public. If a dog or a horse is known to be vicious and the company are informed of this, the company are bound to take not only the usual but extraordinary precautions to prevent it from escaping and so doing injury to the public.(b)

102. Of Reasonable Despatch in Transit.—In the absence of special agreement there is no implied contract on the part of a railway company to deliver with punctuality; but the contract is to deliver within a reasonable time, having regard to all the circumstances; and railway companies are not responsible for the consequences of delay arising from causes beyond their control, and are justified in incurring delay if it be necessary to secure safe carriage. (c) The ordinary course of the journey which is professed by the company to be their route must be observed; (d) and where delay is occasioned by causes beyond the control of the company, as—*e.g.*, by a snowstorm, they are not bound to use extraordinary effort, or incur extra expense, in order to surmount such an obstruction.(e) A railway company, however, must

---

(a) Blackburn and Lush, J.J., in *Gill* v. *M. S. & L. Ry. Co.* 1873, L.R. 8 Q.B. 186.

(b) Per Lord Inglis in *Gray* v. *N. B. Ry. Co.*, 1890, 18 R. 76, 77.

(c) *Taylor* v. *G. N. Ry. Co.*, 1866, L.R. 1 C.P. 385; *Hales* v. *L. & N.-W. Ry. Co.*, 1863, 32 L.J., Q.B. 292; *Myers* v. *L. & S.-W. Ry. Co.*, 1869, L.R. 5 C.P. 3.

(d) Blackburn, J., in *Hales*, cit.; *Johnson* v. *Midland Ry. Co.*, 1849, 4 Ex. 367.

(e) *Briddon* v. *G. N. Ry. Co.*, 1858, 28 L.J., Ex. 51.

K

carry with reasonable despatch,(*a*) all the more so if it is within their knowledge that a horse is going to a special market for sale ;(*b*) and if there be a known cause of danger of delay, the company are bound to warn the consignor of it. "Temporary or accidental detention from unexpected pressure of traffic is a risk incidental to railway traffic, and one of which the customer must to a certain extent take his chance. But it is quite a different thing when the causes of probable detention are known and foreseen, and are not specifically disclosed to the customer when his goods are accepted."(*c*)

What amounts to reasonable time is purely a jury question.(*d*) A falling-off in condition in consequence of delay in delivery, and from want of food and water, amounts to an "injury" under the Railway and Canal Traffic Act.(*e*)

103. Of a Fit Place for Delivery.—Railway companies are bound to keep their stations in a fit and proper state for the safe delivery of the horse, and they cannot relieve themselves of that duty by special conditions ; (*f*) but there is no specific obligation on a railway company carrying live stock to provide fences or guards at the station where the animals are unloaded to prevent their straying on the line. (*g*)

4. Of Delivery to the Consignee.—A common carrier is bound to deliver the horse, in the same condition as he got it, to the consignee, or one authorised to receive it ; (*h*)

(*a*) *M'Connachie* v. *G. N. S. Ry. Co.*, 1875, 3 R. 79 ; *Macdonald & Co.* v. *Highland Ry. Co.*, 1873, 11 M. 614.

(*b*) *Anderson* v. *N. B. Ry. Co.*, 1875, 2 R. 443.

(*c*) Per Lord Justice-Clerk Moncreiff in *M'Connachie*, cit. 85.

(*d*) *Donohoe* v. *L. & N.-W. Ry. Co.*, 1867, 15 W.R. 792. Question as to whether company is bound to send animals by special train.

(*e*) *Allday* v. *G. W. Ry. Co.*, 1864, 34 L.J., Q.B. 5.

(*f*) *Rooth* v. *N.-E. Ry. Co.*, 1867, L.R. 2 Ex. 173.

(*g*) *Roberts* v. *G. W. Ry. Co.*, 1858, 27 L.J., C.P. 266 ; see also *Sneesby* v. *L. & Y. Ry. Co.*, 1875, 1 Q.B.D. 42. For the circumstances of this case, see § 170.

(*h*) See § 93, authorities there cited ; Macnamara, Art. 100. As to goods delivered by mistake, see *Caledonian Ry. Co.* v. *Harrison*, 1879, 7 R. 151.

or, if necessary, to some other carrier to complete the transit,(*a*) or to the consignor stopping it *in transitu ;* (*b*) and in the absence of any direction as to delivery, a carrier may deliver to a named consignee at a different place from that to which he contracted to carry it.(*c*) Accordingly, the carrier is not discharged of his liability until delivery to the consignee or his assignee, or until a reasonable time has elapsed after the consignee has notice of arrival for him to come and take delivery ; (*d*) but if the consignee delays taking delivery within a reasonable time, the liability of the carrier is reduced to that of an ordinary custodier.(*e*) Where express directions are given as to delivery, railway companies are bound to follow them ; and if, in doing so, they observe their usual course of business, they are not liable if they deliver to a person the consignor did not intend.(*f*) If there be no one to receive a horse at the end of its journey, the company may put it into a livery stable, and recover livery charges from the consignee. (*g*)

105. Of Through Booking.—Where a horse is received by a railway company for transmission to a place beyond the terminus of its own lines, in the absence of special conditions the company is liable for its safe carriage during the whole of the transit ; (*h*) the persons to whom they hand it over being considered their agents for delivery,(*i*) unless there is evidence by special contract(*j*) to show that their responsi-

---

(*a*) See § 105.

(*b*) B. Pr. 168.

(*c*) *Cork Distillery Co.* v. *G. & S.-W. Ry. Co.*, 1874, L.R. 7 H.L. 269 (Ireland) ; *L. & N.-W. Ry. Co.* v. *Bartlett*, 1861, 7 H. and N. 400.

(*d*) *Bourne* v. *Gatliff*, 1844, 11 C. and F. 45.

(*e*) *Chapman* v. *G. W. Ry. Co.*, 1880, 5 Q.B.D. 278 ; see also Martin, B., in *Heugh* v. *L. & N.-W. Ry. Co.*, 1870, L.R. 5 Ex. 51, 57.

(*f*) Martin, B., in *M'Kean* v. *M'Ivor*, 1870, L.R. 6 Ex. 36.

(*g*) *G. N. Ry. Co.* v. *Swaffield*, 1874, 43 L.J., Ex. 89. As to the company's duty when the consignee refuses to take delivery, see *G. W. Ry. Co.* v. *Crouch*, 1858, 3 H. and N. 183 ; also *Hudson* v. *Baxendale*, 1857, 2 H. and N. 575.

(*h*) *Caledonian Ry. Co.* v. *Hunter*, 1858, 20 D. 1097.

(*i*) *Muschamp* v. *L. & P. Ry. Co.*, 1841, 8 M. and W. 421.

(*j*) *Fowles* v. *G. W. Ry. Co.*, 1852, 22 L.J., Ex. 76.

bility is to cease when the goods are beyond their own
lines ; (a) but to claim exemption under a condition relieving
them of responsibility for damage occurring beyond their own
lines, a company must show that some other company, who
would be responsible, had obtained custody before the injury
or loss occurred.(b)   The liability of the company to whom
horses are given for transit in such cases depends upon
whether there is in the stipulation they have made with the
consignor anything to exclude their liability beyond their
own lines. (c)

By § 14 of the Regulation of Railways Act, 1868,(d) it
is provided that where a company by through booking contracts to carry animals, &c., partly by railway, or partly by
canal and partly by sea, they shall have power to exempt
themselves from the usual sea risks if they give due notice
at their office or by freight note.

By the Regulation of Railways Act, 1871,(e) § 12, it is
enacted that when a railway company under a contract for
carrying animals, &c., by sea, sends them in a vessel not
belonging to them, their liability is the same as if the
vessel had been their own, provided the injury happens
in such vessel, the *onus* of proof to the contrary lying
upon the company.   A company having no powers to work
steam vessels, contracted in Dublin to convey cattle by sea
to Liverpool, and thence by rail to St. Ives, upon conditions repudiating liability for danger of the sea, or for " any
default or negligence of the master or any of the officers or
crews of the company's vessels ; " the cattle were lost on the
passage to Liverpool by the negligence of the crew of a vessel
with whose owners the company had a booking arrangement.
It was held that the condition was unreasonable, and that

(a) *Muschamp, cit.* ; *Aldridge v. G. W. Ry. Co.*, 1864, 33 L.J., C.P. 161.

(b) *Kent v. Midland Ry. Co.*, 1874, L.R. 10 Q.B. 1.

(c) See *Coxon v. G. W. Ry. Co.*, 1860, 5 H. and N. 274 ; *Gill v. M. S. L. Ry. Co.*,
1873, L.R. 8 Q.D. 186 ; *Combe v. L. & S. W. Ry. Co.*, 1874, 31 L.T., N.S. 613.

(d) 31 & 32 Vict. c. 119.

(e) 34 & 35 Vict. c. 78.

the words " master, &c., of the company's vessels " applied to all vessels the company should employ. (a)

106. Termination of the Company's Responsibility.(b)— Should the consignee reject the horse, or delivery to him be impossible, the liability of the company extends to re-delivery of it to the consignor's order. (c) Even after the transit has ceased this responsibility of a railway company does not terminate till the owner or consignee had, or might have had, an opportunity of removing the horse carried. (d) The company, however, are bound to keep the horse for a reasonable time for the consignee to come and fetch it, during which period of time their liability continues. After a reasonable time this liability ceases, and they are merely custodiers, and not liable as carriers; (e) and the amount of time is a question of circumstances. (f) But in one case a company was held not liable even when slightly in fault, there being also fault on the part of the sender. A horse was sent from Newbury to Windsor. No one appeared to claim it; it was forgotten, left tied up in a horse box for twenty-four hours, and was found seriously injured. It was held that the company was not liable, the true cause of injury having been the neglect of the sender to inform the consignee that the horse was coming. (g)

(a) *Doolan* v. *Midland Ry. Co.*, 1877, L.R. 2 App. Ca. 792. Where it was also decided that the effect of 31 & 32 Vict. c. 119, § 16, taken with 34 & 35 Vict. c. 78, § 12, was to extend all the provisions of the R. and C. Traffic Act, 1854, to railway companies carrying goods in vessels not belonging to them. See also *Moore*, cit. § 114, p. 143.

(b) See § 104 as to the company's duty if there be no one to receive the horse.

(c) *Metzenburg* v. *Highland Ry. Co.*, 1869, 7 M. 919. As to carrier's duty in such a case, see *G. W. Ry. Co.* v. *Crouch*, 1858, 3 H. and N. 183.

(d) *Shepherd* v. *B. & E. Ry. Co.*, 1868, L.R. 3 Ex. 189 ; *Gordon* v. *G. W. Ry. Co.*, 1881, 8 Q.B.D. 44. See also Macnamara, Art. 96, 105, 293.

(e) *Chapman* v. *G. W. Ry. Co.*, 1880, 5 Q.B.D. 278 ; *Taff Vale Ry. Co.* v. *Giles*, 1853, 2 E. and B. 822 ; *Cairns* v. *Robins*, 1841, 8 M. and W. 258.

(f) *Coxon* v. *N.-E. Ry. Co.*, 1883, 4 R. and C. Tr. Ca. 284.

(g) *Wise* v. *G. W. Ry. Co.*, 1856, 1 H. and N. 63. In this case there was a notice protecting the carrier from injury ; but still it seems difficult to reconcile the decision with those in *Chapman* and *Taff Vale*, cit. *supra*.

107. Legal Presumption in Case of Loss or Injury.—
When loss or damage occurs in transit, there arises a presumption that it occurred at the carrier's hands ; and the burden of proving that it did not is laid upon him ;(a) and a common carrier, if not protected by express contract, is responsible for all loss and damage to a horse entrusted to him for carriage, unless he can establish that the loss was due to inevitable accident,(b) or solely to some inherent vice in the horse carried.(c) Thus, a common carrier by sea received a mare for transit from London to Aberdeen. There was a rough passage, and the mare received such injuries that she died. The jury found that the injury was due partly to more than ordinary bad weather and partly to the fright of the mare, and that there was no negligence on the part of the carrier or his servants.(d) It is not necessary for the carrier to prove that it was absolutely impossible to prevent it, but it is sufficient to have proof that by no reasonable precaution under the circumstances could it have been prevented.(e)

108. *Damnum fatale.*—The inevitable accident(f) which will free a common carrier from liability for loss must be due exclusively to natural causes without human intervention. Thus, neither theft(g) nor the fraud of servants are any excuse ;(h) but, in order to show that the cause of the loss was irresistible, it is not necessary to prove that it was absolutely impossible to prevent it ; it is sufficient to prove that by no reasonable precaution under the circumstances could

(a) § 93; for form of issue see *Wood & Co.* v. *Peebles Ry. Co.*, 1860, 22 D. 1393 ; *Hudson* v. *Baxendale*, 1857, 2 H. and N. 575.

(b) Ersk. iii. 1, 28 ; Stair, i. 13, 3 ; B.C. i. 495 ; § 108.

(c) § 109. *Paxton* and *Ralston*, cit. p. 128.

(d) *Nugent* v. *Smith*, 1875, L.R. 1 C.P.D. 423.

(e) Per L.J. Mellish in *Nugent*, cit. p. 441.

(f) See also §§ 93, 160.

(g) *Forbes* v. *Steel*, 1687, M. 9233 ; *Chisholm* v. *Fenton*, 1714, M. 9241.

(h) Stair, i. 13, 3, but the goods must be given regularly so as to charge the master. See § 96.

it have been prevented ; and a carrier in such a case has done all that is reasonably to be required of him, if he has used all the means to which prudent and experienced carriers ordinarily have recourse to insure the safety of goods entrusted to them under similar circumstances.(*a*)   A fall of snow is an accident such as will free a railway company for liability from delay, and a common carrier is not bound to use extraordinary efforts or incur extra expense to surmount the obstruction.(*b*)   Railway companies, when common carriers, are liable for loss of horse by fire.(*c*)   Carriers, moreover, are not liable for accidents happening to an animal from its inherent vice, when there is no fault or negligence attributable to them.

109. Inherent Vice.(*d*)—The leading case on this subject was one in which the Great Western Railway Company were sued for failure in delivery of a bullock delivered to them at Dingestow Station, to be carried to Northampton.   In the course of the journey the animal escaped from the truck in which it was placed, and was killed.   In a case stated by the County Court judge, it was found that the escape was wholly attributable to the efforts and exertions of the animal itself, and not to any negligence on the part of the company, and that the truck was in every respect proper and reasonably sufficient for the conveyance of cattle.   The Court held that, upon this state of facts, the judge ought to have directed a verdict for the defendants ; and Willes, J., observed:—" The bullock was received by the company under the terms of a notice which is assailed by the plaintiff.   It is unnecessary to consider whether or not the notice was a reasonable one. The question for our decision is, whether the defendants, upon the facts and findings of the County Court judge, are

(*a*) See Cockburn, C.J., in *Nugent* v. *Smith*, cit., p. 438, but irresistible force occasioned by robbers and mobs will not free the carrier ; *Coggs* v. *Bernard*, 1 Smith's L.C., p. 215.

(*b*) *Briddon* v. *G. N. Ry. Co.*, 1858, 28 L.J., Ex. 51.

(*c*) 19 & 20 Vict. c. 60, § 17.

(*d*) § 100.   Cases of *Paxton* and *Ralston*, p. 128.

liable as common carriers for the loss of this animal. . . .
The question as to their liability may turn on the distinction
between accidents which happen by reason of some vice
inherent in the animals themselves, or disposition producing
unruliness or phrensy, and accidents which are not the result
of inherent vice or unruliness of the animals themselves. It
comes to much the same thing whether we say that one who
carries live animals is not liable in the one event but is liable
in the other, or that he is not a common carrier of them at
all, because there are some accidents other than those falling within the exception of the act of God and the Queen's
enemies, for which he is not responsible. By the expression
'vice,' I do not, of course, mean moral vice in the thing itself
or its owner, but only that sort of vice which, by its internal
development, tends to the destruction or the injury of the
animal or thing to be carried, and which is likely to lead to
such a result. If such a course of destruction exists, and
produces that result in the course of the journey, the liability
of the carrier is necessarily excluded from the contract between
the parties."(a)

In another case, decided in the same year, the circumstances were as follows :—A horse, saddled and bridled, was
taken to Waterloo Station to be carried to Ewell. It was
attempted to be shown that the railway company's servants
were guilty of negligence in not tying up the stirrups ; but,
as the plaintiff acquiesced in their being allowed to hang
down, and there being evidence that that course was usual
and proper, the contention was abandoned. No accident
happened to the train, nor anything likely to alarm the
horse, which was one accustomed to travel by rail ; but at
the end of the journey it was found to have sustained considerable injuries, and an action was brought against the
company. The Court held that the defendants were not
liable, since it was to be inferred that the injuries resulted
from inherent vice of the horse. Bramwell, B., said: " There

(a) *Blower v. G. W. Ry. Co.*, 1872, L.R. 7 C.P. 655, 662.

is no doubt that the horse was the immediate cause of its own injuries. That is to say, no person got into the box and injured it. It slipped, or fell, or kicked, or plunged, or in some way hurt itself. If it did so from no other cause than its inherent propensities, ' its proper vice '—that is to say, from fright, or temper, or struggling to keep its legs—the defendants are not liable. But if it so hurt itself from the defendants' negligence, or any misfortune happening to the train, though not through any negligence of the defendants —as, for instance, from the horse-box leaving the line owing to some obstruction maliciously put upon it—then the defendants would, as insurers, be liable."(a) Where the vice, however, is brought out by the negligence or fault of a railway or shipping company, the liability attaches.(b)

110. Limitation of Carriers' Responsibility under Statute.

—Under various statutes the common law responsibilities of common carriers have to a certain extent been limited. By the Carriers Act of 1830,(c) common carriers were exempted from liability for injury to certain goods when their value exceeded £10, unless their description and value were declared, and an increased charge, according to notice, paid at the commencement of the carriage ; but special contracts were not affected by this Act ;(d) and this exception led to the abuse of carriers being able to contract themselves out of almost all liability whatever. By § 4, common carriers could no longer by public notice limit their responsibility in respect of articles not within the Act ; and, accordingly, they were liable to the full value of the loss to horses injured or lost in transit. These defects were removed by

---

(a) *Kendall* v. *L. & S.-W. Ry. Co.*, 1872, L.R. 7 Ex. 373, 377.
(b) *Gill* v. *M. S. & L. Ry. Co.*, 1873, L.R. 8 Q.B. 186.
(c) 11 Geo. IV, and I Will. IV. c. 68, § I.
(d) *Ibid.* § 6.

the passing of the Railway and Canal Traffic Act.(*a*)   Under § 7 of this statute, railway and canal companies (*b*) shall be liable for the loss of or for any injury done to horses or other animals in receiving,(*c*) forwarding, or delivering them, occasioned by the neglect or fault of such company or its servants,(*d*) notwithstanding any notice, condition, or declaration made and given by such company contrary thereto, or in anywise limiting such liability, every such notice being declared null and void.   Power is reserved, however, to companies under the Act to make by a special contract with the consignor such conditions with regard to receiving, forwarding, or delivering animals, &c., as the Court shall adjudge to be just and reasonable, provided it is in writing, and signed by the consignor, or the person delivering the animals for carriage ; and a limit of £50 is fixed as the amount of damage to be recovered for the loss of a horse, unless a declaration of its value, if higher than £50, shall be made at the time of delivery, and a reasonably (*e*) higher charge paid for carriage.   It is further provided that the notice of increased rates shall be publicly notified as under the Carriers Act,(*f*) and that the *onus* of proof of value of such animals, and the amount of injury done thereto in all cases, lies with the person claiming compensation for such loss or injury.   Where the sender fills up and signs a receiving note on which conditions of carriage are printed, it is presumed that he has assented to them.(*g*)   The leading case(*h*) regarding the interpretation of this section settled that the validity

(*a*) 17 & 18 Vict. c. 31, § 7.

(*b*) And this liability attaches when they carry in vessels not belonging to them in the absence of special contract. See also § 105.

(*c*) *Hodgman* v. *W. Mid. Ry. Co.*, 1865, 6 B. and S. 560 ; see also § 95.

(*d*) *Harrison* v. *L. B. Ry. Co.*, 1860, 2 B. and S. 152 ; *Van Toll* v. *S.-E. Ry. Co.*, 12 C.B., N.S. 75.

(*e*) This is a jury question, *Harrison*, cit.

(*f*) 11 Geo. IV. and 1 Will. IV. c. 68, § 2.

(*g*) *Lewis* v. *G. W. Ry. Co.*, 1860, 29 L.J., Ex. 425. Cockburn, J., in *Zunz* v. *S.-E. Ry. Co.*, 1869, L.R. 4 Q.B. 539, 544.

(*h*) *Peek* v. *N. St. Ry. Co.*, 1863, 10 H. of L. Ca. 473.

of conditions limiting the common law liability of the carrier
is subject to their being both adjudged "just and reasonable," and embodied in a signed special contract; and, also,
that the *onus* of showing them to be reasonable lies with the
company alleging them to be so.(*a*)   In regard to the signature
of the contract, it is settled that the company cannot
repudiate a special contract on the ground of its not being
signed by the consignor ;(*b*) that an agent or servant signing
binds his principal,(*c*) whether the servant can read or
not,(*d*) but that mere initials are not equivalent to signature
under the Act.(*e*)

The value must be truly declared, otherwise the owner is
barred from recovering damages ;(*f*) and if it be declared of
less value than £50, the sender cannot recover a sum greater
than the declared value.   Further, where a very valuable
horse was injured through the negligence of a railway company in their yard before the value was declared, it was held
to be an injury while "receiving," and that the owner of
it could not recover more than £50, even though it was the
practice to put horses into horse-boxes before declaring their
value or paying the fare.(*g*)

111. Of "Just and Reasonable" Conditions.(*h*) — The
Court is always the judge of this matter, and the *onus* of
proving a condition reasonable lies upon the company.(*i*)
The justice and reasonableness of conditions are purely a
question of circumstances, and no definite rule can be laid
down.(*j*)   In construing them the Court will give effect

(*a*) See also *M'Manus* v. *L. & Y. Ry. Co.*, Ex. Ch. 1859, 4 H. and N. 327,
349 ; *Simons* v. *G. W. Ry. Co.*, 1857, 2 C.B., N.S. 620.

(*b*) *Baxendale* v. *G. E. Ry. Co*, 1869, L.R. 4 Q.B. 244.

(*c*) Baron Martin in *Kirby* v. *G. W. Ry. Co.*, 1868, 18 L.T., N.S. 658.

(*d*) *Foreman* v. *G. W. Ry. Co.*, 1878, 38 L.T., N.S. 851.

(*e*) *Peebles* v. *Cal. Ry. Co.*, 1875, 2 R. 346.

(*f*) *M'Cance* v. *L. & N.-W. Ry. Co.*, 1861, 7 H. and N. 477.

(*g*) *Hodgman* v. *W. Mid. Ry. Co.*, 1865, 6 B. and S. 560.

(*h*) See this fully treated in Macnamara, Art. 171.

(*i*) *Harrison* v. *L. B. & S. C. Ry. Co.*, 1860, 2 B. and S. 122, 152.

(*j*) *Gregory* v. *N.-W. Ry. Co.*, 1864, 33 L.J., Ex. 155.

to the plain meaning of the language without implying
any limitation or exception not expressed.(a)   In judging of
it, all the circumstances of the contract and transit will be
considered ; such—*e.g.*, as the conduct of the sender and
his servants who accompany the horse sent by rail.(b)   The
leading case on this point with regard to horses is *M'Manus*
v. *Lancashire & Yorkshire Railway Company*.(c)   A horse
was placed by the railway in a truck which was insufficient.
In the journey the horse put its foot through a hole in the
floor, by which it was injured, and the case turned upon
the reasonableness of the following condition :—This ticket
is issued, subject to the owner's undertaking "all risks of
conveyance, loading, and unloading whatsoever, as the company will not be responsible for any injury or damage (however caused) occurring to live stock of any description
travelling upon the Lancashire and Yorkshire Railway Company, or in their vehicles."   The Court found this condition
neither just nor reasonable ; and Justice Williams observed :
—"It is unreasonable that the company should stipulate for
exemption from liability, from the consequence of their own
negligence, however gross, or misconduct, however flag-
rant."(d)   Again, a condition that a company shall not be
liable for any damage or delay "in any case," has been held
unreasonable.(e)   Thus, also, a condition that a company is
not to be answerable for "any consequences arising from
over carriage, detention, or delay in, or in relation to, the
conveying or delivery of said animals, however caused," was
held unreasonable,(f) and Chief Justice Cockburn observed :
—"It might, perhaps, be reasonable if they had given the
plaintiff the choice of two rates, and had made a special

(a) *M'Nally* v. *L. & Y. Ry. Co.*, 1880, 8 L.R., Ir. Ex. App. 81.

(b) *Rain* v. *G. & S.-W. Ry. Co.*, 1869, 7 M. 439.

(c) *M'Manus* v. *L. & Y. Ry. Co.*, 1859, 4 H. and N. 327.

(d) § 110, see also *Paxton* v. *N. B. Ry. Co.*, 1870, 9 M. 50 ; and *Rooth* v.
N.-E. Ry. Co., 1867, L.R. 2 Ex. 173.

(e) *Ashendon* v. *L. B. & S. C. Ry. Co.*, 1880, L.R. 5 Ex. D. 190 ; *Harrison* and
Gregory, cit. p. 139.

(f) *Allday* v. *G. & W. Ry. Co.*, 1864, 34 L.J., Q B. 5.

contract limiting their liability in consideration of the lesser rate being paid. But a condition that a company is not to be liable for loss beyond the limits of its own lines, and that money received for the journey beyond its own lines is received for the consigner's convenience is reasonable.(a) A condition disallowing a claim of damages unless made within a specified time,(b) or unless the value be truly declared,(c) is reasonable.

112. Alternative Rates.—When there is an option of having animals carried at a higher rate, rendering the company liable, and the horse is carried at the lower rate, the company will not be liable except for their own negligence or fraud, but to contract against that is unreasonable. Lord Wensleydale observed : " A carrier can't say, ' I won't be liable for *any* loss, unless you pay me a fixed sum to indemnify against all.' "(d) But where the sender knows of a company having a certain rate for carrying horses in horse-boxes by passenger train, and lower rate if carried in waggons by goods train, and sent his horse by goods train, it was held a reasonable condition that they should be carried entirely at the owner's risk; and that such a condition would protect the railway if the horses were injured, but not from delay.(e)

In another case of carriage of cattle there were alternative rates, one the ordinary rate, where the company undertook

(a) *Aldridge* v. *G. W. Ry. Co.*, 1864, 33 L.J., C.P. 161 ; see also *Wise* v. *G. W. Ry. Co.*, 1856, 1 H. and N. 63.

(b) *Simons* v. *G. W. Ry. Co.*, 1856, 26 L.J., C.P., 25.

(c) *Lewis* v. *G. W. Ry. Co.*, 1860, 5 H. and N. 867.

(d) *Peek* v. *N. S. Ry. Co.*, 1863, 10 H. of L. Ca. 473, 578 ; see also *M. S. & L. Ry. Co.* v. *Brown*, 1883, 8 App. Ca. 703.

(e) *Lewis* v. *G. W. Ry. Co.*, 1877, 3 Q.B.D. 195 ; *Robinson* v. *G. W. Ry. Co.*, 1865, 35 L.J., C.P. 123 ; *Harris* v. *Mid. Ry. Co.*, 1876, 25 W.R. 63. See also *Moore* v. *G. N. Ry. Co.*, 1882, 10 L.R., Ir. 95, where it was also held that a condition exempting the company "in all cases from liability for injuries caused by fear or restiveness of animals," did not embrace cases in which the injury immediately flowed from these causes directly occasioned by negligence and want of care on the part of the company, but applied to injury from these causes in ordinary transit without negligence on the part of the company, and that it was "reasonable" in this limited sense.

the ordinary liability of a carrier; the other a reduced rate, where the company were to be free from all responsibility (including liability for loss, injury, delay), unless such injury should be occasioned by the intentional and wilful neglect or misconduct of the company's servants. The train arrived late, and some of the cattle died, others were injured, and loss of market was also incurred. *Inter alia*, a condition in the following terms was held reasonable :—" The company will in no case be responsible for any injury sustained by reason of the overcrowding of waggons, or by such overcrowding and delay in transit, where such overcrowding takes place at the instance of the owner or sender, or person in charge of animals." It was also held that the reasonableness of the alternative rate was for the judge and not for a jury. (*a*)

113. Conditions where Free Pass is given to Groom.— Further, a condition where a pass is given for a drover to ride with his animals, that the company is to be held free " from all risks in respect of any damages arising in the loading or unloading, from suffocation or being trampled upon, bruised, or otherwise injured in transit, from fire, or from any other cause whatsoever," was held reasonable, the drover having means of ascertaining the sufficiency of the vehicle supplied. (*b*)

But a condition that an " owner undertakes all risks of loading, unloading, and carriage, whether arising from the negligence or default of the company or their servants, or from defect or imperfection in the station platform, or other places of loading, . . . or of the carriage, . . . or from any other cause whatever," is unreasonable, and its unreasonableness is not destroyed by granting free passes to persons having care of live stock. (*c*)

(*a*) *Sheridan* v. *M. G. W. Ry. Ir. Co.*, 1888, 24 L.R., Ir. 146. In this case there will be found six conditions all held reasonable.

(*b*) *Pardington* v. *S. W. Ry. Co.*, 1856, 1 H. and N. 392.

(*c*) *Booth* v. *N.-E. Ry. Co.*, 1867, L.R. 2 Ex. 173.

114. Unreasonable Conditions.(*a*)—The following condition about cattle transit was held unreasonable, viz. :—" That the owner or his representative is required to see to the efficiency of such waggon before he allows his stock to be placed therein, and complaint must be made in writing to the station inspector or clerk in charge as to all alleged defects, either at the time of booking or before the waggon leaves the station."(*b*) Again, a condition that "all goods delivered to a company will be received and held by them subject to a general lien for all money due to them, whether for carriage of such goods or for other charges," was held not just and reasonable.(*c*) Again, it has been held unreasonable for a company, carrying partly by sea and partly by land, to exempt itself from liability from the consequences of the negligence of the captain and crew of the steamer engaged in the sea transit, which was worked by and belonged to a steam packet company working under an arrangement with the railway company.(*d*)

Where cattle were prepaid at "owner's risk," and detained by a company for a lien which turned out to be unfounded, the company was found liable in damage.(*e*) When there is an exemption from damage of a special kind, it will not relieve the company when loss or damage is distinctly traceable to their fault. Thus, damage by leakage or breakage is not covered by the exemption if negligence supervene on the part of a railway company,(*f*) or those who are agents for them to complete a journey.(*g*) Where a consignee delays unreasonably, after receiving his horse, to give notice of damage done to it in course of transit, he is barred from objecting to its condition.(*h*)

(*a*) See also §§ 111, 112, 113.
(*b*) *Gregory* v. *W. M. Ry. Co.*, 1864, 33 L.J., Ex. 155.
(*c*) *Peebles* v. *Cal. Ry. Co.*, 1875, 2 R. 346.
(*d*) *Moore* v. *M. Ry. Co.*, 1875, 9 Ir. C.L. 20.
(*e*) *Gordon* v. *Gt. W. Ry. Co.*, 1831, 8 Q.B.D. 44.
(*f*) *Phillips* v. *Clark*, 1857, 2 C.B., N.S. 163.
(*g*) § 105.
(*h*) *Stewart* v. *Cal. Ry. Co.*, 1878, 5 R. 426.

115. The Limit of Damage Recoverable.—Under the Act no more than £50 can be recovered from a railway or canal company for damage to or loss of a horse, unless under declaration of a higher value,(a) and the declared value is taxative.(b) The chance of obtaining a prize is too remote a ground for damage.(c) If recovery is sought at the price of a sub-sale rendered ineffectual by the injury, there must have been an actual contract to purchase at that figure.(d) If, on failure to provide proper horse-boxes, the customer has to provide other means of transit for horses out of condition, the company is bound to make good only the deterioration which the horses would have suffered if they had been in good condition, and the expenses for time and labour on the road ;(e) and it is a jury question whether the customer would not be entitled to a special train for their conveyance, if there were no ordinary trains for delivery within reasonable time.(f)

116. Responsibility of Carriers by Water.—When the carriage is by canal it is under the same rules as carriage by railway companies.(g) Common carriers by water are under the obligations already referred to and explained, so far as they are applicable to this description of transit.(h) Where carriage is by a special contract, the owner is bound to supply a seaworthy vessel, properly manned and navigated, with all necessary equipments and documents for safety.(i) The vessel(j) must not be overloaded, and the horse must be kept safe from all perils, such as concussion or

---

(a) See § 110 ; 17 & 18 Vict. c. 31, § 7.
(b) *M'Cance* v. *L. & N.-W. Ry. Co.*, 1864, 3 H. and C. 343.
(c) *Watson* v. *A. N. & B. Ry. Co.*, 1851, 15 Jur. 448.
(d) *Hart* v. *Baxendale*, 1867, 16 L.T., N.S. 390, Martin, B.
(e) *Waller* v. *M. G. W. Ry. Co.*, 1879, L.R. 4 Ir. 376.
(f) *Donohoe* v. *L. & N.-W. Ry. Co.*, 1867, 15 W.R. 792.
(g) §§ 93-108.
(h) § 93.
(i) B. Pr. 408.
(j) Regulations for conveyance of horses in passenger steamers, Appx. vi.

explosion,(a) and there must be no deviation from the usual course of the voyage,(b) and the vessel must be reasonably fitted and prepared for the carriage of animals.   Thus, where a vessel which had carried cattle with foot-and-mouth disease was not properly cleansed before a fresh lot were put on board, and, owing to this, they took the disease and died, the shipowners were found liable in damages.(c)

A common carrier by sea is not liable at common law for loss which is the result of inevitable accident caused by the act of God, the Queen's enemies,(d) or inherent vice of the horse carried, unless aggravated by himself(e) or by the fault of the consignor or his servants travelling along with the horse conveyed.   Perils of the sea,(f) when unavoidable, come under the category of accidents, and are a valid defence to the carrier, but they cannot be pleaded in answer to a claim of damage caused by deviation from the usual course of the voyage.(g)   Perils of the sea include such unavoidable dangers as stress of weather, winds, waves, lightning and tempests, rocks, sand banks, collisions,(h) and a common carrier is not bound to restore what is thrown overboard for common safety.(i)   The exceptions, however, do not excuse the carrier where he has deviated from the course of the voyage,(j) or has been negligent,(k) or has failed to obviate loss when it was in his power to do so ;(l) nor where the loss is caused by the ship's unseaworthiness.(m)

(a) B. Pr. 167.
(b) *Davis* v. *Garrett*, 1830, 6 Bing. 716.
(c) *Tattersall* v. *N. Steamship Co.*, 1884, L.R. 12 Q.B.D. 297.
(d) § 108, p. 135, note (a).
(e) § 109 ; Carver, § 13.
(f) See Abbot, 13th ed., p. 450, *et seq.*
(g) B. Pr. 241 ; as to *onus* shifting in case of stress of weather, see *Williams* v. *Dobie*, 1884, 11 R. 982.
(h) Carver, § 93.
(i) *Ibid.* § 15.
(j) Davis, cit.
(k) *Phillips* v. *Clark*, 1857, 2 C.B., N.S. 156 ; *Siordet* v. *Hall*, 1828, 4 Bing. 607.
(l) *Notara* v. *Henderson*, 1872, L.R. 7 Q.B. 225; *The Freedom*, 1871, L.R. 3 P.C. 594.
(m) *Steel* v. *State Line S. S. Co.*, 1877, 3 L.R. App. Ca. 72.

L

It has been held that this strict rule of the liability of a common carrier, applies to the case of a vessel used exclusively for the purposes of one person who engaged her services for the voyage.(*a*)

By the Merchant Shipping Act, 1854, § 388: "No owner or master of any ship shall be answerable to any person whatever for any loss or damage occasioned by the fault or incapacity of any qualified pilot acting in charge of such ship, within any district where the employment of such pilot is compulsory by law," but if the master is guilty of contributory fault this provision does not free him.(*b*) The mere fact that the pilot is on board does not relieve the master and crew of their liability.(*c*)

117. Statutory Limitations of Liability of Carrier by Sea.

—By the Merchant Shipping Act, 1854,(*d*) Part xi. sec. 503 : "No owner of any sea-going ship(*e*) or share therein shall be liable to make good any loss or damages that may happen without his actual fault or privity . . . to any goods, merchandise, or other things whatsoever taken in or put on board any such ship by reason of any fire happening on board such ship." This section does not apply to foreign ships,(*f*) nor lighters used in landing from a ship.(*g*) By the Merchant

(*a*) *Liver Alkali Co.* v. *Johnson*, 1872, L.R. 7 Ex. 267 ; Carver, § 5 ; but it has been held that a bailee of a horse was excused from re-delivering it when it had become sick and died without any neglect on his part, on the ground that this happened by the act of God. Cases of this kind are now generally excepted, on the ground that the loss is by a defect in the thing itself. But such a case may fall within the definition of "act of God," if the defect or disease which has caused the loss has been in no way caused by the act of man (*Williams* v. *Lloyd*, W. Jones' Rep. 179, cit. Carver, 10) ; *The Ida*, 1875, 32 L.T., N.S. 541.

(*b*) *The Iona*, 1867, L.R. 1 P.C. 426 ; *Clyde Nav. Co.* v. *Barclay*, 1876, L.R. 1 App. Ca. 790 ; Brett, L.J., in *Guy Mannering*, 1882, 7 P.D. 132-134.

(*c*) Carver, § 32.

(*d*) 17 & 18 Vict. c. 104.

(*e*) Ship includes every kind of vessel not propelled by oars. See *Ex parte Ferguson*, 1871, L.R. 6 Q.B. 280 ; *The C. S. Butler*, 1874, L.R., 4 Ad. and Eccl. 238 ; *The Mac*, 1882, 7 P.D. 126.

(*f*) *Cope* v. *Doherty*, 1858, 27 L.J., Ch. 600.

(*g*) *Morewood* v. *Pollok*, 1853, 22 L.J., Q.B. 250 ; *Hunter* v. *M'Gown*, 1819, 1 Bligh. App. Ca. 573. These cases were under Geo. III. c. 86, § 2.

Shipping Amendment Act, 1862, section 54: "The owners of any ship, whether British or foreign, shall not, where any of the following events occur without their actual fault or privity, that is to say, . . .

>(2.) Where any damage or loss is caused to any goods, merchandise, or any other thing whatsoever on board any such ship,(a) . . .

>(4.) Where any loss or damage is, by reason of the improper navigation of such ship, as aforesaid, caused to any other ship or boat, or to any goods, merchandise, or other thing whatsoever on board any other ship or boat,

be answerable for loss or damage . . . to goods, to an aggregate amount exceeding £8 for each ton of the ship's tonnage," such tonnage to be registered tonnage in the case of sailing ship, and in the case of steamships the gross tonnage.

This benefit is extended by the Regulation of Railways Act, 1871, to railways carrying partly by rail and partly by sea, provided the loss happened during carriage by the vessel, and the *onus* of showing that it did so is laid on the railway company.(b)

118. Carriage by Sea by Special Contract.—The contract of affreightment which contains the specification of the animal or animals to be carried, the freight and the modifications of the common law responsibilities of the shipowner may be by charter-party or by bill of lading.(c)   The former occurs when the ship itself is chartered, the latter is usually adopted in the carriage of horses; and the bill of lading is the ordinary document embodying evidence of a contract of carriage between the shipowner and the shipper.   Under the present state of the law, shipowners, as has already been pointed out, are liable as common carriers to make good all

---

(a) This does not apply to loss after transhipment into another ship in consequence of a collision, *Bernina*, 1886, 12 P.D. 36.

(b) 34 & 35 Vict. c. 78, § 12.   See also § 105.

(c) See form, Appendix vii.

loss or damage to horses entrusted to their custody for carriage.(a) They are protected at common law from losses due to inevitable accident,(b) and, in certain cases, inherent vice of the horse carried.(c) They are protected by statute from loss by fire, or loss due to the fault of a pilot when his employment is compulsory by statute.(d) The Carriers Act, 1830, (e) moreover, has no application in carriage by water ; nor is there any provision under the Merchant Shipping Act (f) under which a shipowner may assume the responsibility for safe carriage of animals on a declaration of their value and payment of an increased rate by the shipper ; accordingly, shipowners are left free to limit their responsibility by notices which are now framed, fencing them against almost every possible contingency.(g)

A shipowner, by contracting to carry horses, impliedly undertakes that his ship is seaworthy at the time of sailing,(h) and this arises from his position as a shipowner, and not as a common carrier ;(i) but even this implied warranty has been the subject of limitation in a bill of lading.(j) The seaworthiness required depends on the nature of the voyage,(k) and extends in the case of animals to a reasonable fitness for their carriage with safety.(l) Thus, a shipper shipped cattle under a bill of lading, agreeing that the shipowner was not to be liable for accidents, disease, or mortality, and under no circumstances for more than £5 per head. The ship, after having carried a cargo of cattle with foot-and-mouth disease on a previous voyage, was left improperly cleansed, the shipper's cattle took the disease, and the plaintiff suffered

(a) § 93.   (b) §§ 93, 116.   (c) § 109.   (d) § 117.
(e) 11 Geo. IV. and 1 Will. IV. c. 68.
(f) 17 & 18 Vict. c. 104.
(g) See notice in form of bill of lading, Appendix vii. See § 105 and *Doolan* there cited ; also §§ 111, 114.
(h) *Cohn* v. *Davidson*, 1877, 2 Q.B.D. 455.
(i) *Kopitoff* v. *Wilson*, 1876, 1 Q.B.D. 377 ; Lord Shand in *Cunningham* v. *Colvils & Co.*, 1888, 16 R. 295.
(j) *The Laertes*, 1887, 12 P.D. 187.
(k) *Daniels* v. *Harris*, 1874, L.R. 10 C.P. 1.
(l) See § 98.

damage amounting to more than £5 per head.   It was held that the provision limiting liability to £5 per head did not apply to damage occasioned by the defendants not providing a ship reasonably fit for the purpose of the cattle they had contracted to carry.(a)   Similarly a shipping company were held liable for the loss by suffocation of some cattle carried under a bill of lading, excluding them from liability "for any loss arising from suffocation or other causes occurring to horses, dogs, or other animals," they having sent the ship to sea with insufficient ballast.(b)   A ship to be seaworthy must be really fit for the sea, and the shipowner will not be discharged of the implied obligation of seaworthiness on showing he has done his best to make the ship fit, if it is not so in fact ;(c) and where a shipper discovers unseaworthiness before the commencement of the voyage, he may throw up the contract if he should have to wait an unreasonable time for the fault being remedied.(d)   A shipowner is liable in damages for loss caused by unseaworthiness at starting, unless this is excepted in his contract ;(e) for unseaworthiness on the voyage not covered by exceptions, even though he has no opportunity of repairing ; and when covered by exceptions if he has an opportunity of repairing but proceeds without doing so.(f) When a horse is delivered in a damaged condition under a bill of lading with a clause, "shipped in good condition," the shipper must give *primâ facie* evidence either that it was shipped in good order or that the damage resulted from some cause within the control of the shipowner.(g)   He must negative inherent vice ;(h) for evidence which leaves it doubtful whether the loss is due to an excepted peril or not does not

(a) *Tattersall* v. *Nat. S.S. Co.*, 1884, L.R. 12 Q.B.D. 297.

(b) *Leuw* v. *Dudgeon*, 1867, L.R. 3 C.P. 17, n.

(c) *Daniels*, cit.

(d) *Stanton* v. *Richardson*, 1875, 45 L.J. H.L. 78.

(e) But the exceptions will not always avail him.   *The Glenfruin*, 1885, 10 P.D. 103 ; *The Undaunted*, 1886, 11 P.D. 46 ; *Seville & Co.* v. *Colvils & Co.*, 15 R. 616.

(f) *Worm* v. *Storey*, 1855, 11 Ex. 427.

(g) *The Ida*, 1875, 32 L.T., N.S. 541.

(h) § 109.   *Williams* v. *Dobbie*, 1884, 11 R. 982.

render the shipowner liable.(*a*) The arrival of the ship without the horse would be *primâ facie* evidence against the shipowner.(*b*)

Even though a shipowner is saved by express exemption in a bill of lading, he is nevertheless bound to take all reasonable care of horses entrusted to him ; and when they are damaged by a cause for which he is not responsible, he is bound to use all means to mitigate the consequences of any disaster they may have met with.(*c*) Whether shipowners can contract themselves out of liability for loss due to their own personal fault is not clear.(*d*) Attempts have been made to do this, but their effect is not to render them the less liable, but merely to shift the *onus probandi* on to the shipowners to show that the loss did not happen through their fault. Various other exemptions have been made in bills of lading regarding other classes of goods which have been the subject of decision, and these, in the absence of express rulings in horse cases, in some measure indicate the lines upon which the exemptions usually found in bills of lading of horses would in all likelihood be construed.

Thus, where goods were delivered in a damaged condition the bill of lading containing a stipulation that the shipowners should not be answerable "for damage, leakage, lighterage, breakage, corruption, &c.," the owner of the goods (sugar) sued the shipowners for damages, and the jury returned a special verdict that the sugar was damaged, but that it had not been established by evidence what was the cause of the damage. It was held that the verdict should be entered for the shipowners, in respect that the only damage found to be proved was damage for which the shipowners were by the terms of the contract exempted from liability. Lord Justice-Clerk Inglis said:—"If we had had here an ordinary bill of lading with the usual exceptions or with

(*a*) Lord Halsbury in *Wakelin* v. *L. & S.-W. Ry. Co.*, 1886, 12 App. Ca. 41, 45.

(*b*) *The Xanthos*, 1886, 2 *The Times'* L.R. 704.

(*c*) *Notara* v. *Henderson*, 1870, L.R. 5 Q.B. 346.

(*d*) Abbot, 13th ed., pp. 477-8. *Phillips* v. *Edwards*, 1858, 3 H. and N. 813.

additional exceptions of the same kind, I should have held that the burden of proof lay upon the shipowner. But the whole peculiarity and difficulty of this case arises on a different clause in the bill of lading, and a clause of exception which appears in an unusual place. The adding of the clause appears to have occurred as an after-thought to the framer. There is one part of the clause which I read thus:—' Not answerable for breakage.' Now, what does that mean? In the first place it is the shipowner who is not to be answerable. He is not to be answerable for breakage. This does not mean that he will not be answerable for breaking the goods. The word breakage is not used here in an active sense, it means the broken condition of the goods. If this be so the clause must mean that the shipowner is not to be responsible for the broken condition of the goods at the port of delivery. This is an exception not of a cause of damage but a stipulation of non-liability for a certain state of the goods. . . . The question is, Does the *onus* lie upon the owner of the goods to prove neglect, or upon the shipowners to prove that there was no neglect? Now, in my opinion, the shipowner has not that burden. I think the burden of proof lies upon the pursuers, and my reason is that the liability for negligence is not a liability which rests upon them in their capacity of carriers, for it lies upon every custodier. I think the bill of lading discharges them from all liability for breakages in their capacity of carriers, but leaves them under the common law liability of custodiers." (a)

Again, a bill of lading bore that the shipowners should not be responsible "for any of the following perils, whether arising from negligence, default, or error in judgment of the pilot, master, mariners, engineers, or persons in the service of the ship or for whose acts the shipowner is liable, or otherwise, namely, risk of craft, &c." An action was raised for damaged wheat, and a special verdict finding, *inter alia*,

(a) *Moess, &c.* v. *Leith, &c., Co.*, 1867, 5 M. 988-991.

that the wheat had been damaged by sea water, and that
through the negligence of some of the crew one of the orlop-
deck ports was insufficiently fastened, and that in consequence the sea water was thereby admitted to the hold
after the ship had been five days at sea.   It was held that
they were not liable in virtue of the exempting clause, and
that the exemption of their liability for negligence of the
crew was a perfectly lawful contract to make.   The House of
Lords upon appeal held that if the circumstances which the
jury found in their verdict existed at the beginning of the
voyage the ship was then unseaworthy and the exceptions in
the bill of lading did not protect the shipowner as they do
not apply till the voyage has begun, and though they found
that the special verdict did not exhaust the case as it did
not find whether the ship was or was not seaworthy at the
commencement of the voyage, yet they held that the bill of
lading contained an implied undertaking of seaworthiness.(a)

Again, where a charter-party excluded the shipowners from
liability for "the accidents of navigation . . . even when
occasioned by the negligence" of their servants, but the
master neglected the duty of at once communicating the fact
of the accident to the pursuer, thereby depriving him of the
power of preventing further damage by immediately removing the cargo, it was held that the shipowners were on that
account liable for damage caused by the delay, but the
opinion was stated that the *onus* of proving that the damage
to the cargo had not been increased by the neglect of the
master to communicate the fact of the accident to the pursuer was upon the defenders.(b)

**119. The usual Exemptions from Liability in the Con-
tract.**—The exemptions from liability vary of course with
each shipping company, and with the goods to be carried.
Those usual in an ordinary bill of lading are those arising

(a) *Steel* and *Craig* v. *State Line Co.*, 1877, 4 R. 657 (H.L.) 103.
(b) *Adam* v. *Morris*, 1890, 18 R. 153.

from perils of the sea, the act of God, and the Queen's enemies, fire . . . &c. But where horses or live stock are to be carried there are usually these further exemptions, —viz. "not liable for mortality, contagion or injury." These exceptions it is thought would not free the shipowner from any damage due to his own fault. Thus, if the contagion were the result of the owners having carried diseased animals in the same ship and not having properly disinfected it previous to allowing the animals to be put on board, or if mortality or injury were the result of an unseaworthy ship, or of deviation where that is not specially excepted, or due solely to faulty arrangement for carriage, the shipowner would still be liable.(*a*)

120. Freight when the Horse Dies or is Damaged.— Freight, as a general rule, is due on delivery in the absence of special agreement ; and the shipowner must be willing and able to deliver on payment of his just charges before he can claim freight.(*b*) "Freight is earned by the carriage and arrival of the goods ready to be delivered to the merchant."(*c*) Express agreement regarding payment of freight overrules the common law ; thus, if the agreement be for lading and undertaking to carry, the subsequent death of the animal does not deprive the owner of his reward ; but if the agreement be to pay freight for *transport*, then no freight is due for those that die on the voyage, because as to them the contract is not performed.(*d*) If the shipowner has been prevented from carrying the horse to its destination, although by causes beyond his control, he cannot claim any part of the freight, for he has not earned it. So " freight would not be payable upon animals which died during a voyage and were thrown overboard. Nor probably would it be payable although the carcasses were carried to the desti-

(*a*) *Tattersall* and other cases cited, § 118.
(*b*) *Johnson* v. *Greaves*, 1810, 2 Taunt. 344.
(*c*) Per Willes, J., in *Dakin* v. *Oxley*, 1864, 33 L.J., C.P. 115, 119.
(*d*) Maclachlan, 4th edition, p. 490.

nation, for the thing for the carriage of which freight was to be paid was the living animal."(a)   A contrary opinion, however, is maintained that, in the absence of express agreement, freight is payable for the dead as well as for the living.(b) If the horse has been carried to its destination, and is there ready to be delivered, it is no answer to a claim for freight that it is damaged or deteriorated, and not in the condition it was in when shipped; even though the damage is so great that the horse is not worth the freight payable upon it, and though the damage has arisen owing to the fault of the master and crew.(c)   The consignee may claim for damages, but is liable for the freight in full.(d)

(a) Carver, § 548 ; see also *L. & N.-W. Ry. Co.* v. *Hughes*, 1889, 26 **L.R. Ir.** 165, 175.

(b) Maclachlan, p. 490, 492.

(c) *Dakin*, cit. *Shields* v. *Davis*, 1815, 6 Taunt. 65 ; *Hotham*, 1 Douglas, 272.

(d) *Meyer* v. *Dresser*, 33 **L.J.**, C.P. 289.

CHAPTER VI.

RESPONSIBILITY FOR THE NEGLIGENT USE OF HORSES.

1. Criminal.

121. Grounds of Responsibility.—In the management of carriages and horses a driver is answerable for that degree of attention which persons of ordinary care and experience exercise in that capacity, and for due observance of the rules of careful driving ; and in cities and crowded places a driver or rider is bound to be more vigilant than in less frequented districts. (a) The rules applicable to drivers are—to ride and drive at a moderate pace ; to abstain from running races with other vehicles or horses on the road ; to keep the horse well in command ; to keep a proper look out against accidents ; to observe the rules of the road ; and not to leave the horse unattended when stopping.(b) Any negligence in regard to these rules is criminal ; and, according to the degree of culpability, the

(a) Alison's Prin. 116 ; *Miller*, 1828, Alison's Prin. 118 ; *Reg. v. Murray*, 1852, 5 Cox's Cr. Ca. Ir. 509.
(b) Alison's Prin. 116.

offence may vary from a police offence to culpable homicide, and even murder if it be wilful.(*a*)

122. Furious and Reckless Riding and Driving.—It is not in every one's power either to be a good rider or driver, or to manage his horse dexterously on every occasion ; but the law considers it incumbent on every person to know his own deficiencies, and take care that he does not proceed along the highway on a horse that he cannot control, or ride at such a rate as to endanger the safety of others upon the road. Furious driving or riding(*b*) is accordingly an indictable offence if it lead to the over-turning or injury of carriages, to the maiming or hurting of individuals, or to injury to property.(*c*) Thus, on a charge of "culpable and furious driving," two drivers of carts of empty barrels were sentenced to twelve months' imprisonment for driving furiously past carts loaded with furniture, whereby some furniture was damaged, and a servant on the cart had her leg broken.(*d*) When furious driving causes death it is culpable homicide, and numerous cases have occurred where drivers have been found guilty of culpable homicide.(*e*) Thus, a hackney-coachman was convicted of culpable homicide for having, in a state of intoxication, driven over and killed an old woman.(*f*)

123. Racing along the Road.—To race along a road at such a pace as to endanger the safety of the lieges is criminal; and if a fatal accident occur, both of those engaged in the race are equally guilty, though only one cause the injury.

(*a*) Lord Raymond, i. 143 ; 1 East. Cr. Pleas, 263 ; Hume, i. 192, 193.

(*b*) *Grant,* 1830, Alison's Prin. 122, 626.

(*c*) Hume, i. 193 ; 1 Geo. IV. c. 4 ; 50 Geo. III. c. 48, § 15.

(*d*) *Bartholemew, Somerville and Watson,* 1825 ; Hume, i. 193. See also *Johnstone and Alexander,* 1829 ; *Davidson and Train,* 1829 ; *Bolton,* 1828 ; and *Grant :* cit. Alison's Prin. 626.

(*e*) *Colquhoun,* 1804 ; *Andrew and Adam Scott,* 1805 ; Hume, i. 192, 193.

(*f*) *Liddell,* 1818 ; Hume, i. 193.

Thus, two carters were convicted of culpable homicide for having run a race in their carts, and thereby killed an old woman.(*a*) And this rule applies equally whether the injured party is within or without either of the racing vehicles.(*b*)

124. Failure in keeping look out and control.—Sitting in a vehicle and not keeping a good look out is a criminal offence, falling under a charge of culpable and reckless driving.(*c*) Thus, a driver was found guilty of culpable homicide, his negligence consisting in driving over a child three years old in a street in Glasgow. He was seated in his cart, the horse only going at a walking pace, and his negligence only reached the length of failing to keep a due look out.(*d*) Again, a driver was similarly convicted for causing the death of a child, his negligence consisting in having stayed behind his horse talking with other carters ; he had not the reins in his hand, and the horse turned a corner, and killed the child. Lord M'Kenzie laid it down that here there was a clear case of neglect, inasmuch as the carter should have been at the horse's head, and with the reins in his hands, and that it was not sufficient to relieve him of criminal responsibility that the horse was only walking at the time.(*e*) But it is a good defence to a charge of criminal negligence that the accident was caused by the injured party getting in front of the horse,(*f*) or that the injured party interfered with the driving.(*g*)

125. Leaving the Horse Unwatched when Stopping is relevant to infer a charge of reckless driving, and even

---

(*a*) *Crichton and Morrison*, 1822 ; Hume, i. 193 ; *M'Millan and Others*, 1831 ; *Forfar*, 1829, and *Brown*, 1827 ; Alison's Prin. 118 ; *Reg. v. Swindall*, and *Osborne*, 1826, 2 C. and K. 230.

(*b*) *Rex v. Timmins*, 1836, 7 C. and P. 499.

(*c*) *Matheson*, 1837 ; 1 Swin. 593.

(*d*) *Miller*, 1828 ; Alison's Prin. 118 ; see also *Macdonald*, 1826 ; Alison's Prin. 119.

(*e*) *Scott*, 1829 ; *Johnstone*, 1823 ; Alison's Prin. 119, 120.

(*f*) Alison's Prin. 120.

(*g*) *Reg. v. Jones*, Lush, J., 1870, 22 L.T., N.S. 217.

culpable homicide, if death ensue. Thus a carter, who left his cart and horses on the road while he went into an alehouse to drink, and the horses merely proceeded along the road, without running off, and killed an old woman, deaf, and nearly blind, was convicted of culpable homicide.(a) Further, it has been held, that recklessly whipping a pony so as to make it run away with its rider, and throw him or fall with him, is relevant to infer a charge of assault.(b)

126. Police Regulations regarding Horses. — For the purposes of the General Police and Improvement (Scotland) Act, 1862,(c) the word "cattle" includes horse, mare, gelding, colt, filly, ass, mule ;(d) and it is provided that any constable or officer of police, or any person residing within the burgh, may seize and impound cattle found at any time without a person to take charge of them in any street of the burgh, and detain them till the owner pays to the Commissioners a penalty not exceeding 40s., besides the reasonable expenses of impounding and keeping them ;(e) and, on the failure of the owner to pay within three days, the stray animal may be sold for penalty and expenses, after seven days' notice to the owner.(f) It is also enacted that every person who exposes for show, hire, or sale . . . any horse, . . . or shoes, bleeds, or farries any horse (except in cases of accident), or cleanses, dresses, exercises, trains, breaks, or turns loose any horse, or slaughters it, in any street or private street, is liable to imprisonment for a period not exceeding fourteen days, or a fine not exceeding 40s.(g) A similar penalty may be imposed on any one who, having the care of a vehicle, rides upon the shafts, or who rides or

(a) *Jackson*, 1810, Hume, i. 192 ; *Fleming*, 1866, 5 Irv. 289.

(b) *Keay*, 1837, 1 Swin. 543.

(c) 25 & 26 Vict. c. 101.

(d) *Ibid.* § 3.   (e) *Ibid.* § 249.

(f) *Ibid.* § 250.   (g) *Ibid.* § 251.

drives without a bit in the horse's mouth, or is at such a distance from the horse as to have no control over it, or who fails to observe the rule of the road, or wilfully prevents other vehicles from passing him ; or who rides or drives furiously ; or who rides or drives on the footpath ; or who fastens a horse so that it stands across a footpath. Any one who causes any public carriage (other than hackney carriages or those animals or vehicles specially permitted by the Commissioners) to stand longer than is necessary for loading and unloading of goods, or for taking up or setting down passengers,(a) shall be liable to a fine not exceeding 40s. for each offence, or imprisonment for fourteen days.

Vehicles for the conveyance of goods or plying for hire must have the name of the owner painted upon them ;(b) and such vehicles are not to be driven by persons under fourteen years of age, under a penalty.(c) If a horse is shown to be an annoyance to the neighbourhood, the magistrate has power to summarily order its removal.(d)

127. Hackney Carriages and Omnibuses.—The same Act (Part V.), provides for the licensing of hackney carriages, which it defines as "every wheeled carriage, whatever be its form or construction, used in standing or plying for hire in any street within five miles from the principal post-office of the burgh," or any carriage having the prescribed plate applicable to hackney carriages required by the Act, or a plate resembling it.(e) It regulates the fees (f) to be paid for licenses, and specifies the conditions under which licenses are to be granted,(g) providing for what shall be specified in the license,(h) and for the registration (i) and duration of licenses.(j) A fine not exceeding 40s. may be imposed on pro-

---

(a) 25 & 26 Vict. c. 101, § 251 ; *Black* v. *Simpson*, 1883, 5 Coup. 212.
(b) *Ibid.* § 252. (c) *Ibid.* § 253. (d) *Ibid.* § 256.
(e) *Ibid.* § 278, 279. (f) *Ibid.* § 280. (g) *Ibid.* § 281.
(h) *Ibid.* § 282. (i) *Ibid.* § 283. (j) *Ibid.* § 284

prietors allowing such vehicles to ply for hire without a license,(*a*) and drivers driving them without a license are liable to a fine not exceeding 20s.(*b*) Provisions are made for a plate specifying the number of persons to be carried in a hackney carriage (*c*) being conspicuously placed on the carriage, and a penalty not exceeding 40s. may be imposed on any proprietor neglecting to do so, or refusing, when required by the hirer, to carry the prescribed number.(*d*) Penalties are also imposed upon drivers refusing to drive, when required by a member of the public,(*e*) for over-charging,(*f*) or permitting persons to ride without the consent of the driver,(*g*) and for being intoxicated or driving furiously,(*h*) for leaving a hackney carriage unattended at places of public resort,(*i*) and for improperly refusing to give way to or obstructing any other driver, or depriving him of the chance of being hired.(*j*) Damage done by a driver may be recovered before a magistrate to the extent of £5 from the proprietor.(*k*)

Penalties are also imposed on the hirer for driving a hackney carriage without the consent of the pro-prietor,(*l*) and for wilfully injuring the carriage,(*m*) and provisions are made for recovery of compensation to drivers for loss of time in attending to answer complaints not sub-stantiated.(*n*)

Power is reserved to magistrates for regulating the use of hackney carriages, the fixing of cab stances and rates and fares, and for the prevention of the use of unsafe omnibuses.(*o*)

Local Acts have from time to time been passed, under which these provisions are applied to different burghs, and

---

(*a*) 25 & 26 Vict. c. 101, § 286.   (*b*) *Ibid.* § 288.
(*c*) *Ibid.* § 292.   (*d*) *Ibid.* § 293.   (*e*) *Ibid.* § 294.
(*f*) *Ibid.* § 298.   (*g*) *Ibid.* § 299.   (*h*) *Ibid.* § 301.
(*i*) *Ibid.* § 302, see *Shaw* v. *Croall*, 1885, 12 R. 1186.
(*j*) *Ibid.* § 304.   (*k*) *Ibid.* § 303.   (*l*) *Ibid.* § 300.
(*m*) *Ibid.* § 307.   (*n*) *Ibid.* § 305.   (*o*) *Ibid.* § 309.

the leading provisions have been adopted with slight variations in various burghs and populous places.(a)   A case occurred in which the magistrates of a burgh, having framed and enacted a bye-law that all omnibuses should stand in and depart from County Square, a proprietor who started his omnibuses from his own yard, without standing in County Square, was convicted and sentenced.   On appeal it was held to be *ultra vires* of the magistrates to compel all omnibuses to stand at the stance fixed, when the proprietors desired that they should start from some other place.(b)

It has also been held that the bye-laws made by the magistrates of a burgh for the regulation of hackney carriages " plying for hire within " the burgh, do not apply to all hackney carriages passing through its streets, but only those licensed by the magistrates of the burgh.(c)

128. Cruelty to Horses.—The Prevention of Cruelty to Animals Act, 1850,(d) provides that " Any person who shall, from and after the passing of this Act, cruelly beat, ill-treat, over-drive (and this includes over-ride (e)), abuse, or torture, or cause or procure to be cruelly beaten, ill-treated, over-driven, abused, or tortured, any animal, shall be guilty of an offence, and shall for every such offence be liable to a penalty not exceeding £5, and any vehicle or any animal may be detained by a constable in security of penalty and expenses of keep, and the magistrate may order sale thereof in default of payment."(f)   Under this Act a complaint was relevantly laid, which set forth the designation and residence of the accused, and that on certain dates and at a certain place where he conducted part of his business, he caused certain oxen to be kept without food, although the complaint did

---

(a) 25 & 26 Vict. c. 101, § 7.
(b) *King* v. *Hart*, 1882, 5 Coup. 16.
(c) *Gairns* v. *Main*, 1888, 15 R. (J.C.) 51.
(d) 13 & 14 Vict. c. 92 § 1.
(e) *Ibid.* § 11.
(f) *Ibid.* § 9.

not set forth personal knowledge of the facts complained of.(a) It was argued that the statute was intended to strike only at wanton and intentional cruelty, but this was over-ruled. Lord Neaves observed :—" I would certainly say that it is not necessary by the statute, in order to establish the offence, that any such intention should be proved. If a person neglect to do a thing which is his duty and within his power, and thereby ill-treat, torture, or abuse any animal, that would equally fall within the scope of the statute as where there is wilful and wanton cruelty." In another case, a charge of cruelty by a cab-driver, " by causing or allowing his horse to remain yoked to a cab on the public road, during the night of the 18th, and morning of the 19th October, 1881, said horse suffering severely from hunger, cold, and exposure, in consequence of which said horse suffered great and unnecessary pain," was held relevantly libelled (diss. Lord Young), and the interpretation of the statute in *Wilson* v. *Johnson* was held sound.(b) But where a conviction was obtained against A, the owner of a horse, for contravening the statute by causing his horse to draw a cart when it was unfit to be worked owing to an open sore beneath the saddle, it was set aside on appeal on the ground that at the time of the alleged cruelty the horse was worked by A's servant, and that it was not proved that A had any personal knowledge of the condition of the horse at the time—such personal knowledge, or at least good reason to believe that suffering would be caused to the animal, being regarded necessary to the commission of the offence.(c) The mere fact of the servant over-driving his master's horse, will not absolve the master from blame, if he knows of its being over-driven, and there is reasonable evidence of its having been over-driven, such as the death of the horse from sheer exhaustion.(d)

(a) *Wilson* v. *Johnston*, 1874, 1 R. (J.C.) 16.
(b) *Anderson* v. *Wood*, 1881, 9 R. (J.C.) 6.
(c) *Wright* v. *Rowan*, 1890, 17 R. (J.C.) 28.
(d) *Carmichael* v. *Welsh*, 1887, 1 White, 333.

129. Slaughter-houses.—"No person shall keep any house or place for the purpose of slaughtering or killing any horse . . . without first taking out a license for that purpose" from the Sheriff. A board with the words, "Licensed for slaughtering horses, pursuant to an Act passed in the session of Parliament in the thirteenth and fourteenth years of the reign of Her Majesty Queen Victoria," must be placed over the gate of slaughter-houses for horses, under penalty of a fine of £5, and a further penalty of £5 for every day the board is not so placed.(a) A description of the horses slaughtered is to be kept in a book for the purpose, under a penalty of 40s. ;(b) and no one can simultaneously hold a license to slaughter horses and exercise the trade or business of a horsedealer.(c) Under the General Police Act, 1862, police commissioners may license slaughter-houses,(d) and make bye-laws for their regulation ;(e) and where such slaughter-houses are provided by the commissioners, no other places within two miles beyond the boundaries are to be used for slaughtering.(f)

2. CIVIL LIABILITY FOR ACCIDENTS.

130. Grounds of Responsibility.—The law protects the personal safety of individuals against negligence, and the gross disregard of it, by other members of the public. The remedy of jury trial is peculiarly applicable to this class of cases, as furnishing the best means of deciding whether there has been negligence, and if so, what amount of damages should be given ; but, in the majority of cases, evidence is led before either a Sheriff or Lord Ordinary, who are judges both of law and fact, subject to the right of ordinary

---

(a) 13 & 14 Vict. c. 92, § 3.
(b) Ibid. § 4.
(c) Ibid. § 5, amended by 41 & 42 Vict. c. 79, sched. 1.
(d) 25 & 26 Vict. c. 101, § 358.
(e) Ibid. § 360.
(f) Ibid. § 363.

appeal to the Superior Courts.(a)   To ground an action for
reparation for injuries caused by riding or driving, there are
two requisites :—*Firstly*, the injury received must have been
caused by the fault or negligence of the injurer, or some one
for whom he is responsible ; and, *secondly*, the injury must
not have been materially contributed to by the fault or negligence of the injured party.(b)   The negligence in horse cases
for which the law gives redress usually consists in furious
driving, or in losing command of the horse, or in failure to
observe the rule of the road ; or, in the case of owners of
public vehicles, in failing to provide safe horses, vehicles, and
drivers.   Although a carrier of persons does not insure his
passengers as he does his goods, he is bound to take the very
greatest care of them, and his civil responsibility is cor-
respondingly strict.(c)   Where there is a contract for the
carriage of persons, and an accident is proved or admitted to
have happened, there arises a presumption against the person
in charge of the horse, and the *onus* of proving that he was
not responsible for it lies upon him ;(d) but where no such
contract exists between the parties, there is no such presumption, and the injured party must not only state precisely
the fault of the injurer, but prove it, and prove that it was
the cause of the accident.   The injured party cannot recover
if he has materially contributed to bring about the accident,
nor if by ordinary care he could have avoided it, nor if the
injury is shown to have been due to inevitable accident.(e)
Redress is given not only against the one who causes the
injury, but also against those who are responsible for him.
Further, one is not permitted to hunt over lands possessed
by another ;(f) or to let his horse stray into adjoining fields,

(a) Mackay's Pr. ii. 13.
(b) *Hawkins* v. *Cooper*, 1838, 8 C. and P. 473 ; L.P. Inglis in *M'Naughton* v. *Cal. Ry. Co.*, 1858, 21 D. 160, 163, *et seq.*
(c) § 147 ; B. Pr. 170.
(d) *Lyon* v. *Lamb*, 1838, 16 S. 1188.
(e) See §§ 160, 161.
(f) Unless he be his landlord.   *Ronaldson* v. *Ballantyne*, 1804, M. 15,270.

but must keep it secure in its field or stable. It is trespass to allow such straying ;(a) and the statute of 1686, c. 11, enacts that " all heritors, liferenters, tenants, cottars, and other possessors of lands and houses shall cause herd their horses . . . the whole year," under a penalty of half a merk for each beast " they shall have upon their neighbour's ground, by and attour the damage done to the grass or planting ;" and the possessor of the ground has power to detain the animal for the penalty and expense of keep. This Act is still in observance ;(b) but the usual remedy where no damage has been done is interdict, which, however, will only be granted when there is reasonable apprehension that the offence will be repeated.(c) If injury is done by a straying animal, the owner of it is liable in damages, but the mere fact of ownership does not of itself render him liable, although it raises a presumption that the injury was due to his fault in not keeping it secure.(d)

Again, stables must be used reasonably, so as not to annoy neighbours. Thus, where the ground floor of a dwelling-house, in a street in London, had been converted into a stable, by a previous occupier, and the new occupier increased the number of horses kept, so that the noise thereby occasioned had an injurious effect on the value of adjoining property, it was held that a nuisance was created.(e)

131. Furious Riding and Driving.—Riders(f) and drivers of vehicles are bound to go at a moderate pace. The speed at which they may go depends upon a variety of circumstances—the time of day or night, the state of the traffic, and the like ; and negligence in the management of horses is

(a) Rankine's Land-Ownership, 123, 534, et seq.

(b) M'Arthur v. Miller, 1873, 1 R. 248.

(c) Hay's Trs. v. Young, 1877, 4 R. 398.

(d) Lord Neaves in Campbell v. Kennedy, 1864, 3 M. 121-125.

(e) Ball v. Ray, 1873, L.R. 8 Ch. App. 467 ; Broder v. Saulliard, 1876, L.R. 2 Ch. D. 692.

(f) Brown v. Fulton, 1881, 9 R. 36.

purely a jury question. Thus, a driver of a pony carriage who, on a dark night in January, between seven and eight o'clock, while driving, without lights, at the rate of about six miles an hour, knocked down a foot passenger on the carriage-way of a public road which had a footpath on one side, was found liable in damages, it being proved that he saw the passenger about fifteen yards off, and that he neither called out nor slackened his pace.(a) If the streets be more than usually crowded, there is greater care necessary on the driver's part.(b) Again, when snow is on the ground, drivers are bound to exercise more caution,(c) and also when coming to a crossing,(d) and if a frail or old person is in his way, there is an additional degree of vigilance required of a driver,(e) and in turning a corner a stricter care is required than in going straight along a road.(f) " Where the driver of a vehicle drives over a person, in broad daylight, there is the strongest presumption, both in fact and in law, that the driver was in fault,"(g) and "where a person, driving a carriage, notices another in front for the first time, when he is only ten or twelve yards off, it almost raises a presumption that he was in fault in not keeping a better look-out."(h) Again, in an action for injuries, received by a young child, through being run over in the street by a milk van, it was proved that the accident happened in daylight, that the driver was seated on the shaft, and not on the driving seat, and that the van was driven at a considerable pace, the Court held the owner of the cart liable in damages.(i) Lord Young observed :—" We may almost take judicial

(a) *Gibson* v. *Milroy*, 1879, 6 R. 890.

(b) *Reg* v. *Murray*, 1852, 5 Cox's Cr. Ca. 509.

(c) *Cotton* v. *Wood*, 1860, 29 L.J., C.P. 333.

(d) *Williams* v. *Richards*, 1852, 3 C. and K. 81.

(e) *Boss* v. *Litton*, 1832, 5 C. and P. 407.

(f) Per Chief-Justice Denman in *Mayor of Colchester* v. *Brooke*, 1845, 7 Q.B. 339-359.

(g) Lord Justice-Clerk Moncreiff in *Clerk* v. *Petrie*, 1879, 6 R. 1076 ; *Anderson* v. *Blackwood*, 1886, 13 R. 443.

(h) Lord Gifford in *Clerk*, cit. p. 1078.

(i) *Grant* v. *Glasgow Dairy Co.*, 1881, 9 R. 182.

notice of the fact that, when two lads are in charge of a light
van like this, they drive at a furious pace.   In fact, the
thing is so notorious that, against such a van as this, driven
by boys who are laughing and chatting together, and which
has run over a person in daylight, the presumption is
irresistibly strong, and I think it wholesome, in the interests
of the public, that masters who send out boys with such
vans, should be held responsible for the injuries inflicted by
the recklessness of these drivers.(a)   And Lord Justice-Clerk
Moncreiff said :—" The driver of the dairy cart was not in his
right place—the driving seat—and when the driver is not in
his right place, I assume he takes some risk for what may
happen through want of sufficient command over his
horse."(b)   Where two vehicles are racing along the road,
an action is relevant against both or either of the wrong-
doers.

132. Neglecting to Warn and Pull-up.—When a foot-
passenger is in front of a vehicle, as—*e.g.*, in crossing the
street, the driver of it is not entitled to drive on regardless
of consequences.   He must not only give a warning, but
also see that his warning is attended to.   This rule was
established in a case where the driver of a dogcart, driving
at a speed of five or six miles an hour, in daylight ran over
an old woman of ninety-four.   He called out to the old
woman, but she could not hear him.   The Court held him
liable in damages ; Lord Gifford observing :—" A driver who
is approaching a person whom it is necessary to warn is
bound either to stop or to slacken speed, so as to be able to
stop if the warning should not be heard or should be mis-
understood.   He is bound to wait to see whether his warning is attended to ; the defender failed to do this, and there
was thus fault on his part.   He should have been able to
avoid the old lady whether she heard him or not."(c)

(a) *Grant*, cit. p. 185.
(b) *Ibid.* p. 185.
(c) *Clerk* v. *Petrie*, 1879, 6 R. 1076-1078.

Again, where a man, while walking in a carriage way, with pavement on each side, was knocked down by a van coming up in broad daylight, the driver was held liable in damages. Lord Young observed :—" My opinion is not founded on the pace. The driver was going at such a pace that he could without difficulty have pulled up in time; if not, that itself would have been fault. The appellant was walking along the road where he was entitled to be, and he was knocked down and hurt. The driver was not entitled to knock him down ; it was his duty to avoid him. He could quite well have done so ; and that he could, but did not, seems to have been because he thought the man must get out of his way. There is *primâ facie* fault leading to liability if a driver of a carriage so knocks up against a passenger. It is his duty to be able to pull up, and to do it, and not just to run over one who, even from stupidity, does not get out of the way."(a) But where a driver of a van called out to an old man, who halted, and then tried to cross in front of the van, which, however, knocked him down and killed him, it was held the man's death was not caused by the negligence of the driver, but in consequence of what was merely a misunderstanding. (b)

133. Horse too Large for Van. — A person was driving a sixteen-hands horse along the highway in a van which was far too small for such a horse, and, in consequence, the horse's hocks rubbed against the crossbar of the shafts of the van. The plaintiff's omnibus was standing at the kerb, on its proper side. The defendant's horse was startled by a slight collision with a cab, and afterwards violently collided with the plaintiff's omnibus, producing damage ; the judge's opinion being that no accident would have happened if the horse had not been too large for the van. It was held that the harnessing of the horse to such a van was the negligence

(a) *Anderson* v. *Blackwood*, 1886, 13 R. 443-445.
(b) *Docherty* v. *Watson*, 1884, 21 S.L.R. 449.

which materially led to the accident, and the defendant was
found liable, notwithstanding that he did his best as far as
driving was concerned in the circumstances. (a)

134. Driving too Close to another Vehicle.—The driver
of a second vehicle must keep a reasonable distance between
his own and the one in front.   Thus, two omnibuses were
driving along a narrow road at a moderate speed, and a
number of children were running after the first omnibus.
One of the children, a boy of six years old, having fallen,
the driver of the second omnibus was so near that he could
not pull up his horses in time, and the wheel of his omnibus
went over the boy, and killed him.   The driver was found
liable in damages.   Lord President Inglis said :—" It is
extremely vexatious and provoking for drivers of all kinds that
children should get in their way.   But I am afraid that it is
part of the disposition of boys and girls to get in the way of
carriages, and that it is a fact in the natural history of young
people which must be taken into account in dealing with the
duty of drivers.   Drivers must take account of this disposition as an incident inseparable from their occupation.   The
question is, whether the driver followed his duty in respect
of these children, or whether he failed in his duty ?   Now,
my opinion is that he failed in his duty.   The result of the
whole evidence is that he was too near the other omnibus.
If he had been twenty or thirty yards farther back this accident would not, or might not, have happened. . . . It was
impossible for the driver to pull up the horse, even with the
assistance of the passengers beside him, before the wheels
passed over the boy.   This proves that he was too near."(b)
Again, where the driver of a tram car, having observed a cab
at a stance from a distance of fifty yards off, and whistled on
approaching it, but yet ran into it, and injured the horse and
cab, the defence that the driver expected the cab to be driven

(a) *Burkin* v. *Bilezikdji*, 1889, 53 J.P. 760.
(b) *Auld* v. *M'Bey*, 1881, 8 R. 495.

out of his way was not sustained, and the tramway company were found liable in damages. (a)

135. Leaving a Horse Unattended.—If one leaves a horse and cart standing in the street, or his servant does so,(b) he must take the risk of any mischief that may ensue. Thus, an owner was found liable in these circumstances though the damage was occasioned by the act of a passer-by in striking the horse,(c) and also where a child was injured who was partly to blame.(d)   But where a driver of a cab at a stance at a railway station got down from his box, took a bag of oats and filled his horse's nosebag and turned to put the bag in its place which was only ten feet off, and meanwhile the horse bolted, causing injury; it was held there was no fault on the driver so as to make his master liable, notwithstanding a regulation by the magistrates that the driver when on his stance must be either on the box or at the horse's head.(e)   In another case, where injury was done to a horse by a pony and chaise running against it, there was evidence in defence that the defendant's wife was holding the pony by a bridle, and that a Punch-and-Judy show came past and frightened the pony which ran off with the chaise and caused the damage; it was held that if this were true the defence was good.(f)

136. Entrusting a Horse to an Incompetent Party.— Negligence will also be inferred from entrusting a fractious horse to one unaccustomed to horses and unskilful in their management.   Thus, where a father in the knowledge that his son, a boy of fourteen, had neither strength nor experience

---

(a) *M'Dermaid v. Edinburgh Street Tramways Company*, 1884, 12 R. 15.

(b) *Fraser v. Dunlop*, 1822, 1 S. 258 ; *Baird v. Hamilton*, 1826, 4 S. 790 ; see also *M'Laren v. Rae*, 1827, 4 Mur. 382 ; *Miller v. Harvie*, 1827, 4 M. 385.

(c) *Illidge v. Goodwin*, 1831, 5 C. and P. 190.

(d) *Lynch v. Nurdin*, 1841, 1 Q.B. 29, where the English decisions are collected.

(e) *Shaw v. Croall*, 1885, 12 R. 1186.

(f) *Goodman v. Taylor*, 1832, 5 C. and P. 410.

to command a horse, entrusted it to him, and a foot-passenger was injured by the horse when ridden by the boy, an issue was allowed against both father and son.(a)

137. Failure to take care of a Vicious Horse.—When animals of a vicious or obstreperous nature are taken along the public thoroughfare, especial care must be taken that they do no injury, and if they are not reasonably kept in subjection their owners are liable for any damage that may thereby ensue ;(b) but merely riding a restive horse which is not known to be so is no ground of action ;(c) and generally with respect to animals either savage by nature or easily infuriated, like a bull or a stallion, the owner takes the risk of their straying in the highway unattended, or getting into a field through which there is a right of way. His blame or fault consists in not securing them adequately against danger to the community, and he is answerable if any harm happen to a member of the public.(d) If one keeps a horse or any other animal and has no reason to suppose that it is ferocious, the mere fact that it has turned out so would not make him liable for anything that it has done. But if ferocity is established and known,(e) and especially if notice be given that it is fierce or vicious, one keeps such an animal at his peril, and the keeper of it is not discharged by using diligence which turns out to be ineffectual.(f) Reasonable diligence is no defence to a civil action in such a case,(g) but will be considered where the keeper of such an animal is

(a) *Brown* v. *Fulton*, 1881, 9 R. 36.

(b) See *Harpers* v. *G. N. Ry. Co.*, 1886, 13 R. 1139. So are carriers, see § 101, p. 129.

(c) *Hammock* v. *White*, 1862, 11 C.B., N.S. 588.

(d) *Clark* v. *Armstrong*, 1862, 24 D. 1315 ; but the duty of the owner of such animal is different in regard to servants about his own place, where the animal is kept in an enclosure, Lord Benholme in *Clark*, cit. p. 1320.

(e) *Renwick* v. *Von Rothery*, 1875, 2 R. 855 ; *Fraser* v. *Bell*, 1887, 14 R. 811.

(f) *Blackman* v. *Simmons*, 1827, 3 C. and P. 138.

(g) *Burton* v. *Moorhead*, 1881, 8 R. 892 (dog) ; *Cowan* v. *Dalziels*, 1877, 5 R. 241 (dog) ; *Hennigan* v. *M'Vey*, 1882, 9 R. 411 (boar) ; see also *Phillips* v. *Nicoll*, 1884, 11 R. 592, where a butcher was found liable for not using extreme precautions when leading a cow to a slaughter-house ; *M'Intyre* v. *Carmichael*, 1870, 8 M. 570 (dog).

sought to be made criminally responsible.(a) So, if a horse escape from its stable,(b) or through a gate the owner is bound to repair, and it thereby does injury, he is liable,(c) and similarly, if one break a young horse in a public thoroughfare, he will be liable if damage ensue.

138. Making Noises which Frighten Horse.—Where a person negligently makes a noise, which frightens a horse, he is liable for injury sustained through his wrongful act. Thus, where an engine-driver blew off steam at a level crossing, with the result of frightening horses waiting to cross, and the place was one where there was considerable traffic, it was held to be actionable negligence on the part of the company.(d) In another case against a railway company, it appeared that the plaintiffs were leaving a station belonging to the defendants, in a carriage, when the horse was frightened by the sight and sound of a locomotive engine at the station, which was blowing off steam, and the carriage was upset, and the plaintiffs injured. It did not appear that the engine was defective, or that it was used in an improper manner, or that the approach to the station was inconvenient, but the jury found that the defendants were guilty of negligence in not screening the railway from the roadway to the station, and that such negligence had caused the accident. It was held, on appeal, that the defendants were not liable, as there was no evidence of any obligation on their part to screen the railway from the road.(e) And where a plaintiff's horse took fright and injured itself, in consequence of the defendant's dogs barking at him, a verdict was obtained, with damages,

---

(a) See Lord Young in *Burton*, cit. *supra*, p. 896.

(b) *Michael* v. *Alestree*, 2 Lev. 172.

(c) See *Lee* v. *Riley*, 1865, 18 C.B., N.S. 722 ; *Ellis* v. *Loftus Iron Co.*, 1874 L.R. 10 C.P. 10, where the horse itself is thereby injured.

(d) *M. S. J. & A. Ry. Co.* v. *Fullarton*, 1863, 14 C.B., N.S. 54.

(e) *Simkin* v. *L. & N.-W. Ry. Co.*, 1888, 21 Q.B.D. 453, and the strong doubt expressed by Lord Fry to the judgment ; see also *Ramsden* v. *L. & Y. Ry. Co.*, 1888, 53 J.P. 183, noise in the pump-house of a railway causing horses to bolt.

for the plaintiff.(a) Where an action is brought against the owner of a dog, in consequence of its having done injury to sheep or cattle, it is not necessary for the pursuer to prove a previous propensity in the dog to injure sheep and cattle,(b) and under a similar statute in England, horses and mares have been held included under "sheep and cattle."(c) The occupier of the house or premises, in which the sheep and cattle have been injured, is considered the owner of the dog unless he can prove the contrary, and that it was kept on his premises without his sanction or knowledge.(d)

139. Leaving Obstacles in the Road.—One who negligently leaves anything on the road, which should not be there, is liable if a horse takes fright from it and damage be sustained. Thus, to leave on the road a fire-basket,(e) or van attached to a steam plough, on the grassy side of the highway,(f) or a heap of manure,(g) lime,(h) or stones(i) on the road, are acts amounting to negligence. But "a party is not to cast himself upon an obstruction which has been made by the fault of another, and avail himself of it, if he do not himself use common and ordinary caution to be in the right"(j); and where an ass was left fettered in the highway, and killed by the driver of a waggon, Baron Parke observed:— "Although the ass may have been wrongfully there, still the defendant was bound to go along the road at such a pace as would be likely to prevent mischief. Were this not so, a man might justify the driving over goods left on a public

---

(a) *Read* v. *King*, Guildhall, 1858, cited Oliphant, p. 351 ; see also *Wakeman* v. *Robinson*, 1823, 1 Bing. 213.

(b) 26 & 27 Vict. c. 100, § 1.

(c) *Wright* v. *Pearson*, 1869, L.R. 4 Q.B. 582.

(d) 26 & 27 Vict. c. 100, § 2.

(e) *Lambert* v. *Harrison*, Guildhall, 1853, cited Oliphant, 302.

(f) *Harris* v. *Mobbs*, 1878, L.R. 3 Ex. D. 268.

(g) *Gassiot* v. *Carpmeal*, 1852, 19 L.T. 64, 94.

(h) *M'Lean* v. *Russell*, 1850, 12 D. 887.

(i) *Gunn* v. *Gardiner*, 1820, 2 Mur. 194.

(j) Lord Ellenborough in *Butterfield* v. *Forrester*, 1809, 11 East. 59 ; see also Chief-Justice Cockburn in *Clark* v. *Chambers*, 1878, L.R. 3 Q.B.D. 327.

highway, or even over a man lying asleep there, or the pur-
posely running against a carriage going on the wrong side of
the road."(a) Road trustees and police commissioners are
liable for damage caused by heaps of rubbish or other
material wrongously left by them on the road.(b) In one
case, police commissioners pleaded no liability, having contracted with a third party to clean the streets, and that the
negligence, if any, was his, not theirs. Upon the contract,
it was held that they retained control over the operations,
and were, therefore, liable; and the question was raised
whether they could free themselves from liability by delegat-
ing this statutory duty, even if the contractor had had sole
control of the works.(c) In another case, where fog prevented police commissioners from removing mud heaps, they
were held not liable for injury caused from their being left
where they were.(d)

140. Neglecting to Fence Dangerous Places.—What is
sufficient fencing is a question of circumstances (e); but a
railway is bound to keep its disused line duly fenced,(f) and
it has been held negligence, on the part of road trustees, to
fail to shut up an old road.(g) Public railways may cross
roads if they have the statutory gates, but where a private
railway crossed a public road on the level, and was not shut
off by gates, and a horse strayed on it and was killed, the road
trustees were held liable, it being in their power to protect
themselves by refusing to proprietors of private railways
permission to cross their roads on the level or by imposing

(a) *Davies* v. *Mann*, 1842, 10 M. and W. 546.

(b) *Watson* v. *Scott*, 1838, M'F. 146; *Virtue* v. *Alloa Police Commissioners*,
1873, 1 R. 285.

(c) *Stephen* v. *Thurso Police Commissioners*, 1876, 3 R. 535; see also *Harris* v.
Magistrates of Leith, 1881, 8 R. 613.

(d) *Barton* v. *Kinning Park Commissioners*, January, 1892, 29 S.L.R. 329.

(e) *Greer* v. *Stirlingshire Road Trustees*, 1882, 9 R. 1069; *Morran* v. *Waddel*,
1883, 11 R. 44.

(f) *Simpson* v. *Cal. Ry. Co.*, 1878, 5 R. 525.

(g) *Maclacklan* v. *Road Trustees*, 1827, 4 Mur. 216.

such conditions as they thought necessary.(*a*) In cases of danger, railway locomotives must give an alarm whistle.(*b*)

141. Collisions.—Collisions are subject to the ordinary laws of negligence, already treated—viz., that the injurer is answerable, but the injured party must exercise due care. They may occur in three different ways. First, one party may be to blame only ; second, both parties may be to blame ; and third, neither party may be to blame. If a collision occur, and the injured party can prove negligence on the part of the injurer, and that he himself took reasonable and proper care to avoid the injury, the other party is answerable. But although there may have been negligence on the part of the injurer, yet, if by ordinary care the injured party could have avoided the injury, and he fail to avoid it, he is the author of his own wrong, and cannot recover.(*c*) Where both parties are to blame, neither party can recover ; and where neither party is to blame, the injury arises from an accident,(*d*) and the injurer is not liable.

3. The Rule of the Road.

142. Foot-passengers.—The footpath at the side of a road is for the accommodation of foot-passengers only, and the use.of it is forbidden to horses and vehicles ; (*e*) but a foot-passenger has a right not only to cross a road, but also to walk along the carriage way, and it is the duty of drivers to avoid injuring foot-passengers when doing so ; and if a driver cannot pull up in time because his reins break, it is no defence, as he is bound to have proper tackle.(*f*) Where a foot-passenger walks

(*a*) *Matson* v. *Baird*, 1878, 5 R. (H.L.) 211 ; *Charman* v. *S.-E. Ry. Co.*, 1888, 21 Q.B.D. 524.

(*b*) *Russell* v. *Cal. Ry. Co.*, 1879, 7 R. 148 ; *Ireland* v. *N. B. Ry. Co.*, 1882, 10 R. 53.

(*c*) *Butterfield* v. *Forrester*, 1809, 11 East. 59 ; see also § 161.

(*d*) See § 160.

(*e*) 41 & 42 Vict. c. 51, § 96.

(*f*) *Cotterill* v. *Starkey*, 1839, 8 C. and P. 691,

on the carriage way in the most crowded thoroughfare he does so entirely at his own risk, and such an act is strong evidence of his going in face of a known danger. When passengers and vehicles are on the road, there arise reciprocal duties of keeping out of each other's way. Thus Chief-Justice Pollock observed :—" It is the duty of persons who are driving over a crossing for foot-passengers to drive slowly, cautiously, carefully; but it is also the duty of a foot-passenger to use due care and caution in going upon a crossing at the entrance of a street so as not to get among the carriages, and thus receive injury,"(a) and Chief-Justice Erle said :—" It is as much the duty of foot-passengers in crossing the street or road to look out for passing vehicles as it is the duty of drivers to see that they do not run over foot-passengers."(b) The tendency of recent decisions in Scotland, however, is that the driver must avoid the foot-passenger. Thus Lord Justice-Clerk Moncreiff said :—" There is no doubt as to the relations between wheeled vehicles and persons on the road. . . . There is no doubt that it lies on the driver to keep clear of foot-passengers. If a person is guilty of such fault as to increase the burden of that obligation, that is another matter, but the primary obligation is undoubted to keep clear of foot-passengers ;"(c) and Lord Young to the same effect said:—" A man may stupidly get into the way of a carriage. I express no opinion on such cases as that, for each case of that kind must be judged by its own circumstances, and it may be that a driver having a clear road before him may count on an intelligent, and even an unintelligent, being not getting in before his horse, and might not be responsible for his doing so, but here the man was walking steadily along the road, and the van came up behind him and knocked him down. And my verdict is, that the driver was to blame for not pulling up or turning aside, but going straight on, leaving

(a) *Williams* v. *Richards*, 1852, 3 C. and K. 81.

(b) *Cotton* v. *Wood*, 1860, 8 C.B., N.S. 568, 571. See also *Hawkins* v. *Cooper*, 1838, 8 C. and P. 473.

(c) *M'Kechnie* v. *Couper*, 1887, 14 R. 345.

it to the appellant to get out of the way or take the consequences.(*a*)

This duty is all the more strict if the person in the road
be frail,(*b*) old,(*c*) deaf or very young.(*d*) And accordingly a
negligent driver cannot escape liability by proving that if the
injured party had gone to the one side or the other, or had
stood still, no accident would have happened, the principle
being that a person who by his misconduct places another in
such a dilemma is responsible for what happens.(*e*) But if
the passenger, by his own want of caution, come in front of
a vehicle and is injured, as—*e.g.*, by getting out on the wrong
side of a tramcar, the driver of the vehicle is not liable.(*f*)

143. Vehicles.—The Roads and Bridges Act, incorporat-
ing a clause in the General Turnpike Act, rendered statutory
the general rule that when vehicles meet they must pass each
other on the left side, and enforced this by a penalty not
exceeding £5 over and above the damages occasioned by
failure to observe it.(*g*) In crossing, the driver must bear to
the left and pass behind the other carriage,(*h*) and one overtak-
ing another must pass on the right.(*i*) In theory the rule of
the road is this : "The highway is divided into two parts,
half of it being appropriated to the traffic going the one way
and half to the traffic going the other way.' When the two
traffics meet they are bound to keep each other on the whip or
right side ; thus each is restricted to one half of the highway.
When one vehicle is coming in the same direction as another

(*a*) *Anderson* v. *Blackwood*, 1886, 13 R, 443, 445.

(*b*) *Boss* v. *Litton*, 1832, 5 C. and P. 407, where a paralytic was run over, and
cases cited in § 131.

(*c*) *Clerk* v. *Petrie*, 1879, 6 R. 1076.

(*d*) See § 162, contributory negligence of pupil children.

(*e*) Lord Ellenborough in *Jones* v. *Boyce*, 1816, 1 Stark. 493, 495 ; *Clerk*, cit.

(*f*) *Ramsay* v. *Thomson & Sons*, 1881, 9 R. 140 ; see § 160; *Jardine* v. *Stonefield
Laundry Co.*, 1887, 14 R. 839.

(*g*) 41 & 42 Vict. c. 51, § 123 (Sch. C, § 97).

(*h*) *Wayde* v. *Lady Carr*, 1823, 2 Dowl. and R. 255.

(*i*) *Chaplin* v. *Hawes*, 1828, 3 C. and P. 554 ; Lord Young in *Ramsay* v. *Thomson & Sons*, cit. *supra.*

N

and the one behind is going faster than the one in front, the rule is, not that the one behind is to go across the *medium filum* to the other half of the road, but that the one in front shall draw to the side and let the faster vehicle pass ; and this is essential, because if there is an obstruction in the centre of the road, then the one coming behind is not bound to take the right side ; he must take the vacant part of his side of the road. This is the *rationale* of the rule of the road where the thoroughfare is crowded."(a) The rule applies both to saddle-horses and carriages.(b) This rule, however, is subject to exceptions. If an injury can be averted by departing from it, a driver is liable if he cause an injury by adhering to the rule of the road ;(c) but when parties meet suddenly and an injury results, the party on the wrong side is held answerable unless it appear clearly that the party on the proper side had ample means and opportunity to prevent it ;(d) and a person riding or driving upon the wrong side of the road must use more care and keep a better look-out than if he is on the proper part of the road.(e)

144. Tramcars.—The general rule of the road suffers another exception in the case of tramway cars. Tramway cars must be treated as if they were permanent obstructions.(f) "When a carriage is coming up behind a tramway car, and the car stops, the driver of the other vehicle shall pass upon the left hand side. That is the opposite of the old rule. . . . If vehicles were to pass a car on the right hand side there would be very great danger of their coming into

---

(a) Per Lord Justice-Clerk Moncreiff in *Ramsay* v. *Thomson & Sons*, 1881, 9 R. 140, 145.

(b) *Turley* v. *Thomas*, 1837, 8 C. and P. 103.

(c) *Turley*, cit. ; *Finegan* v. *L. & N.-W. Ry. Co*, 1889, 53 J.P., 663, before Lord Chief-Justice Coleridge.

(d) *Chaplin*, cit. ; *Clay* v. *Wood*, 1803, 5 Esp. 44 ; *Lloyd* v. *Ogleby*, 1859, 5 C.B., N.S. 667.

(e) *Pluckwell* v. *Wilson*, 1832, 5 C. and P. 375.

(f) Lord Craighill in *Ramsay*, cit.

collision with another car coming the opposite way."(a)
Where a vehicle is legitimately stopped on tramway rails,
the driver of the car coming immediately behind it must
stop also, and if injury be occasioned by his not doing so the
tramway company is liable.(b) The promoters or lessees of
tramway companies are, by the General Tramway Act, 1870,(c)
answerable for all accidents, damages, or injuries happening
through their act or default, or of any person in their
employment, by reason or in consequence of any of their
works or carriages, but the Act does not enlarge their common
law liabilities. Thus, where a steam car, without negligence
on the part of its driver, caused a horse to take fright and
injured it, the company were not held liable.(d)

145. Traction Engines.—The legislature has, from con-
siderations of public safety, introduced certain regulations(e)
for the construction of traction engines, and for their
conveyance along public roads ; and persons who use these
vehicles are liable for injuries to horses, &c., if they fail to
use the precautions prescribed by statute or local authorities.
Those applicable to the safety of horses and those using them
are :—That, as far as practicable, they shall consume their
own smoke;(f) that road authorities may make bye-laws
as to the hours during which these engines may pass over
roads ;(g) that three persons at least must be employed to
conduct the locomotive, and if more than two waggons or
carriages be attached thereto, an additional person shall be
employed, who shall take charge of such waggons or carriages ;(h) that one of such persons, while the locomotive is

---

(a) Lord President Inglis in *Jardine* v. *Stonefield Laundry Co.*, 1887, 14 R.
830 ; see Lord Justice-Clerk Moncreiff in *Ramsay,* cit.
(b) *M'Dermaid* v. *Edin. Street Tramways Co.*, 1884, 12 R. 15.
(c) 33 & 34 Vict. c. 78, § 55.
(d) *Brocklehurst* v. *Manchester, &c., Tramways Co.*, L.R. 17 Q.B.D. 118.
(e) 24 & 25 Vict. c. 70 ; 28 & 29 Vict. c. 83 ; 41 & 42 Vict. c. 58 ; 41 & 42
Vict. c. 77 (England).
(f) 41 & 42 Vict. c. 58, § 5.   (g) *Ibid.* § 6.   (h) 28 & 29 Vict. c. 83, § 3.

in motion, shall accompany the locomotive on foot, and shall, in cases of need, assist horses and carriages drawn by horses passing the same ;(a) that drivers of such locomotives shall give as much space as possible for the passing of other traffic ; that the whistles shall not be sounded, nor the cylinder taps opened, nor steam blown off, within the sight of those in charge of horses on the road ; that every locomotive shall be instantly stopped on any person with a horse putting up his hand as a signal for that being done ; and that two lights shall be carried by the locomotive between one hour after sunset and one hour before sunrise.   " Nothing in this Act contained shall authorise any person to use a locomotive which may be so constructed as to be a public nuisance at common law, and nothing herein contained shall affect the right of any person to recover damages in respect of any injury he may have sustained in consequence of the use of a locomotive."(b).   The mere presence of such a locomotive on the road, however, will not render the user of it liable if he has observed the statutory regulations, unless there be other fault traceable to the men in charge, or unless the injured party can prove the locomotive a nuisance at common law. (c)

146. Lights.—There is no obligation at common law that vehicles driven by horses must carry lights at night, but such a precaution should be adopted, the want of them being evidence of negligence.(d)   Bicycles must carry lamps at night.(e)

147. Responsibilities of Owners of Public Vehicles.— In addition to the duties of safe driving already discussed, there lies upon drivers of public vehicles the further obliga-

(a) 41 & 42 Vict. c. 58, § 4.

(b) 28 & 29 Vict. c. 83, § 12.

(c) *Galer* v. *Rawson*, 1890, 6 T.L.R. 17 ; see also *Powell* v. *Fall*, 1880, L.R. 5 Q.B.D. 597 ; *Watkins* v. *Reddin*, 1861, 2 F. and F. 629 ; *Jones* v. *Festiniog Ry. Co.*, 1868, 3 Q.B. 733 ; *Rex* v. *Pease*, 1832, 4 B. and Ad. 30.

(d) *Gibson* v. *Milroy*, 1879, 6 R. 890 ; *Cruden* v. *Fentham*, 1799, 2 Esp. 685.

(e) 52 & 53 Vict. c. 50, § 58.

tion of providing a safe means of transit for passengers. The obligations of proprietors of vehicles for the carriage of persons are quite different from those that belong to them as carriers of goods. In the latter case fault need not be proved, and carriers must restore goods without enquiry, because the owner cannot see or know what is done with them ; but with passengers it is quite different. They, to a certain extent, take care of themselves, and therefore cannot recover unless they can prove fault on the part of the carrier.(*a*) A coach proprietor is bound to supply a road-worthy vehicle and appurtenances reasonably fit for the purposes of transit.(*b*) Reasonably fit, however, denotes something short of absolutely fit, but the standard of fitness is " as fit and proper as care and skill can make it."(*c*)

148. *Onus* **of Proof.**—The general rule is that the injured party must prove fault on the part of the proprietor of a public vehicle or his servant ; but where the coach itself breaks down, the presumption is against the proprietor, and he must show that " all that man could do was done to provide against the accident."(*d*) In the case of breakage of bolts or other fittings of his machine, it is not sufficient to show that he had no reason to suppose there was any defect, or that it could not have been discovered by ordinary inspection. He must show that due inspection was made :(*e*) but if it be shown that the accident is due solely to a defect which no care or skill could detect, that will exonerate him from liability.(*f*) If, however, the cause of the accident could have been known by the proprietor, and he takes no precautions to prevent it, he will be liable. Thus, where a passenger

---

(*a*) Per Lord President Inglis in *Ferus* v. *N. B. Ry. Co.*, 1872, 9 S.L.R. 652 ; *Crofts* v. *Waterhouse*, 1825, 3 Bing. 319.

(*b*) *Jones* v. *Boyce*, 1816, 1 Starkie, 493.

(*c*) *Hyman* v. *Nye*, 1881, L.R. 6 Q.B.D. 685.

(*d*) *Lyon* v. *Lamb*, 1838, 16 S. 1188.

(*e*) *Hyman*, cit. *supra* ; *Bremner* v. *Williams*, 1824, 1 C. and P. 414.

(*f*) *Redhead* v. *Midland Ry. Co.*, 1867, L.R. 2 Q.B. 412.

in an omnibus was injured by a blow from one of the horses, which had kicked through the front panel of the vehicle, and there was no evidence on the part of the passenger that the horse was a kicker, but it was proved there were marks of other kicks on the panel, and that no precaution such as a kicking strap was adopted to avert the consequences of a horse kicking out, it was held there was evidence of negligence to go to a jury.(a)

149. Insufficient Vehicle and Appurtenances.—A coach proprietor is liable if an accident occur from his using horses of a vicious temper, or from his having a careless driver, or from an ill-constructed coach.(b)   Thus, where a mail coach breaks down, as—e.g., by the breaking of the axle tree and consequent fracture of a bolt ; (c) or where the coach(d) or harness is faulty in construction ; (e) or where the driver is intoxicated,(f) or drives recklessly,(g) or starts his horses suddenly,(h) unless there be proof of contributory negligence, or that everything possible was done to avert the accident, the proprietor is liable.   Thus, in one case, the pole of a mail coach broke, but did not snap through ; the guard, without repairing it, desired the coachman to go on.   He proceeded at the usual rate and the coach upset, either from the deficiency of the pole or from the carelessness of the driver.   It was held that the owners were liable in damages for an injury sustained by a passenger.(i)   Moreover, it will not liberate the proprietors that the injured party excited the coachman to over-drive ;

(a) *Simson* v. *L. G. Omnibus Co.*, 1873, L.R. 8 C.P. 390.

(b) Lord President Inglis in *Ferns* v. *N. B. Ry. Co.*, 1872, 9 S.L.R. 652.

(c) *Lyon* v. *Lamb*, 1838, 16 S. 1188; *Anderson* v. *Pyper*, 1820, 2 Mur. 261 ; *Hyman* v. *Nye*, 1881, L.R. 6 Q.B.D. 685.

(d) *Curtis* v. *Drinkwater*, 1831, 2 B. and Ad. 169.

(e) *Cotterill* v. *Starkey*, 1839, 8 C. and P. 693, 694, *n.*

(f) *Gunn* v. *Gardiner*, 1820, 2 Mur. 194.

(g) *Gunn*, cit. ; *Elder* v. *Croall*, 1849, 11 D. 1040.

(h) *Annand* v. *Aberdeen Tramways Co.*, 1890, 17 R. 808.

(i) *Spiers* v. *Drysdale*, 1813, Hume, 316.

though it is relevant to diminish damages.(a) Convictions for reckless driving were held admissible evidence to meet a defender's plea of having supplied a competent driver, where the pursuer's witnesses had been cross-examined as to the driver's general character.(b) Again, where an omnibus, on the top of which the plaintiff was, was struck by the defendant's omnibus, with the result that the omnibus the plaintiff sat on ran against an obstacle, and the plaintiff was injured, it was held the defendant was liable.(c) A public coach-driver is bound to limit his passengers to the number his vehicle will accommodate with safety, even though he may be allowed to carry more by statute,(d) and also to avoid any approaching danger to the passengers, such as low archways,(e) branches of trees, and the like ; and if by reason of failing to do so, a passenger is placed in such a dilemma as to choose between jumping off and being thrown off a coach, the wrong-doer is responsible for what happens whichever alternative the passenger adopts.(f)

4. Liability of Master to Third Parties for the Fault of his Servant.

150. Master's Liability.—A master is bound in the interest of members of the public to employ careful and competent servants, and is in general answerable to third parties if he knowingly employs a drunken or inexperienced coachman to drive his carriage ; (g) and also if he authorise his servant to drive with dangerous rapidity in a public place. (h) The law enables a master to protect himself in

(a) *Alan* v. *M'Leish*, 1819, 2 Mur. 158.
(b) *M'Arthur* v. *Croall*, 1852, 24 Sc. Jur. 170.
(c) *Ryby* v. *Hewitt*, 1850, 5 Ex. 242.
(d) *Irael* v. *Clark*, 1803, 4 Esp. 259.
(e) *Lidley* v. *Smith*, 1808, 1 Camp. 167 ;
    M'Fee v. *Police Commissioners of Broughty Ferry*, 1890, 17 R. 764.
(f) *Jones* v. *Boyce*, 1816, 1 Stark. 493.
(g) *Tanstall* v. *Pooley*, 1841, 6 Cl. and F. 910, *n.*
(h) *Fraser*, M. and S 261.

this respect by giving him a power of dismissing his servant when his orders are not obeyed; and a coachman may be dismissed even for driving other people in his master's carriage contrary to orders.(*a*) " Although a master will be liable if his coachman negligently runs down or injures a pedestrian in a public street, he will incur no liability to a friend whom he has invited to ride with him in his carriage, and who is injured by the carelessness of his generally competent coachman. The foot-passenger on the public road is a stranger, but the friend or acquaintance who has accepted a drive in the carriage will not be considered as such. . . . He takes the risk himself, provided only that the servants were competent, and selected with reasonable care.'(*b*) A master is also responsible for injury occasioned by his servant in negligently obeying a lawful command,(*c*) and also for a wanton and reckless discharge of duty by his servant within the scope of his employment, but not for wanton or malicious acts of the servant to serve his own ends,(*d*) or for illegal acts wilfully done;(*e*) still less for the unauthorised act of a third party.(*f*)

" If a servant, driving his master's carriage along the highway, carelessly runs over a bystander . . . the person injured has a right to treat the wrongful or careless act as the act of the master, *qui facit per alium facit per se.* If the master himself had driven his carriage improperly . . . he would have been directly responsible, and the law does not permit him to escape liability because the act complained of was not done with his own hand."(*g*) Thus, masters have

(*a*) *Thomson* v. *Stewart*, 1888, 15 R. 806.

(*b*) Lord Gifford in *Woodhead* v. *Gartness Mineral Company*, 1887 4 R. 469, 505 ; see also *Moffat* v. *Bateman*, 1869, L.R. 3 P.C. 115.

(*c*) *Faulds* v. *Townsend*, 1861, 23 D. 437.

(*d*) Lord Glenlee in *Baird* v. *Hamilton*, 1826, 4 S. 790.

(*e*) *Patteson*, J., in *Lyons* v. *Martin*, 1838, 8 A. and E. 512; *Bramwell*, J., in *Degg* v. *Midland Railway Company*, 1857, 1 H. and N. 773.

(*f*) *Moyes* v. *Greig*, 1841, 3 D. 1058, where the owner of a cart and horse was found not liable for damage caused by its being interfered with without his authority.

(*g*) Per Lord Cranworth in *Bartonshill Coal Co.* v. *Reid*, 1858, 3 M'q. 266, 283.

repeatedly been found liable for injury caused by a horse and cart, or other vehicle, under the care of their servants. (*a*)

Again, a master was found liable for his groom negligently using spurs, and causing the horse he was riding to kick and injure a waggoner ; (*b*) and where a servant in the course of his employment gives the reins to a stranger, and a person is injured through his careless driving,(*c*) or if a servant leave a horse and cart unattended, and a third party strike it,(*d*) and damage ensue, his master is liable. In another case, however, a defendant's horse, by the negligence of his servant, ran away with a cart, and turned into the yard of the defendant's house, which opened on to the highway: and the plaintiff's wife, who happened to be paying a visit at the defendant's house, ran out into the yard to see what was the matter, when she was met and knocked down by the horse and cart. It was held that, as the defendant's servant was not bound to anticipate that the plaintiff's wife would be in the yard, there was no duty on the part of the defendant towards the plaintiff's wife, and that the action therefore was not maintainable. (*e*)

151. Acts within Scope of Employment.—But to render the master so liable the act must be in the regular course of the servant's duty, and it must arise from want of skill or attention, and not from a wilful act ; for a criminal act will not subject the absent and innocent master.(*f*) The master's liability rests on implied mandate, and therefore has no place where the limits of the mandate are exceeded. Hence a master is not liable for the crime or trespass of his servant, unless committed by express command, or unless it is the necessary consequence of the orders given by him. (*g*) Thus,

(*a*) *Fraser* v. *Dunlop*, 1822, 1 S. 258, overruling *Dalrymple* v. *M'Gill*, 1804 ; Hume, 387 ; *Baird*, cit., and cases cited in § 131.

(*b*) *North* v. *Smith*, 1861, 10 C.B., N.S. 572.

(*c*) *Booth* v. *Mister*, 1835, 7 C. and P. 66.

(*d*) *Illidge* v. *Goodwin*, 1831, 5 C. and P. 190.

(*e*) *Tolhausen* v. *Davis*, 1888, 58 L.J., Q.B. 98.

(*f*) *M'Laren* v. *Rae*, 1827, 4 Mur. 381 ; *Miller* v. *Harvie*, 1827, 4 Mur. 385.

(*g*) *Young* v. *Colt's Trustees*, 1832, 10 S. 666 ; *Fraser*, M. and S. 261, 274.

where a servant, driving his master's cart-horse, whips a man out of private spite, the master is not liable; (*a*) but if a coachman negligently strikes a passenger with a whip, intending to strike someone who has jumped on his omnibus, it is a jury question whether this is done to serve his own purpose, or in the furtherance of his master's interest.(*b*) Again, if the guard of an omnibus use undue violence in ejecting a passenger whom he supposes to be drunk, the master is liable. (*c*) Thus, a coachman, where his master's carriage was entangled with another, struck the horses of the other carriage, and damage ensued from their bolting, the jury considered he was acting within the scope of his employment, because they held that the entanglement arose from his fault, and they held the master liable.(*d*) Again, if a horse falls in a street, and the footman from another carriage comes to the assistance of the servants who are in charge of the horse, it is quite plain that in volunteering friendly assistance he is not doing his master's work, and will not make his master responsible for any consequences that may arise from his interference. (*e*)

In another case, a shopkeeper instructed his salesman to remove articles from one shop to another. The salesman borrowed a van from a friend, who came with it to drive it, and the articles were placed in the van with the shopkeeper's knowledge and assent. While the van was passing through the streets the salesman took the reins from the vanman, who was intoxicated, and owing to his careless driving an accident occurred. It was held that the shopkeeper was not liable, because the salesman was acting outwith his duty in undertaking to drive the van.(*f*)

(*a*) Lord Glenlee in *Baird* v. *Hamilton*, 1826, 4 S. 790.
(*b*) *Ward* v. *General Omnibus Company*, 1873, 42 L.J., C.P. 265.
(*c*) *Seymour* v. *Greenwood*, 1861, 7 H. and N. 355.
(*d*) *Croft* v. *Alison*, 1821, 4 B. and Ald. 590.
(*e*) Lord Justice-Clerk Moncreiff in *Gallacher* v. *Burrell*, 1883, 11 R. 53, 56.
(*f*) *Martin* v. *Wards*, 1887, 14 R. 814.

152. Acts done for the Master's Benefit.—A master is only liable for acts done by his servant for his benefit if the servant is acting within the scope of his employment. In the leading case of *Limpus* v. *General Omnibus Company*,(a) Baron Martin thus charged the jury, and his charge was held to be right by all the Judges of Appeal, with one exception : —" If the jury believed that the defendants' driver acted recklessly, wantonly and improperly, but in the course of the service and employment, and doing that which he believed to be for the interest of the defendants, then they were responsible."(b) In approving of this charge, Mr. Justice Blackburn, in referring to the act being done in the course of the servant's employment, observed :—" It is not universally true that every act done for the interest of the master is done in the course of his employment. A footman might think it for the interest of his master to drive the coach, but no one could say that it is within the scope of the footman's employment, and that his master would be liable for damage resulting from the wilful act of the footman in taking charge of the horses."(c)

153. Servant making Detour with Master's Horses.(d) —When a servant drives his master's horses on his master's business and makes a detour to call upon a friend, and an accident happen, the master is liable,(e) but not if the servant be on a frolic of his own, and not on his master's business ;(f) yet the master is liable if he takes a circuitous route to suit his own purpose in executing his master's order.(g) But if the servant acts contrary to his trust, and without his master's knowledge takes his horse and vehicle after his day's

(a) *Limpus* v. *Gen. Omnibus Co.*, 1862, 1 H. and C. 526.
(b) *Ibid.*, cit. p. 529.
(c) *Ibid.*, cit. p. 542.
(d) See hackney coachmen as servants of proprietor, § 156.
(e) *Joel* v. *Morrison*, 1834, 6 C. and P. 501.
(f) Parke, B., in *Joel*, cit.
(g) *Sleath* v. *Wilson*, 1839, 9 C. and P. 607.

work with it is done and drive it on his own purposes, the
master is not liable.(a) Thus, a carman, whose duty it was
to deliver wine and bring back empty bottles to his master's
warehouse, was induced to turn aside from the direct road to
drive a clerk home. The plaintiff was knocked down by the
cart when they were about two miles out of the way, and the
master was not found liable.(b) The deviations, however,
which will divest the master of liability must be such as to
make them separate journeys, and in all such cases this is a
question of degree.(c) Thus, a contractor's servant, against
express orders not to leave his horse or to go home for his
dinner, took his master's horse and cart to his home, a
quarter of a mile away, and left it unattended. It bolted
and caused injury, and it was held that a jury were justified
in finding the driver as acting within the scope of his employment.(d) If a servant, however, deviates materially from his
master's employment, and on returning to the course of it an
accident happens, if the return to the master's employment is
established, the master is liable, but not if the servant is on
his own errand.(e) Nor is a master liable if his servant,
without his authority, rides some one else's horse and injury
ensue.(f)

154. Effect of Master's Orders.(g)—General orders by
the master to a coachman not to drive when he is drunk,(h)
or not to drive too fast,(i) or not to leave his van unattended,(j)
or not to obstruct other vehicles,(k) will not free the master

(a) *Mitchell* v. *Crasweller*, 1853, 22 L.J., C.P. 100.
(b) *Storey* v. *Ashton*, 1869, L.R. 4 Q.B. 476.
(c) Cockburn, C.J., in *Storey*, overruling Erskine, J., in *Sleath* v. *Wilson*, *sup.*, contra.
(d) *Whatman* v. *Pearson*, 1868, L.R. 3 C.P. 422.
(e) *Rayner* v. *Mitchell*, 1877, 2 C.P.D. 357.
(f) *Goodman* v. *Kennell*, 1827, 3 C. and P. 167.
(g) See on this subject Fraser, M. and S. 282.
(h) Willes, J., in *Limpus* v. *Gen. Omnibus Co.*, 1862, 1 H. and C. 526, 539.
(i) Cresswell, J., in *Brown* v. *Copley*, 1844, 7 M. and G. 558, 566.
(j) *Whatman* v. *Pearson*, 1868, L.R. 3 C.P. 422.
(k) *Limpus*, cit.

from liability if what is done is within the general scope of
the servant's employment.   A servant, when doing what he
is either expressly or tacitly authorised to do by his master,
has a right to use his own judgment and skill, and even in
some cases take a wrong way of doing a thing and the master
must trust to it.   But if a master has expressly forbidden a
particular act to be done at all, there is no ground for attaching liability to him.(*a*)

**155. The Relationship of Master and Servant must
exist to render the Master Liable.**—When the parties are
not in the relation of master and servant at the time of the
injury, the master is not liable for injury caused by his
servant.   Thus, a master was not liable where the servant
had his master's permission to go to a fair and use his horse
and gig for his own pleasure ;(*b*) nor where the master had
allowed his servant to work for a third party whose control
he was under when the injury happened.(*c*)   In another case,
a driver of a coach was killed by a heap of lime negligently
left unprotected on the road.   The proprietor of the house
had contracted with builders to make repairs on it, and the
builders sub-contracted for the plaster-work with the plasterer,
who left the heap of lime unfenced.   An action was brought
against the proprietor, builder, and plasterer, and it was held
that liability only rested against the plasterer.(*d*)   Again, if
a man sends his servant a message and he meets a friend who
lends him his horse to ride, and an injury happens, the master
is not liable ; but if the master authorise the use of the horse,
he is liable.(*e*)

The relationship may be proved by general evidence infer-

(*a*) *Fraser* v. *Younger & Sons*, 1867, 5 M. 861 ; *Stevens* v. *Woodward*, 1881,
L.R. 6 Q.B.D. 318.

(*b*) *Cormack* v. *Digby*, 1876, 9 Ir. C.L.R. 557.

(*c*) Cockburn, C.J., in *Rourke* v. *Whitemoss Colliery Co.*, 1877, L.R. 2 C.P.D.
205-208.

(*d*) *M'Laen* v. *Russell*, 1850, 12 D. 887.

(*e*) *Goodman* v. *Kennell*, 1827, 3 C. and P. 167.

ring its existence, as—*e.g.*, the occasional or frequent use of the master's gig by the servant.(*a*) The contract of service itself may afford evidence, or the periods of payment of wages, or the fact of special agency for a particular business ; or the intervention of the authority of a contractor, or assumption of control of driving by a third party. But these are not conclusive, the true test in all cases being whether the alleged master had or had not direct or implied control over the servant's actions when the injury occurs ; whether the servant received his wages from the master and could be removed by him for misconduct, and was bound to obey his orders.(*b*) If one hire a carriage and horses and the owner orders his own servant to drive them, the owner is responsible for his servant's negligence ;(*c*) and where the owner of a carriage hires horses and a driver by the day, the jobmaster is liable for the driver's negligence ; (*d*) and it makes no difference that the owner of the carriage has always been driven by the same driver, he being the only coachman employed by him ; or that he was paid a fixed sum for each drive, or that he wore his livery.(*e*) If two persons hire a carriage, each is jointly liable for the damage caused by either, as they are joint possessors at the time ; but if it be hired by one only, the hirer and not the passenger is liable ; (*f*) and to make a third party liable for the negligence of a driver, the relation of master and servant must exist between them.(*g*) Again, when the lessor and the servant of the owner of a hired horse and carriage drive together, if the lessor might have controlled the

(*a*) *Patten* v. *Rea*, 1857, 2 C.B., N.S. 606.

(*b*) Parke, B., in *Quarman* v. *Burnett*, 1840, 6 M. and W. 499 ; *Shiells* v. *E. & G. Ry. Co.*, 1856, 18 D. 1199 ; and Lord Gifford in *Stephen* v. *Thurso Police Commissioners*, 1876, 3 R. 535.

(*c*) *Smith* v. *Lawrence*, 1828, 2 M. and Ry. 1 ; *Sammel* v. *Wright*, 1805, 5 Esp. 263.

(*d*) *Smith*, cit.

(*e*) *Quarman*, cit., which decided this point left open in *Laugher* v. *Pointer*, 1826, 5 B. and C. 547.

(*f*) *Davey* v. *Chamberlain*, 1802, 4 Esp. 229.

(*g*) *Moffat* v. *Bateman*, 1869, L.R. 3 P.C. App. 115 ; see also *Martin* v. *Wards*, 1887, 14 R. 814.

servant and failed to do so, he is liable.(a)   Questions of this
sort are purely jury questions—"no satisfactory line can be
drawn at which, as a matter of law, the general owner of a
carriage, or rather the general employer of a driver ceases to
be responsible and the temporary hirer becomes so.(b)

156. Cab-Driver is the Servant of the Proprietor.—
Under the General Police Act, hackney carriage drivers are
so far regarded as the servants of the proprietors that provision is made for the recovery of damage done by the driver
from the proprietor ;(c) and generally, at common law, the
proprietor of a public vehicle is liable for personal injury
caused by the negligence of the driver,(d) even though the
injury occur during a slight deviation on the driver's
account ; (e) but the presumption of relationship in such a
case yields to proof of the contrary.(f)

5. LIABILITY OF MASTER TO HIS SERVANT.

157. General Liability. — A servant on entering his
master's employment is considered as contemplating and
taking the chance of all ordinary risks properly incident to
the particular employment in which he engages. The master
is bound to take all reasonable precautions which ordinary
prudence would suggest, but is not an insurer against all
risks.(g)   Thus, a butcher's servant, ordered by his master
to drive his van, alleged that an accident occurred owing to
the master's failure to see that the van was in a proper

(a) *M'Laughlin* v. *Pryor*, 1842, 4 M. and G., 48 ; *Gordon* v. *Rolt*, 1849, 4 Ex.
365.

(b) Lord Abinger in *Brady* v. *Giles*, 1835, 1 M. and Rob. 494.

(c) 25 & 26 Vict. c. 101, § 303 ; see also § 127.

(d) *Powles* v. *Hider*, 1856, 25 L.J., Q.B. 331 ; *Fowler* v. *Lock*, 1872, L.R.
7 C.P. 272.

(e) *Venables* v. *Smith*, 1577, 2 Q.B.D. 279 ; see also § 153.

(f) *King* v. *Spur*, 1881, L.R. 8 Q.B.D. 104, 108.

(g) *Fraser*, M. and S. 175.

state of repair and not overloaded, but it was not alleged that the master knew of the defect. It was held that the action was not maintainable.(a) Lord Abinger in that case observed:—"The mere relation of the master and the servant never can imply an obligation on the part of the master to take more care of the servant than he may reasonably be expected to do of himself. . . . In fact, to allow this sort of action to prevail would be an encouragement to the servant to omit that diligence and caution which he is in duty bound to exercise on behalf of his master to protect him against the misconduct or negligence of others who serve him, and which diligence and caution, while they protect the master, are a much better security against any injury the servant may sustain by the negligence of others engaged under the same master than any recourse against his master for damages could possibly afford." Nor is the master liable if the servant is in full knowledge of the risk he encounters, or neglects to take proper precautions for his own safety.(b) And where the master promises to remove the danger, and induces the servant to continue working in face of the danger, it is a question of circumstances whether the servant can or cannot recover ;(c) but where a horse, alleged to be dangerous and unfit for work, was supplied to a servant who, induced by the master's promises to procure a horse fit for its work, to continue working it, was injured, Lord Justice-Clerk Inglis observed :—"If a servant, in the face of manifest danger chooses to go on with his work, he does so at his own risk, and not at the risk of his master. The averments of the pursuer as to the condition of the horse are such as if true would have entitled him to refuse to continue working; and I cannot, in such circumstances, allow the servant to say to his master, 'I went on at your

---

(a) *Priestly* v. *Fowler*, 1837, 3 M. and W. 1 ; *Riley* v. *Baxendale*, 1861, 30 L.J. Ex. 87.

(b) See cases cited in § 164.

(c) *Holmes* v. *Clarke*, 1862, 31 L.J. Ex. 356 ; see also § 164.

risk.' " (*a*)   The master is not liable if there is contributory negligence on the part of the servant,(*b*) nor if the servant is injured when acting clearly outwith his employment, even under the order of the master ;(*c*) but the master is liable if the injury is clearly the result of an act of negligence on his part, the servant being in such a case in the same position as a third party, both as regards the claim and the *onus* of proof;(*d*) and this holds when the servant is so injured by a danger which was not obvious, or when the risk is not incidental to his employment.(*e*)

158. Fellow-Servants Causing Injury.—One of the risks a servant runs in contracting service with his master is the negligence of fellow-servants.(*f*)   Accordingly the master is not liable for injuries to a servant caused by a fellow-servant, provided he has taken reasonable care to provide competent servants ; still less when the injured servant is only casually assisting the master's other servants.(*g*)   This relation of fellow-servant must be clearly established to exempt the master from liability, and it has been held that in an action to recover damages for injury caused by the negligence of the defender's servant, the defence of common employment is not applicable, unless the injured person and the servant whose negligence caused the injury were not only engaged in a common employment, but were in the service of a common master.(*h*)   Again, a man was engaged in delivering his master's cattle to a railway company for carriage, and

(*a*) *Crichton* v. *Keir*, 1863, 1 M. 407, 411.

(*b*) See § 161.

(*c*) *Sutherland* v. *M. Ry. Co.* 1857, 19 D. 1004 ; *M'Naughton* v. *Cal. Ry. Co*, 1858, 21 D. 160.

(*d*) See § 150.

(*e*) *Fraser*, M. and S. 187, 188.

(*f*) Lord Cranworth in *Bartonshill Coal Co.* v. *Reid*, 1856, 3 M'Q. 266 ; Alderson, B., in *Hutchinson v. Y. N. & B. Ry. Co.*, 1850, 19 L.J., Ex. 296.

(*g*) Erle, C.J., in *Potter* v. *Faulkener*, 1861, 31 L.J., Q.B. 30.

(*h*) *Johnson* v. *Lindsay* [1891] A.C. 371 (over-ruling *Woodhead* v. *Gartness Iron Co.*, and disapproving *Macguire* v. *Russell*, and explaining Lord Cairns in *Wilson* v. *Merry*).

O

was being assisted by the company's servants in trucking
them, when, through the fault of the company's servants, a
train struck the truck and injured the driver of the cattle.
The company pleaded in defence to an action by the injured
man that he was a volunteer in their service for the time ;
the defence was repelled, and it was held that the railway
company were liable in damages.(a)   But if the master
himself is acting as fellow-servant, he is answerable for injury
caused to his servant, because a servant is entitled to expect
from his master " the care and attention which the superior
position and presumable sense of duty of the latter ought to
command."(b)   The Employers Liability Act, 1880,(c)
while giving a workman the same right of action as a third
party against his master, for injuries sustained while in his
service, by reason of deficiency of plant, or negligence, or
improper rules, provides that the master is no longer to be
allowed to plead that the negligence causing the accident
was the negligence of a fellow-servant, if the person to blame
was a foreman or other person exercising superintendence, or
if the person injured was at the time under the orders of
another workman, and the injury was due to his having
obeyed that person's orders.(d)   Under this statute horses
have been held " plant,"(e) and an injured party must be
able to show that the horse which caused him injury was
defective and unfit for use ; but if there be mere surmise
upon this point, the pursuer's *onus* is not discharged.(f)
Where a company are necessarily in the knowledge that one
of their horses used by their employees is unsafe, they are
liable if they negligently permit it to be used, and any one
of the employees is injured thereby.(g)   It has also been

(a) *Wyllie* v. *Cal. Ry. Co.*, 1871, 9 M. 463 ; see also *Calder* v. *Cal. Ry. Co.*, 1871,
9 M. 833.

(b) Crompton, J., in *Ashworth* v. *Stanning*, 1861, 30 L.J., Q.B. 183.

(c) 43 & 44 Vict. c. 42, §§ 1, 2.

(d) *Ibid.* §§ 1, 2.

(e) *Huston* v. *Ed. Tram. Co.*, 1887, 14 R. 621 ; *Fraser* v. *Hood*, 1887, 15 R.
178 ; *Yarmouth* v. *France*, 1887, 19 Q.B.D. 647.

(f) *M'Farlane* v. *Thomson*, 1884, 12 R. 232.   (g) *Huston*, cit.

observed that the employer is answerable for any defect in the condition of " plant " hired for the day,(a) but in such a case he has relief against the owner unless the defect was undiscoverable by any ordinary or reasonable means of enquiry and examination. If there be any improper system or rules for the management of "plant," they will infer negligence against the master, and if a horse be known to be dangerous, and this fact be concealed from an injured workman, the master is liable. (As to the bearing of this Act upon the pleas of contributory negligence and *volenti non fit injuria*, see § 164.)

159. Proof of Negligence.—To make out a case of liability for negligence the Court or jury must be satisfied—not only that there was fault on the part of the defenders; but also, that the fault was the natural or proximate cause of the injury.(b)

The fault complained of must be distinctly made out and not left to mere conjecture. " A *scintilla* of evidence, or a mere surmise that there may have been negligence on the part of the defendants clearly would not justify the judge in leaving the case to the jury."(c) There must be evidence upon which they might reasonably and properly conclude that there was negligence. Where the evidence is equally consistent with either view—with the existence or non-existence of negligence—it is not competent to the judge to leave the matter to the jury. Thus, a plaintiff attended a sale of horses at the defendant's sale-yard. In order to show the animal's pace, a servant of the defendant led it with a halter between a blank wall and a row of spectators, there being no barrier to protect buyers from injury. Another servant of the defendant struck the horse with a

(a) *Jones* v. *Burford*, 1884, 1 T.L.R. 137.

(b) § 170.

(c) Williams, J., in *Toomey* v. *L. B. & S. C. Ry. Co.*, 1857, 3 C.B., N.S. 146; *Cotton* v. *Wood*, 1860, 8 C.B., N.S. 568 ; *Cox* v. *Burbidge*, 1863, 13 C.B., N.S. 430, child kicked.

whip, and the animal swerved round, and kicked and injured the plaintiff. It was proved a customary thing for a man to be stationed with a whip at the particular point where the servant was ; but there was no evidence as to the kind of blow given, nor the character of the horse, nor how it was being led, nor that protecting barriers were customary in public horse sale-yards. It was held there was no evidence of negligence to go to a jury.(*a*)

There are certain cases where the mere occurrence of an event is *primâ facie* evidence of fault—*e.g.*, where a public vehicle breaks down.(*b*) In such cases, *res ipsa loquitur ;* the *onus* is shifted ; and the defender has to show that he was free from blame ; and if a defender can prove that the injury was not preventable by any care or skill, he will not be liable.(*c*)

(*a*) *Abbot* v. *Freeman*, 1876, 35 L.T., N.S. 783.

(*b*) *Lyon* v. *Lamb*, 1838, 16 S. 1188 ; see also *Byrne* v. *Boadle*, 1863,[33 L.J., Ex. 13 ; *Kearney* v. *L. B. & S. C. Ry. Co.*, 1871, L.R. 6 Q.B. 759 ; *Macaulay* v. *Buist*, 1846, 9 D. 245.

(*c*) *Christie* v. *Griggs*, 1809, 2 Camp. 79.

CHAPTER VII.

DEFENCES TO ACTIONS OF DAMAGES FOR INJURY TO HORSES AND CAUSED BY THEM.

Inevitable Accident, 160. Contributory Negligence, 161-163. *Volenti non fit injuria*, 164. *Mora*, 165. Trespass, 166. [Remoteness, see Chap. VIII., § 170.]

160. Inevitable Accident. — A defender is entitled to absolvitor in an action by one personally injured by him, or one for whom he is responsible, if he can show that the injury was not due to any *culpa* on his part ; and, in all cases where there is an *onus* of proof on the defender to show that the injury was not due to his fault or negligence, inevitable accident is a good defence to an action of damages. To establish a defence of inevitable accident a defender must, in the first place, disprove allegations of negligence, and show that the occurence was due to natural causes beyond his control, or that the event was so unlikely to occur that it could not reasonably have been anticipated. (a) The event need not be unique, (b) nor is it necessary that it should never have occurred before. (c) Thus, it will be sufficient for one not otherwise in fault to show that a horse bolted from being frightened by thunder or lightning, or some unforeseen cause ; (d) or that it bolted from being whipped

(a) *Nitro-phosphate, &c., Co. v. L. & St. K. Docks Co.*, 1878, L.R, 9 Ch. D. 503 ; *Nichols v. Marshland*, 1876, L.R. 2 Ex. D. 1.
(b) *Pirie v. Magistrates of Aberdeen*, 1871, 9 M. 412.
(c) *Nitro-phosphate, &c., Co.*, cit.
(d) *Pluckwell v. Wilson*, 1832, 5 C. and P. 375.

by some other person ; (a) or that a fog was so thick that
the coachman could not keep the road ; (b) or from fright
caused by another vehicle running into his own ; (c) or to
a misunderstanding between a driver who has called out
and the party injured by the van he was driving.(d)
Again, it has been held an inevitable accident if a horse
from inherent vice(e) suddenly become restive, and the
driver can prove that there was no fault in his want of
control over it; mere restiveness is not *primâ facie* evidence of negligence.(f)   Also, where a carriage horse
suddenly bolted, notwithstanding the coachman's utmost
efforts to control it, swerved on the footpath, and injured
a passenger, it was held there was no evidence of fault
to go to the jury, even although it was proved that the
horse cast a shoe shortly after bolting, and that the
driver gave no warning.(g)   Thus also, damage caused by
a horse's taking an obstinate fit of backing has been held
an accident.(h)   Again, it was held to be an accident where
a horse, which had strayed into a wheat field, and was driven
back, while leaping a fence fell on a stake and was killed,
there being proof that the servant who drove it away did not
intend to injure it.(i)   In a somewhat similar case, a stallion
broke out of a field in pursuit of some mares, and entered
the farm-close of a neighbouring farm, and a farm servant
beat it with a stake in order to drive it away ; the horse
died from a wound alleged to have been inflicted by a nail
in the stake, and it was held that the servant was not liable

---

(a) *Gibbons* v. *Pipper*, 1 Lord Raymond, 38.

(b) Best, C.J., in *Crofts* v. *Waterhouse*, 1825, 3 Bing. 319.

(c) *Wakeman* v. *Robinson*, 1823, 1 Bing. 213 ; *Goodman* v. *Taylor*, 1832, 5 C.
and P. 410.

(d) *Docherty* v. *Watson*, 1884, 21 S.L.R. 449.

(e) See § 109.

(f) *Hammack* v. *White*, 1862, 11 C.B., N.S. 588.

(g) *Manzoni* v. *Douglas*, 1880, L.R. 6 Q.B.D. 145 ; see also *Holmes* v. *Mather*,
1875, L.R. 10 Ex. 261.

(h) *Pyper* v. *Thomson*, 1843, 5 D. 498.

(i) *Herriot* v. *Unthank*, 1827, 6 S. 211.

for the value of the horse. (a)   But the least proof of negligence will upset the theory of accident, as—*e.g.*, the failure to examine the axles of a public coach before the journey, or taking a horse known to be restive to a public place.   If, however, in leading animals, such as bulls or stallions, along the public thoroughfares, every reasonable precaution is taken, the fact that damage is done gives no right of action. (b)

161. Contributory Negligence generally.— When damage has been proved to have been occasioned by negligence, the party causing it will be absolved from blame if he can show that the injury has been contributed to by the negligence of the injured party ; (c) but his contribution to the injury must be material.   Thus, a plaintiff who had left his ass tethered in a highway, and, therefore, unable to get out of the way of the defendant's waggon, which was going smartly along the highway, and ran into it, was found entitled to recover ; the charge given to the jury was held correct upon appeal—viz., " that though the act of the plaintiff in leaving the donkey on the highway so fettered . . . might be illegal, still if the proximate cause of the injury was attributable to the want of proper conduct on the part of the driver of the waggon, the action was maintainable against the defendant." (d) Again, where a cabman attempted to lead his horse over some rubbish wrongously left in a lane, he was not found disentitled to recover because he had at some hazard created by the defenders brought his horse out of the stable. (e) The principle of contributory negligence is thus explained by Lord President Inglis :—" When an event is brought about directly by the *culpa* of two persons, whether joint or several, where the *culpa* of each has contributed to produce the event, and the event would not have been produced but for the

(a) *Cumming* v. *Turnbull*, 1840, 2 D. 579.

(b) *Harpers* v. *G. N. Ry. Co.*, 1886, 13 R. 1139 ; *Phillips* v. *Nicoll*, 1884, 11 R. 592 ; see also § 137.

(c) *Greenland* v. *Chaplin*, 1850, 5 Ex. 243.

(d) *Davies* v. *Mann*, 1842, 10 M. and W. 546.

(e) *Clayards* v. *Dethick*, 1848, 12 Q.B. 439.

culpa of both, there can be no claim as between these persons for reparation for injury flowing from that event;" (a) and Lord Fitzgerald thus defines it :—" Contributory negligence seems to me to consist in the absence of that ordinary care which a sentient being ought reasonably to have taken for his own safety, and which, had it been exercised, would have enabled him to avoid the injury of which he complains, or the doing of some act which he ought not to have done, and but for which the accident would not have occurred." (b) What amounts to ordinary care is purely a jury question ; so is contributory negligence, and each case depends on its own circumstances. (c)   Thus, a person crossing a street, (d) or leaving a tramcar, is bound to look about him to see that he does not go in front of a vehicle, (e) and the failure to do so amounts to contributory negligence. (f)   In regard to what amount of contributory negligence is sufficient to bar a claim of damages at the instance of an injured party or his representatives, the rule in *Radley* v. *L. & N.-W. Ry. Co.* is authoritative. (g)   Lord Penzance in that case observed :—
" The first proposition is a general one to this effect, that the plaintiff in an action for negligence cannot succeed if it is found by the jury that he has himself been guilty of any negligence or want of ordinary care which contributed to cause the accident.   But there is another proposition equally well established, and it is a qualification upon the first—namely, that although the plaintiff may have been guilty of negligence, and although this negligence may in fact have contributed to the accident, yet if the defendant could, in the

---

(a) *M'Naughton* v. *Caledonian Railway Company*, 1858, 21 D. 160, 163.

(b) *Wakelin* v. *L. & S.-W. Ry. Co.*, 1886, L.R. 12 App. Ca. 41, 51 ; see also *Tuff* v. *Warman*, 27 L.J., C.P. 322.

(c) *Greenland*, cit. ; *Clayards*, cit.

(d) Coleridge, J., in *Woolf* v. *Beard*, 1838, 8 C. and P. 373.

(e) *Ramsay* v. *Thomson*, 1881, 9 R. 140; *Jardine* v. *Stonefield Laundry Company*, 1887, 14 R. 839.

(f) But see as to aged persons, Lord Justice-Clerk Moncreiff in *Clerk* v. *Petrie*, 1879, 6 R. 1076 ; and pupil children, see § 162.

(g) *Radley* v. *L. & N.-W. Ry. Co.*, 1876, L.R. 1 App. Ca. 754, 759 ; see also cases of *Cotton*, *Hawkins*, *Williams*, and *Boss*, cited § 142.

result by the exercise of ordinary care and diligence, have avoided the mischief which happened, the plaintiff's negligence will not excuse him "—*i.e.*, the defendant.   Thus, where a tramway driver, going down an incline whistled so that a cab, which was standing in the way, might get out of the way, but nevertheless ran into it, and injured it, it was held that there was no contributory negligence on the part of the cabman, who did not drive off immediately, but was waiting to pick up a passenger.(*a*)   Again, where the negligence of the injurer consisted in his servant's leaving a horse and cart unattended in the street, and it would not necessarily have been followed by damage had there not been great negligence on the part of the child injured by amusing itself with the wheel, Lord Denman observed :—" The most blameable carelessness of his servant having tempted the child, he ought not to reproach the child with yielding to that temptation.   He has been the real and only cause of the mischief ; he has been deficient in ordinary care ; the child, acting without prudence or thought, has, however, shown these qualities in as great a degree as he could be expected to possess them.   His misconduct bears no proportion to that of the defendant who produced it."(*b*)   Where negligence of the injured party subsequent to the accident aggravates the amount of damage, it is pleadable in mitigation of damage.(*c*)   (As to the bearing of the Employers Liability Act on this plea, see § 164.)

162. Contributory Negligence of Pupil Children.—Young children have as much right to be on the public street and highways as adults ; and their disposition to get in front of vehicles is one of the risks drivers must specially guard against.(*d*)   Thus, where two children, one three, and the other five, years of age, were driven over in a crowded street

(*a*) *M'Dermaid v. Edinburgh Street Tramways Company,* 1884, 12 R. 15.

(*b*) *Lynch v. Nurdin,* 1841, 1 Q.B. 29, 37.

(*c*) *Moffat v. Park,* 1887, 5 R. 13.

(*d*) *Auld v. M'Bey,* 1881, 8 R. 495 ; see also § 142.

in Glasgow, the Court held it not to be a good defence that
the father had contributed to the accident by allowing them
to be there unprotected.(*a*) If, however, a child rushes
suddenly in front of an advancing vehicle, and it is impossible for the driver to pull up, the driver will be free.(*b*) The
question as to what age a child can be guilty of contributory
negligence depends on the negligence alleged. Thus, where
a child was killed on a private line of railway by a passing
engine, Lord President Inglis observed :—" To allow a child
of two and a-half years of age to wander about in so dangerous a place, without anyone to take charge of it, showed
great carelessness on the part of the parents," and the father
was not found entitled to recover for its death.(*c*) Again,
where a child, four years old, was injured while meddling
with a dangerous machine, negligently left unprotected,
Lord Young said :—" There can be no contributory negligence by a child of four years."(*d*) A child is only guilty of
contributory negligence when it neglects the care that is
usually to be expected from children of its age.(*e*)

163. Proof of Contributory Negligence.—Proof of contributory negligence is subject to the same rules as proof of
negligence.(*f*) What a defender has to prove is that the
pursuer has been negligent. If he succeeds, the pursuer
will not recover ; but if it is clear that the defender had been

---

(*a*) *Martin* v. *Wards*, 1887, 14 R. 814.

(*b*) *Frasers* v. *Edinburgh Street Tramways Co.*, 1882, 10 R. 264. In this case a
new trial was granted, on the ground of the jury having ignored evidence of contributory negligence of the boy, who was six years old, rushing in front of a tramcar. It resulted in a verdict for the defenders, on the ground of no fault, the
speed not being excessive.

(*c*) *Morran* v. *Waddell*, 1883, 11 R. 44 ; *Grant* v. *Caledonian Ry. Co.*, 1870, 9
M. 258 ; see also *Davidson* v. *Monklands Ry. Co.*, 1855, 17 D. 1038 ; *Greer* v.
Stirlingshire Road Trustees, 1882, 9 R. 1069, where defenders were found liable for
the death of an infant of twenty-two months old, who, accompanied by a child
of three and a-half years, crept through an insufficient fence, and was drowned.

(*d*) *M'Gregor* v. *Ross*, 1883, 10 R. 725, 731 ; see also *Campbell* v. *Ord*, 1873,
1 R. 149.

(*e*) *Lynch* v. *Nurdin*, 1841, 1 Q.B. 29.

(*f*) See § 159.

negligent, and merely doubtful if the pursuer has, the pursuer will be entitled to recover. The defence of joint negligence must be as clearly established as the ground of action requires to be.(*a*)

164. *Volenti non fit Injuria.*—It is also a good defence where fault or negligence is established, to prove that the injured party voluntarily chose to run the risk. Wherever one is not physically constrained, where he can, at his option, do a thing or not, and he does it, this maxim applies.(*b*) It differs from the plea of contributory negligence in respect of its being a matter of voluntary acceptance of a known risk, not mere carelessness in presence of danger.(*c*) Mere knowledge of the risk does not involve consent to it. "The question in each case must be, not simply whether the plaintiff knew of the risk, but whether the circumstances are such as necessarily to lead to the conclusion that the whole risk was voluntarily incurred by the plaintiff."(*d*) The mere fact that a workman undertakes, or continues, in a dangerous employment, with full knowledge and understanding of the damage, is not conclusive to show that he has undertaken the risk so as to make the maxim, *volenti non fit injuria*, applicable in the case of injury. The question, whether he has so undertaken the risk, is one of fact and not of law. And this is so both at common law and in cases arising under the Employers Liability Act, 1880.(*e*) "The question which has most frequently to be considered, is not whether he voluntarily and rashly exposed himself to injury, but whether he agreed that, if injury should befall him, the risk was to be his and not his master's."(*f*) Thus, a servant was not allowed to recover damages against a railway com-

---

(*a*) Lord Neaves in *M'Martin v. Hannay*, 1872, 10 M. 411.

(*b*) *Membery v. G. W. Ry. Co.*, 1889, L.R. 14 App. Ca. 179.

(*c*) Chief-Justice Cockburn and Lord Justice Mellish in *Woodley v. M. D. Ry. Co.*, 1877, L.R. 2 Ex. D. 384.

(*d*) Justice Lindley in *Yarmouth v. France*, 1887, 19 Q.B.D. 647, 660.

(*e*) *Smith v. Baker* [1891] A.C. 325.

(*f*) Lord Watson in *Smith*, cit. p. 355.

pany for furnishing him with a horse unfit for work, on the ground that he was aware of the danger of working with it.(*a*)   In another case, a plaintiff was employed for a wharfinger, who, for the purposes of his business, employed horses and carts, the plaintiff's duty being to drive the horses and load and unload the carts.   One of the horses supplied was so vicious as to be unfit to be driven, even by a careful driver.   The plaintiff objected to drive this horse, and told the foreman that it was unfit to be driven, to which the foreman replied that he must continue to drive it, and that his employer would be responsible if any accident happened. The plaintiff continued to drive the horse, and whilst sitting in his proper place was kicked by it, and his leg was broken. It was held, *inter alia*, that the horse was "plant," under the Employers Liability Act, and that upon the facts a jury might find the defendant to be liable, for there was evidence of negligence on the part of his foreman, and that the circumstances did not show conclusively that the risk was voluntarily incurred by the plaintiff.(*b*)   Again, a stable boy was ordered by his master to tie up an entire horse in its stable, and was bitten by it.   He raised an action against his master, averring that the horse was vicious and dangerous, that it had previously bitten other people, and that he had been five years in his master's employment as a carter, and five months as stable boy.   The action was held irrelevant, on the ground that the stable boy, of his own choice, continued to work in face of the danger.(*c*)   In another case, under very similar circumstances, the question of known danger was not raised, the evidence turning on whether or not the horse of a tramway company was a dangerous animal.(*d*)   Again, where an injured carter sued his employer

---

(*a*) *Crichton* v. *Keir*, 1863, 1 M. 407.

(*b*) *Yarmouth* v. *France*, cit.

(*c*) *Fraser* v. *Hood*, 1887, 15 R. 178 (where it was held that horses are "plant," under the Employers Liability Act); see also *Thomas* v. *Quartermaine*, 1887, L.R. 18 Q.B.D. 657.

(*d*) *Haston* v. *Edinburgh Street Tramways Co.*, 1887, 14 R. 621.

as blameworthy, in having a horse in his possession, for use by his carters, not broken to steam engines, the jury found that he "knew of its condition and character, and the risk he ran in taking charge of it," and accordingly, on the instructions of Lord Young, who presided at the trial, gave their verdict for the defenders, which was upheld in an application for a new trial.(a)

The effect of the Employers Liability Act(b) upon the defences of the master, when sued by a workman, is thus stated by Justice Smith, concurred in by Justice Matthew:—"The workman, when he sues his master for any of the five matters designated in it, shall be in the position of one of the public suing, and shall not be in the position a servant theretofore was when he sued his master; in other words, that the master shall have all the defences he theretofore had against any one of the public suing him, but shall not have the special defences he theretofore had when sued by his servant; . . . the defence of contributory negligence is still left to the employer, but the defence of common employment, and also the defence that the servant had contracted to take upon himself the known risks attending upon the engagement, are taken away from him when sued by a workman under the Act. . . . The Legislature, while stating for the employer the two defences above-mentioned, has given him a statutory defence under § 2, sub.-sec. 3, which, theretofore, did not exist. It is this—the employer, when sued for a defect, ways, or machinery, may set up that the servant knew of the defect, and did not communicate it to him (the employer), or to some other person superior to himself in the service of the employer."(c)

165. Mora.—A pursuer must make his claim for reparation timeously. Thus, where a claim of damages for personal

(a) *Wilson* v. *Boyle*, 1889, 17 R. 62.
(b) 43 & 44 Vict. c. 42.
(c) *Weblin* v. *Ballard*, 1886, 17 Q.B.D. 122.

injury was unduly postponed, the Court said :—" The word *mora* suggests mere delay, but I am free to admit that in the ordinary case delay of itself is not sufficient to establish a plea of *mora*, and that abandonment must be implied in the delay. But when the claim is one which requires constitution . . . the plea of *mora* will be justified by delay for a certain length of time in constituting the claim. . . . It is unfair that a man should be allowed to keep back a claim of this kind until it suits him to bring it forward, when all means of rebutting it may have been lost.(*a*)

166. Trespass.—Where the injured party is trespassing where he has no business to go, and is injured, he cannot recover, as he is the author of his own wrong, and this applies also to children. (*b*) When a party's horses or cattle break in among the crop or stock of a neighbour, the servants of the latter are entitled and bound to use ordinary and reasonable compulsion to drive them away, and if any accident happen to the animals trespassing from the means used, it is a casualty which the owner must take upon himself.(*c*)

(*a*) *Cook* v. *N. B. Ry. Co.*, 1872, 10 M. 513.
(*b*) *Balfour* v. *Baird*, 1857, 20 D. 238, see § 162.
(*c*) *Cumming* v. *Turnbull*, 1840, 2 D. 579 ; *Herriot* v. *Unthank*, 1827, 6 S. 211.

CHAPTER VIII.

DAMAGES.

167. Who may Recover.—Where any one is injured either in person or property he has a claim of damages against the party negligently injuring him ; but a master has no claim in Scotland against the injurer of his servant on account of loss of service ; (a) this remedy, however, is competent in England.   Should the injured party survive for a time, his right of action, unless discharged or barred by *mora*, transmits to his representatives.(b)   When the injury causes death, the children or parents, or the husband or wife of the deceased injured party, but not his collateral relations, acquire in their own right a claim for damages and solatium.(c)   The parents of an illegitimate child, however, have no such claim.(d)   Again, if an injured party receive a sum in name of damages, and grant a receipt bearing that it is "in full of all claims competent," he has no further recourse against the wrong-doer ; (e) and when one has received reparation or brought an action to judgment for a delict or

(a) *Allan* v. *Barclay*, 1864, 2 M. 873.

(b) *Auld* v. *Shairp*, 1874, 2 R. 191 ; Lord Adam in *Wight* v. *Burns*, 1883, 11 R. 217.

(c) *Greenhorn* v. *Addie*, 1855, 17 D. 860 ; *Eisten* v. *N. B. Ry. Co.*, 1870, 8 M. 981 ; *Horn* v. *N. B. Ry. Co.*, 1878, 5 R. 1055.

(d) *Clerke* v. *Carfin Coal Co.*, 1891, 18 R., H.L. 63 ; *Weir* v. *Coltness Iron Co.*, 1889, 16 R. 614.

(e) *N. B. Ry. Co.* v. *Wood*, 1891, 18 R., H.L. 27.

breach of contract, he cannot again sue on the ground of a
subsequent increase or development of the damages arising
from the same act.(a) If, however, damage be done to property and also to goods by the same act of negligence, there
is a different cause of action, and recovery of compensation
for the damage to property is no bar to an action subsequently commenced for injury to the person.(b) Lord
Bramwell put the case thus :—one " cannot maintain an
action for a broken arm, and subsequently for a broken rib,
though he did not know of it when he commenced his first
action. But if he sustained two injuries from a blow,
one to his person, another to his property, as, for instance,
damage to a watch, there is no doubt that he could maintain
two actions in respect of the one blow."(c)

Under the Employers Liability Act a workman injured by
any of the five enumerated causes in § 1, or, in case of his
death, his legal representatives,(d) has the same right of
compensation and the same remedies against the employer
as if he had not been a workman under the master's employment, and had been a member of the public. The statute
expressly excludes " domestic and menial servants."(e) In
Scotland, a tramway conductor has been held entitled to the
benefit of the Act ;(f) but in England an omnibus conductor
engaged at daily wages, and paid daily, was held not entitled
to the benefit of it.(g) A huntsman(h) and a " general
garden and stable hand " have been held to be menial
servants,(i) and thus not within the Act ; but a dairy-maid

(a) *Stevenson* v. *Pontifex*, 1887, 15 R. 125.

(b) *Brunsden* v. *Humphrey*, 1884, L.R. 14 Q.B.D.141.

(c) *Darley Main Colliery Co.* v. *Mitchell*, 1886, L.R. 11 App. Ca. 127-144. See
a strong dissent from this doctrine in *Brunsden* cit. by Lord Coleridge at
p. 153.

(d) 43 & 44 Vict. c. 42, § 1.

(e) *Ibid.* § 8 ; 38 & 39 Vict. c. 90, § 10.

(f) *Wilson* v. *Glasgow Tramways Co.*, 1878, 5 R. 981.

(g) *Morgan* v. *L. Gen. Omnibus Co.*, 1883, 12 Q.B.D. 201 ; aff. 1884, 13 Q.B.D.
832.

(h) *Nicoll* v. *Greaves*, 1864, 17 C.B., N.S. 27.

(i) *Johnson* v. *Blenkensopp*, 1841, 5 Jur. 870.

has been held to be a "servant in husbandry," and so within the Act.(a)

168. Against whom Damages are Recoverable.—Though a wrong-doer is liable in damages if he injure any one, no one, with the exception of a master who is liable in certain cases for the negligence of his servant,(b) is responsible for the fault of a third party.   On the death of the wrong-doer a claim of damages may be made effectual against his representatives, such a claim being of the nature of a civil debt.(c) Administrative bodies, such as royal burghs,(d) statutory trustees,(e) police commissioners,(f) navigation trustees,(g) corporations,(h) and other local authorities, are answerable for the negligence of their servants, just as if they were those of a private individual; and claims against them are to be met, not by the members of the board individually, but out of the funds which the board administers.   Public and private companies, also, are responsible for their own negligence or that of their servants.   Thus, the two proprietors of a stage-coach were held liable, along with the driver, for his negligence in driving the coach.(i)   And where a horse was killed by falling during the night into an old ironstone pit, which lay within a yard of the public highway, and was insufficiently fenced, it was held that an action lay against the judicial factor on the estate in which the pit was situated, without calling the tenant, who, for all the judicial factor knew, might have been working the minerals when the accident happened.(j)

(a) *Ex parte Hughes*, 1854, 23 L.J., M.C. 138.
(b) See §§ 150-155.
(c) *Wight v. Burns*, 1883, 11 R. 217.
(d) *Harris v. Mags. of Leith*, 1881, 8 R. 613.
(e) *Mersey Docks and Harbour Board v. Gibbs*, 1864, L.R. 1 H.L. 93.
(f) *Virtue v. Alloa Police Coms.*, 1873, 1 R. 285.
(g) *Buchanan v. Clyde Lighthouses Trs.*, 1884, 11 R. 531.
(h) *Scott v. Mayor of Manchester*, 1856, 1 H. and N. 59.
(i) *Moreton v. Hardern*, 1825, 4 B. and C. 223.
(j) *Mack v. Allan*, 1832, 10 S. 349.

All parties committing a wrong are liable *singuli in soli-dum* in pecuniary reparation,(a) and there is no relief among wrong-doers.(b) If an injured party has obtained full indem-nity from any one, he cannot sue the others in a separate action ; but if he releases any without indemnity, he does not thereby lose his remedy against the rest.(c) In the case of master and servant, a servant injured by his fellow-servant may recover against him, for a person is none the less answer-able for a wrongful act because it is done by the order or authority of another.(d)

169. What may be recovered as Damages for Breach of Contract.—It depends whether an action is founded on breach of contract or on delict what may be recovered. Though the general rule is that consequential or remote damages are never allowed, whatever be the ground of the action, yet the application of this rule suffers a more strict interpretation in contract than in delict. Direct damage only, and the expenses of obtaining reparation, are all that can be recovered under a breach of contract, where there has been no fraud ; but, if there has been fraud, certain losses are considered as direct which would have been regarded as too remote, had there been no fraud ;(e) and, even in that case, purely speculative and hypothetical sources of benefit are not allowed to be computed, on the ground of their not being the natural and proximate consequences of the loss. Therefore, where a cattle dealer fraudulently represented a cow to be free from infectious disease when he knew that it was not so, and the purchaser placed it with five others which caught the disease and died, the latter was held entitled to recover as damages, in an action for fraudulent misrepresentation, the

(a) *Ferguson* v. *E. of Kinnoul*, 1842, 1 Bell's App. 662 : *Western Bank* v. *Bairds*, 1862, 24 D. 859.

(b) Ersk. iii. 1, 15.

(c) *Ferguson*, cit. See also L.J.C. Inglis in liq. *Western Bank* v. *Douglas*, 1860, 447, 476.

(d) *Mackenzie* v. *Goldie*, 1866, 4 M. 277. See also § 150.

(e) B. Pr. 33.

value of all the cows.(a) The same principle was applied where a cow was warranted free from disease, and both parties contemplated its being placed with other stock.(b) But though it is illegal in England to bring a glandered horse into a public market, there is nothing illegal in the simple sale of it; therefore one who sold a glandered horse without a warranty, and without fraudulent misrepresentation, was held not responsible for disease communicated to other horses belonging to the purchaser in the stable to which he removed it.(c) Again, the *pretium affectionis* or fancy value placed on a horse by its owner, would not be allowed in computation of its value, unless fraud were established ;(d) and where damages are claimed for breach of contract, nothing will be allowed except the direct loss upon the thing itself, and what would reasonably be considered as in contemplation of the parties at the time of making the contract as the natural result or reasonable consequence of a probable breach.(e) Thus in breach of sale, in the absence of more precise evidence of value, the highest price which might have been got for a horse after the day of sale, or the average value between the stipulated day of delivery and date of action, or the price at which the buyer could procure a similar one at the stipulated time of delivery, are the usual criteria for determining the amount of damages. There is no absolute rule as to market value in Scotland, and in determining the amount (f) each case is to be considered according to its own circumstances. If there have been a subsale disclosed to the seller, he will be liable for the difference between the price contracted for and the price of the intimated sub-

(a) *Mullett* v. *Mason*, 1866, L.R. 1 C.P., 559.

(b) *Smith* v. *Green*, 1875, L.R. 1 C.P.D. 92.

(c) *Hill* v. *Balls*, 1857, 2 H. and N. 299 ; see also *Ward* v. *Hobbs*, 1878, 4 App. Ca. 13.

(d) Ersk. iii. 1, 14.

(e) *Hadley* v. *Baxendale*, 1854, 9 Ex. 341 ; *Keddie* v. *N. B. Ry. Co.*, 1886, 14 R. 233 ; *Elbinger, &c.* v. *Armstrong*, 1874, L.R. 9 Q.B., 473.

(f) *Dunlop* v. *Higgins*, 1848, 6 B. App. Ca. 195.

sale.(a)   And where the seller resells, he cannot charge the
buyer with the difference between the contract price and
market value, unless he sell immediately.(b)   If, however,
there is any special loss known to the parties which will ensue
as the result of a breach of the contract, such loss will be
estimated in assessing the damages, whether it be loss of
profit or not.(c)   So also, in the contract of hiring, where an
inn-keeper contracted to provide stabling for twelve horses
for a plaintiff during a particular fair, and failed to do so, it
was held that damages could be recovered for injury caused to
the horses by exposure to the weather while he was engaged
in finding other stables for them.(d)   Again, in the contract
of carriage, the damages are usually confined to the value of
the horse lost or damaged, and in estimating this, the market
value at the time and place at which it ought to have been
delivered is the usual test of its value, which is taken in full
if the animal be killed, but in the case of injury, from this
will be deducted what it will fetch in the market.(e)   If
there be no means of testing the market value, the real value
must be ascertained as a fact by taking into consideration the
circumstances which would otherwise have influenced the
market price, if there had been one, such as costs of carriage and a reasonable sum for the consignee's profit where
he is a dealer in the goods.(f)   Where a sender of animals
brings it under the notice of the carrier that they must be
in time for a certain market, or the carrier must necessarily
be aware of this fact, loss of market is to be considered in
estimating damages, even when caused by an accident which
the carrier cannot show could not have been avoided by
ordinary care and foresight on his part.(g)

(a) Bell's Pr. 31, *Hadley*, cit. ; *Grebert-Borgnis* v. *Nugent*, 1885, 15 Q.B.D., 85.
(b) *Warin & Craven* v. *Forrester*, 1876, 4 R. 190 ; aff. 4 R.H.L. 75.
(c) *Hammond & Co.* v. *Bussey*, 1887, 20 Q.B.D. 79.
(d) *M'Mahon* v. *Field*, 1881, L.R. 7 Q.B.D. 591.
(e) *Rice* v. *Baxendale*, 1861, 7 H. and N. 96 ; *Wilson* v. *L. & Y. Ry. Co.*, 1861,
9 C.B., N.S. 632 ; *O'Hanlan* v. *G. W. Ry. Co.*, 1865, 6 B. and S. 484.
(f) *O'Hanlan*, cit.
(g) *Anderson* v. *N. B. Ry. Co.*, 1875, 2 R. 443.

170. Damages in Delict and Quasi-delict.—The general rule is that a wrong-doer is liable for all the consequences that may reasonably be expected under ordinary circumstances to result from his misconduct, but not for remote contingencies happening therefrom. The distinction between damage for breach of contract and that occasioned by delict is that, in the former, direct damage only can be recovered, but in the latter, the highest advantage which, but for the delict, would have been enjoyed.(a) The damage must be so related to the injurious act that it follows it as its effect naturally and in the ordinary course of events,(b) and each case must be judged of by its own circumstances. Thus, a servant washed a van and allowed the waste water to run down a gutter towards a grating leading to a sewer, about twenty-five yards off. The grating was obstructed by ice, and the water flowed over the causeway and froze. A horse passing the place slipped on the ice and broke its leg. This was held to be a consequence too remote to be attributed to the wrongful act of the servant.(c) But where a carriage belonging to A was driven against the wheel of B's chaise, and the collision threw a person in the chaise on to the dashing board, and the dashing board falling on the back of the horse caused it to kick, and the chaise was thereby injured; it was held that B was entitled to recover against A damages commensurate with the whole injury.(d) Again, a defendant left a van and ploughing gear four or five feet from the metalled part of the road to stand there for the night; the deceased drove past it, and his mare, which it appeared in evidence was a confirmed kicker, shied at the van, kicked, and in kicking got her leg over the shaft which caused her to fall, and in falling the deceased received the kick which caused his death. It was held by Justice Denman that the defendant's act of leaving the van where he did was an unreasonable use of the highway,

(a) B. Pr. 545.
(b) Mayne on Damages, pp. 44, 45.
(c) *Sharp* v. *Powell*, 1872, L.R. 7 C.P. 253.
(d) *Gilbertson* v. *Richardson*, 1848, 5 C.B. 502.

and that the death was the proximate and natural result thereof.(a)

As illustrating the principle of liability attaching for only such damage as is the natural result of a wrongful act, the following cases may also be referred to :—Where the gate-keeper of a railway company had invited the plaintiff to drive over a level crossing when it was dangerous to do so, and the jury, although an actual collision was avoided, assessed damages for physical and mental injuries occasioned by the fright, it was held that damages for a nervous shock or mental injury caused by fright at an impending collision were too remote.(b)   In another case a horse had strayed on a highway and kicked a child, and the plaintiff sued for damages.   There was no evidence why it kicked the child further than that it occurred through no fault of the child. The Court assumed the horse to be a trespasser, and held that the owner would be liable for all the natural results of such trespass, such as eating grass or trampling down the soil ; but they regarded the act of kicking a child as an act unnatural to a horse which was not known to be vicious; and, there being no proof that the owner knew the horse was vicious, he was held not liable for the injury.(c)   This case may be contrasted with two other cases where the sufferer was a horse instead of a child.   A mare belonging to a defendant strayed through a gate which he was bound to keep in repair and got into plaintiff's field.   A conflict between the plaintiff's horse and mare ensued, in which the mare kicked the plaintiff's horse and killed it.   It was held that it was a natural consequence of horses meeting that the one might kick the other, and as there was sufficient evidence of negligence in leaving the gate unfenced, the defendant must be liable for what ensued as the approximate cause of the negligence.   The direction of the judge to the jury,

(a) *Harris* v. *Mobbs*, 1878, L.R. 3 Ex. D. 268.

(b) *Victorian Ry. Coms.* v. *Coullas*, 1888, L.R. (P.C.) 13 App. Ca. 222.

(c) *Cox* v. *Burbridge*, 1863, 13 C.B., N.S. 430.

to the effect that it was not necessary to prove that the owner knew that the horse was vicious, and that it did not matter which horse began to kick, was approved of.(a)   In the other case, the plaintiff's and defendant's fields were separated by a wire fence.   In the plaintiff's field was a mare, and in the defendant's a stallion.   The animals came together at the fence, and the stallion bit the mare, and damages were brought for the injury.   On evidence that the defendants had been warned to keep their stallion away from the mare, the Court held them liable for the damage, on the ground that the damage, though not the necessary result of the trespass, was the direct and natural consequence of the defendant's negligence in not duly restraining an animal known by him to be vicious.(b)   Again, damages to animals have been considered the natural or probable result of negligent fencing, and have been recovered on that ground in the following cases :—where a horse escaped into the defendant's close, and was there killed by the falling of a haystack,(c) it was held a natural result of the defendant's failure to fence his property :—similarly, where a defendant was bound to fence the plaintiff's property, and as the result of a breach of the obligation, two cows strayed through the fence, ate some leaves off a yew tree, in consequence of which they died.(d)   Again, a defendant had allowed a wire fence to fall into disrepair, so that small pieces of iron broke off and lay hidden in the grass.   A cow ate some of the iron and died, and the owner of the cow was held entitled to recover its value from the defendant.(e)   In another case, where a defendant planted upon his own ground yew trees which in course of time spread over the plaintiff's ground, and a horse ate some of the leaves and was poisoned ; the defendant was found liable, on the general principle that one who brings on his land any

(a) *Lee* v. *Riley*, 1865, 18 C.B., N.S. 722.

(b) *Ellis* v. *Loftus Iron Co.*, 1874, L.R. 10 C.P. 10.

(c) *Powell* v. *Salisbury*, 1828, 2 Y. and J. 391.

(d) *Lawrence* v. *Jenkins*, 1873, L.R. 8 Q.B. 274.

(e) *Firth* v. *Bowling Iron Co.*, 1878, L.R. 3 C.P.D. 254.

noxious agent, is bound at his own risk to prevent it doing injury to his neighbour.(a) Again, a plaintiff hired of the occupier of some land adjoining the defendant's line of railway a stable for his horse. The horse was allowed to graze during the day on the land. One night it escaped from the stable on to the land, and thence, through a defective fence, on to the defendant's line, where it was run over and killed.(b) Thus also, where a herd of cattle were being driven at night along an occupation road to some fields. The road crossed a siding of the defendant's railway, on a level, and while the cattle were crossing the siding, the defendant's servants negligently sent some trucks down an incline into the siding, with the result that the cattle were divided into two lots. The animals being frightened, rushed away, and the drovers after them. The drovers were unable to recover six of the herd, which were ultimately found lying dead or dying at another part of the railway. There was no evidence to show when the train had run over the cattle, but it appeared that the animals had gone along the occupation road up to an orchard about a quarter of a mile from the level-crossing, had got into the garden through defect in the fences, and so on to the line.(c) In each of these two cases the defendants were held liable.

171. Damages where a Hired Horse has been Injured. —Where a horse has been injured by negligent driving, the damages include the expenses of curing it and its keep from the time of the accident till recovery, in addition to the difference in its value due to the injury. Thus, where a horse so injured was sent to a farrier's for treatment for six weeks, and at the end of that time was damaged to the extent of £20, Mr. Justice Coleridge held that the proper measure of damage was the keep of the horse at the farrier's, the amount of the farrier's bill, and the difference between the value of the horse at the

(a) *Crowhurst* v. *Amersham Burial Board*, 1878, L.R. 4 Ex. D. 5.
(b) *Dawson* v. *Mid. Ry. Co*. 1872, L.R. 8 Ex. 8.
(c) *Snesby* v. *L. & Y. Ry. Co*. 1875, L.R. 1 Q.B.D. 42.

time of the accident and at the end of six weeks, but no allowance was made for the hire of another horse during the six weeks.(a)

172. Elements to be considered in Assessing Damages in case of Personal Injury.—(A.) *When the pursuer survives.* In a recent case of negligent driving where a pursuer obtained a verdict of £800 in an action of damages against a tramway company, Lord M'Laren observed :—"There are three elements to be taken into consideration in arriving at the amount of compensation which ought to be awarded in a case of this kind. In the first place, it must be given for expenses to which the pursuer has been put on account of the accident, for medical attendance and lodging ; in the second place, it must be given for the physical suffering which has been thereby occasioned, whether temporary or permanent ; and in the third place, it must be given for the loss of business which has resulted so far as that has been proved.(b) The first and third of these elements are as a rule capable of fairly accurate ascertainment by proof ; but the second, termed solatium, is more difficult to fix.

The method of computing solatium is " by the jury taking into their consideration the whole circumstances of the case, looking at both the present suffering and permanent injury, and without trying to put a money value upon each separately, to fix a sum which will do justice between the parties."(c) It is impossible to doubt that it is a material element for the jury to consider, both in the question of reparation and solatium, whether the accident resulted from very gross, or from a lesser degree of negligence.(d)

The fact that a deceased injured party was a burden to those who are suing for reparation, will not affect their

(a) *Hughes* v. *Quentin*, 1838, 8 C. and P. 703 ; but see § 69, p. 94.
(b) *Young* v. *Glasgow Tramways Co.*, 1882, 10 R. 242-243.
(c) Lord Shand in *Young*, cit.
(d) Per Lord President Boyle Hope in *Cooley* v. *Ed. & Gl. Ry. Co.*, 1845, 8 D. 288, 291.

right to sue, but may be proved by the defender in mitigation of damages. Thus in an action of damages at the
instance of an adult son against the proprietor of a coach by
which his father, an old man on the poor's roll, was driven
over and killed, Lord President Boyle in charging the jury
said :—"You have been told that this man was in great
poverty indeed, that he was actually on the poor's roll ; but
the pursuer is not less entitled to a solatium for his wounded
feelings although he may not be able to show any pecuniary
loss through his father's death." (a) Damages for death or
personal injury are not to suffer diminution on account of
sums received or to be received by the injured party or his
representatives from a friendly society, or under a policy of
insurance ; (b) but " a jury may take into account provisions
made by a deceased in favour of a widow, where these are settled
directly upon her ; but where they are provided by a policy
on the husband's life in the wife's favour, the amount is not to
be deducted from the damages assessed, because the benefit
derived from the acceleration of the payment may be com-
pensated by deducting from their estimate of the future earnings of the deceased the premiums he would have had to
pay had he lived to keep up the premium."(c)

(B.) *Where the pursuer dies after raising an action.*
—The further consideration of shortening of life is an
element to be considered. A lad of sixteen, earning twelve
shillings and sixpence a-week, received injuries on a railway
and died seven months afterwards from the effects of the
accident. He had previously brought an action of damages
against the railway company, and after his death his father
was sisted as pursuer in his place. A verdict of £400 was

(a) *Elder* v. *Croall*, 1849, 11 D. 1040 ; see also *Brown* v. *M'Gregor*, 1813, F.C.;
cited in *Richmond* v. *Russell*, 1849, 11 D. 1038 ; *Brash* v. *Steele*, 1845, 7 D. 539;
diligence allowed to recover documents to prove that a deceased did not support
his family who averred deprivation of parental care and support.

(b) *Hicks* v. *N., &c., Ry. Co.*, 1857, 4 B. and S. 403, *n* ; *Bradburn* v. *G. W. Ry.
Co.*, 1874, L.R. 10 Ex. 1 ; *Yates* v. *White*, 1838, 4 Bing. N.C. 272.

(c) *Grand Trunk Ry. Co.* v. *Jennings*, 1888, L.R. 13 App. Ca. 800.

returned, and on a motion for a new trial on the ground of
excessive damage, Lord President Inglis said :—" It was
contended upon the part of the defenders that the whole
damage which the pursuer could possibly demand or receive
in such an action, as executor of the injured person, was the
loss actually sustained—the pecuniary loss actually sustained
—by the deceased, and a sum by way of *solatium* for the
suffering which he endured during his survivance.   Now,
I am not satisfied that that is necessarily the limit of the
damage. . . .   If it had been foreseen that the man was to
die very shortly after the occurrence of the injury, or very
shortly after the time when the trial was to take place, there
may be a question whether he would not have been entitled
to damages for the shortening his life.   And so it may be a
question whether his executor, as now representing him, is
not entitled to damages for that very same thing, it being
now ascertained beyond all dispute that his life was shortened
in consequence of the injury."   The Court refused to disturb
the verdict;(a) stating that the jury properly had all the
circumstances before them, and that their verdict, though
large, was not so large as to call for judicial interference.
Other elements to be taken into account are the worldly
circumstances of the pursuer ; and also the degree of fault
which caused the injury.   " When a party receives a severe
personal injury, in consequence of an accident to a coach or
other public conveyance, ought he not to receive a greater
compensation when the accident is caused by gross misconduct than when the conveyance is well regulated, and
there has been proper care and attention, and the accident is
of a nature which almost no possible precaution could have
averted ?   And in like manner, is not larger *solatium* to be
given when the life of a parent is lost through gross and
reckless misconduct ? " (b)   and, accordingly, it has been

(a) *M'Master v. Cal. Ry. Co.*, 1885, 13 R. 252.
(b) Lord Justice-Clerk Hope in *Morton v. Ed. & Glas. Ry. Co.*, 1845, 8 D. 288,
294.

held that evidence of the manner in which an injury has been caused, is not to be excluded by an admission of liability.(*a*)

173. New Trial.—A new trial will be granted if the verdict of the jury is contrary to evidence,(*b*) or inconsistent or self-contradictory ; (*c*) but the Court will not interfere with a verdict except in very special circumstances on the ground of excess or deficiency of the sum awarded. "The remedy of setting aside the verdict of a jury is provided for the purpose of preventing a miscarriage of justice, and it is granted only in cases where the damages are so large that the jury must be held to have taken into account elements which they ought not to have considered, or to have given too large a sum from leaving out of consideration elements which ought to have been kept in view." (*d*)   Lord President Inglis observed :—"It seems to me that unless it can be said that the verdict ought not to have been for more than one-half of the sum awarded, there is not, according to our practice, any room for interference." (*e*)

174. Damages Recoverable under the Employers Liability Act.—Under the Employers Liability Act, 1880,(*f*) § 3, the sum recoverable is not to exceed such sum as may be found to be equivalent to the estimated earnings during the three years preceding the injury, of a person in the same grade employed during those years in the like employment, and in the district in which the workman is employed at the time of the injury. The action is not maintainable unless notice that injury has been sustained is given within six

(*a*) *Morton*, cit. ; *Dobie* v. *Aberdeen Ry. Co.*, 1856, 18 D. 862.
(*b*) Mackay, ii. 66.
(*c*) *Stewart* v. *Cal. Ry. Co.*, 1870, 8 M. 486.
(*d*) Per Lord M'Laren in *Young* v. *Glasgow Tramways Co.*, 1882, 10 R. 242, 243.
(*e*) Per Lord President Inglis in *Young*, cit. 245.
(*f*) 43 & 44 Vict. c. 42, § 3.

weeks, and it must be commenced within six months of the accident, or in case of fatal accident, within twelve months ; and it is only in the latter case that the notice may be dispensed with on cause shown.(a)   The notice must state the cause of the injury, but need not specify the ground of action, and there are no formalities necessary to its efficacy.(b)

(a) 43 & 44 Vict. c. 42, § 4.
(b) *Ibid.* §§ 3, 7 ; *Spens & Younger*, " Employers and Employed," 152 *et seq.*, 319, 326 *et seq.*

CHAPTER IX.

INSURANCE.

175. Nature of Contract.—Insurance is a consensual contract to indemnify against possible or probable loss in consideration of a sum paid as premium.(*a*) Under the contract the insurer undertakes to be responsible for certain risks, such as—*e.g.*, perils of the sea, fire, death, accident, disease, &c., to which the property of the insured may be exposed ; being assured in doing so that he is free from such other risks as may arise from the natural or actual condition of the subject, or from the crime or fault of the insurer. Thus, one who beat his mare with an iron rod so that she died, was held not entitled to recover on a policy.(*b*)

The essentials of the contract are a subject in which the insured has an interest, a premium, and a risk ; (*c*) and these are embodied in a written or printed stamped(*d*) document termed the policy, subscribed by the insurers or their agents, and specifying the name of the insured. A policy usually incorporates by reference the limitations of the insurance company's charter; but if this is not done, and the charter allows only a certain class of insurance, and the policy goes beyond it, the policy is void. Thus, a policy of

(*a*) B.C. i. 645, May on Insurance, i.

(*b*) *Western Horse, &c., Ins. Co.* v. *O'Neill*, 21 Neb. 548, cited in Lawson's Rights, Remedies and Practice, § 2206.

(*c*) B. Pr. 457.

(*d*) B.C. i. 649-650; 33 & 34 Vict. c. 97, § 118.

insurance of horses with a company authorised to insure against loss and damage by fire, lightning and inland navigation and transportation, is void if it be taken against death and disease.(*a*) But where the charter in a mutual insurance company confines the insurance within certain counties, the loss of a horse insured in one of the included counties, and removed to another, is covered by the policy.(*b*)

176. Horses as the subject of Insurance.—The horse insured must be clearly specified in the policy so as to leave no doubt as to its identity, except in the case of floating policies,(*c*) when a similar precision is requisite in defining the premises in which the horse is kept. An unborn foal may be the subject of insurance.(*d*) The horse insured also must be at hazard ; and it is held to be so even though it may have perished, or been injured, if this be unknown on entering into the contract ; the insurer in such a case takes the risk of past losses ; that is to say, the risk attaches from a date anterior to the date of the contract. (*e*) It is not necessary that the horse belonged to the insured ; for any one who has an insurable interest in it may insure it.(*f*) Horses are usually identified in a fire or horse insurance policy by description of them, or of the building, stable, or farm they are in when insured ; in a marine policy, by the ship, or by description ; and when a consignment of horses are sent by sea, they should be sent " by ship or ships," if it is not known by what vessels they are to travel.(*g*)

Horses are not " goods " in the sense of being general cargo, and when so sent a special declaration on the policy that it

(*a*) *Insurance Co.* v. *Martin*, 13 Mian, 59, cited in Lawson's Rights, Remedies and Practice, § 2206.

(*b*) *Coventry Mut. Live Stock Ins. Association* v. *Evans*, 102 Pa. St. 281, cited in Lawson, *ut sup.*

(*c*) § 182.

(*d*) B. Pr. 459 ; § 188.

(*e*) B. Pr. 458 ; Brett, J., in *Bradford* v. *Symondson*, 1881, L.R. 7 Q.B.D. 456-463, 4.

(*f*) § 177.

(*g*) B. Pr. 470.

is to cover loss to horses seems necessary.   It has been held
that a general insurance on "cargo" will not cover provender
taken on board for live stock constituting the greater part of
the cargo, nor will it cover the live stock itself.(a)   Thus
where a policy on goods was intended to cover live stock, the
insurance was declared, at the foot of the policy, "to be on
thirty mules, ten asses, and thirty oxen;(b) and in another
case, where a policy was effected "on goods as per annexed
statement valued at £2800," the horses, a loss on which was
claimed under this policy, were specially valued in the statement.(c)

177. Of Insurable Interest.—Whoever has an interest in
a horse may insure it.(d)   The interest may be that of a proprietor, creditor, the holder of a lien, a consignee, and even a
temporary custodier, such as a grazier or livery stable-keeper,
who, in such a case, can recover the full value, being regarded
as trustee for the owner so far as the sum insured exceeds
his interest in respect of his own charges ; but a mere
agent, without possession or lien, could not effect a fire
policy.(e)   The interest an insurer has extends to every real
and actual advantage arising out of, or depending upon, the
thing to which it refers, and must be "such that the peril
would, by its proximate effect, cause damage to the
assured."(f)   It need not be expressed in the policy ; (g) and
must be proved by evidence other than the mere words of
the policy.(h)

178. Of Risk Generally.—The risks undertaken in policies

(a) *Wolcott v. Eagle Insurance Co.*, 4 Pickering, 429, cited by Arnould, p. 29 ;
see also *Brown v. Stapylton*, 1827, 4 Bing. 119.
(b) *Lawrence v. Aberdein*, 1821, 5 B. and Ad. 107.
(c) *Gabay v. Lloyd*, 1825, 3 B. and C. 793.
(d) See May on Insurance, § 80.
(e) Bunyon on Fire Insurance, p. 17.
(f) *Seagrave v. Union, &c., Insurance Co.*, 1866, L.R. 1 C.P. 305.
(g) *Crowley v. Cohen*, 1832, 3 B. and Ad. 478.
(h) B. Pr. 461 ; *Murphy v. Bell*, 1828, 4 Bing. 567.

of insurance vary according to the subject of the contract, and commence at the time and place mentioned in the policy, or from the date of the policy, if there be no mention of time.

179. Of the Risk in Fire Insurance.—The risks in fire insurance are against fire, or by means of fire, such—*e.g.*, as by smoke, occurring within the stipulated period and not excepted in the policy.(*a*) But where there is no ignition the loss is held not to be caused by fire ; and, accordingly, injury by the over-heating of a flue,(*b*) or by explosion in neighbouring premises, is not covered ;(*c*) there must be actual ignition. But incidental damage to a horse, occasioned directly by a fire, such as its taking cold by being removed from a burning stable into the open air, or by water(*d*) used to extinguish a fire, or damage by a wall or beam, injured by fire, falling on it, would be recoverable under " loss by means of fire."(*e*) Where, however, the cause of injury is too remote from the damage sustained, it will not be recoverable ; thus, a claim for loss of hire,(*f*) or use of a horse damaged by fire, would not be covered, except by express stipulation to that effect, nor the loss of possible profits by sale.(*g*)

The usual exceptions in fire policies are loss occasioned by, or happening through invasion, foreign enemy, riot, or civil commotion.

Loss by ignition resulting from lightning is covered by a policy insuring against danger by fire, or by fire from light-

(*a*) Justice Cushing in *Scripture* v. *Lowell, &c., Insurance Co.*, 10 Cush. (Mass.) 356, cited in May on Insurance, p. 620, note 5.

(*b*) *Austin* v. *Drew*, 1815, 4 Camp. 360.

(*c*) *Everett* v. *London Assurance Co.*, 1865, 19 C.B., N.S. 126 ; but see opinion of Justice Cushing, *ut sup.*

(*d*) May on Insurance, § 404.

(*e*) *Johnston* v. *W. Scot. Insurance Co.*, 1828, 7 S. 52.

(*f*) *Wright* v. *Pole*, 1834, 1 A. and E. 621.

(*g*) *Menzies* v. *N. B. Insurance Co.*, 1847, 9 D. 694.

Q

ning. But loss by being torn to pieces by lightning, without
combustion, is not.(a)

Frequently, in American policies, and in some British
policies also, there is what is called a "lightning clause," in
which the insurer takes the risk of animals being struck by
lightning. This risk is entirely separate from fire insurance ;
it is sometimes found in fire policies, but more frequently
in horse and other live stock policies, which do not cover
fire.(b)

Where a horse, described as in a certain barn, was
insured, the policy containing a lightning clause, and the
horse was struck at pasture, the company were held liable ;
(c) and where a clause ran "on horses and colts while in
barn, and by lightning only when in use, or running in
pasture or yard on his farm, in the town of L.," it was held
not limited to the farm occupied by the plaintiff at the date
of the issue of the policy, but extended to any place in the
town.(d)

180. Duration of the Fire Policy.—The efficacy of the
policy is limited to a certain day ; and the whole of the last
day is covered when mentioned in the policy.(e) Where a
certain number of days (generally fifteen) is added, within
which it is declared the policy shall subsist on payment of
the premium, it has been held that this only gives an option
to the insured to continue the insurance by paying the
premium within the fifteen days, notwithstanding any inter-
vening loss, provided the insurance company had not already
given notice that they would not renew the contract.(f)

(a) *Hillier* v. *Allegheny, &c., Co.*, 1846, 45 Am. D. 656, collecting the American
authorities upon what is included in loss by fire. See also May, § 406.
(b) § 188.
(c) *Haws* v. *Philadelphia Fire Association*, 114 Pa. St. 431, cited in Lawson's
Rights, Remedies, and Practice, v. § 2206.
(d) *Boright* v. *Springfield, &c., Insurance Co.*, 34 Minn, 352, cited in Lawson,
ut sup.
(e) *Isaacs* v. *Royal Insurance Co.*, 1870, L.R. 5 Ex. 296.
(f) *Tarleton* v. *Staneforth*, 1796, 1 B. and P. 471 ; *Salvin* v. *James*, 1805,
6 East, 571.

181. Conditions in Fire Policy.—The usual conditions are —that the insurer shall not be liable for loss arising by foreign enemy, or military or usurped power, such as riot, tumult, or civil commotion, and that he shall give notice of any other insurance effected on his horse.

182. Floating Policies.—Horse dealers, auctioneers, and others frequently effect a general or floating policy applicable to all the live stock, carriages, or other goods that may be in their stables or steading. The owner of the horse cannot sue on such a policy, if it be not taken in his name ; but the insured may sue, if he can show that by his usual course of dealing or usage he is liable to the owner for the animals.(*a*) The liability under a policy upon " live stock in premises" is not avoided by the fact that the horse killed was not assured when the policy was issued, but was afterwards acquired by the insured in exchange for others on the premises.(*b*)

Fire policies are not valued policies. They limit the amount of loss recoverable ; but they do not measure the liability for loss ; the amount of the loss must be proved.(*c*) The underwriter pays, not for what has been expended, but only for what is lost to the amount of the sum insured, which may be ascertained amicably, judicially, or by arbitration. Frequently an option may be reserved to the insurer to pay the loss or re-instate,(*d*) and the impossibility of fulfilling the obligation to re-instate after election is no defence to the company.(*e*) In the case of a " floating policy," the loss recoverable is usually limited by the policy to not more than a certain sum for each animal destroyed.

(*a*) B. Pr. 517. As to insurable interest, see § 177.
(*b*) *Mills* v. *Insurance Company*, 37 Iowa, 400, cited in Lawson's Rights, Remedies and Practice, v. § 2206.
(*c*) B. Pr. 515.
(*d*) *Sutherland* v. *Sun Fire Office*, 1852, 14 D. 775.
(*e*) *Brown* v. *Royal Insurance Company*, 1859, 1 E. and E. 853.

183. Of Risks in Marine Insurance.—A marine policy to cover all risks is usually so costly as to prohibit its being taken, except in the case of the most valuable horses, and such a contract is invariably embodied in a special policy ; but the ordinary marine policy insures against the risks of perils of the sea, men-of-war, fire, enemies, pirates, rovers, jettisons, takings, arrests, restraints and detainments of all kings, princes, and people, of what nation, condition, or quality whatsoever, and all other perils, losses, or misfortunes that have or shall come to the hurt, detriment, or damage of the said goods and merchandises, &c., or any part thereof during this adventure.(*a*)

184. Of Losses not Covered by the Policy.—Loss which is due to inherent vice(*b*) alone is not recoverable under an ordinary marine policy ; nor is loss due to the fault of the insured ;(*c*) nor are underwriters liable for losses solely attributable to death from natural causes. As, for instance, if it be owing to any infectious disorder which might equally have seized them on land, or to some disease which, though probably in part occasioned by the confinement and other usual circumstances of the voyage, is yet not proximately caused by any extraordinary, violent, or immediate agency of the perils insured against, the underwriters are undoubtedly not liable for the loss.(*d*) "The insurers answer for the death of animals insured, if it proceeds from tempest, from the fire of an enemy, from jettison, or any other accident, but not if from sickness. Horses had been shipped on board a *pinque*. Some of them died on the voyage. The insurers, proceeded against for payment of this average, had sentence in their favour, 21st March, 1759. It would have been otherwise had the horses been struck by lightning, or killed by the fire of an enemy, or drowned in stranding, &c."(*e*)   Again, where

(*a*) See *Arnould*, 232.
(*b*) § 109 ; *Arnould*, 722 ; but the *onus* is on the insurer to prove that the loss was attributable to this cause, *ibid.*
(*c*) *Arnould*, 731.   (*d*) *Arnould*, 724.   (*e*) *Emerigon*, ch. xii. § 9 fin.

thirty mules, ten asses, and thirty oxen were insured " at and from Cork to Barbadoes and St. Vincent, warranted free of mortality and jettison," Chief-Justice Abbot was of opinion that if the ship had been driven out of her course by the perils of the sea so as to protract the voyage and exhaust the provisions, then the words " warranted free from mortality " in the policy would have protected the underwriters from liability for loss arising from such cause.(a)   Where the perils of the sea are a conducing cause of the loss, it is often a matter of great difficulty to determine whether the underwriter is liable. In the case just cited, where the underwriters expressly stipulated not to be liable for loss caused by mortality, and it appeared that all the animals insured, except five mules and one ass, died on the voyage of severe bruises, lacerations, and injuries arising from the violent pitching and rolling of the ship occasioned by a furious storm and the consequent agitation of the sea, the Court decided, though not without some doubt, that this was a loss by perils of the sea, for which the underwriters were liable, and against which they were not protected by the warranty to be " free from mortality ;" for the word " mortality " in its ordinary sense never means violent death, but death arising from natural causes. If living animals be deliberately thrown overboard to save the rest, in consequence of scarcity of provisions occasioned by the gross ignorance of the captain in mistaking his course, and thus protracting the voyage, this is not properly described as loss by perils of the sea, the proximate cause of the loss being the incapacity of the captain.(b)   And if they were to perish for want of food and water, owing to the extraordinary and unavoidable prolongation of the voyage in consequence of bad weather, this would be considered a loss by mortality, and not by perils of the sea.(c)   But it was held to be loss from perils of the sea where several horses, in consequence of

(a) *Lawrence* v. *Aberdein*, 1821, 5 B. and Ad. 107, 110.

(b) *Greyson* v. *Gilbert*, 1783, 3 Doug. 232 ; Marshall, Mar. Ins. 375, 386.

(c) *Tatham* v. *Hodgson*, 1796, 6 T.R. 656 ; *Lawrence*, cit.

the labouring of the vessel in a violent storm, broke down the support slings and partitions, and kicked each other so severely that they died in the course of the storm from the injuries thus received. (a)   And under a policy for safe carriage of live stock, covering, with the usual exceptions, the perils of railroad and river, the insurers are liable for a loss occurring in a necessary transhipment from cars to steamboat, upon the route, if not caused by a peril excepted. (b) Further, the underwriter is not liable for any loss not proximately caused by the perils insured against ; (c) nor for loss which might by ordinary care and prudence on the part of the shipowner have been averted. (d)

185. Losses Covered by the Policy. — "Perils of the sea" (e) include the common perils of storms, and their direct consequences, by striking on a rock, stranding, springing a leak, shipping great seas, collision, (f) and such injury as happens to horses from the agitation of the ship due to the action of the sea, which it was not in the power of the master to provide against, or the owners to obviate by means of supplying a seaworthy ship and appurtenances.   Thus, where loss is directly attributable to failure of the shipmaster to take precautions by shifting the position of animals in his custody so as to avert injury to them, or to faulty arrangements for carriage, the underwriter is not liable, there being in the latter case a breach of the implied warranty of seaworthiness. (g)   But provided perils of the sea are the proximate cause of loss, the assured is not precluded from recovering under an allegation of such cause merely because the negligence, unskilfulness, or misconduct of the master and mariners have been the remote occasion of it. (h)

(a) *Gabay* v. *Lloyd*, 1825, 3 B. and Cr. 793.

(b) *Ætna Insurance Company* v. *Stivers*, 1868, 95 Am. D. 467.

(c) *Ionides* v. *Universal, &c., Insurance Company*, 1863, 14 C.B., N.S. 259.

(d) *Arnould*, 733.

(e) Arnould's Mar. Ins., Part III., chap. ii. 744-759.

(f) *Arnould*, 756.   (g) See § 116.

(h) *Arnould*, 753 ; *Davidson* v. *Burnard*, 1868, L.R. 4 C.P. 117.

" Enemies " applies to capture by public enemies in war ; " detention of princes " signifies not that of enemies only, but those in amity, and of the nation of the assured also. "Acts of piracy" refer to all hostile depredation, such as would, if committed on land, amount to felony.   " Jettison " is strictly loss by dangers of the sea, and the clause for indemnity is not limited to the strict case of average contribution, but extends to all jettison which arises on just cause of throwing overboard goods for the common safety.   Under " other perils " come such risks as a ship fired on by mistake from a British cruiser,(a) the explosion of a steam boiler,(b) or the bursting of a pump,(c) and damage to cargo by sea water through a waste pipe having been negligently left open.(d)

186. Exemptions under the ordinary "Cattle Clause." —There is frequently inserted what is termed the " cattle clause " in a marine policy when horses are carried.   It is generally in these terms (e):—" To cover the risk of death or loss in consequence of the stranding, sinking, or burning of the vessel, or owing to collision with any other vessel, but warranted free from mortality, contagion, and loss or injury arising from other causes."   The effect of this clause in a policy is to free the underwriter in all cases when the loss is not directly due to shipwreck, stranding, burning, or collision. Under the customary live stock policy at Lloyd's, with a clause " warranted to be free from mortality and jettison," underwriters are not considered liable for any loss arising from death where the ship arrives safe ; but only where the ship is lost, and the animals are drowned.   But this being

(a) *Cullen* v. *Butler*, 1816, 5 M. and S. 461.

(b) *West India Telegraph Company* v. *Home, &c., Insurance Company*, 1880, 6 Q.B.D. 51.

(c) *Hamilton* v. *Thames, &c., Insurance Company*, 1886, 17 Q.B.D. 195.

(d) *Davidson*, cit., where doubt was expressed whether this was due to perils of the sea, but fell at all events under " other perils."

(e) A list of twenty-two different forms of cattle clauses will be found in Owen's *Marine Insurance Notes and Clauses*, pp. 144, 241.

mere usage, it is not binding unless it can be shown to be within the knowledge of the assured.(a)

187. Loss Recoverable in a Marine Policy.—The loss must have been within the policy; and it is either total loss, or, if the policy be not valued, partial loss to the amount claimed. The burden of proving the loss lies upon the insured, the general rule being that the best proof is to be given which can be had in the circumstances.(b) In claiming total loss it is sufficient to prove that the horses were embarked, that the ship sailed and never arrived at her port. If it be proved that the ship was reported to be lost and her crew saved, that is held *primâ facie* proof of loss, without the necessity of calling or proving the absence of the crew.(c)

The loss on horses in a valued policy will be estimated as in the case of other goods, by the invoice price, with charges, premium, broker's commission, and charges of moving.(d) In an open policy there are two methods of valuation. Either the invoice is taken with premium, &c., and the net proceeds of the sale are deducted, or the amount of the sales is compared with a *pro forma* account of the same horses had they arrived in proper condition.(e)

188. Risks in a Horse Insurance Policy.—These usually are :—Accidental death as—*e.g.*, by lightning,(f) or an accident necessitating the immediate destruction of the horse while in the charge of the assured or his paid servant, and death from disease : but glanders and farcy are invariably excepted. The ordinary British horse insurance policy also excludes the risks of death, when the horse is out of Great Britain and Ireland, or when death ensues from neglect or

---

(a) §§ 11, 40 ; *Gabay* v. *Lloyd*, 1825, 3 B. and Cr. 793 ; *Arnould*, 843, 844.
(b) B. Pr. 496, *Ferrier* v. *Sandieman*, 1809, 15 F.C. 373.
(c) *Koster* v. *Reid*, 1826, 6 B. and Cr. 19.
(d) B. Pr. 502.   (e) B. Pr. 504.   (f) See § 179.

improper use, or unskilful treatment, from overloading, or improper loading of any vehicle to which it may be harnessed or attached, or from breaking of the harness, or by reason of the horse being left unattended, or by the intoxication of its rider or driver, or from poison, or malicious injury, or by reason of the horse being loose ; or loss occasioned by invasion of foreign enemy, or by civil commotion, riot, or any military or usurped power. The risks of hunting, foaling, castration, and fire are also, as a rule, excluded; and, if desired to be covered, are undertaken only at special rates. These contracts are usually the subject of separate policies, as are also contracts of indemnity against the risks of driving accidents, and insurance of vehicles against loss by collision.

Such policies are invariably "valued" ones, the amount recoverable for loss to a horse being considerably below the declared value, generally two-thirds of it ; and, in estimating the loss, the declared value is taxative, and the company reserve to themselves the salvage.

The usual conditions in such a policy are, that when a claim is made under the policy, the company shall contribute only rateably along with other insurers of the same interest and risk; that in the case of illness, accident, or death, the company shall receive notice of it, with full particulars ; and that in such a case the assured shall immediately secure the services of a "duly qualified" veterinary surgeon,(a) and send his report to the company, and give notice also to the company's veterinary surgeon, if any in the district. A horse insured under a policy containing these conditions sustained a fracture of the leg, and the owner, on advice of a veterinary surgeon, who was not registered as such, had it killed at once, and by telegraph intimated to an agent of the company that the horse had broken its leg, and had been condemned. This intimation was at once communicated by the agent to the manager of the company, by whom liability was repudiated. No report by a veterinary surgeon was forwarded to the company. It

(a) See Appendix i.

was admitted that the accident to the horse was of such a character that death was inevitable, and that the only humane course was to kill it.(a)   Lord Justice-Clerk Kingsburgh observed :—"The pursuer, under such a policy as this, if he adopts the alternative of putting the animal to death, undertakes the *onus* of showing that death was inevitable under the circumstances.   He undertakes that risk, and if he fails, he loses his case.   But if he succeeds in proving that the result, the only result sooner or later of the injury, would be the death of the animal, and that its immediate destruction is the only humane course to follow, then I think we must take the case on the footing that the animal had been killed outright, and not merely fatally injured."(b)   There was evidence held sufficient to prove that the pursuer was justified in killing the horse, that the notice was received by the company's manager before he repudiated liability in case of its being destroyed by the owner without the written consent of the company.   The company under these circumstances pleaded want of notice to the office of the company, and that they received no report by a qualified veterinary surgeon, but it was held— (1) that as it had been proved that the horse was fatally injured, and that in the circumstances the proper course was to kill it at once, the case was to be taken as one of death, and not of injury in the sense of the condition ; (2) that although the notice had been sent only to an agent of the company, yet as it had *de facto* reached the manager timeously, it was sufficient ; (3) that the instant repudiation of liability by the company had rendered it unnecessary for the pursuer thereafter to send the report required by the condition, and barred the company from objecting to the want of it.

The other usual conditions are that when accidental death shall occur by reason of the negligence, carelessness,

(a) *Shiells* v. *Sc. Ass. Corporation*, 1889, 16 R. 1014.
(b) *Shiells*, cit. p. 1019.

or wrong-doing of any person, the company may sue in the name of the assured for recovery of compensation; that the company's officials may visit the premises where the insured horse is kept, and the assured shall furnish them with such information regarding the horse as they may require; and also, that if the horse be put to any other uses than are specified in the proposal, the assured shall forfeit his benefit under the policy. Such conditions will be literally construed and enforced.(a)

(a) B. Pr. 513.

APPENDIX.

APPENDIX.

I.—THE VETERINARY SURGEONS ACT, 1881.

(44 & 45 Vict. c. 62.)

This Act was passed with the view of enabling persons requiring the aid of veterinary surgeons to distinguish between qualified and unqualified practitioners. Its leading object is the establishment of a register of veterinary surgeons. The register of the Royal College of Veterinary Surgeons incorporated by charters 1844, 1876 and 1879 (§ 2) is now styled and kept as The Register of Veterinary Surgeons (§ 3); and the Royal College is bound to make provisions for the examination of students attending in England, the Royal Veterinary College, and in Scotland, the several Scottish Veterinary Colleges; and to admit them to be registered as members of the Royal College on passing the necessary examinations (§ 4). Provisions are made for the correction of the register (§ 5); and for removal of names therefrom by request or with the consent of the party, or where a name has been incorrectly or fraudulently entered, or where the party has been convicted of an offence which in England would be a misdemeanour or higher offence, or is shown to have been guilty of any conduct disgraceful to him in a professional respect (§ 6). Names may on certain conditions and formalities be restored to the register (§§ 7, 8): and the appearance of any one's name on the register is declared to be *primâ facie* evidence of his qualifications (§ 9). Provision is also made for the registration of colonial and foreign practitioners with recognised diplomas (§ 13). The following penalties are imposed by the Act:—

11. Any person who wilfully procures or attempts to procure himself to be placed on the register of Veterinary Surgeons by making or producing or causing to be made or produced any false or fraudulent declaration certificate or representation either in writing or otherwise, and any person aiding and assisting him therein, shall be deemed guilty in England or in Ireland of a misdemeanour and in Scotland of a crime or offence punishable by

fine or imprisonment, and shall on conviction thereof be liable to a fine not exceeding fifty pounds or to be imprisoned with or without hard labour for any term not exceeding twelve months.

12. If the Registrar wilfully makes or causes to be made any falsification in any matter relating to the register of veterinary surgeons he shall be deemed guilty of a misdemeanour, and shall be liable to a fine not exceeding fifty pounds, or to be imprisoned with or without hard labour for any term not exceeding twelve months.

16. If after the passing of this Act any person not being a fellow or a member of the Royal College of Veterinary Surgeons takes or uses any name, title, addition, or description, by means of initials or letters placed after his name, or otherwise, stating or implying that he is a fellow or a member of the Royal College of Veterinary Surgeons, he shall be liable to a fine not exceeding twenty pounds.

17.—(1.) If after the thirty-first day of December one thousand eight hundred and eighty-three any person, other than a person who for the time being is on the register of veterinary surgeons, or who at the time of the passing of this Act held the veterinary certificate of the Highland and Agricultural Society of Scotland, takes or uses the title of veterinary surgeon or veterinary practitioner, or any name, title, addition, or description stating that he is a veterinary surgeon or a practitioner of veterinary surgery or of any branch thereof, or is specially qualified to practise the same, he shall be liable to a fine not exceeding twenty pounds.

(2.) From and after the same day a person other than as in this section mentioned shall not be entitled to recover in any court any fee or charge for performing any veterinary operation, or for giving any veterinary attendance or advice, or for acting in any manner as a veterinary surgeon or veterinary practitioner, or for practising in any case veterinary surgery, or any branch thereof.

The proceedings for fines and imprisonment are summary :—

19. Fines and imprisonment under this Act may be recovered and imposed summarily, that is to say—

In England, in manner provided by the Summary Jurisdiction Act 1848 and the Summary Jurisdiction Act 1879, and any Act amending either of those Acts ;

In Scotland, before the sheriff or sheriff-substitute or two justices, in manner provided by the Summary Procedure Act 1864, and any Act amending the same.

II.—CLAUSE IN A SHERIFF COURT PETITION FOR A JUDICIAL WARRANT TO SELL,

(*a.*) An unpaid horse at the seller's instance.

"To Grant warrant to any licensed auctioneer to sell by public roup the bay horse referred to in the said condescendence, and to apply the proceeds of sale in payment *pro tanto*—(1) of the expenses thereof, and of the horse's keep and of process, and (2) of the sum of forty-five pounds : to Reserve all action competent to the pursuer for the balance of said sum and expenses, and to the defender his defences as accords: and to Find him liable in expenses in the event of his offering opposition hereto."

The condescendence sets forth the sale, the price, the refusal to take delivery, and the expediency of present sale.

PLEA IN LAW :—"The defender having purchased said horse but having refused to take delivery of it, warrant ought to be granted for its sale as craved."

(*b.*) An unpaid horse at the buyer's instance :—

"To Grant warrant to A.B., auctioneer, Edinburgh (*or* any licensed auctioneer), to sell by public roup the brown cob, put by the pursuer into the custody of C.D., livery stable keepers, Edinburgh, on (*date*), and which is presently in their custody : and to Appoint the proceeds of sale after deducting the expenses thereof, and of the horse's keep and of process, to be consigned with the clerk of court, to abide the orders of court ; and to Find the defender liable in expenses in the event of his offering opposition hereto."

The condescendence sets forth the sale, with its conditions and warranty (*if any*), the trial, the fact of horse's unsoundness, and of its having been tendered back, the seller's refusal to accept it, and its consequent removal to livery, and the expediency of present sale.

PLEA IN LAW :—"The said horse having been rejected by the pursuer as disconform to warranty, but the defender having refused to take it back, the pursuer is entitled to have it sold under authority of court for behoof of whom it may concern."

(*c.*) Of a paid horse at the buyer's instance :—

"To Grant warrant, &c., *ut supra* (*b.*) . . . custody and to apply the proceeds of sale *pro tanto*—(1) in payment of the expenses thereof, and of the horse's keep and of process, and (2) in repayment to the pursuer of the sum of forty-five pounds, &c., *ut supra*." (*a*)

The condescendence sets forth the sale price and payment, the trial and disconformity to warranty, the tender and refusal, and consequent removal to livery, and the expediency of present sale.

PLEA IN LAW :—Same as in (*b*) . . . court, and the proceeds applied in manner craved.

R

III.—ISSUES.

1. Issues adjusted to try a question as to breach of special warranty, where repayment of the price was demanded :—

"Whether, on or about the 9th day of June, 1852, the defenders sold and delivered to the pursuer a bay gelding for the price of £180 sterling, then paid by the pursuer to the defenders : and whether the defenders warranted the soundness of the near fore-foot of the said gelding in the following terms :—' His near fore-foot we warrant for six months.'

"Whether the said gelding, within the said period of six months, was not sound in the near fore-foot, contrary to the true intent and meaning of said warranty, and whether the pursuer duly and timeously offered back the said gelding to the defenders : and whether the defenders are indebted and resting-owing to the pursuer in the said sum of £180 the price of the said gelding, with interest thereon from the said 9th day of June, 1852, and in the sum of £50, for the keep of said gelding or in either of the said sums or any part thereof." —*Maule* v. *Laing*, 1853, 15 D. 778.

2. Issues to try the question whether horses were sold under an express or implied warranty :—

"(1.) Whether, on or about the 1st day of March, 1854, the pursuers purchased two horses, as a pair, from the defender, at the price of £94, under an express warranty of soundness : and whether one of the said horses was at the time of the said sale unsound.

"(2.) Whether, on or about the 1st day of March, 1854, the pursuers purchased two horses, as a pair, from the defender, at the price of £94, under an implied warranty of soundness : and whether one of the said horses was at the time of the sale unsound."—*Croall* v. *Hunter*, 1855, 17 D. 652.

3. It has been held that horses being "goods" under the Mercantile Law Amendment Act, 1856, sec. 5, a pursuer must take an issue of express warranty. "An issue of implied warranty will not do now, but it will come out at the trial from what circumstance an express warranty will be inferred."—Per Lord President M'Neill. The following issue was approved :—" It being admitted that on 31st October the defender sold to the pursuer a horse at the price of £60, and that the horse was delivered and the price paid—Whether the defender gave an express warranty that the said horse was sound : and whether the horse was at the time of the sale unsound, and the defender is due and resting-owing to the pursuer the sum of £60

with interest from the date of citation to this action."—*Young* v. *Giffen*, 1858, 21 D. 87.

4. Issue and counter issue in an action upon a warranty given at a sale of a horse in Scotland, the buyer averring that he had taken the horse to England, and had there, upon discovering his unsoundness, sold him, admittedly without judicial authority, after an offer of return to the seller, which was declined.

"Issue for the pursuer.—It being admitted that on the 18th July, 1862, the pursuer bought from the defender a horse and pony for the price of £115, and that the said price was then paid, and that the horse and pony were delivered to the pursuer by the defender under an express warranty that they were 'sound up to delivery,' in terms of document No. 7 of Process,— whether the said horse and pony were, or either or which of them was, unsound at delivery: and whether the defender is indebted and resting-owing the pursuer the sum of £112, 3s. 6d., or any part thereof, with interest as per schedule annexed?" (The schedule stated the price paid by the pursuer, and the expenses of keep, &c., and credited the defender with £20, the proceeds of the sale.) "Counter issue for the defender.— Whether the pursuer failed duly to return the said horse and pony, or either of them, to the defenders?"—*Robson* v. *Thomson*, 1864, 2 M. 593.

5. Issue to try the question whether a warranty was given that a mare was "a good worker," see this case referred to, § 27.

"It being admitted that, on 2nd January, 1862, the defender sold to the pursuer a grey mare, at the price of £27, and that the mare was delivered, and the price paid—Whether the defender expressly warranted the said grey mare to be a good worker, and whether at the time of said sale, the said grey mare was not a good worker; whether the pursuer returned the said mare to the defender; and whether the defender is bound to pay back to the pursuer the said sum of £27, or any part thereof, with interest thereon from 9th January, 1862."—*Ferrier* v. *Dods*, 1865, 3 M. 561; see also *M'Bey* v. *Reid*, 1842, 4 D. 349, and *Fisher* v. *Ure*, 1846, 9 D. 17.

6. Issue to try the question whether a horse was unsound, either at the date of sale or of the demand for repetition of the price where a pursuer kept and used it for five weeks, and it was pleaded that he was not entitled to return it.

"It being admitted that the defender, on the 10th day of November, 1852, sold and delivered to the pursuer a roan gelding at the price of £25, which was then paid by the pursuer :—Whether at the time of the said sale, the defender specially warranted the said gelding to be sound ? Whether at the time aforesaid, the said gelding was not sound ? Whether the pursuer, within reasonable time, gave notice to the defender of the alleged unsoundness ? And whether the defender is indebted and resting-owing to the pursuer in the sums set out in the annexed schedule, or either or any part thereof ?"

The schedule set forth the price and expenses of keep, loss and damages.—*Balfour* v. *Wordsworth*, 1854, 16 D. 1028.

For forms of issues on a breach of contract to supply goods fit for a specific purpose, see *Hutchison* v. *Henry*, 1867, 6 M. 57.—*M'Farlane* v. *Taylor*, 1868, 6 M. (H.L.) 1. Observations on alternative form of issues, "fraud and circumvention" and "force and fear."—*Love* v. *Marshall*, 1870, 9 M. 291 ; and for form of issue where an action for the price of moveables (a picture) was met by an averment of fraud.—*M'Lennan* v. *Gibson*, 1843, 5 D. 1032.

IV.—CONDITIONS OF AUCTION SALES.

Scott, Croall & Sons, Royal Horse Bazaar, Edinburgh.

Regulations and Conditions.

1st.—The highest bidder to be the purchaser, and should any dispute arise between two or more bidders, the lot so disputed shall be immediately put up and re-sold. Owners shall have the option of bidding once for each lot in the course of the sale, but not oftener.

2nd.—Purchasers to give in their names and places of abode, and to pay Five Shillings in the Pound (if required) as earnest and part payment ; in default of which, the lot may be put up and re-sold.

3rd.—Each lot to be at the risk of the purchaser after being sold ; and the price to be paid on the day of sale.

4th.—In the event of non-fulfilment of the foregoing conditions, such lot or lots may be re-sold by public or private sale, and any deficiency or expenses connected therewith shall be made good by the defaulter.

5th.—When any warranty is given, the owner shall be solely responsible for the same, and the auctioneers shall not be liable as a party in any action or dispute between the seller and the purchaser.

6th.—The purchaser of any lot who objects to the subject of purchase as disconform to warranty given, must intimate the precise grounds of disconformity founded on in writing, to Messrs. Scott, Croall & Sons, on or before noon of the second day after the sale, and return the lot objected to as aforesaid, to them within the same period ; and only the objections lodged in writing as aforesaid, and no others, shall be pleadable against the lot objected to. Failure to comply with these provisions shall bar all objections to the purchase, and the lot shall be conclusively held to be conform to the warranty given. Nothing herein contained shall affect the mode of *determining* the special objections referred to in article 10th hereof.

7th.—The seller shall be entitled to receive the purchase money on the third day after sale, provided no objection has been made, and that Scott, Croall & Sons have then received the price.

8th.—When a horse is returned as not being conform to warranty given, the seller must nevertheless pay the usual commission on the purchase price.

9th.—Any Horse returned as not being conform to warranty given in Catalogue, in respect of soundness or age, must be accompanied with a V.S. certificate.

10th.—Any Horse returned as not being conform to warranty given, as regards riding or driving shall be tried by Messrs Scott, Croall & Sons, or some one appointed by them, whose decision in all cases shall be final, and not subject to review in any Court of Law.

11th.—No warranty given as to height of horses, purchasers being required to satisfy themselves previous to sale.

12th.—The usual commission shall be payable on all horses, carriages, &c., brought to Scott, Croall & Sons' Bazaar, and sold privately either by them or the owners.

13th.—Scott, Croall & Sons will not be accountable for bridles, saddles, &c., unless specially given into the hands of their hostler.

14th.—All horses must be in stalls by 10 o'clock on the morning of sale and remain at the risk of seller until sold.

15th.—The auctioneers do not guarantee any lot entered for sale being brought forward, whether arising from having been sold privately or other circumstances.

V.—"ANIMALS ORDER OF 1886, Part IV., Chap. 26.

"Every railway truck, horse-box, or other railway vehicle used for carrying animals, horses, asses, or mules on a railway shall be provided at each end with two spring buffers, and the floor thereof shall, in order to prevent slipping, be strewn with a proper quantity of litter or sand or other proper substance, or be fitted with battens or other proper footholds."

(*Part IV., Chap. 26, Art.* 123.)—" A Railway Company shall not allow any railway-truck, horse-box, or other vehicle used for carrying animals, horses, asses or mules on the railway to be over-crowded so as to cause unnecessary suffering to the animals, horses, asses or mules therein."—(*Ibid. Art.* 124.)

"If anything is done or omitted to be done in contravention of the foregoing provisions . . . the railway company carrying animals on or owning or working the railway on which,—and also in case of the over-crowding of a railway truck, horse-box, or other vehicle on a railway . . . the consignor of the animals in respect of which,—the same is done or omitted, shall, each according to and in respect of his or their own acts or omissions, be deemed guilty of an offence against the Act of 1878."—(*Ibid. Art.* 126.)

" *Horse-Boxes.*

"(1.) A horse-box used for horses, asses, or mules on a railway shall, on every occasion after a horse, ass, or mule is taken out of it, and before any other horse, ass, or mule, or any animal is placed therein, be cleansed as follows:

"(i.) The floor of the horse-box, and all other parts thereof with which the droppings of horses, asses, or mules have come in contact shall be scraped and swept, and the scrapings and sweepings, and all dung, sawdust, fodder, litter, and other matter shall be effectually removed therefrom ; and

"(ii.) The sides of the horse-box and all other parts thereof with which the head or any discharge from the mouth or nostrils of a horse, ass, or mule has come in contact shall be thoroughly washed with water by means of a sponge, brush, or other instrument.

"(2.) The scrapings and sweepings of the horse-box, and all dung, sawdust, fodder, litter, and other matter removed therefrom, shall forthwith be well mixed with quicklime."—(*Ibid. Part III., Chap.* 18, *Art.* 103.)

" *Horse-Boxes, Guards' Van and other Vehicles.*

"(1.) A horse-box or a guard's van or other railway vehicle (not being a railway truck) if used for animals on a railway shall, on every occasion after an animal is taken out of it, and before any other animal, or any horse, ass, or mule is placed in it, be cleansed and disinfected as follows:

"(i.) If the animal is accompanied by a declaration in writing of the owner or consignee or his agent to the effect that it is intended for exhibition or other special purpose therein stated, and has not, to the best of his knowledge and belief, been exposed to the infection of disease, the vehicle shall be cleansed as follows :

"(*a*) The floor of the vehicle, and all other parts thereof with which the droppings of the animal have come in contact, shall be scraped and swept, and the scrapings and sweepings, and all dung, sawdust, fodder, litter, and other matter shall be effectively removed therefrom ; and

"(*b*) The sides of the vehicle, and all other parts thereof with which the head or any discharge from the mouth or nostrils of the animal has come in contact shall be thoroughly washed with water by means of a sponge, brush, or other instrument ; but

"(ii.) If the animal is not accompanied by such a declaration, the vehicle shall be cleansed and disinfected as follows :

"(*c*) The floor of the vehicle, and all other parts thereof with which the droppings of the animal have come in contact, shall be scraped and swept, and the scrapings and sweepings, and all dung, sawdust, fodder, litter, and other matter shall be effectually removed from the vehicle ; then

"(*d*) The same parts of the vehicle shall be thoroughly washed or scrubbed or scoured with water ; then

"(*e*) The same parts of the vehicle shall have applied to them a coating of lime-wash.

"(2.) The scrapings and sweepings of the vehicle, and all dung, sawdust, fodder, litter, and other matter removed therefrom, shall forthwith be well mixed with quicklime, and be effectually removed from contact with animals."—(*Ibid. Art.* 104.)

" *Trucks.*

"(1.) A railway truck, if used for animals on a railway, shall, on every occasion after an animal is taken out of it, and before any other animal, or any horse, ass, or mule, or any fodder or litter, or anything intended to be used for or about animals, is placed in it, be cleansed and disinfected as follows :

"(i.) The floor of the truck, and all other parts thereof with which animals or their droppings have come in contact shall be scraped and swept, and the scrapings and sweepings, and and all dung, sawdust, litter, and other matter shall be effectually removed therefrom ; then

"(ii.) The same parts of the truck shall be thoroughly washed or scrubbed or scoured with water ; then

" (iii.) The same parts of the truck shall have applied to them
a coating of lime-wash.

" (2.) The scrapings and sweepings of the truck, and all dung,
sawdust, litter, and other matter removed therefrom shall forthwith be well mixed with quicklime, and be effectually removed from
contact with animals."—(*Ibid. Art.* 105.)

" *Vans.*

" (1.) A van, if used for containing animals, horses, asses, or mules
while carried on a railway, shall, on every occasion after a diseased or
suspected animal, horse, ass, or mule is taken out of it, and as soon as
practicable, and before any other animal, horse, ass, or mule is placed
in it, be cleansed and disinfected as follows :

"(i.) The floor of the van, and all other parts thereof with which
animals, horses, asses, or mules, or their droppings have
come in contact shall be scraped and swept, and the
scrapings and sweepings, and all dung, sawdust, litter,
and other matter shall be effectually removed therefrom ;
then

"(ii.) The same parts of the van shall be thoroughly washed or
scrubbed or scoured with water ; then

"(iii.) The same parts of the van shall have applied to them a
coating of lime-wash.

" (2.) The scrapings and sweepings of the van, and all dung,
sawdust, litter, and other matter removed therefrom shall forthwith
be well mixed with quicklime, and be effectually removed from
contact with animals."—(*Ibid. Part III., Chap.* 18, *Art.* 106.)

PROVISIONS OF THE CONTAGIOUS DISEASES (ANIMALS) ACT, 1878,
41 & 42 VICT. 74, § 33.

33.—(1.) Every railway company shall make a provision, to the
satisfaction of the Privy Council, of water and food, or either of
them, at such stations as the Privy Council from time to time, by
general or specific description, direct, for animals carried, or about to
be or having been carried, on the railway of the company.

(2.) The water and food so provided, or either of them, shall be
supplied to any such animal by the company carrying it, on the
request of the consignor, or of any person in charge thereof.

(3.) As regards water, if, in the case of any animal, such a request
is not made, so that the animal remains without a supply of water for
twenty-four consecutive hours, the consignor and the person in charge
of the animal shall each be guilty of an offence against this Act ; and

it shall lie on the person charged to prove such a request and the time within which the animal had a supply of water.

(4.) But the Privy Council may from time to time, if they think fit, by order prescribe any other period, not less than twelve hours, instead of the period of twenty-four hours aforesaid, generally, or in respect of any particular kind of animals.

(5.) The company supplying water or food under this section may make in respect thereof such reasonable charges (if any) as the Privy Council by order approve, in addition to such charges as they are for the time being authorised to make in respect of the carriage of animals. The amount of those additional charges accrued due in respect of any animal shall be a debt from the consignor and from the consignee thereof to the company, and shall be recoverable by the company from either of them, with costs, by proceedings in any court of competent jurisdiction. The company shall have a lien for the amount thereof on the animal in respect whereof the same accrued due, and on any other animal at any time consigned by or to the same consignor or consignee to be carried by the company.

VI.—STATUTORY REGULATIONS FOR THE CARRIAGE OF HORSES IN PASSENGER STEAMERS.

By the "Passengers Act (Amendment Act), 1863," 26 & 27 Vict. c. 51, § 8, it is provided: "Notwithstanding the Prohibition contained in the Twenty-ninth Section of the said 'Passengers Act, 1855,' Horses and Cattle may be carried as Cargo in Passenger Ships, subject to the following conditions:

"(1.) That the Animals be not carried on any Deck below the Deck on which Passengers are berthed, nor in any Compartment in which Passengers are berthed, nor in any adjoining Compartment, except in a Ship built of Iron, and of which the Compartments are divided off by Water-tight Bulkheads extending to the upper Deck:

"(4.) That in Passenger Ships of less than Five hundred Tons registered Tonnage not more than Two Head of large Cattle be carried, nor in Passenger Ships of larger Tonnage more than One additional Head of such Cattle for every additional Two Hundred Tons of the Ship's registered Tonnage, nor more in all in any Passenger Ship than Ten Head of such Cattle: The Term "large Cattle" shall include both Sexes of horned Cattle, Deer, Horses, and Asses; Four Sheep of either Sex, or Four Female Goats, shall be equivalent to,

and may, subject to the same Conditions, be carried in lieu
of One Head of large Cattle :

"(5.) That proper Arrangements be made, to the Satisfaction of the
Emigration Officer at the Port of Clearance, for the Housing,
Maintenance, and Cleanliness of the Animals, and for the
Stowage of their Fodder :

" (6.) Not more than Six Dogs, and no Pigs or Male Goats, shall be
conveyed as Cargo in any Passenger Ship : For any Breach
of this Prohibition, or of any of the above Conditions, the
Owner, Charterer, and Master of the Ship, or any of them,
shall be liable for each Offence to a Penalty not exceeding
Three hundred Pounds nor less than Five Pounds."

But they may be carried, notwithstanding these provisions, by order
of the Secretary of State as naval and military stores.—(33 & 34
Vict., c. 95, *Peramble and* § 3.)

VII.—BILL OF LADING AND NOTICE OF CONDITIONS OF SHIPMENT.

ORDINARY BILL OF LADING.

𝖲𝗁𝗂𝗉𝗉𝖾𝖽 in good order and well-conditioned by
in and upon the Steam Ship called the   , whereof
                              is Master for the present Voyage, or
whoever else may go as Master in the said Ship, and now lying in the
Port of LEITH, and bound for ROTTERDAM, with Liberty to call at
any Port or Ports,

being marked and numbered as in the margin (with liberty to tranship
the said Goods or Specie on board any other craft or Steamer), and
are to be delivered in the like good order and well-conditioned, at the
aforesaid Port of ROTTERDAM [*The Act of God, the Queen's
Enemies, Pirates, Robbers, Thieves, Vermin, Barratry of Master or
Mariners, Restraints of Princes, Rulers, or People, Loss or Damage
resulting from Insufficiency in Strength of Packages, from Sweating,
Leakage, Breakage, or from Stowage or Contact with other Goods, or
from any of the following Perils (whether arising from the negligence,
default, or error in judgment of the Pilot, Master, Mariners,
Engineers, or others of the Crew, or otherwise howsoever), excepted,
namely, Risk of Craft, Explosion, or Fire at Sea, in Craft, or on
Shore, Boilers, Steam, or Machinery, or from the consequence of any*

Damage or Injury thereto, howsoever such Damage or Injury may be caused, Collision, Stranding, or other Peril of the Seas, Rivers, or Navigation, of whatever nature or kind soever, and howsoever such Collision, Stranding, or other Peril may be caused, with liberty in the event of the said Steamer putting back into any port, or otherwise being prevented from any cause from proceeding in the ordinary course of her voyage, to tranship the Goods by any other Steamer belonging to or chartered by the Leith and Rotterdam Steam Shipping Company, and with liberty to sail with or without Pilots, and to tow and assist Vessels in all situations], unto

or to his or their Assigns, Freight, Charges, &c., for the said Goods being payable by Consignees as per Margin, with Primage and Average accustomed. In Witness whereof, the Master or Agent of the said Ship hath affirmed to One Bill of Lading, of this tenor and date, the one of which Bills being accomplished, the others to stand void.

In the event of the Steamer being prevented by ice, blockade, or the hostile act of any Power, from reaching her destined port, the Master reserves the liberty of either landing her cargo at the nearest unblockaded port he can reach with safety, or of bringing her cargo back to port of shipment; in either case at Consignees' risk and expense, but charging Outward Freight only. Landing and transshipping expenses to be paid by Consignees. The Ship and Owners are not liable for any negligence, default, or error in judgment of the Pilot, Master, Mariners, Engineers, or others of the Crew, in navigating the Ship.

Freight payable on weight delivered.* Double Freight will be charged when Goods are found to weigh more than stated on Bills of Lading, Consignees paying freight and weighing expenses on all overweight found.

Steamer not to be responsible for any delay to Cargo caused by Strikes, Lock-outs, or combinations of Officers, Engineers, Crew, Dock Labourers, Stevedores, Lightermen, or any other hands connected with the loading or discharge of the Steamer.

* Instead of this the following is common :—
Freight on live Stock payable on the number of animals embarked, without regard to and irrespective of the number loaded, and the owners of the vessel are not to be responsible for any general or other average contribution based on the destruction of such live Stock by jettison, or by any other cause ordinarily giving rise to a claim for average contribution, or for accident, injury. or death arising from any other cause whatever.

Weight, Contents, Measure, Quantity, and Value unknown, and not answerable for Leakage, Lighterage, Breakage, Corruption, Rust, Torn Wrappers, *Decay and Mortality, Contagion or Injury*, and the Wrong Delivery of Goods, caused by error or by insufficiency in marks or numbers. The Goods to be taken from the Ship by the Consignees immediately after arrival, or the same will be transhipped into Lighters, landed on the Quays, or Warehouse, at the expense and risk of the Owners of such Goods. If the discharging of the Goods is detained by the Entry not being passed, the Agents of the Steamer will have the power to enter them, for account and risk of the Owners of such Goods. All Goods shipped on Deck, at Shippers' risk.

DATED IN LEITH,   189   *For the Master*,

                       (Signed)

NOTICE OF CONDITIONS OF SHIPMENT.

The following conditions appear almost universal in bills, notices and bills of lading of the various Shipping Companies in Edinburgh and Glasgow, and may be taken as typical :—

" Owners will not be responsible for loss or injury to horses, cattle, or other live stock of any kind, and such must be accompanied by some one in charge ; and freight paid before shipment.

" Shippers ought to insure all Goods ᵃⁿᵈₒᵣ *Live Stock*, covering the following conditions, being the terms on which they are carried, viz. :—

" The Owner, Charterers, or Agents shall not be deemed or held to be common Carriers. They do not engage to ship the Goods in the first or in any particular Steamer, or on the days of delivery to them, or on any particular day, but may send them in any Steamer on any day, and at any time, or may tranship them from one Steamer to another.

" Nor will they be accountable for the number of Live Stock entered in the Manifest (such numbers being taken on the representation of the shippers), nor for the correct selection of each owner's respective stock on landing. Nor for inward condition, leakage, breakage, contents or weights of packages, nor for incorrect delivery of Goods from insufficiency of addresses.

" The Steamers, Owner, Charterers, or Agents, are not liable for any damage or loss that may occur to Goods, before or at Shipment, during the passage, whether on deck or in the hold, or at landing, or while otherwise in their custody, from any of the following causes howsoever arising, or from any consequence of said causes—viz., losses of any kind by delay by the Steamers not sailing according to appointment, putting back, being detained, or making deviations, accidents, losses, or damage arising from the Act of God, the Queen's enemies, pirates, restraints of princes, rulers, and people; jettison, barratry, collision, stranding, vermin, fire on board, or in hulk, craft, shed, store, or on shore; perils of the sea, rivers, and navigation, from machinery, boilers, oil, steam, or steam navigation; breaking down of ship or machinery; *overcrowding of Horses or Live Stock, kicking, plunging, vice, or restlessness of Live Stock or Horses;* breakage, short weight, deficiency in number, leakage, rust, stains, decay, sweating, smell, or contact with other Goods, insufficiency of packages, want of or insufficiency or inaccuracy in address or marks, or from any act, neglect, or mistake in judgment of the master, mariners, engineers, or other of the crew of the Steamers, or of persons connected with the management of the Ships, or with the loading, discharge, stowage, storage, carriage, or handling of the Goods, whether before, after, or during the voyage.

"*Carriage and Horses previously arranged for (and in all cases entirely at Owner's risk*), will be taken by Passenger Steamer, provided there are suitable persons in charge. Dogs are carried entirely at Owner's risk, both as to any injury or damage whatever, done to themselves, or any injury or damage they may do to any one in any way. In cases of transhipment, Owners require to see to their Dogs themselves.

"The public are requested to keep the above conditions in view in effecting their insurances.

"No Agent or Servant of the Owner has authority to dispense with any of these Conditions, and all Passengers' Tickets and Bills of Lading and other Receipts for Live Stock and Goods, signed by any Agent or Servant of the Owner, shall be subject to these Conditions, whether or not the same be repeated therein."